## "Don't go, Gwynne," he said.

His whispered entreaty made the ache inside of her blossom into pure agony; her body began to tremble, a faint shivering that she did her best to conceal as she dragged her gaze slowly from where his hand rested on her arm, up to his face, feeling the pain rock through her.

"I must," she said finally, mustering all the dignity she could into that hoarse reply. "You have your duty to fulfill. . ." She gazed into the warm depths of his eyes one last time, unable to stop herself, even though it made her feel like he probed the wounds in her heart with a red-hot knife. ". . .and I have mine."

With that, she very carefully raised her shoulder, lifting her arm up and away from his touch. And then, even though it was the most difficult thing she would ever have to do, she turned her back on Aidan de Brice—the one man who would ever hold her heart and soul in his hands . . .

And she walked away.

D1005159

*Other* **AVON ROMANCES**

His Scandal *by Gayle Callen*
The Lily and the Sword *by Sara Bennett*
The MacKenzies: Jared *by Ana Leigh*
A Necessary Husband *by Debra Mullins*
The Rake: Lessons in Love *by Suzanne Enoch*
A Rebellious Bride *by Brenda Hiatt*
Tempt Me With Kisses *by Margaret Moore*

*Coming Soon*

A Game of Scandal *by Kathryn Smith*
Lone Arrow's Pride *by Karen Kay*

*And Don't Forget These*
**ROMANTIC TREASURES**
*from Avon Books*

After the Abduction *by Sabrina Jeffries*
Marry Me *by Susan Kay Law*
When the Laird Returns: Book Two of
The Highland Lords *by Karen Ranney*

---

# MARY REED McCALL

# THE MAIDEN WARRIOR

AVON BOOKS

*An Imprint of HarperCollinsPublishers*

This is a work of fiction. Names, characters, places, and incidents are products of the author's imagination or are used fictitiously and are not to be construed as real. Any resemblance to actual events, locales, organizations, or persons, living or dead, is entirely coincidental.

AVON BOOKS
*An Imprint of* HarperCollins*Publishers*
10 East 53rd Street
New York, New York 10022-5299

Copyright © 2002 by Mary Reed McCall
ISBN: 0-380-81787-X
**www.avonromance.com**

First Avon Books paperback printing: June 2002

Avon Trademark Reg. U.S. Pat. Off. and in Other Countries, Marca Registrada, Hecho en U.S.A.
HarperCollins ® is a registered trademark of HarperCollins Publishers Inc.

Printed in the U.S.A.

10  9  8  7  6  5  4  3  2  1

For six legendary women in my life: my sisters—Linda, Cindy, Susan, Sandy, Deb, and Carolyn. From first introducing me to the mystical fantasy of Merlin, with his strange language and gift of sweets that "fell from the sky," to infinite hours jumping off the back porch playing Wonder Woman, singing in the kitchen as we cleaned up after supper, or tap dancing across the state in competitions and county fairs—you have helped to make my life a rich tapestry of happy memories and special times. Thank you for being such wonderful sisters—I love you all . . .

And for two other women who are legendary in their own right: Ruth Kagle and Lyssa Keusch. You have given freely and generously of your time, expertise, and support to help me pull my writing into the best shape possible; your ability to make wonderful—and tactfully offered—suggestions for smoothing over the rough spots never ceases to amaze me. You would be any author's dream agent-and-editor team, and I'm so thankful that you've been mine!

# Acknowledgments

My sincere gratitude:

To my dear friend and colleague, Kathie DeKalb, Registered Master Teacher, Usui Shiki Ryoho Reiki healing methods, for invaluable insights to ways of accurately portraying the healing process and its physical manifestations on the healer. I wanted to get it right, and I couldn't have without you. Gwynne and I both thank you!

To my husband, my children, my mother-in-law Norma, Judy, Richard, Donald, and the rest of my family and friends for encouragement, understanding, and help during the often crazy times that go along with this writing life. You make it all a lot easier—and a lot more fun as well. Thank you.

And to my parents, for, as always, reading my work in its roughest form and giving me vital feedback—and for continued love and support. This book never would have made its deadline without your offer of unlimited babysitting! I don't know what I'd do without you . . .

# THE MAIDEN WARRIOR

# Prologue

*A forest in Northern Wales, 1163*

**H**e was coming.

Gwendolyn heard the baying of Owain's hounds; they were close now, and their frenzied howls helped her to cover the distance to the clearing. Finally stumbling to a halt, she leaned against a tree, her legs numb and her breath rasping as she opened the fold of her tunic to check the babe nestled against her breast. Despite the jostling pace they'd been forced to take, her child still slept peacefully, one tiny thumb tucked into its rosebud mouth.

A rush of love so great that it threatened to stop what little breath was left in her swept through Gwendolyn; she blinked away her tears and leaned down to kiss the babe's ebony curls. But as she moved, a tangled lock of her own golden hair fell forward, and with a mewling sound the child stirred, as if it would begin to cry.

1

"Hush, now, angel," Gwendolyn murmured, stroking the silken cheek, even as her gaze frantically searched the wood around them. This was the spot; it had to be. A gnarled tree, bent almost to the ground with age, loomed ahead of her just as they'd described. A small circle of oddly shaped stones jutted from the mossy earth nearby. 'Twas the Druid place of worship, and 'twas here that she'd been told to bring her babe.

The clamoring of the dogs filled Gwendolyn's ears again, their howls closer than before. They'd picked up her scent for sure. Panicked moans rose to her throat as she took a few more running steps, clinging to the soft, warm weight of her child; her tear-filled gaze swung from one end of the tiny clearing to the other. Sweet Jesu, what if the Druids hadn't come?

At that moment a rustling noise drew her attention; as if fashioned from the forest itself, a woman stepped into the stone circle. She was dressed in a coarse bliaud of brown and green, and strange tattoos—Druid honor marks—rimmed her fingernails and continued up her hands to her arms.

With a kind nod, the woman reached out, saying softly, "Give me the babe now, my lady. There isn't much time."

Gwendolyn paused, but the hounds' chorus rose again, vicious in its intensity. With a choked cry, she reached into her tunic and took her child from its haven against her skin. Murmuring wordless sounds of love, she cradled its head and pressed her lips once more to its downy curls. Tears blinded her as she kept up the sing-song humming, nuzzling her babe and breathing in its sweet, milky fragrance.

Knowing that she'd never have the chance again.

Too soon it was time. Her arms trembled violently as the Druid woman took the child from her with a gentle touch; her sobs gained in force while she watched the woman back away. As if from the end of a long tunnel, she heard the quiet assurance that this was for the best. That they would keep the babe safe and secure. And then the Druid was gone, melted back into the woodland as if she were part of the trees and leaves that whispered their melancholy song to the sky.

Gwendolyn sank slowly to the ground, emptiness engulfing her—a huge black hole that had once been filled with the tender miracle of her child. All that kept her from curling up in the dirt and letting Owain's dogs have her was the knowledge that she wasn't done yet. A realization that told her she could still do more to protect her babe, still draw attention away from the Druid woman's presence.

Dragging herself to her feet, Gwendolyn ran back toward the brutal howling of the dogs, the crashing sounds of the army Owain led in quest of her. She veered suddenly to the left, her feet flying over roots and stones, her heart thumping, and her chest aflame as she sought to divert her pursuers' attention to her.

Before long the burning in her lungs forced her to stop again. She could go no farther, but she hoped against hope that it would be enough.

An eerie stillness settled over the woodland as she bent over, gasping for air. Dimly, she realized that it was odd to hear no chattering of animals or birds high in the trees. Even the baying of the dogs had fallen silent.

In the next instant, she knew why.

With a violent snapping of branches, Prince Owain strode into view before her. Slowly, she straightened and pushed aside her tangled hair to look up at him—the massive, stunning warrior that was her lord husband.

For a while he gazed at her without speaking, his face grim under the blue war designs painted on his cheeks and brow. Far off through the trees, she could see the sun winking on the weapons and shields of his vast army, kept at a distance so that he could confront his errant wife in private. A shaft of light slanted down on him as well, turning his ebony hair to a blue-black halo above him, making him look like some kind of dark angel come to gain vengeance on her for her sins.

"What have you done with our child?" he finally asked, his voice gruff with suppressed emotion.

"Our babe is not the Legend, Owain," she whispered, searching him with her gaze, trying to make him understand. "Why can't you see? The birthmark, the signs . . . they mean nothing. The child is innocent, and I could not let you—"

"Where is she?" he growled, taking a threatening step toward her, his obsidian eyes glittering. "Do not toy with me, Gwendolyn. Give her to me now. I vow that you will not relish the consequences of disobeying me further."

A kind of calm filled her as she faced this powerful man who'd once professed to love her above all else. This Welsh prince who'd bargained away nearly half of his fortunes only a year ago in order to gain the privilege of wedding her.

She raised one shaky, dirt-smeared hand to her face, brushing her fingers over her eyes. But her mind was clear, her heartbeat steady at last. He wouldn't get her child. Nay, little Gwynne was safe from his plots and his obsessions. His dreams of war and glory. Nothing else mattered.

"She is gone, Owain. Gone for good, to a place that is safe from the bloodshed you planned for her. You will never see her again." She paused, glancing away and blinking back her tears before adding huskily, "And neither will I."

A metallic scraping sound pulled her gaze to her husband again. Light glinted off the deadly length of his blade, reflecting the dangerous shadows shifting in his eyes.

"You are wrong, Gwendolyn," he murmured, his voice all the more menacing for its softness. "I *will* see her again. Our child is the Legend reborn, and once I have finished what must be done here, I will scour every mountain, search beneath every rock and tree in all of Wales. I will move heaven and earth if need be—and I promise you, I will find her."

He strode forward, then, coming at her with the confident gait of a predator who has finally cornered his prey.

Gwendolyn froze for an instant before gasping and leaping into action, spurred on by an impulse as old as time. Spinning away from him, she began to run again, though the branches whipped back to scratch her and sharp stones cut into her feet. She took final, hopeless flight, because she knew exactly what was happening here. She'd seen it in Owain's eyes . . .

# Chapter 1

*The wood beyond Dunston Castle*
*The border of England and Wales*
*Fourteen years later*

**S**he hadn't come.

Frowning, Aidan ducked around one of the towering stones that ringed the clearing. The ancient circle stood as a remnant of times long ago—days of myth, sorcery, and legend. And it *was* magic, their secret meeting place. Here he and Gwynne had spent countless hours, free from the weight of prying eyes or the restraints others might wish to impose upon a gentle Welsh lass and her forbidden English suitor.

"Gwynne, are you here?" he called out, appalled to hear the quaver in his voice. He quelled his weakness with a grimace, saying more firmly, "Gwynne, answer me!"

That was better. It wouldn't do for him to sound uncertain. Not today of all days. Today he must be confident

6

and strong, as befitted the fifteen-year-old son of Dunston's lord. He must be sure of himself if he hoped to convince Gwynne that what he planned for them was right.

"Gwynne!" He stalked forward so quickly that the edge of his tunic caught on a felled branch, snapping the wood with a resounding crack.

"For goodness' sake, Aidan, I'm over here. You needn't bellow," Gwynne scolded, making him jump as he spun to face her.

She sat cross-legged on top of one of the ancient stones only a few paces away, looking down at him with mischief in her silver gaze. The sun caressed her face and glinted on the fall of raven hair that hung past her waist like a cloak, concealing what she held cupped in her palms. He saw with a flush of pleasure that she wore the circlet of wildflowers he'd woven and left for her here this morning, when he'd departed Dunston on a pretext of hunting. Perching atop the stone, she looked like some kind of fey lass come to him through the misty veils of time.

Just beyond the stone, a crow with a splinted wing— one of the many creatures he knew she relished taking in and healing—hopped a little ways off, as if nonplussed by his thunderous entrance. She glanced at it, crooning softly before directing her sparkling gaze at Aidan once more.

He couldn't help but smile at her daring. She was a fearless thing, he thought, biting the inside of his cheek. Especially for a girl.

"What are you doing up there?" he demanded with mock ire.

She didn't respond, instead grinning as she shrugged her shoulders and arched her brow in that maddening way of hers.

"Well, you must come down at once. We may be almost of an age, but that doesn't mean your bones won't break as badly as a child's if you fall from there."

"Nay, I'll not come down." She shook her head, her hair rippling about her. " 'Tis too good an angle."

"For what?"

By the time his bemused mind caught up with his instincts, it was too late. With a shriek of glee, Gwynne sat up straight and began pelting him with the handfuls of acorns she'd been hoarding. He shouted as the nuts found their mark with stinging accuracy; then yelling a playful war cry, he launched himself at her and pulled her from the stone. She fell on him, scattering the flower petals from her circlet all around, and they laughed and rolled together on the soft grass, coming to rest, finally, with him lying half atop her.

Breathless, he smiled and gazed into her eyes as he brushed a tendril from her brow. He could wait no longer. Leaning down, he tasted her lips as he'd been aching to. His mouth slid smoothly against hers, and he was gratified when she lifted herself into him. She threaded her cool fingers through his hair, causing tingles of pleasure to tighten his groin and jolt every inch of his skin to full awareness.

No matter how many times he kissed her, he knew he'd never get enough. He knew it with the burning certainty of youth; he'd never stop feeling this rush of sensation—or the tantalizing thoughts that followed of what he wished to do with her, ways he wanted to touch her.

But that must needs come later, he reminded himself. Later, after he'd made her his own in truth and by law.

With a groan, he rolled away, settling for lying at her side. Wordlessly, she slipped her hand into his, and their fingers intertwined as naturally as the breeze wafting through the trees near their magic circle. Together they gazed up at the smooth blue canopy of the sky above them.

The splinted crow disturbed their peace for a moment

when he hopped over to peck at Gwynne's tiny, expended weapons, but they ignored him. The late summer sun blanketed them with warmth; insects hummed, the grass felt soft beneath them, and the wind swished through the trees, adding music to the scented air around them.

It was time, Aidan decided.

"Gwynne, I have something to ask of you."

"Aye?" she said softly, tilting her head to look at him.

He held his breath, focusing on her gaze; then he just let the words tumble out. "Marry me, Gwynne. Marry me here and now, in the circle. If we betroth ourselves in the age-old way, no one will ever be able to part us. Ever."

"*Marry* you?" Gwynne sat up slowly. The smile faded from her face, replaced by an expression of wonder.

"Aye. Marry me today!" Aidan pushed himself up next to her. "I love you, Gwynne. I've loved you since the day I found you picking berries in the glen—so long that I cannot remember what my life was like before you. I want to pledge myself to you, if you'll have me."

"You wish to wed me?" Gwynne asked, her voice laced with tears and such heartbreaking uncertainty that he reached up to cup her face and gaze into her eyes again.

"Aye, love, truly. If you feel as I do, then this day we can become one."

"Oh, Aidan, I wish it more than anything!"

Relief flooded him, and he leaned in to kiss her again. But she pulled back suddenly, taking his hands and frowning.

"What of your father? Will he not oppose this?"

Aidan stiffened.

"Mam will be furious when she learns that we've wed," she continued, "and she has nothing to lose. But Lord Sutcliffe—"

"My father needn't know anything of our betrothal," he broke in harshly. "Not yet, anyway."

She looked like she was going to cry again, and Aidan cursed himself. Softening his tone, he added, "I know my duty to my father and my family well, Gwynne. It has been bred into me from the cradle—whether I wish it or nay, I must become a knight without peer for King Henry, a warrior to carry on the de Brice name and reputation in England." He looked down. "In truth, I learned only this morn that I must leave Dunston Castle within the week to foster as a squire with my father's cousin, Rexford de Vere, the Earl of Warrick, so that I may begin to fulfill my service and my destiny."

"*Leave*?"

Now 'twas Gwynne's turn to press her gentle palms to his face, pulling him to her, forcing him to meet her gaze. Her eyes welled with tears; one crystalline drop escaped, its liquid path marring the silk of her cheek. "You will leave Dunston in a week, Aidan? You will leave *me*?"

"I must leave Dunston, Gwynne, aye," he answered, his chest tightening as he said it. "But never you. Not in my heart. 'Tis why I wish to wed you here and now, in our magic circle, so that no matter how far I must go, or for how long, you will know that I am yours. Then, when the time comes and I am a man in my own right, we will make our union known. And then none, including my father, will dare deny it."

Aidan clenched his fists as he spoke, as if by willing it so, it could be. By God, he would *make* it so. Only a few years more . . .

A few years more and his father would no longer be able to bargain with him as a political tool, valuing him for his promise of manhood and offering it to the highest bidder amongst the fathers of England's many young heiresses. Nay. Then his father would have to accept that he was wed, bound body and soul to the gentle Welsh girl who'd captured his heart in the peace of this magic wood.

"I will make a good life for us, Gwynne, I swear it. But I must first make my way and free myself of the plans my father has laid for me."

She swallowed hard, her face vulnerable with uncertainty and the hope that struggled against it. "If only it could be so, Aidan," she whispered. She flung her arms around his neck and pulled him tight to her, breathing against his ear, "Yet only say it is, and I will believe."

"Aye, Gwynne," he answered huskily, cupping her head and threading his hands through her exquisite, silken hair. He breathed in her scent, fresh as the new leaves of spring, kissing her cheek and the tender spot at the top of her jaw.

"I vow that I will make it so."

Pulling back, he gazed at her solemnly. Then he reached into his tunic and drew out a length of rich emerald-hued cloth, embroidered with colorful flowers woven through the openwork pattern of a snow-white cross. Gwynne gasped at the beauty of it, and Aidan took her hand and helped her to her feet before draping the fabric over her fingers.

" 'Tis a length of de Brice sacramental cloth, taken from our chapel," he said, placing his fingers beneath hers and wrapping the material round, encircling their joined hands. " 'Twill serve as a sign of God's presence in our union."

Wide-eyed, Gwynne nodded. He reveled in the warmth of her palm against the back of his hand, held together by the sacred band. Her lips trembled, and she caught the tender, ruby fullness of the lower curve with her teeth. The sight of it made Aidan long to kiss her again, to soothe her cares away with the loving caress of his mouth.

Instead he dragged his gaze from her lips and up to her eyes, their distinctive color muted now with the depth of her emotions. She blinked, and he smiled, coaxing a smile from her as well. Then he took a deep breath and began their vows.

"I, Aidan de Brice, son of Gavin de Brice, second Earl of Sutcliffe, do take thee, Gwynne ap Moran, to be my wife. I love thee with all my heart and soul, and will bind myself to thee forever, with this my eternal vow. I do so swear it."

She smiled tremulously. "And I, Gwynne ap Moran, take thee, Aidan de Brice, to be my husband. I love thee with all that I am, and will keep only unto thee until the end of time. This I so swear and will abide, heart and soul, until I die."

They stood for a moment, just gazing at each other. Finally, Aidan said quietly, "Then it is done, Gwynne. By the laws of England and Wales, we are husband and wife." He swallowed. "All that remains now is the final consummation of our vows."

Her cheeks flushed an enchanting pink, and she gave him a shy look before glancing away. Aidan grinned, his heart thudding madly in his chest as he considered their boldness and the joy he felt in what they'd just done—in what they had yet to do.

He loosened the embroidered fabric from their hands and pressed it into her palm. "Take this cloth as my pledge, Gwynne. I wish 'twas more, but it must needs suffice until I can earn a proper gift for you."

"Nay, Aidan, 'tis far too costly."

" 'Tis yours, Gwynne," he insisted gently. "Take it and know of my love for you each time you look upon it."

"I do not know what to say," she murmured at last, bringing the folded fabric to her breast. She gazed at him, emotion full in her gaze, and another burst of tenderness shot through him.

"I—I want to give you something too," she said softly. Tucking the cloth into her over-tunic, she reached down and slid his dagger from the sheath at his waist before he could speak against it, then brought it up to cut off a hand's-length lock of her hair. With deft fingers, she braided the top to a close, so that when she handed it to him, the end curled around his palm like dark silk.

" 'Tis not so fine a gift as yours," she said, "but 'twill serve to comfort you, I hope, as your gift will comfort me during the time we must be parted."

Aidan was speechless for a moment. He thought his breath might never flow freely again for the lump that seemed to have settled in his throat. "Gwynne . . ." he murmured hoarsely. He swallowed a few times. "I will treasure it always, Gwynne." Then, tipping her chin up, he lowered his mouth to hers, melding their lips in a sacred kiss. A kiss that spoke more eloquently than his clumsy words ever could.

She pressed close to him, and he felt her sigh of longing shudder through every inch of his sensitized flesh. She reached her arms around him, sliding her palms up his back; the gentle swell of her breasts seemed to brand his chest, her thighs warm against his. He deepened their kiss, readying to lower her to the tender grasses within the circle, aching to complete the now consecrated promise of their love at long last . . .

Until a piercing scream rent the air.

A slight rumbling sound began to swell in the distance, increasing in power until the wood around them erupted into a cacophony of noises: branches breaking and men shouting. Men with wildly painted blue faces.

Sweet Lord in heaven . . .

Aidan stood stunned for a moment. Everything seemed to slow to a maddening, surreal pace as he swung his gaze to Gwynne; she was staring at him, wide-eyed, her mouth open in horror as she twisted her fingers into the front of his tunic.

Oh, God, he had to get her out of here.

Swallowing his panic, he tried to shout, but 'twas clear that she couldn't hear him. He settled on jerking his head in the direction of her mother's cottage, praying that she understood. Grasping her hands, he led her, stumbling at first, toward the edge of the stone circle . . .

And then they ran.

# Chapter 2

*Near Craeloch Castle, Western England*
*June, twelve years later*

The nightmare had come again last night, choking him with how real it had seemed, how painful it had been to relive . . . the blue-faced devils attacking, Gwynne clinging to him in fear, her screams going on and on as the warriors swarmed into the clearing, their weapons held aloft—the arrow piercing his chest, and what came after . . .

Aidan rubbed the back of his neck, inhaling sharply of the early morning mist in an effort to shake the memories. 'Twas fitting, he supposed, that it had come again now; today of all days he needed to remember exactly why he was here. Of why he had vowed to spend the rest of his life, if need be, stopping the Welsh rebels from doing to anyone else what they'd done to him.

To him and Gwynne . . .

He leaned over his steed's neck, the vapor of his breath mingling with the cool air as he awaited his prey. Any moment now the warrior the Welsh called the Dark Legend would emerge from the forest with his band of rebels to claim the rich prize he expected to find outside of Craeloch's walls—payment in gold, offered in return for leaving the people in peace, their property and lands undisturbed.

The bastard would find naught but a trap.

Aidan shifted in his saddle, his muscles tense, his thoughts racing. It had been a long year hunting these Welsh outlaws and their powerful, elusive leader. A year during which the rebellious inhabitants of Wales had gathered in ever increasing numbers, rallying behind the Dark Legend in raid after raid against English barons and Marcher lords. Against King Henry himself.

They had to be stopped.

But the Dark Legend was no ordinary enemy. Nay, he was an opponent of the most deadly kind. A man who'd risen to mythic proportions in the minds and hearts of the people who followed him—for according to the bards who sang of him, he was no ordinary man. They claimed him to be none other than King Arthur, come back from his rest in Avalon. The Dark Legend of prophecy, returned to lead them to freedom from English rule.

Such dangerous fancy could not be allowed to continue. The man could be the devil himself, as far as Aidan was concerned; if all went as planned, this day would be his last.

"There," Kevyn murmured next to him, nodding toward the glint of metal that shone through the trees across the clearing. "They approach."

Aidan swung his gaze to the spot, honing in on his quarry. "Ready the men for attack," he answered quietly, never losing sight of the edge of the forest. As he heard the soft call of warning pass down the ranks, his hands tightened, anticipation thrumming through his blood with every beat of his heart. It was almost time for the battle to begin—the culmination of all he'd worked so hard to accomplish.

Almost time for another chance at redemption.

Suddenly, the chain mail of one of the rebel warriors caught the morning sun, throwing flashes of light as more than two dozen Welshmen rode from the wood and into the clearing, some of them wearing blue war paint, others helms. Their leader sat proudly atop his steed in front of them, clasping a magnificent golden shield with the emblem of the legendary Arthur—a red dragon, rampant—emblazoned on its front, going forth as if no one would dare to oppose his will. As if none possessed the right or the power to stop him. Aidan watched him, his gaze narrowing as he watched his progress across the field.

*Strange.* He wasn't as large as Aidan had imagined he'd be. Then again, the bard's tales told not of a brawny man, but of a dark-haired youth, lean and tall. A mythic Arthur with sword skills that dazzled the mind and strange, otherworldly combat moves that froze his disbelieving opponents into dangerous immobility. Immobility that got them killed.

Tamping down that ridiculous notion, Aidan caressed the hilt of his sword; he needed to be patient. A few moments more and he would face the celebrated enemy himself. Move in for the kill. And then he would find out just how much was legend and how much was mere flesh and blood.

A feral smile edged Aidan's lips. Aye, he relished the thought of crossing blades with this opponent. The Dark Legend was about to meet the Scourge of Wales, and he wagered the results would not be pretty.

Only a few more seconds—just a little longer and the

rebels would be far enough into the clearing that they'd not be able to flee back to the forest when he attacked.

Just a little longer . . .

"Now!"

Aidan's command ripped through the silence, sending the full three score of his men hurtling onto the field. He led the solid wall of horseflesh and shouting warriors toward the Welsh, who reined their mounts in sharply at the explosive sound and movement of the attack.

Keeping his gaze trained on their leader, Aidan closed the gap, feeling a pang of disappointment when he realized that the man's helmet with its concealing face-guard would undoubtedly mask his enemy's expression of fear and surprise. 'Twas a look Aidan had long relished in his imagination.

But in the next instant the clash of battle overcame any idle thoughts. Instinct roared to life as Aidan slashed out at any Welsh warrior unfortunate enough to get between him and his prey. Bleeding from a fatal wound, one of the Welshmen fell off his mount, allowing Aidan to see a path through the writhing, battling forms of the warriors around him.

A path that led directly to the Dark Legend.

Kicking his destrier forward, Aidan charged at him, lifting his bloodied sword to begin the combat that would remove his enemy forever from the light of day. But as he approached, the Legend swung his steed around, and Aidan's mount rammed into him, the force of impact knocking both men to the ground.

Black spots blinded Aidan's vision; his chest felt afire, but he knew he had little time to recover. Looking up, he saw the Dark Legend spring to his feet with uncanny ease, his growl of rage audible even through the din of fighting around them.

Ignoring the answering flash of apprehension that shot

down his spine, Aidan rolled to stand just in time to meet a savage thrust, his blade glancing off of his enemy's sword with bone-jarring force. It deflected up to the man's head, catching his helmet and sending it flying off at the same time that it knocked him sideways and onto one knee.

He was down.

As if in the slower motion of a dream, Aidan pulled back, preparing to deal the killing strike his king had commanded of him. But before he could commence the blow, the Dark Legend swung his head to glare at him, a snarl twisting his features as he locked gazes with Aidan for the first time.

And at that moment, Aidan felt like he'd been impaled right through the heart; he froze, unable to move a limb. If not for his own men flanking either side of him as they fought, he would surely have been killed by one of the Welsh. All the energy seemed to drain from his arms. They dropped to his sides, the tip of his blade gouging uselessly into the dirt of the field. Even knowing 'twas impossible, there was no mistaking what he saw.

A smooth, beardless face stared back at him. An oval face, topped by raven curls chopped short like a boy's. But that didn't mask the fact that this was no youthful King Arthur looking at him, grimacing in anger. Nay, Aidan would recognize those silver eyes anywhere. They belonged to a *woman*—a woman he'd loved long ago.

A woman named Gwynne ap Moran.

But before he could bring himself to voice her name, she leaped from her crouched position, moving so fast that she was almost a blur as she tucked and spun in a complete revolution before landing on her feet in front of him. Her gaze pierced him, her expression flat. Unknowing.

"You will regret this day, Englishman," she muttered, her voice a husky growl as she lashed out at him with her weapon.

He managed to pull back and twist enough so that the blade missed his vitals, instead catching his upper arm. The flare of pain from the cut banished the last of the strange weakness that had dominated him since he first saw her face; angrily, he lunged back at her, but she'd already disappeared behind one of the riderless Welsh steeds. Swinging atop it, she wheeled around, flashing another hate-filled glare at him before looking away to shout a war cry of retreat to her men.

Then turning, she thundered from the field, leading her remaining warriors back into the forest—and leaving Aidan to stand there bleeding, more shaken than he'd been since that day twelve years ago when he'd thought he'd seen her die . . .

Vaguely, he heard his men gather around him, heard Kevyn's anxious voice questioning him as if from afar as he examined the wound on his arm. But it blended into the background of his mind, twisting and turning with all manner of haunting images and agonizing scenes. With bloody, horrific memories.

He swallowed the bitter lump in his throat, only one thought managing to shine clear in the muddled mess of his brain; for he couldn't help but acknowledge that the stories wafting down from the Welsh mountains had been right on one point, at least . . .

The dead, it seemed, had indeed risen to new life.

# Chapter 3

 ❧ ❧

Aidan clenched his fists, staring into the woods into which Gwynne and her men had disappeared. His breath rasped heavy, his gaze suddenly narrowing to a pin-prick of black—his vision obscured by the rush of images. By the unbearable memory from that day so long ago . . .

"Aidan! Christ, man, what is it?"

Aidan jolted to awareness as Kevyn growled the question again and shook his arm, the brutal vision receding again to the dark corners of his brain. He breathed deep and saw that he stood, still frozen, on the bloody field. Slowly, sound and life returned to his senses. He pulled his gaze away from the wood. Kevyn waited, staring at him anxiously, while nearby, Derik ordered some of the men to bring bandages from the supplies they'd hidden at the field's edge; swinging his gaze further, Aidan saw that Cedric and Bryan tended to a fallen comrade not far off, backed by another four or five of his men who combed the field for survivors.

"Kev, it was her," Aidan managed to say quietly, his mouth still stiff from shock.

"*Her*?" His friend stiffened at the word and then snapped, "Christ's blood, Aidan, the Dark Legend just slipped our snare, and he was most definitely not a her." He let out his breath in a whistle. "I knew that gash was more serious than you let on. It's addled your brain. I'll tell one of the men to bring some thread to stitch it."

"Nay," Aidan answered, shaking his head. "My wound is not the problem." He saw young Cedric glance up from his position tending the injured man.

" 'Twas Gwynne, Kev," he said in a low voice. "Gwynne is the Dark Legend."

"Gwynne?" His friend looked confused for a moment before his face went slack. "You don't mean—?"

Aidan nodded. "Aye. 'Twas her. I'll not deny that she was different, but I'd recognize those eyes, that face, anywhere."

"Impossible," Kevyn scoffed. "For a woman to fight like that? 'Tis impossible. You need to sit in the shade for a while, my friend, then it will all seem clearer."

"I'm not addled, Kev. She saved my life twelve years ago—I think I'd recognize her, disguise or nay."

"The woman who saved you is dead. She broke her neck struggling against the bandits when they carried her away. You saw it with your own eyes, man! She is long gone—but the Dark Legend is very much alive, and we're under orders from the king to bring him down. This is no time to let fantasies overthrow your reason."

Aidan clenched his jaw and stalked from the field toward his steed. "I'm telling you, 'twas her, Kev—and like it or not, I'm going after her."

"Going after—?" Kevyn sputtered, coming to a dead halt before he was forced to scramble to catch up to Aidan. "You can't mean to track the rebels into Welsh territory? The bastards have traps set all over the bloody mountains!"

"You said it yourself—'tis the king's orders." Aidan reached up to check his steed's bridle strap. "I am to defeat the Dark Legend by death or by capture. Our trap here failed, so I will follow her to her camp and stop her there."

"Oh, aye, 'tis as simple as that."

"I'd have had her on the field today had I not been so surprised at seeing her."

Kevyn scowled, arms crossed over his massive chest. "You're insane, do you know that? The Dark Legend is a man, Aidan, not a woman. A *man*. He most certainly was not Gwynne ap Moran."

When Aidan didn't offer anything more, Kevyn rolled his eyes. "Fine. Let us say for the sake of argument that by some miracle it was Gwynne, and you *do* manage to track her to her stronghold. What then?"

Aidan saw the question in his friend's gaze, the same question that had been pounding through his own skull since that moment on the battlefield. How far would he go to stop her? It was a question for which he had no answer. Not yet, anyway.

"I'll do my duty," Aidan said finally, steeling himself against the burning memories that slashed again through his mind. "How remains to be seen, but I'll fulfill my vow to defeat the Welsh rebels."

"Aye, but this particular rebel is what inspired your vow in the first place."

"She wasn't one of them twelve years ago, Kev." Aidan looked away, jabbing his hand through his hair. "She's changed, that much is obvious. On the field she stared at me with a look to chill the blood in my veins. I don't think she even knew me."

"All the more reason to be careful," Kevyn said, gesturing to the bloody gash on his arm. "If 'tis her and you hunt her down, you'd be wise to remember what she's capable of."

Aidan's jaw tightened, but he remained silent, and Kevyn finally sighed. "All right. Whether the Dark Legend is a man or a woman doesn't seem to matter much right now. Your mind is obviously made up, so I suppose I might as well hear it sooner rather than later. When exactly do you plan to attempt this foray into Welsh territory?"

"Within the hour."

His friend let go a colorful stream of curses. "I should have known it. Blast it, but you don't believe in patience, do you? I'll need to start right away if I'm to ready the men and mounts in time."

Aidan just raised his brow and smiled, and Kevyn gave him a good-natured shove and another curse before shaking his head and stalking off to complete his task.

But exactly three quarters of an hour later, they were all ready to go. Aidan gave the signal to ride, and Kevyn, Cedric, Bryan, and more than a score of his loyal warriors set out into the perilous mountain climes. They rode, resolute and committed, as he knew they would; to the last man they'd spill their blood for his sake, and he would for theirs.

But as he led them into the thickening forest, Aidan's nagging thoughts of what to do with Gwynne once he found her returned with a vengeance. Neither of the two most obvious choices—killing her or capturing her—seemed possible. Taking her life, even in battle, was out of the question. No matter what had happened to her in the last twelve years, she was still a woman—a woman he'd loved, and who, in return, had once loved him enough to save him from a brutal death.

And as for capturing her . . .

After what he'd seen of her fighting skills and the abilities of her men, he'd wager that outcome stood the same chance as the king's prize pear trees bearing fruit in January.

He shook his head, focusing his attention on the trail. There had to be another way. He only prayed that their journey would be long enough for him to figure out what the devil it was.

Gwynne hunched over Damon's body, her arms aching as she pressed against the gaping wound on his side. Her hands slipped, and she cursed under her breath. Using her shoulder, she tried to clear her eyes, but 'twas useless. The slick heat of blood was everywhere, pumped out by the fading force of Damon's heart. She blinked, willing the sting away.

'Twas so hard to concentrate.

She cursed more loudly this time before closing her eyes and breathing in again. She bade the power to form, the heat to spread through her and swell from her palms—struggled to make it surge forth and seal his gash.

Nothing.

*Damn, damn, damn . . .*

"*Chwedl*," one of her men murmured. "Let him go. 'Tis over now. He is gone."

"Nay." She gritted her teeth and kept pressing against Damon's side. She wouldn't give up. Her powers had worked before. Healed the dying, stopped the bleeding.

*Work, damn it, work!*

He was so young. Only sixteen and on his first mission, one that should have been safe. She'd been sure 'twould be safe. A simple gathering of tribute to keep her people clothed and fed for a few more months.

Her men clustered around her, silent in the shade of the copse where they'd been forced to stop after Damon fell from his mount. The foolish lad had hidden the wound he'd received battling the English; he'd ridden high into the mountain forest behind her, trying to be strong, wanting to return to camp with the rest of his warrior comrades and *Chwedl*, their legend.

With a growl Gwynne finally admitted defeat, pushing herself up and dragging her sleeve across her mouth. After a long moment, she pulled her gaze from Damon's lifeless body and turned away, stalking to the edge of the glade to yank off her blood-spattered hauberk. It didn't do much good; her woolen tunic and shirt beneath were soaked crimson.

The men kept their distance as she stood very still and just concentrated on breathing, trying to cool the rage, the hatred she felt before it spiraled out of control. It would do no good. Not now, anyway. Not until she faced the English bastards again.

After a moment, Dafydd, her chief guardsman, dared to come up to her and put his hand on her shoulder. She flinched from the contact but didn't pull away.

" 'Tis not your fault," he said gently. " 'Twas Damon's time. Even a legend cannot stop the hand of God."

Gwynne clenched her jaw, staring straight ahead into the shadows of the woodland. "I thank you for saying so, and yet I do not think that will comfort his Mam when we return to camp with his body in tow." She glanced at Dafydd, who nodded somberly before she pulled away and walked back toward the corpse.

"Come," she called to the men standing nearby. "Help me secure him to his mount."

She was readying to lift the body when she suddenly stiffened. A chill went up her spine, and her senses seemed to pitch higher as she spun to glare into the woodland again.

"Isolde!"

Her combined bellow and scowl made a few of the younger men of the raiding party back away, while Dafydd and the more seasoned of her guard stood firm, prepared from years of service with her to witnessing this more uncanny aspect of her powers.

"Curse it—Isolde, I know you're near. Show yourself!"

A slight rustling of branches revealed a shadowy shape that stepped forward into the light of the clearing. Isolde's cobalt robes looked strangely brilliant in the murky glade; her chestnut braids, shot through with silver, dangled over her shoulders, and she wore an expression Gwynne knew well: a hard, cold look that warned of her displeasure before she ever uttered a word.

"What is this?" Isolde finally snapped, flicking both her gaze and her slender fingers toward the corpse. "Another lad gone to waste thanks to your carelessness, *Chwedl*?"

Gwynne stiffened, and she felt the men around her pull in tighter, but no one murmured an answer to the sorceress.

Holding her robe close to her with one hand, Isolde frowned and moved in her odd, floating way toward Damon's body. "You ought to take more care when you go into battle with green warriors," she complained. "My sight cannot always be trusted to foretell such weighty matters."

"Aye, and yet you bandy it about as the only truth when it suits you," Gwynne muttered.

Isolde turned her icy glare on her again. "It has suited you in the past, *Legend*. You'd do well to—"

"Enough of your nagging, woman!"

The command came from one of the two fully geared warriors who stomped into the clearing with enough noise to make Gwynne and her men reach for their weapons. Upon sight of their faces, however, everyone relaxed and called out greetings before setting again to the task Gwynne had asked of them. Isolde just glowered at the intruders—her husband, Marrok, and their grown son, Lucan.

"Marrok," Gwynne called, as she strode toward the man who was both the clan's leader and her mentor in the arts of war. She clasped his forearm with her own, feeling a surge of gladness to see him. He was her rock, the only one she could truly rely on. He alone had trained her from the first day she'd held a sword, and aside from herself, he was the most gifted and respected warrior in the clan. She glanced at the younger man beside him, nodding acknowledgment. Lucan only jerked his head in response before shifting his gaze to his mother, who had slowly crossed the length of the clearing to stand beside him.

"What are you doing back so soon?" Gwynne asked them. "I thought your negotiations would keep you away for another fortnight at least."

"Bah!" Marrok scowled. "The Welsh prince wants peace with the English, blast him. He talks of freedom, then in the next breath demands we stop our assaults on the border lords. We'll get no aid from Rhys ap Gruffyd, *Chwedl*; we must rethink our tactics."

"I won't give up. Too many of our people have lost too much for us to stop the fight now."

Marrok glanced beyond Gwynne to Damon's pale corpse.

" 'Twas a trap," she said quietly, swinging around to view her men's progress at securing him to his mount. "The English knew we were coming. They set us up and attacked us in the open. We lost five men in the ambush—six, counting Damon."

Isolde made a disgruntled sound. "You should have been more careful. Those you fought must possess their own power. An ability that helped them to hide their true purpose from my sight."

"They were Englishmen," Gwynne growled. "The only power they can claim is their ability to grovel at King Henry's feet."

"All right, enough," Marrok chided, pulling Gwynne aside, even as he directed Isolde back. When they could talk privately, he asked, "How many English were there?"

"At least three score, led by that bastard who calls himself the Scourge of Wales. I recognized him by the device on his shield—a hawk swooping to pierce the neck of a dragon. 'Twas he who set the offering as a trap, I'm sure of it."

"Then they know of our condition and the poverty that hampers our cause."

"Aye, and they used it as bait against us." Gwynne flashed a dark look. "But I left them with a few remembrances of my own. And I wounded their leader before we were forced to flee."

"The Scourge himself?"

Gwynne made a scoffing sound. "He was less a Scourge than an idiot; he stood there stiff-legged, allowing me to swing at him before he even flinched to move out of my way."

Marrok was silent for a long moment, and Gwynne felt a tingle of unease as her mentor's gaze settled hard on her. Finally he murmured, "Where is your helm, *Chwedl*?"

She looked away and slipped her hauberk back over her head again before shrugging. "I lost it in the battle."

Marrok muttered a curse. "He saw your face, didn't he? 'Tis why he stood like one bewitched; he knows you're a woman."

"He knows nothing," Gwynne answered, jerking her gaze back to him. "I was covered in blood, dirt, and sweat. Even without my helm, there is no way the English bastard could have known me for what I am."

"Ah, but that is where you are wrong, *Legend*," a man's voice called from behind her.

Gwynne whirled around and backed up, the sound of her and Marrok's weapons clearing their sheaths drowned out by the metallic hiss of the rest of her men's swords, as they all turned to face the owner of that imposing voice. Her comrades silently moved into position around her, even as the English leader stepped into the clearing, flanked by more than twice her number in soldiers.

All went still as the opposing forces faced each other down. Tension filled the clearing, prickling up Gwynne's back like a thousand needles of fire.

"I take it you are prepared to die this day, Englishman," Gwynne said, her voice dangerously soft as she fixed her gaze on the warrior whose trap had caused the deaths of six loyal men. Her hand tightened on her hilt, lust for battle swelling in her blood.

"I could ask the same of you, *Legend*, considering the outcome of our last meeting and the numbers you face here now—but I would much rather ask something else."

She said nothing, only keeping her gaze hard upon him.

Reaching up, he pulled off his helm, and a little shock went through her, followed fast by hollow panic. A full half of her life was a blank in her memory, and the sight of his square-jawed face, his eyes, and the thick, dark hair that fell to his shoulders sent a prickle of warning through her—a maddening sensation of something she couldn't quite place.

She heard Marrok's sharp intake of breath, felt him stiffen beside her, and her heart began to thud more wildly.

The Englishman cocked his brow.

"Do you know me, Gwynne?"

The sound of his voice uttering her true name lanced through her like a stinging arrow, and she glared at him, trying to quell her reaction. "Aye, I know you, *marchog*— you call yourself the Scourge of Wales, but you're no different from the rest of the soft-bellied English dogs that I dispatched today."

She thought he might smile for a moment, but then his expression shifted, a dangerous glint darkening his eyes.

" 'Tis an unfortunate answer, Gwynne, for there is much more you ought to know about me."

"I know only that you toy with me, Englishman," she said, her anger building, "and I don't like it. Just who the devil are you, and why are you here, if 'tis not to fight?"

"Ah, now we come to it." This time the corners of his mouth lifted into a mocking smile.

"Allow me to oblige. I am Aidan de Brice, the third Earl of Sutcliffe and a loyal servant to King Henry II, as well as an English warrior under oath to defeat all Welsh rebels . . ."

His gaze locked with hers, scorching and chilling her at the same time.

"And I am here to claim you as my lawful bride."

# Chapter 4

〜〜⟨⟩〜〜

Aidan's men swung their heads to stare at him, their mute expressions of disbelief echoing the cries of denial rising from the Welsh side. Kevyn finally looked away and muttered a curse, but Aidan kept his gaze forward, watching Gwynne's face, seeing her magnificent eyes spark with rage.

Those eyes were all that remained of the girl he'd once known. The rest of her was as fierce and sharp as any battle-hardened warrior. Aye, she'd changed. But he knew she'd sensed something familiar about him. In that second after he'd removed his helm, something had glimmered to life in her memory—fleeting, perhaps, but real.

"You must be out of your mind, Englishman," Gwynne growled at last, taking several steps forward. "I'm no man's *bride,* nor will I ever be. Now, use that sword you're holding to defend yourself, or suffer being cut down where you stand."

"If you attack me now, 'tis possible that you may reach

me," Aidan answered, "but you are outnumbered, and
'twill go badly for your men in the aftermath." He flicked
his gaze to the corpse strapped atop one of the mounts behind the Welsh group. "Think of them, Gwynne, if not of
yourself."

"Every one of my men would gladly risk death for the
pleasure of slicing through an English cur, never fear it."

Aidan cocked his brow again at the savage howling of
support that rose from the Welsh side. Without another
word, he tipped his sword down and pressed the point into
the dirt, very slowly, before lifting his hands up, palms
forward. The Welsh cries died down at his unexpected action, and when it was finally quiet, he offered Gwynne a
half-smile. "Call it a sign of good faith. I have an offer to
make that I think even you will approve."

"You might as well save your breath for battle."

"Patience, Gwynne. You see, I need to *dissolve* the betrothal that is between us, so that I may marry another—an
English lady who has already agreed to become my wife."

"You can marry any milksop you like," she gave him a
feral look, "provided you're alive to do it."

*Christ, she wasn't making this any easier.*

Aidan clenched his jaw, trying to decide what he could
say to make her listen, when the older-looking warrior
near her stepped forward and murmured something in her
ear. As the man talked, her face went white before settling
into the lines of the blackest scowl Aidan had ever seen.
Then she swung her head and whispered angrily, her
weapon still gripped tightly in her fist. The heated exchange continued for a moment before she once again directed her icy glare at Aidan.

"Whether or not such an agreement may have ever ex-
isted between us, de Brice—and I am not saying it did,"
she flicked a dark look at the man behind her, "it has no
bearing now."

"The law says it does, whether you wish it or nay."

"*English* law does not bind me."

Aidan bit back another retort and looked past her to the older man who had talked with her; his gaze settled hard on him, studying him. Aye, he looked familiar. It had been many years, and time had blurred those hours into nightmarish images in his memory, but 'twas possible that he was one of the Welsh warriors who had attacked Gwynne's cottage so long ago and taken her away from him.

He nodded toward the man, deciding to take a chance on it. "Your friend there knows I speak the truth. He's seen me before."

The warrior glared at him. "My name is Marrok, Englishman. And perhaps you forget, but we are at war. Your woman troubles do not interest us."

Aidan shook his head and made a clicking sound with his tongue, as he leaned his forearm onto his hilt. "Ah, but they should, Marrok, since the vows Gwynne and I made were uttered under the law of handfasting, and sworn to within a sacred circle of stones."

Renewed grumblings and murmurs arose from the Welsh, and Gwynne scowled deeper. "If 'tis a release from this phantom betrothal you seek in your own addled mind, Englishman," she called, "then consider it done, so that we may get on with the matter of war between us."

" 'Tis not so simple as that. Our betrothal must be dissolved *legally*." Aidan steeled himself to finish what he had to say. "And that means you must return to English soil with me to do it."

Shocked silence greeted him. Jesu, but she was angry now—more so than he'd seen her yet this day. Rage fair spilled from her in waves, scorching him with heat.

"You can go to hell, de Brice," she finally growled. "I spit on England. The only reason I would go there would be to kill Englishmen." She cocked her head and impaled him with her gaze. "Like you."

"Even if it meant sparing your people the fear of attack for three months?" he countered, undaunted. "Even if it meant food, warmth, and security—a chance for your clan to rebuild its strength to wage war more effectively against its enemies?"

As he spoke, he gestured behind him to Cedric, who handed him a large sack of coin, which he threw into the clearing. It landed with a heavy, metallic sound, leaving no doubt as to the king's ransom in gold it contained.

Marrok's mouth twisted sardonically, and he stepped closer to Gwynne. "You're good at throwing money about, de Brice, but it will gain you no more today than it did when you were a lad. You must be daft to think we would let *Chwedl* return to England with you. 'Tis a trap, clear as day."

"There is no trap, I assure you. I promise her safety while she is with me."

"Why would you want to aid us, even for a short time?" Gwynne broke in, scoffing. "Our people are enemies, and yet you offer money and a temporary peace—why would you do so if not for the fact that you have greater plans for my destruction while I am in your keeping?"

Aidan considered how to respond, finally settling on telling what was in most part the truth. "The situation that I mentioned earlier, the one with the English lady, is . . . imperative. Until this day I did not know that you still lived, but now I cannot go forward with my own plans until what is between us is dissolved. I will do whatever is necessary to clear my way to that end."

"You could always just try to kill me. 'Twould rid you of your problem as completely." She gave him a cold smile. "If you succeeded, that is."

He saw her silver eyes spark with heat and realized that she would relish just such an attempt on his part. But he could never do it.

"Dark Legend or nay, you are still a woman I once knew," he allowed, leaving out the part about once loving her as well, "and I will not try to kill you. I have principles, and I give you my word that you will be treated well if you come with me. No harm will come to you, I swear it."

"Your word means nothing," Gwynne muttered.

"It means everything," he ground out.

By God, he was rapidly losing patience with her.

"I vow that you'll be safe in my keeping for the space of the three months it will take to dissolve our union. At the end of that time I will return you to your people unscathed, and you can then prepare to wage war again if you so choose."

He thought she might throw his words back at him as she'd done each time he'd mentioned their betrothal, but suddenly her expression shifted, her eyes narrowing for an instant. Without answering him, she turned to Marrok and murmured something.

This time it was Marrok's turn to scowl. He shook his head sharply, muttering something in Welsh that Aidan couldn't understand. Gwynne argued back, and Aidan knew by the rigid line of her jaw that she meant to have her way. She said something more, and Marrok tensed before nodding once, his hands fisted at his sides.

Gwynne faced Aidan again, her face still unreadable. "What kind of assurance would I or my people have that you will honor your word, Englishman? For though you claim that it alone is enough, it is not."

Aidan paused, biting back a retort at her insult to his honor. He was close to victory, now, he sensed it. Very close.

"What kind of assurance do you seek?"

"A trade." Her jaw tipped higher, her hand clenched, white-knuckled, on the hilt of her blade. "An exchange of warriors. Four of your best men for me."

"*Four* of my men?"

"Aye." Her brow arched, and a shock went through him. 'Twas the same expression she'd made at him countless times in their magic circle. So long ago, when they'd still loved each other . . .

"I am my people's leader in battle," she continued, seemingly unaware of her effect on him. "Equal to you, at the least. But then, if the trade was you for me, it would defeat the purpose, wouldn't it?" She lifted her brow a little higher, sending that stabbing ache of longing into his heart again.

He swallowed. "I suppose it would."

"If we agree on this, then when I am returned to my people, your men will be restored to you in like condition."

He was readying to reject her offer when Cedric stepped forward. "Allow me to go, my lord," he said. He was followed by Gareth, Bryan, Kevyn, and another half score of his men, each boldly asserting their willingness to participate in the trade that would allow their leader to bring home the Dark Legend.

Speechless for a moment, Aidan viewed them, pride filling him. This could well be a fatal mission, and they all knew it—none better than Aidan himself. The trade might stop the Dark Legend, but only temporarily; his duty to King Henry would remain. And by the terms Gwynne suggested, if she wasn't given back to the Welsh alive and well at the end of their agreement, his men would be unmercifully slaughtered by their Welsh captors.

An idea that had flickered to life as he'd led his forces into Welsh territory bloomed in full now. 'Twas possible, he supposed. It would mean complicating his life, but he could do no less with his men's safety hanging in the balance.

And three months was a fair amount of time . . .

"Very well," he said, finally. "I accept your terms. Four of my men for you."

"Nay," Marrok called out before Gwynne could answer him. "She must be allowed two of her *teulu*, her bodyguards, to accompany her, or she does not go at all."

"Then I'll be trading you four for three," Aidan said.

"So be it," Marrok growled, crossing his arms over his chest and ignoring Gwynne's glare.

"Well, Gwynne? What say you?" Aidan directed a pointed look to her.

She paused, tight-lipped, for a moment, before jerking her head once. "Agreed. Let's get on with it, then."

With a grimace she sheathed her sword; the Welsh reluctantly followed suit, as did Aidan's men. In the end, Cedric, Bryan, Edward, and Gareth crossed to the Welsh side, while Gwynne came over to the English, accompanied by a seasoned-looking warrior named Dafydd, and a younger man she called Owin. Marrok walked over with her as well, pulling away to approach Aidan. He stopped to stand face to face with him, for a moment just studying him, seeming oblivious to the activity around them.

"Before you leave, know this, Englishman," Marrok finally said, his voice as unflinching as the stony set of his jaw. "If you go back on your word—if anything happens to *Chwedl* in your keeping—I swear to you on my last breath that I will hunt you down and drain the life from you drop by drop. Do not mistake me."

"And do not mistake me, old man," Aidan answered evenly. "I live by my honor and my word. 'Tis not *I* who pillage homes and kidnap unsuspecting young women.

You'd do well to remember that. Gwynne ___
fear from me."

Marrok didn't answer, only staring at Aidan ___ a ___
ment more before making a noise in his throat and ___ ing
away to have a few final words with Gwynne.

Kevyn came up next to Aidan, handing him his helm
and leaning in to talk with him as the others around them
finished preparations for their departure.

"Christ's blood, I can't believe 'tis really her. But even
so, what in hell were you thinking to publicly claim a betrothal with her?" he asked quietly. " 'Tis ancient history.
You're risking all you've worked so hard to gain with Helene and her father if they learn of it."

"I know." Aidan tried to ignore the burning ache of the
old wound in his chest. "But I could think of no other way
to make her come with me peacefully."

He shifted his gaze to the cause of this day's troubles.
She was in heated conversation with Marrok and unaware
of his stare. "I had to do it, Kev; I can't explain why, except
to say that I owe her a life-debt—and I couldn't very well
repay it by trying to kill her." He pulled his gaze back to
his friend. "You're right, though; it will be risky. I'll need
your help in making sure the men remain silent about who
she really is and why she's with me once we're home."

"What do you want them to say about her, then?"

"I don't know yet. I'll figure out a story before we arrive at Dunston."

"It had better be a good one," Kevyn said, following
Aidan's stare back to Gwynne. "Though I can't pretend to
understand why you're doing this. It won't matter in a few
days. Once the king learns you've captured the Dark Legend, he'll demand her surrender—and you know the
likely outcome of that. Cedric and the other lads might as
well make their peace with God now."

Aidan paused. "I'm not going to tell the king."

"What?" Kevyn fixed him with an incredulous look.

"Not yet, anyway."

"Christ, Aidan, 'tis not as if you can hide her. She's a warrior, for God's sake. She'll fit into English society about as easily as a wolf mingles with sheep."

"That's why I'm going to keep her secured at Dunston, at least until I have a chance to work on her for a while."

He watched Gwynne, saw the graceful movement of her hands, the quick way she tilted her head, and memory upon memory slammed into him—of Gwynne, young and lithe, bending over to heal a bird's broken wing. Gwynne, her hair rippling down blue-black in the sun where she sat atop a stone in the ancient circle, playfully pelting him with acorns. Gwynne, wrapping her arms around his neck and smiling up at him as she slid her lips sweetly across his.

He swallowed hard, banishing the images. "She knew me once, Kev. Better than anyone. She may not remember it now, but I intend to bring it back for her. To help her remember her life before the rebels stole her away."

Kevyn choked. "Jesu, Aidan, you might as well rip up your betrothal to Helene right now. You cannot go courting another woman under her nose and expect her or her father to ignore it."

"I'm not going to court Gwynne, I'm just going to help her remember," Aidan grated. "Think about it. She's not likely to continue leading the Welsh in battle once she realizes how they used and betrayed her. 'Tis the perfect way to repay my debt to her. Her life will be spared, and the king will get exactly what he wants."

His friend's expression didn't waver. "So you make her remember—make her recall *loving* you, by all that's holy—and then expect her to walk away quietly so that you can marry another woman? Are you daft? She's more likely to pull out her blade and lop off your head than turn against the Welsh for it."

"What would you have me do, then?" Aidan countered. "Hand her over to the Court, and certain execution? Let her stay with the Welsh so that I can face her in battle again and try to kill her myself? I won't do it, Kev. I can't."

His friend didn't respond at first. Shaking his head, he finally muttered, "You're playing with fire, Aidan, mark my words. 'Twill be a bloody inferno, and you yourself are setting the blaze."

Aidan clenched his jaw, his mood turning blacker by the second as Kevyn stalked off to rejoin the other men. This plan was the only way open to him, damn it. It was. Difficult or nay, he had no other choice.

And yet a part of him wondered if his friend might be right after all . . .

Because he swore that he could already feel the first tiny flames rising up to lick at the tender scars of his heart.


Gwynne scowled at Marrok as she stepped away from him to check her mount's girth strap. It was clear that he was worried about her—more so than she'd ever seen him, even counting the times she'd ridden into what promised to be a vicious battle.

" 'Tis the perfect opportunity to see their defenses up close, without risking anything," she said to him over her shoulder. "I'll be led straight to the heart of de Brice's lands, inside his castle. Once there, I can gather information to plan our next attack after I return home."

" 'Tis the returning part that I'm worried about," Marrok said.

"Why? Do you doubt me?" Gwynne stopped what she was doing and fixed her attention on him. "I need no memory of my childhood to have listened well whenever you told the tale of rescuing me from the English. I go back now to learn their weaknesses. To use the knowledge I gain against them."

" 'Twill be a great risk," her mentor argued. "We cannot know what kind of treachery awaits you."

"I will be careful. The months it takes to dissolve this supposed betrothal will afford me an opportunity to learn de Brice's habits and routines, so that we may strike at him more surely once I lead our people in battle again."

Marrok was silent for a moment before finally murmuring, "You cannot trust him, *Chwedl*—or believe him. Never forget that. Once he has you in his keeping, he will try to delve beneath your defenses. I see it in his eyes."

"There's naught to fear, Marrok. You trained me well. I can outfight any man who tries to harm me, including de Brice." She forced herself to grin, hoping to ease his mind. "None can pose a threat to my safety, old friend, thanks to you."

He shook his head. " 'Tis not only your physical wellbeing that concerns me. You must promise me to be more careful than usual and keep all of your skills at their peak while you stay with the English."

"Aye, Marrok. I promise."

After another moment he nodded once, his face resigned. "Go, then. But keep Dafydd and Owin near to you. They will serve to carry messages back and forth between us. I'll not have you in that nest of snakes for three months with no word."

"Agreed," Gwynne said, clasping his hand in hers. Marrok squeezed back in affection, and a final look of understanding passed between them before he moved off to give his parting advice to Owin and Dafydd.

Gwynne watched him go, trying to quell the uneasy feeling that prickled deep in her gut. Finally she just shook her head, rubbing the back of her neck as she turned to ready herself for her departure. But at that moment, the English leader turned around as well, apparently finished with a conversation he'd been having with one of his men near the edge of the clearing; his gaze locked with hers, and it sent a jolt of some strange emotion through her, unsettling her as it had before.

"There's naught to fear," she murmured to herself, when she was able to pull her stare from the man who both enraged her and set her blood racing every time she looked at him.

But the words rang false in her heart—for she felt, suddenly, that there might be something to fear after all. Something she could not explain or grasp.

'Twas foolish, she knew. She was the Dark Legend. A fierce warrior, destined to lead her people to freedom.

And yet she couldn't suppress the tingle of apprehension every time she felt the heat of Aidan de Brice's gaze on her—for the way he looked at her belied that knowledge, telling her in no uncertain terms that she was a woman first in his eyes.

A woman who had once belonged to him.

# Chapter 5

Gwynne hunched over the fire, blowing on her fingers to ease the sting of the sizzling grease. The spitted pheasant had already begun to crisp on the edges; 'twould be ready soon. Dafydd sat close by, but Owin had moved off to check their mounts. Sounds of laughter and talking came from behind her where the English soldiers, including their maddening leader de Brice, clustered around their own fires; still, she knew by the hot tingle up her neck that she was the focus of much of their attention.

"I expected Owin to be back by now," she murmured to Dafydd, trying to ignore the weight of the enemy stares on her.

Dafydd shrugged. "He always takes his time with the horses. He swings his blade with the best of them, but let any harm come to one of his animals, and he goes wild. In truth, I think he finds their company more comforting than people's. 'Tis his way."

Gwynne smiled. "I understand that."

But just as quickly her smile faded as a flash of memory shook her—a murky glimpse of a crow with one of its wings in a splint, hopping through a clearing of grass inside an ancient circle of stones.

Shaking her head to banish the image, she prodded the fire with a stick. After turning the roasting fowl so that the fat dripped hissing to the flames, she handed the spit to Dafydd. "Here. Take some of the meat to Owin once it's done. I'll eat later."

Dafydd nodded and remained at the fire while she stood and walked over to some nearby branches, to check the wet tunic and shirt she'd hung there. On the way to this resting point, de Brice had surprised her by insisting that they stop at a stream so that she and her men could wash out their blood-soaked garments. At first she'd refused, galled to accept even a hint of kindness from the Englishman. But when he'd tossed her three shirts to use while their clothing dried, she'd been forced to comply. Cooperating with him vexed her, to be sure, but she'd decided that easing Dafydd and Owin's obvious discomfort was more important than her pride.

Now she had to admit that she was glad she'd done it. 'Twould be good to get into her own clean clothing again.

She tested the sleeve of her shirt, brushing her palm over its rough surface. Still damp, but dry enough. She was just readying to pull it from the branch and slip into the wood to change when a low voice startled her.

"You might as well let it dry completely."

She spun to face Aidan's dark-eyed gaze. Her surprise at not having sensed his approach sent a stab of irritation through her. *Lugh*, 'twas not like her to miss such a thing, and yet this was the second time he had managed to sneak up on her today.

"I'd rather wear my own shirt," she muttered, reaching to take the garment down anyway.

" 'Tis a waste. You'll not be wearing it long enough to warrant dirtying it again."

"Why, do you intend to keep me locked away in sack-cloth at your castle?" she asked, half mocking.

"Nay. I intend to have you dress as you must to ensure your safety while you reside with me in England—you'll be clothed in a gown, chemise, and circlet."

He might as well have told her she'd be parading around naked.

"Not likely," she said, carefully keeping her voice even. "We never agreed to such terms. I'll wear my own clothes during the time I'm forced to stay in England."

"You'll wear what I tell you to, or you will find yourself a prisoner to the king, awaiting trial in his Tower."

Dafydd glanced over at them during this last exchange, and she met his gaze for an instant, acknowledging his readiness to lend his support at any time.

Looking back to Aidan, Gwynne met his implacable expression with one of her own. "You should realize by now that I don't respond well to threats, Englishman."

"Damn it, Gwynne, it isn't a threat. Don't you see? You are a wanted criminal in England. If anyone learns who you really are, the king will hear of it and dispatch his entire army to take you captive."

Several of his men ceased talking around their fires and looked over at them. He lowered his voice, scowling. "My own men may be sworn to keep your identity secret thanks to their loyalty to me, but I cannot say the same for the rest of the country."

Gwynne frowned, uncertainty pricking her. "If I dress as a female, 'twill draw attention to the fact that you, a betrothed man, are bringing an unknown woman into your household. Suspicions will arise concerning your intentions—unless you plan to present me as a servant. And *that*, Englishman, I will never abide. I agreed to live with you while you dissolve this betrothal you claim between us, but I didn't agree to serve you."

"You won't need to serve me, Gwynne," Aidan murmured.

An odd tingle shot through her at the softening she saw in his gaze. She crossed her arms over her chest, pretending not to notice it.

"I've thought of a story that will ensure you're treated as a noble guest in my home," he continued. "As a relative, actually. I will present you as a distant cousin whose entire family was slaughtered in the warring up north. Everyone will believe that I'm taking you in to live with me at Dunston since you've no one left to care for you."

Gwynne almost laughed at that absurd prospect. Instead she raised her brow. "How do you plan to explain my departure back to Wales in three months, then?"

"We'll have to deal with that when the time comes."

He looked away for a moment before piercing her again with his gaze—and she got the distinct impression that she wasn't going to like what he was about to say next.

"In the meantime, we must make your stay with me as believable as possible, for both your sake and mine. While you're at Dunston, I must make it look like I'm trying to arrange a marriage for you with one of my fellow nobles."

Gwynne choked.

"At least, try to pretend an interest in it," Aidan added, ignoring her glare. "As you've said, your presence in my home would appear suspect otherwise." A muscle in his jaw tightened. "And I will not endanger my betrothal to Lady Helene by allowing any colorful rumors about you to reach her ears."

*Lady Helene.* So that was her name.

Annoyed, Gwynne tossed her head and reached up to her shorn hair. "What of this?" she demanded. "Will it not be difficult to pass me off as a lady, seeing that I don't possess the silken tresses that seem to be the pride and joy of every weak-minded English female?"

He didn't rise to her bait.

"We can explain that away by saying you've recently suffered from a fever that required its cutting. 'Tis far less dangerous to have you act the part of a gentle-born woman than a man. No one will suspect a female of being the Dark Legend."

Gwynne scowled again. Damn him and his irrefutable arguments.

"Just when will I have to begin this farce?" she muttered.

"Tomorrow. We'll be passing through another demesne where I can get you some suitable garments to wear before we reach Dunston by late afternoon."

"Wonderful." She gritted her teeth. "But I will consent to this only if you ensure that my own clothing and weapons be kept accessible to me. I still need to train during the time I live with you."

"Agreed—with the exception of your shield. It marks you too clearly as the Dark Legend. It will have to be sent back to your people for safekeeping." He studied her for a moment with what might have been a glimmer of understanding in his gaze. "Never fear, Gwynne. It won't be so bad, you'll see."

She glared at him. "Imagine yourself donning a smock and skirt, Englishman. That's how bad it will be."

"Ah, but you used to wear such garments all the time. 'Twill be like revisiting old habits."

"So you claim." She clenched her fists tight.

A smile edged his lips, sending a jolt of anger through her. The bastard was enjoying this far too much.

Flashing him a dark look, she leaned forward. "Just remember this, de Brice: appearances can be deceiving. I may be forced to wear a dress while I'm with you, but I will still be exactly who I am." She slapped the place on his arm where she'd wounded him, relishing his wince as she added, "If you decide you want this stitched, just let me know."

Then she stalked away, pretending she didn't hear his quiet chuckle—or feel the strange, hot fluttering in her belly that came from knowing he watched her every step as she made her way back to the fire.

*The woodland looked misty in the moonlight, fingers of fog reaching out, veiling Gwynne's sight as she strode forward. The vapor clung to her, wetting her cheeks, her hair, coating her chain mail with its damp touch. But still she kept on, drawn by the same irresistible force that pulled her each time: the siren's song that echoed through the depths of her soul.*

*Her heart beat thickly, her breathing harsh as she pressed forward, searching the wood. The woman was here, she knew it. She was calling out, her haunting refrain filling Gwynne's head. But it blended and swirled with the howling wind until it was lost, tangled in the dark canopy of branches and sky above.*

*Her eyes stung. She tried to answer, but her throat clenched tight, the words strangled before they reached her mouth. She thrust forward one gauntleted arm, moving aside a branch thick with rain-drenched leaves . . .*

*And saw her there.*

*The woman floated in a shaft of moonlight, her form pale, her delicate hands reaching out to Gwynne. She was so beautiful. Long, golden hair cascaded to past her hips from the jeweled circlet she wore on her brow; her white gown glowed in the moonlight, lustrous and pristine.*

*All except for the blood.*

*So much blood.*

*It besprinkled the folds of diaphanous fabric and dripped down to the forest floor. The woman held one hand up to her ravaged throat, the other reaching out again, her expression pleading, her mouth moving soundlessly . . .*

With a sharp intake of breath, Gwynne lurched to a sitting position, her eyes wide, her fists clenched tight. The fragments of her dream dissolved and scattered into the night air as her surroundings came into focus.

It was dark. Moonless. The dusky forms of men were spread around her on makeshift pallets, some of them snoring. An owl sounded its cry on a breeze that carried the scent of burning wood. Swiveling her gaze to the spot, she froze. Aidan de Brice sat staring at her, motionless next to the dying fire. 'Twas difficult to tell, but it seemed that a shadow of concern passed over his face before he masked it. Then one of his brows arched, and he nodded to her, lifting the cup of whatever he was drinking in her direction.

Gwynne stared back for a moment before looking away with a scowl. She threw herself down on her pallet and rolled over on her side. Damn the man. Damn him for what he was doing to her—for stirring up such troubling feelings, such needling sensations. Damn him for coming into her life at all. It had been nearly a year since she'd had the nightmare. Nearly a year since she'd been forced to wake herself from that choking sense of emptiness. But now because of him, it was back, as vivid and disturbing as ever.

Letting her breath escape in a rush, she squeezed her eyes shut and resolved not to think about the dream anymore . . . to concentrate instead on other, more pleasant things—like all the ways she was going to make de Brice pay.

Reaching under her pallet, she checked to see that the cool, hard length of her blade was still there and at the ready. Then, pulling her woolen cloak up under her chin, she set her jaw in a grim line and slept.

Aidan stood next to his steed, struggling to remain patient as he waited for Kevyn and Colin to return from the village. Ribbons of golden light filtered through the trees, belying the chill and setting the dew-soaked grass to a sparkling tapestry of green beneath their feet.

But even the sun couldn't dispel the storm clouds he'd seen in Gwynne's eyes when he'd been foolish enough to glance her way a few moments ago. She'd glowered at him, then, her silver gaze crackling, filling the clearing with foreboding. His men had felt it too, he knew, by the way they shifted uneasily around their mounts and talked to each other under their breath, though her own guards, Dafydd and Owin, seemed unconcerned about her black mood.

Would that he could be as nonchalant. Clenching his jaw, he checked the fit of his stallion's bridle strap for the fifth time this morning.

Curse this incessant waiting . . .

"They return, my lord," Stephen, his squire, murmured, gesturing toward the pathway.

" 'Tis about time." Aidan strode forward to meet them. Taking action relieved some of his tension, and he nodded to Kevyn as he approached. Colin came close behind, carrying a bundle of what appeared to be dark blue fabric in his arms; he slipped as he came closer and then cursed as a wispy piece of sky blue silk fluttered out of his grasp onto the muddy ground. Snatching it up again, he brushed it off, his expression looking the same as if he'd been made to sit in the dirt and eat worms.

"I see you've found something," Aidan said to Kevyn, even as his gaze flicked to Colin and his burden.

"Aye, though 'twas more of an effort than we anticipated. 'Tis naught more than a woman's hooded cloak and veil, yet we had to use all of the coin we'd brought."

"*All* of the coin?" Aidan looked aghast at his friend. "You're jesting."

"Nay," Kevyn said, shaking his head. " 'Twas the only way to make the lady part with her goods."

"God's wounds, it had better be worth it."

Kevyn shrugged as Aidan took the mantle from Colin's arms and shook it out, shoving the flimsy veil, for now, into the front of his tunic. The cloak was wrinkled, but of a costly weave, long, and of rich color. He glanced from it to Gwynne, eyeing the size. It seemed the right length for her height, he'd warrant, though a bit scant through the bosom and shoulders if she used the clasp; she was a warrior, after all, and her build in those areas matched the activities to which she was accustomed: swordplay and battle.

But it would have to do until they reached Dunston.

Taking a deep breath, he headed toward her with it. She stood motionless, her gaze still stony, her arms crossed over her chest. The only indication that she saw his approach came from the occasional twitch of a muscle above her jaw. When he reached her, he held out the garment wordlessly. Finally, she shifted her gaze to his face, and he almost winced at the animosity he saw there.

He swallowed, standing straighter and reminding himself of the necessity of this part of the plan before he spoke in the most buoyant tone he could muster. "We could find no gown in the village. Until we get to Dunston, you must needs give over your shield and sword and don this. With the hood up, 'twill conceal you well enough."

She still didn't move to take it.

He waited a moment more before adding, "Do you require assistance?"

Though he'd not have thought it possible, her expression sharpened more—enough, he imagined, to draw blood.

Without a word, she snatched the cape from him and stalked toward her men, cursing under her breath as she went; she ceased only to bark out a command over her shoulder for everyone to stay clear of her if they valued their lives.

He watched her unclasp her sword belt and hand it to Dafydd. Owin, in the meantime, unhooked from her saddle her spectacular golden shield, emblazoned with a red dragon, rampant, and began to wrap it in a piece of linen. Both men wore grave expressions, treating Gwynne and her weapons with the same kind of reverence Aidan had witnessed before only during the handling of the Eucharist at Holy Mass.

Facing away from Aidan and his men, Gwynne pulled the sapphire cloak around her shoulders, fastening it the best she could before yanking the hood over her hair. Then she swung astride her mount, letting the gentle folds of fabric settle around her to conceal her form.

Aidan cleared his throat. "Shall we depart, then?"

Gwynne swiveled to glare her answer as Owin and Dafydd mounted their steeds. But he hardly noticed their movements for the ache that suddenly bloomed in his gut. Images hammered at him, of another time, another place—of their betrothal day, when they were both so young, so desperate for each other that they'd ignored everything to undertake their forbidden union.

She'd worn blue that day as well, the same shade of blue that surrounded her now in silky folds, caressing the smooth contours of her cheek . . . that softened the warrior-harsh lines of her expression until he could imagine something almost like before. Like when she'd loved him . . .

"Are you going to stand there gawking, Englishman, or are we going to leave?"

Her sharp question jolted him from his memories. Only the hollow feeling remained. He pulled his gaze from her and mounted, noticing that all of his men were already in position and waiting for him. He ignored the heat that swept up his neck in response to his foolish reaction and barked the order to ride, leading his nemesis—the woman who'd haunted his dreams for the last twelve years—onto the wooded trail and the last stretch toward home.

By the time they neared Dunston's gate, Gwynne felt as prickly and annoyed as a bear besieged by a swarm of bees. 'Twas not that the ride had been difficult. Nay, just the opposite; the English landscape had been a pleasure jaunt compared to the mountainous climes she was accustomed to traversing in Wales.

But in Wales, she'd never had a solemn-eyed Englishman ceaselessly searching her with his gaze—or a rush of irritating images constantly assaulting her mind.

Her jaw throbbed from clenching it, and yet now she bit down harder, determined to banish the strange pictures that kept popping into her head the nearer they got to de Brice's stronghold. This latest vision had been of a shady green circle surrounded by stones, and a handful of acorns thrown into the sun; they'd arced up before pelting down on someone, to the echo of masculine laughter, low and sweet. Laughter that sounded surprisingly like de Brice's . . .

But she had no conscious recollection of ever being with him anywhere before. No inkling at all, but for these disturbing flashes of—well, whatever they were.

It was her imagination, she decided. A lingering result of the nightmare. It had set her on edge, and she was still feeling the effects of it now. Nothing more. Glancing sideways, she tried to catch the English leader staring at her again. Only he wasn't. This time he was looking forward, his generous mouth edging up into a smile.

"We're here," he murmured, almost as if to himself. But then his dark-eyed gaze slipped sideways and connected with hers, making her heart skip and leaving her no room to breathe. She frowned, and his brow lifted above a flash of white teeth. He looked forward again as they rounded a curve in the road—and then she saw it, stretched before them. A solid gray wall, its portcullis in the process of being raised. And behind it, the massive towers of a keep jutted into the sky.

Dunston Castle.

The nagging sensation she'd experienced from that first moment when de Brice had taken off his helm returned now with a vengeance, making her feel like some memory waited right at the edge of her mind. She just couldn't grasp what it was. *Lugh*, it was maddening.

Barely restraining herself from uttering the command to retreat to Wales, she directed her attention to her mount, clicking her tongue to bring him to a canter in order to keep up with de Brice's newly quickened pace. Before long they were riding through the opened gate, to the sound of welcoming halloos and the sight of smiling faces and waving arms.

The courtyard burst into activity as Aidan and his men pulled their steeds to a halt; prosperous looking villagers and castle folk came streaming from doorways and milling among the men, all talking and laughing at once.

Stiffly, Gwynne dismounted, Owin and Dafydd staying close by her as they waited for an indication of what they should do next. But Aidan seemed oblivious to the awkward way he'd left them. Instead, he peered around the courtyard, as if looking for someone in particular.

She shouldn't be surprised, she thought, crossing her arms over her chest and scowling. Why should de Brice care for their comfort? He was naught but an English oaf.

A stable boy came up with a nod and led her mount

away to the stables for a brush down and some food; she
continued to glare at de Brice, hoping he'd look her way
and realize his discourtesy. But he was too engrossed in
his search, undoubtedly awash with lust as he searched for
sign of his precious Lady Helene.

In the next instant, a woman came bursting through the
main doors of the keep, her face wreathed in smiles—and
all Gwynne's worst imaginings were realized.

The creature was the essence of femininity, but of that
sensuous sort that made other women bristle and men
stare with mouths agape. Her rich auburn hair hung to her
waist like rippling silk, a crowning glory for her creamy
skin and seductive, thick-lashed eyes. And though she was
young—no more than seventeen, Gwynne guessed—
she'd been blessed with a figure only the gods themselves
could have crafted: all graceful lines and curves, set off to
perfection by the lush crimson gown she wore.

Forcing herself to pull her gaze from the sight of the
bewitching creature throwing herself into Aidan's arms,
Gwynne dared a glance at Owin and Dafydd and saw to
her annoyance that they too seemed besotted; Owin's eyes
might as well have left their sockets and rolled to the
ground to do homage to the woman, he was gawking so
openly. Gritting her teeth, Gwynne jabbed him none too
gently in the ribs, making him double over and cough.

But at least he'd stopped staring.

Then she looked back to de Brice and his ladylove, and
her initial jab of dislike expanded to a flood of animosity.
The woman had pulled away from Aidan, who had obviously just mentioned the presence of Gwynne and her
men in their party. The lady glared now in Gwynne's direction as if she'd like to flay her alive.

Resisting the urge to scowl back at her, Gwynne instead raised her brow and favored her with a cold look.
Ah, but de Brice seemed to have chosen a jealous woman

as his future mate. If anger wasn't making her gut twist so strangely right now, the knowledge would have made her feel positively gleeful.

With a jerk of her head, she directed Owin and Dafydd to come with her as she approached the pair. The long length of cloak swishing round her legs reminded her that she should attempt to use a more ladylike gait, but her usual saunter came through nonetheless.

When they reached Aidan, he was saying something in hushed tones to his lady—most likely scolding her for her less than welcoming attitude. She'd resorted to pouting, though on that perfect face of hers, the expression still managed to look entrancing. Her elegant nose wrinkled as she flicked her gaze up Gwynne's sapphire-cloaked length, stopping with what might have been surprise, or perhaps just wariness, when she met Gwynne's silver gaze.

With a sigh, Aidan stepped back a little so that the women could see each other better, though he directed his comment to his lady. "Allow me to introduce our Welsh cousin, Gwynne ap Mo—ap Morrison."

Gwynne noticed that his voice sounded rather sharp—not at all the tone she'd have expected a love-besotted man to use with his betrothed. He continued, she saw to her astonishment, with a look on his face almost as if he intended to forcibly compel his fiancée to accept the situation.

"Gwynne will be staying with us for the time being and is in need of understanding and comfort after the ordeal she has been through. She and these, her two serving men, are all that remain of her family after the attack on their estate."

With a nod, he finally looked at Gwynne and waved his hand back from her to the woman. "Gwynne, meet my sister, Lady Diana de Brice."

*Sister*? Gwynne snapped her gaze to Aidan, to see if he

jested with her. He looked nothing less than sincere—and perhaps exasperated. Her brow furrowed in confusion for a moment, until Diana spoke. Then her hand itched to pull out and use the sword that no longer hung at her side.

"I don't see why you need to bring home every stray you find, Aidan," Diana muttered. "And why now, of all times, pray tell? 'Tis not as if we have no worries when it comes to your imminent marriage—or my own betrothal." She gave him another pouting look.

"That will be enough, Diana," Aidan said tightly, gripping his sister's arm and attempting to steer her back toward the castle. "We'll talk about it after dinner."

Diana resisted as Aidan pulled her away, casting one last dark look at Gwynne before adding, " 'Tis not as if we have no other relatives to help carry the burden of destitute kin. Her being here will not please Lady Helene or her father at all."

"Then the feeling will be mutual," Gwynne couldn't resist muttering, tempted as well to charge up the few steps to the main door and throttle the woman senseless.

The gentle pressure of a hand on her arm held her back, though it was all she could do not to whirl and strike the foolish person who'd dared to touch her. It was de Brice's man, Kevyn. His expression was somber, not at all mocking, as she'd expected. That helped to ease her anger a bit. And so when he murmured something about escorting her to her rooms and gestured the way, she decided to clamp her mouth shut and follow.

As they passed into the shadows beyond the castle doors, through the nearly empty great hall, and up a curved set of stairs that led to the bedchambers, she tried to cool her temper further, reminding herself that dealing with conflicts by fighting and using her weapons was no longer an option. Not for the next three months, anyway.

That part was going to take getting used to. She was a

warrior, trained to behave like a man—like a legend—for as long as she could remember, and punished for acting like anything else. Being made to assume the role of a female now was strangely painful, and as awkward as if someone had cut off her hands and told her to accustom herself to doing everything with her feet.

But she'd have to get used to it. She'd agreed to de Brice's plan, after all.

She spent the remainder of the two hours until dinner sitting in her spacious chamber and bemoaning that fact. Wondering what under heaven had possessed her to go along with his schemes in the first place. Only the thought of the respite her sacrifice was giving her people and of the vengeance she'd have on de Brice after she returned to them made any of this even remotely tolerable.

When it was nearly time to descend to the hall, she yanked on the heavy rose-hued gown that had been sent up for her, not caring if it was positioned correctly or not. She fastened the matching gold-embroidered belt low on her hips in what she thought was the proper way and tugged it with enough force that she was disappointed when it didn't snap. Then, jamming onto her head the absurd gauzy veil and cap that had arrived with the gown, she stood and paced over to face her reflection in the polished oval of metal that leaned against the wall in the corner.

*Ridiculous*.

A scowl darkened her face. Stamping away from the mirror, she tripped, caught up in the unfamiliar length of skirts swirling around her legs. *Lugh*, but this was idiotic! Wrenching the fabric back into place, she lifted the hem to see if she'd torn it. A bit of ragged edge dangled an inch or two. Grimacing, she shook the skirts out so that they fell again over the leggings she'd refused to remove.

If it was the last thing she accomplished in this life, she

was going to make de Brice pay for doing this to her.

Yanking open the door, she stomped into the corridor and tried to make her way down the stairs to the great hall without breaking her neck. She set her jaw and breathed deep, her black mood kept in check by that one satisfying thought.

Aye, de Brice would pay. By God, he'd be begging for mercy before she was finished with him.

# Chapter 6

Aidan didn't quite know how to handle what was happening in his once peaceful home. Diana sat picking at her food and using every opportunity to glare at Gwynne, who in turn leaned on her elbows across the table, glaring back and looking as if she'd like to spear his sister through the heart with her eating knife. The current state of affairs was far, far worse than he'd expected.

"You knew it wasn't going to be easy," Kevyn said, daring a glance at the women from his position next to Aidan. " 'Tis awkward at best, whether or not you try to pass her off as your relative. And it doesn't help that she acts like a man in skirts. There doesn't seem to be a feminine bone in her body."

"Oh, yes there is," Aidan murmured. "I remember that far too well."

Kevyn pretended not to have heard him, adding, "Your sister needs time to adjust; she's used to competing with women and doing her best to outshine them, but she has no idea what to do with one like Gwynne."

Aidan scowled into his trencher, absently picking up a piece of roasted fowl and dipping it into the sauce bowl in front of him. " 'Tis not as if Gwynne presents any kind of outward threat to her."

"I don't think Diana is worried about her as a rival. Gwynne does have a rather striking face with those silver eyes of hers, and she's tall enough to attract notice. But her figure seems somehow more thick in skirts than I'd have imagined after seeing her on the field." Kevyn nodded as a page refilled his cup with wine, adding, "Nay, Diana isn't fretting over her for her looks, you can be sure."

A clatter farther down the table drew both men's gazes. Gwynne had knocked over a large bowl of fruit, sending an army of errant winter apples rolling toward Aidan's sister; her expression as she watched Diana huffily replace them made it obvious that she'd done it on purpose.

"You heard what your sister said when we arrived," Kevyn continued, looking back to Aidan before taking a deep drink from his cup. "She fears Lady Helene's reaction to news of Gwynne's presence in your home—and the Duke of Rutherford's even more. 'Tis very near your nuptials, after all."

"My wedding isn't for almost four months."

"Close enough. Especially when the duke continues to seek any reason he can find for dissolving your betrothal with his daughter. And Diana knows that her match with Hugh Valmont hangs in the balance; if the alliance with Helene's family is not secured, Valmont will not make an offer."

"Valmont is a fop."

Kevyn shrugged. "There's no accounting for women's taste in men. But Valmont is powerful, and you cannot deny that settling Diana in his family will protect her from some of the difficulties that have resulted from your father's misfortunes."

"They weren't misfortunes, Kev," Aidan muttered, glaring into his own now nearly empty cup and grabbing the pitcher to refill it. "My father committed treason and was executed—only Mother, Diana, and I paid our own price for it as well."

Kevyn nodded, thoughtful. "Aye, and I know better than most how you've tried to rebuild your family's name and ensure Diana's future ever since. But this latest decision on your part is sure to appear less than satisfactory to her. It puts an already precarious situation at greater risk."

"Damn it, I know that," Aidan said, "which is why I have to resolve this quickly. I have to make Gwynne remember what happened—make her remember what the Welsh did—so that I can settle my debt to her before everything else goes to hell and the king demands my head too."

Kevyn gave a choking laugh, and Aidan turned to see what his friend found so humorous. But the laughter wasn't directed at him; he was looking down the table at Gwynne, who at that moment was leaning back, yawning noisily and swiping a hand over her mouth.

"Perhaps you'd better start by helping her to behave more like the lady she's supposed to be," Kevyn said, coughing back another chuckle.

At that moment Gwynne noticed Aidan's stare. Fixing him with a sarcastic look, she made a show of scratching her belly and belching loudly. Diana sat frozen across from her, looking on in horror. With a smile of satisfaction, Gwynne finally pushed herself away from the table and stalked from the chamber, flanked by her two men.

After a moment of stunned silence, Aidan cradled his head in his hands and groaned. "Sweet Mother Mary, this is going to be more difficult than I thought."

*   *   *

Gwynne kept going down the hall and out toward the rooms her men had been given near the other servants by the stables. Their quarters weren't nearly as large or well appointed as her own rooms inside the main keep, but she'd have preferred them nonetheless. Aye, she'd have given her best blade to be able to switch places with her men during what promised to be a grueling three months.

Owin busied himself with retrieving her sword and Dafydd seemed intent on removing from his tunic a couple of the apples he'd pilfered from the table as Gwynne yanked off her gown and veil and threw them into the corner. A cloud of hay dust rose where they landed.

"No need to turn away," she muttered, stalking up and taking her sword-belt from Owin. "I've kept on my own clothes beneath those ridiculous skirts."

Dafydd seemed relieved, daring a glance at her discarded garments before shifting his gaze back to her. "Won't you need to wear those again when you've finished your training tonight?"

"Aye, curse de Brice's eyes. What of it?" she answered as she tightened the belt around her hips.

Dafydd shrugged. " 'Tis just that they'll likely be wrinkled if you leave them like that until you're finished. They look costly, and de Brice may not appreciate it."

Gwynne paused to consider what he'd said. "I suppose you're right," she said finally, walking over to the garments and picking them up, only to ball them more tightly before cramming them back into the corner. Turning to her men, she wiped her hands on her tunic. "That's better."

They didn't try to suppress their answering grins. She clapped Dafydd on the back before donning a short cape and pulling up the hood—another of de Brice's requirements for her movement about the estate whenever she was out of her female clothing. Then, after taking a last look around, she picked up one of the smaller shields they carried with them to use while her own was unavailable to her.

Heading to the door, she called over her shoulder, "Which one of you will lead the way to the chamber de Brice promised to clear for my training?"

"I will, *Chwedl*," Owin answered, following her. " 'Tis just down the path that goes between the stables and tack chamber. An abandoned room all the way to the castle wall on your left. Dafydd and I looked at it earlier; you should be secluded enough to train without notice." He reached for an extra unlit torch to hand to her. "Will you need a sparring partner this night?"

"Nay," she answered, starting to pull open the scarred wooden door. "I think I'll work alone. I'll just imagine de Brice's head under my blade each time I swing it."

The door creaked open the rest of the way, and she stiffened. Aidan stood there, leaning against the wall opposite them, his arms crossed loosely over his chest.

"That's not a very charitable remark to make about your host," he said smoothly, pushing himself away from the wall to stand straight before her. He wasn't really smiling, but Gwynne sensed the expression hovering around his lips. Humor warmed his dark gaze, and she felt an odd tingle up her spine when one corner of his mouth finally lifted with what might have been the beginnings of a quirky grin.

She scowled and looked past him. "I'm not here for charitable reasons, as well you know," she said, trying to push by. "Now, if you'll get out of my way, I need to go train."

When he didn't budge, she stopped and fixed him with a hard stare. "Unless, that is, you've come to prove yourself a lying Englishman like every other by going back on your agreement to provide me with a place to do it."

He paused, his gaze cooling. " 'Tis clear that for all your *training*, Gwynne, you've failed to master the art of being civil." He lowered his arms to his sides, all hints of his previous good humor vanished. Somehow, he seemed taller and more powerfully built than she'd noticed before, all rippling muscle and sinew beneath the smooth cloth of his shirt.

A burst of familiar battle-heat shot through her at his aggressive stance, and she cocked her head, daring him to take action. Almost hoping that he would give it a try so that she could fight him and dispel some of the prickling energy that seemed to rise in her every time he was near.

"But I'm not here to prevent you from engaging in your exercises," he continued. "I just need to discuss our plans for tomorrow first."

"Our plans?" she taunted. "We have no plans. I am your hostage for three months, and you are my keeper. 'Tis as simple as that." Her mouth tensed, her hand still itching to grip the comforting weight of her sword-hilt. "Stay out of my way, and I'll stay out of yours."

Now he looked more exasperated than he had with his sister when she'd defied him in the courtyard.

"I thought I'd made it clear," he said. "While you reside with me, we have to make a good show of the story I was forced to craft for you." When she didn't react, he added tightly, "That you are a distant relative in need of protection? That I've taken you in to try to find a suitable husband for you?"

Gwynne just looked at him. "Aye. So . . . ?"

A muscle in Aidan's jaw jumped, and she had the sudden urge to smooth her fingertip over the spot—a reaction that nearly choked her when she realized it. She forced herself to loop her thumbs nonchalantly into her sword belt.

"In order to make anyone believe that story, you have to behave as a *lady*," he continued. "Something that, based upon your performance at dinner tonight, it seems you are either unwilling or unable to do."

Gwynne felt her face heat at his gibe, but she held back a retort until he added, "You need to try to act less like a warrior, Gwynne, and more like a woman."

Anger bloomed to the surface then, and she almost flung his words back into his face—but the look in his eyes stopped her. They held such a serious cast, such sincerity, that she found herself glancing away. He'd spoken true— in part, at least. She *had* exaggerated her bad manners at dinner, because she'd wanted to shock Diana and perhaps pay him back just a little for making her wear a dress. But she'd be boiled alive before she'd admit that to him.

"I've done what you asked of me, de Brice," she grated. "I've donned your ridiculous clothes, kept my mouth closed about my true identity, agreed to your scheme to pretend I'm seeking a husband. By God, I don't know what more you want of me."

Owin coughed lightly and ducked back into the chamber, obviously as uncomfortable at witnessing his leader's embarrassment in handling this unfamiliar role as she was in experiencing it.

Aidan waited until he'd closed the door, then met her gaze again. "I know this isn't easy for you, Gwynne, but acting the part is just as important as looking it. And that's why I'm here. Beginning tomorrow, you'll be meeting with one of my most trusted female servants for an hour each morning to practice some of the skills you'll need to make this pretense plausible. Then you and I will meet each afternoon to practice some more."

She stared at him, certain he'd lost what little mind he possessed.

"This had better be your idea of a jest."

"I'm afraid not. 'Tis imperative that all who do not know the truth about you believe you to be as I've described." His expression was deadly serious. "I'll not risk innocent lives by allowing anyone to suspect who you really are and to get word of it to the king."

"Not to mention the difficulties it would raise with your beloved Helene and her father if it was discovered that you were secretly harboring the Dark Legend in your home," she added, flashing him a sarcastic glare.

He had the good grace to look embarrassed. "That is another issue entirely. What's important now is ensuring that everyone believes you to be my distant cousin, come to live with me through the tragic loss of your family."

Blast him, but he was persistent. And a lout. A demanding, unbearable lout, to try to make her cooperate with this. It wasn't enough to force her into wearing silly gowns and veils. Nay, he wanted her humiliation to be more complete. He wanted her to behave in ways that she remembered only from the distant reaches of her memory, when she was first training to be the Legend. Ways she'd been punished for indulging.

Ways she'd learned to despise.

A suffocating feeling swept up to grip her throat, and she swallowed hard against it, battling for control. Damn him to bloody hell . . .

"I can't do it," she finally muttered. " 'Twill have to be enough that I dress accordingly."

"You *will* do it, Gwynne. Curse it, you must," he said, his voice suddenly gone husky with some unspoken feeling. "Don't you see? Even with my men's loyalty, you are in danger of being discovered here. I'm trying to protect you from what may happen if you don't do as I ask." When she tried to push by him again, he gripped both of her arms firmly but gently, almost as if he were going to embrace her, murmuring, "Damn it, Gwynne, you have to listen to me."

She froze, the contact seeming to scorch through her shirt to singe the vulnerable flesh beneath with his heat. Flashes of something, muddled pictures of some sort, shot through her brain, taking her breath away before they faded. Slowly, she dragged her stunned gaze from his hands to his face.

He'd touched her before. Even without a conscious memory of it, she knew it deep in her bones.

But no one touched her like this. No one. Except for the occasional brief grips she exchanged with Marrok, few dared to try, because she never allowed it.

Most thought her reserve was due to her status as the Legend. After all, she was a myth in their midst, far above the reach and comfort of common folk. But it wasn't that. Nay, never that. It was because it hurt too much. Being touched in kindness, in friendship—in anything but cold, hard anger—hurt far too much. It reminded her of all she'd never have, all she'd forsaken in order to be the savior to her people.

Concern and love were not for one such as she. She was built to fight and kill. That was all.

But this . . . this remembered touch . . .

As if coming out of a dream, she wrenched herself free of Aidan's grip, quelling the waves of almost painful sensation his touch had evoked. She didn't trust herself to speak, her throat felt so tight, but she forced herself to anyway, knowing that he'd not let her escape to the cleansing ritual of her training until she answered him.

"I'll think about it," she managed to say, her voice gone as husky as his had been. Then she shoved harder to push past him, desperate to get away from the confusing feelings sweeping through her. He let her go, and she took in deep breaths as she stalked away down the path in the direction that Owin told her. As she tried to will calm and focus back to her frazzled senses.

"Tomorrow morning, Gwynne. We'll begin your other training then," Aidan called out softly after her, and she held herself stiff as she walked, to stop herself from flinching at the gentleness in his tone. "Do not fail me."

Less than a quarter hour later, Aidan stood outside the old tack chamber and watched through a knothole in the wall. He'd chosen this place for Gwynne's training, knowing that no one would come out here. It had been empty for more than two years, ever since they'd built the new tack room closer to the stables.

When they'd first cleaned out this chamber, he'd meant to have the walls torn down and put the space to use in some other way, but now he was glad he hadn't gotten around to it. 'Twas a perfect place for Gwynne to have privacy for her exercises—and with its knot-riddled walls, a perfect way for him to keep an eye on what she was doing.

He stood now, stunned as he watched her, amazed anew at the strange motions and exercises she practiced over and over, until her breath came in heavy rasps and her shirt dampened with sweat. He'd had glimpses of these very moves in action during his battle with her on the field, but it had been a fleeting glance at best, and mitigated by the shock he'd felt when he'd discovered who she really was.

Now he had the chance truly to study her, and her abilities astonished him. He'd not have believed it if he hadn't seen it with his own eyes.

She was using her sword, feinting and jabbing through a series of moves with a speed and strength worthy of any of his best warriors. But she'd added several of the strange, twirling jumps he'd seen her use on the field, her long, lean form tucking and spinning around before she landed on both feet again. Then she'd jab close and hard at her imaginary opponent who, had he been real, would have been preparing himself to slash at her two full sword's-lengths away, making his death an almost forgone conclusion.

Aidan narrowed his gaze, watching her practice the series of motions again and again, her movements quickening in pace. He exhaled his breath slowly, shaking his head in wonderment at her sheer endurance. How in hell did she keep it up—and how many hours of grueling training had it taken her to master a skill like this?

After a few more minutes of fierce activity, she finally slowed, gasping and letting her arms fall limp; the point of her sword dug into the hard-packed floor. When she let go of it, the heavy weapon thudded on the dirt, and she sank down cross-legged next to it, sides heaving, before burying her head in her hands.

She looked so vulnerable sitting there. The curve of her back revealed the toll such rigorous training took, and Aidan watched in silence for a while, listening to her ragged breathing, longing to yank open the door and go to her.

But he knew better than that; if she had the slightest inkling that he was here, that he was watching her in secret, she'd never trust him, and he needed her to if he hoped to complete his mission to make her remember. It was all locked inside her, he knew it. All the memories of their time together, of what they'd felt for each other, and of what the Welsh had done to her—to them—that day. He'd seen glimpses of it flutter to the surface before quickly fading away. But the memories were there.

He just needed to find the key to unlocking them for her.

Suddenly, a broken cry echoed through the chamber, making Aidan's heart wrench as he shifted to press his eye closer to the tiny knothole. Gwynne was crouched over now, arms wrapped around herself and rocking against whatever strong emotion held her in sway. Her breath no longer rasped, though her entire frame shook, as if she held back sobs. Aidan fisted his hands, reminding himself yet again of why he couldn't intervene. Why he couldn't go inside as every fiber and sinew of him demanded, and soothe away whatever caused her pain.

A moment later, she abruptly ceased her rocking movements and lifted her head, swiping her hand across her mouth before jerking to her feet. Her back was to him as she reached down to lift her sword, her spine and shoulders tense. As if she'd done it a thousand times before, she wearily widened her stance, beginning to swing her blade through a new series of motions, more like the kind he and his men practiced when they ran through their own exercises.

Though her face was still concealed from him, Aidan imagined he could see the stoicism of her expression, the rigid determination etching cold, hard lines over her features. And the knowledge of it ripped him apart inside.

God in heaven, what had happened to turn her from the sweet, laughing creature he'd loved so many years ago into this hardened warrior, who drove herself beyond the limits of endurance? What other punishing experiences were behind the impervious front that she worked so hard to maintain, forcing her to keep the truth of her past and the memory of his loving her locked so firmly away?

Aidan swallowed and stepped away from the wall, deciding that he'd better go now before she discovered him spying. But as he made his way back to the castle, one last thought hammered through his brain, swirling around to tempt and prod him, leaving him no rest . . .

Because he couldn't help asking himself just how far he'd be willing to go to bring all her memories of loving him back again.

# Chapter 7

Diana stood up carefully, checking as she did to make sure she was still alone in the corridor. The dull gray light of morning had proved too weak to aid her attempts to peer beneath the chamber door. Undaunted, she leaned in with one ear to the cool wood, keeping very quiet to see if she could at least hear what was happening inside the room.

The Welsh stranger had been in there with old Alana since breaking her fast. Though Gwynne had been considerably more civilized during this morning's meal than she'd been the evening before, Diana still didn't like her. Aside from her strange appearance, there was something about her that sent warning tingles up Diana's spine; something else that just wasn't right.

Holding her breath now, Diana pressed her ear closer, straining to catch any hint of sound or conversation from within the chamber.

What in blazes could she be doing with Dunston's most

trusted servant? Aidan never let old Alana take on extra work. Never. He treated her like a grandmother, allowing her only the easiest of tasks, and those only because she insisted on doing something for her keep.

Alana was a fixture in the castle. Though her condition had worsened over the years, she'd remained with the family through everything. 'Twas she who'd found Aidan in the woods, bleeding and confused after he'd been attacked by the Welsh rebels. And it was Alana who'd stood by them through the horrible nightmare of Father's arrest and execution. She'd stayed through it all, unbroken by the disgrace, even after many of the other servants had left. Even after Mama . . .

Diana bit her lip and frowned. *Mama.* Dear, sweet Mama. What would she think of her daughter lurking in the hallway to eavesdrop? Guilt sent a rush of warmth into her cheeks. *Oh, Mama. How I wish you were still here to hold me. To keep me safe.* But that could never be. Never again.

The day the soldiers had come for Father, Mama's sweet embrace and her comforting lavender scent were all that had kept Diana from screaming aloud. She'd buried her face in Mama's neck, feeling her world spin apart and hearing her mother's soft cries as the soldiers had loaded Father into that horrible cart and driven him away. She'd finally broken away from Mama's arms and run after them, begging them to stop. To give her Papa back. But it had been too late. The gate had shut. He was gone and she'd never seen him again.

And then everything had changed. In the weeks after Papa's execution, Lady Sutcliffe had slowly sunk into a world of her own making, becoming distracted and then distant, holed up alone in her chamber. Her once beautiful hair, a shade darker than Diana's own, had become tangled and unkempt, her spotless gowns ripped and stained.

And then had come that horrible morning . . . the misty dawn when Diana had gone to the pond to gather up some of the pretty swamp iris that grew there, to make a bouquet for Mama—and found a bloated, unrecognizable thing floating in the water. A thing with billowing auburn hair.

Diana grimaced with the memory. The thing hadn't looked like Mama at all. For a long time she'd even refused to believe it was her. But eventually she'd been made to accept the truth. That Mama was dead, just like Father. All Diana had left now was Aidan—and she'd chew nettles before she'd let some backwoods relative come between them and upset their plans.

A crashing sound from inside the room sent Diana skittering into the shadows. Breathless, she slipped behind the edge of the tapestry hanging on the wall and held very still. Suddenly, the door to the chamber was yanked open from inside. Gwynne came stalking out, looking like a thundercloud and mumbling under her breath. She glared once over her shoulder at the open portal, not seeing Diana's hiding place, praise the saints, before she reached the stairs and turned to thump down them into the gloom below.

A moment later, old Alana emerged, her form perpetually bent by her crippled joints, but with a half smile on her lips as she looked in the direction of the retreating figure. She shook her head and began to go back into the chamber, then stiffened.

Without turning around, she murmured, " 'Tis poor behavior from you, lass, to be sneaking about and prying into business that's not your own. Get on wi' you now. If I catch you at it again, your brother will be hearing of it."

Shuffling back into the room, she shut the door firmly behind her.

Diana flounced from behind the tapestry, cheeks hot

with an odd mixture of annoyance and shame. It was all
Gwynne's fault. She was to blame for forcing Diana to
creep about like this. There'd been no choice. *Someone*
had to save Aidan from the trouble the Welshwoman was
going to bring. No one else seemed worried, but Diana
knew better. Gwynne was dangerous—she could feel it.
An unplanned hazard to their plans. Taking a deep breath,
Diana smoothed her hands along the golden girdle slung
low on her hips and headed down the stairs on the same
path Gwynne had taken moments earlier; she was determined to do whatever it took to lessen the damage. Aye,
she would do everything in her power to get Gwynne ap
Morrison out of Dunston Castle before the duke learned
about her, or God forbid actually met her—and found reason to call off his daughter's wedding to Aidan for good.

Gwynne sat on the steps to the main hall at Dunston,
trying to take deep breaths while at the same time avoiding the curious gazes directed at her from the people going about their business around the castle. The sun beat
down on her, soaking into the infernal bliaud and smock
she was wearing and inspiring a renewed burst of annoyance. She tugged at the neck of the blue linen, trying to
catch a bit of breeze, while angry thoughts swirled
through her head.

Curse it, but this morning's humiliation with Alana had
sapped all her patience, and the day wasn't even half over.
Aidan would be meeting her here in a few more minutes to
start the process all over again, only with who knew what
torturous activity.

She shuddered and gave up tugging at her neckline to
lift surreptitiously the ends of her skirt. Part of her wanted
to run and hide—or better yet, to rip off this absurd gown,
jump astride her steed, and gallop like the wind until she
reached the mountains of home.

But she couldn't do that, she knew. 'Twould be the coward's way. She'd faced blood, death, and destruction countless times on the battlefield, dealing the same to others more often than not. Having to face her buried femininity by pretending to be a lady should seem easy by comparison. But it wasn't. It was blasted hard, making something deep inside twist and ache. Something she wanted to forget altogether.

Yet aside from needing to protect herself and her men from the danger of discovery, she knew that her people were counting on her for the three months of truce with the English to restore their strength. That, combined with de Brice's gold, would give them the boost they needed to strike at the heart of their enemy in a way that would not soon be forgotten. A way certain to garner victory.

Trying to calm herself with that thought, she concentrated on folding her hands in her lap as Alana had instructed this morning, checking to see that her knees were at least partway together. She could hear the old woman's rusty voice in her mind, coaxing her to sit like a lady.

Of course, having her own tunic and leggings on under her gown made it harder to remember such niceties, not to mention that it added to the stifling feeling she experienced in the heat, but wearing the skirts alone wasn't an option; the very idea of having her legs bare beneath, of the naked feeling that it would cause, especially when Aidan de Brice directed his prying gaze on her, made her break out in a sweat.

Nay, she'd make due with the leggings on.

She was just getting ready to get up and find her men, de Brice be damned, when Aidan came whistling around the corner of the gatehouse. He stopped when he saw her, his gaze locking with hers; the whistle died on his lips and his eyes lit up, his entire face creasing with a smile.

Gwynne swallowed hard against the warm rush of

pleasure that swept through her. Curse him, but he was handsome when he looked at her like that. She bit the inside of her cheek, the metallic taste of her own blood helping to bring her back to reality, reminding her of her purpose here. He was the enemy, and she couldn't allow herself to forget it.

"I wasn't sure you'd be here," he said, still looking pleased as he approached.

She managed to calm the thudding of her heart, restoring enough order to her senses to shrug and offer, "I've nothing better to do for the next three months—no attacks to arrange, no pillaging or massacres to plan."

Rather than chilling his mood, as she'd expected, her flippant answer only made him grin more deeply.

"Are you ready to go?" He gestured to the gate.

"Where?"

"You'll see."

Pursing her lips, she got up to follow him, clumping down the steps in her usual manner before she remembered to try to walk more genteelly. She glanced at him, catching the twinkle in his eye that told her he'd noticed her efforts. Irritation lanced through her again, and she fisted her hands. *Lugh*, but it was difficult to handle her constantly changing mood where de Brice was concerned. One moment she was angry with him, the next, tingling with a strange sense of excitement.

"I want to know where you're taking me," she demanded, as much to maintain her own sense of control as to find out his plans for her.

"To the wood beyond the castle," he answered, quickening his pace.

She slowed, uncertain about accompanying him alone without her weapons. Noticing her hesitation, he turned and gripped her hand in his to tug her along with him, smiling again and murmuring, " 'Tis not too far, and I've nothing sinister in mind, I promise. There's just something I want to show you."

The shock of his touch raced through her, as it had when he'd gripped her shoulders outside the stables last night; yanking her hand away, she decided to take her chances. She could always just knock him senseless if he tried anything. She sped up to keep abreast of him, hiding the tingling in her fingers by twisting them in her skirts as they made their way out of the castle yard and to the meadow beyond.

Soon, they approached the edge of the woodland. As when they came through this area on their arrival at Dunston, Gwynne felt an odd nagging sensation at the back of her skull—a feeling of familiarity she couldn't quite place. They ducked into the cool shade of the trees, the branches all around them having long since unfurled their sweet green splendor under the force of the June sunlight.

The prickling sensation in her brain increased the deeper they went into the woodland. Uncomfortable, she started to tell de Brice that she'd go no further, when he suddenly slowed, then stopped altogether.

"We're here," he announced. Putting his hands on his hips, he breathed deep and gazed around the little clearing as if it were as spectacular as a king's throne-room.

She crossed her arms over her chest, looking cautiously around, half expecting a hidden army to come charging at her from the trees. She saw nothing but two large woven baskets resting against one thick trunk. "All right. What exactly is it that I'm supposed to be seeing?"

"Strawberries."

"Strawberries?" She stared at him in disbelief; his dark eyes sparkled at her, stunning her with a flood of heat deep in her belly and leaving her with that same breathless feeling as always. Then he grinned, looking supremely pleased with himself.

He walked over to the thick foliage that blanketed most of the clearing, pushing aside some of the leaves to show clusters of succulent red fruits hanging beneath. "Look—there must be a thousand of them, just at the peak of ripeness!"

Gwynne rubbed her nose, staring askance at him. It seemed she'd have to go gently with him. "That's lovely, de Brice, truly it is. But why in God's name have you brought me here to see them?"

"Because you're going to pick them," he answered, as if it were the most logical thing in the world. He bent over and plucked one of the berries from a nearby plant, popping it in his mouth and straightening to chew it with his eyes closed, in obvious bliss. "Delicious," he murmured, not seeming to notice her pointed gaze.

"Ah, de Brice?" she called out, trying to pull his attention to her again. When he didn't respond, she repeated herself more loudly until he finally looked at her, another berry halfway to his mouth, his brows raised in innocence.

"Aye?"

"I told you when I agreed to leave Wales with you that I wasn't going to be your servant. If you want berries, you're going to have to pick them yourself."

He shocked her again by grinning like a fool. "Aye, that I will," he answered. "But you're going to help me."

The afternoon was turning stranger by the second.

"Why would I do that?" she managed to sputter. "Berry picking isn't a skill that you can claim I need to develop. God's blood, 'tis most often a task for little children, not ladies!"

Faint giggling suddenly seemed to echo in Gwynne's ears, and she jerked to look behind her, scrutinizing the woods. All was empty and still, save for the waving of the branches in the breeze. Just a trick of the wind, no doubt . . .

"I think you'll pick them, because I have a wager for you," Aidan said, stepping closer with a soft smile and muddling her senses anew. "Knowing how partial you are, after all, to making deals," he added, offering her a berry and then eating it himself when she refused with a scowl.

"What kind of wager?" she asked grudgingly, willing herself to avoid his gaze in a desperate attempt at self-preservation.

"A contest of sorts. We pick for half an hour; whoever has the most berries at the end of that time wins."

"Wins what?"

"Well, that part is open for discussion," he said, rocking back on his heels and feigning deep thought as he rubbed his chin. "I was thinking of something physical, perhaps."

When he directed his twinkling gaze on her again, she could resist no longer; she met his stare, and the warmth in his eyes made the melting feeling in her belly swell tenfold. Without warning he stepped even closer, and she suddenly found herself unable to breathe. Mesmerized, she watched as he reached out to drag his fingertip lightly down the side of her cheek, leaving behind a path of tingling pleasure.

"Aye, something physical would be perfect, I think," he added, his voice a husky murmur. "A prize of true worth. Something that the winner would find . . . exciting."

Helpless to drag her gaze from his, she swallowed and managed to whisper, "What exactly did you have in mind?"

He wiggled his eyebrows and suddenly stepped back. "Why, the chance to spar with me on the battlefield, of course. It seems to be what you most desire, and I'd allow you to use your choice of weapons—blunted, I should think. I wouldn't want either of us to be truly hurt for the sake of sport."

She was so taken aback that she just gaped at him.

"If you win, you'll have what I overheard you saying you longed for—the opportunity to knock me about a little. A bit of satisfaction for all that I've put you through at Dunston." Grinning, he feinted back and gave a playful jab at her shoulder, making her stumble sideways. "Eh? What say you, Gwynne? Are you game to try?"

She righted herself with a scowl, surprised at the dark rush of annoyance—and emptiness—that filled her. How dared he treat her so . . . well, so much like a *man*? 'Twas his idea that she play the part of delicate female while she stayed with him. He'd brought her out here in almost the same way that she fancied a gallant might escort his lady for an afternoon's stroll, yet now he was proposing that they engage in sport-fighting like any two common soldiers.

Looking away, she muttered, "A sparring match is the prize if I win. What about if *you* win the wager?"

"Ah, yes." He paused for a moment before giving her another half-smile. "If I win, then every afternoon for a week, beginning tomorrow, you'll agree to learn court dancing—with me as your teacher."

More faint giggling tinkled through the clearing again, momentarily overriding Gwynne's shock and setting her instincts afire. Whirling around, she growled, "What in blazes *is* that?"

"What?" Aidan asked calmly.

"That noise," she almost shouted, spinning back to him.

She clenched her fists when she saw that he was looking at her as before, all wide-eyed innocence. He shrugged and murmured, "I don't hear anything," before bending to pick a few more berries to sample.

And he was right. At least for the moment. Whatever she'd heard was gone, and the woodland was as silent as ever, the only sound the faint rustling of the leaves above them.

"Blast it to hell, but I think you're driving me mad," she muttered, yanking off her veil and jabbing her fingers through her hair.

"So, do you accept my wager or not?" Aidan asked, popping the last of the fruits in his mouth, as nonchalant as if her outburst had never happened.

"Aye, I'll take your cursed wager," Gwynne snapped, jamming the veil into the neck of her gown and hiking her skirts to her knees as she stalked to the baskets. "Just let me get started, so that I can get to the part where I'm allowed to crack some sense into that wooden skull of yours."

She snatched one of the baskets up and marched off to a spot in the clearing where the strawberry plants seemed clustered most thickly, muttering all the way about Aidan's stubbornness and his dim-witted ideas. Deliberately, she put her back to him and began to pick as if her life depended on it, ignoring the masculine chuckling that came now from the opposite end of the glade. After a moment she dared a glance and saw Aidan picking the crimson fruits with a passion of his own . . .

With a fervor, she thought, shuddering, that if she wasn't careful, might consign her to the hell of having to spend a whole week of afternoons in the disturbing proximity of his lean, hard form—and locked in the depths of his strangely compelling gaze.

# Chapter 8

Aidan nudged his basket closer to the edge of the clearing, surreptitiously glancing at Gwynne as he did. Her back was still to him, thank God. He hummed a lilting tune and kept picking, pausing to sample some of the juiciest berries as he went. He knew he should stop eating them. She'd already looked over and caught him at it several times, not to mention the fact that his tasting had made quite a dent in what little he'd managed to accumulate. He paused to peer into the depths of his basket, grimacing at the paltry sight.

'Twas a good thing he'd arranged a back-up plan.

By the time the agreed-upon half hour had elapsed, his carefully plotted strategy had borne its expected fruit. Quite literally. He checked the sun's position to be sure that time was up, then looked at his basket again, gratified to see that it was filled to overflowing. In fact, there were so many berries that several plump gems had spilled over the top edge to form a crimson mound on the ground beneath it.

"Time!" he called to Gwynne, who straightened slowly and turned to meet his gaze. She shaded her eyes with her hand, her piercing stare shifting from his face to the abundance of fruit at his feet. At the sight, her mouth went slack, then tightened in wrath. In the next instant she burst into motion.

"What is *this*?" she yelled, pointing at his basket as she dragged her own over to him with angry strides. "You couldn't have picked all of these so quickly. I looked but a few moments ago, and you hadn't enough even to come level with the brim!"

Aidan felt a prickle of guilt, but he raised his hands and tried to look sincere. "Would you believe that I pick more quickly under pressure?"

He blinked a few times, hoping that his innocent look would distract her from scrutinizing his take. But she just kept glaring at his basket as if she was certain that the berries must have appeared from thin air to have accumulated so quickly.

"You couldn't have gathered so many," she said, fisting her hands on her hips as she finally lifted her accusing gaze again to his. " 'Tisn't possible. Not in the amount of time you've had since I last looked."

He swallowed and then coughed, thinking that perhaps he *had* overdone it just a bit.

"Well, I—" he began feebly, trailing off when a renewed sound of giggles echoed through the clearing, followed closely by a swishing and crackling of branches. He closed his eyes and grimaced as two exuberant bundles shot into the glade from where they'd been crouching behind him, concealed in the brush. Little Clara and Ella shrieked with laughter, their chubby, berry-stained fingers curled over their mouths with glee.

Clearly, the two village imps had forgotten the part of his plan that directed them to stay *hidden* from Gwynne's sight.

"*We* did it! *We* did it!" they shouted between giggles, dancing around to a position on either side of Aidan before throwing themselves at his legs to give him a mighty hug.

"Did we do good, Unca Aidan? Did we?" Clara crowed, lifting her cherubic face to gaze at him in adoration.

"Aye, sweet, you did very well," he murmured, tussling first her blond head and then Ella's before directing a helpless look at Gwynne.

She stood open-mouthed for a moment. Then her brows drew together and a storm unleashed in her eyes.

"Damn you, de Brice—you cheated!" she snapped. " 'Tis a forfeit. I win the wager, by rights of your deception."

He was about to try offering some kind of explanation, when a faint sniffle pulled their attention downward again. Clara's bottom lip jutted out, her violet eyes filling with tears. She dragged one grubby hand across her nose and looked up at Gwynne, blinking, even as she continued to cling to Aidan's leg.

"Unca Aidan didn't cheat! We only helped him, is all. We wanted to play our pipes for you, and he said that we could if we helped him gather lots of berries!"

"Aye," the slightly elder Ella chimed in, stepping away from Aidan with a wavering smile. "Uncle Aidan said we'd get to practice our songs if we helped." She pulled a reed pipe from her tunic to blow a few sample notes. "If you give us the chance, we'll make grand music for you to dance by, we promise!"

Aidan's heart lurched. Looking away, he cursed himself for ever thinking to involve children in his scheme to get the better of Gwynne. Damn his eyes for being a selfish brute. He'd have to think of a way to smooth it over once she was done with them. He'd learned far too well in the past few days that when she was angry, nothing and no one stopped her from unleashing her wrath. Poor little

Clara was so sensitive to begin with, not to mention Ella's tender—

" 'Tis not your fault, girls," Gwynne said gruffly.

Aidan looked on in shock, watching as she dropped to one knee and brushed a thumb over Clara's cheek, wiping away the wetness there. Then she patted Ella on the shoulder in turn, giving her a smile before pushing herself to stand and face him, her expression shifting to match the frost in her eyes.

"*Uncle Aidan* and I will work out the details later. But beginning tomorrow afternoon, I'll expect you to be here in the glade and ready to play your pipes for us. So make sure you've practiced well between now and then."

The joyful whoops and shrieks that rose from the girls could have deafened anyone within a league. Aidan couldn't help but smile as they swung around him and Gwynne a couple of times before skipping off down the path from the clearing, yelling back about how well and often they were going to practice.

When they were gone, silence weighed heavy in the glen. Gwynne hadn't moved a muscle since uttering her agreement for the girls to play. Aidan glanced at her sidelong; she stared straight ahead, her expression unreadable.

"Thank you for that," he said quietly.

" 'Twas for the girls' sake, not yours," she answered, locking her arms in their customary position across her chest.

When she finally shifted her gaze, the cold anger he saw there rocked him, reminding him viscerally of the hardened warrior she'd become—a woman very different from the tender girl he'd loved so long ago.

"But you're not off the hook," she continued, slicing him with the steel of her eyes. "By rights, I still won today. I'll go along with the dancing part for the children's sake—but you owe me. I'll let you know how and when you're going to repay me once I decide on the method."

Then, without allowing him to utter a word in his own defense, she turned and headed down the path toward the castle, leaving him to mull over all that had happened here this day . . .

And to wonder how in God's name he was going to reconcile his gentle memories of Gwynne with the harsh reality of the woman who had stalked away from him just now—with all of the love she'd once felt for him seeming to have changed, in the past twelve years, to hate.

Gwynne thumped into her men's quarters a few hours later, still trying to shake off the black mood that the incident with Aidan had inspired. She kept telling herself that her disappointment made no sense. But no matter how she tried to ignore it, it remained, a throbbing ache akin to a feeling she hadn't acknowledged in years. Not since Marrok was first training her to be a warrior.

Not since she was naught but a simple girl instead of a Legend.

"*Lugh's bones,*" she growled under her breath, struggling to pull off her cumbersome gown before throwing herself onto a pile of old sacks that served as a pallet.

The chamber was empty, her men having gone to deliver her shield to the appointed envoy who'd arranged to meet them in the wood outside Dunston each week for news and the exchange of messages. They'd been gone since morning and should have been back by now. Another twist of fate to be annoyed about, she thought, running her hand through her hair before leaning back on the pallet.

She closed her eyes, trying to quiet her turbulent emotions. She had to keep hold of herself. Allowing Aidan de Brice to play havoc with her like this was exactly what Marrok had warned her against. He'd said that Aidan would try to delve beneath her defenses. That he'd work to weaken her in ways that had nothing to do with battle prowess or physical abilities. And her mentor had been right—but in her vast ignorance about the workings of men and women, she'd had no idea what he'd meant. Now she was beginning to understand, and it was unsettling, to say the least.

A creaking sound pulled Gwynne from her musings. Pushing herself to a sitting position, she glanced to the door she'd secured behind her, expecting to hear Owin and Dafydd scratch the sequence that would reveal their identities, so that she could lift the bar and allow them entrance. No one else was authorized to come into their chamber but Gwynne, them, and de Brice; Aidan had made that clear to everyone, and she'd secretly appreciated it, knowing it meant she could be in her masculine garments here if she chose, without fear of discovery.

But no familiar scratching sounded at the door. All was silent, save for the creaking. With a start, she realized that it was coming from behind her, from near the wall.

A mouse, perhaps?

It seemed unlikely, unless it was an awfully big mouse.

Slowly, she stood and made her way to the area from which the noise came, picking up her sword as she went. 'Twas dim outside the ring of rush-light near the pallets, and she squinted, her hand tensing and relaxing out of habit on the hilt of her weapon.

She could see nothing in the gloom, so she stood still and cocked her head to listen. There. The scuffling, creaking noise echoed through the chamber again. Gwynne softened her breathing until it was barely perceptible, so as not to distract from her hearing as she honed in on the source of the sound.

Suddenly, she scowled and headed for the door. The noise was coming from *outside*. Something or someone was on the other side of the wall, trying to get in.

She paused to glance at her gown and veil on the floor where she'd left them, considering whether or not she should put them back on over her own garments before she ventured out to confront the intruder. Her hand flexed again on her hilt. Blast it, but 'twould be difficult to explain her masculine attire and sword if 'twas naught but an errant stable boy out there—but even worse to try to fight hampered by skirts if 'twas indeed someone plotting harm to her or her men.

Mouth tight, she compromised by grabbing the short, hooded cloak Aidan had given her and throwing it on. Suddenly, the familiar cadence of scratching rang out. Cursing under her breath, she lifted the bar on the door and yanked it open, stepping aside to allow Owin and Dafydd entrance.

"What in blazes were you two doing banging around out there like that?" she asked, jamming her sword back into its sheath. "I was about to go out and ambush you, thinking you strangers prying where you didn't belong."

Owin frowned. "We made no noise, *Chwedl*. We only just now returned from delivering your shield," he said, looking as confused as Dafydd at her chiding.

In the next instant, all three locked gazes and as quickly ducked outside, drawing their weapons as they went. Gwynne followed her men, throwing her hood up as they sneaked around the building to ferret out the real interloper. Their search yielded naught but a scrap of green fabric, torn away, apparently, when the person who'd been wearing it had fled at Owin and Dafydd's approach. It fluttered there, snagged on a splinter of wood that poked from the wall.

Gwynne picked the bit of cloth from its mooring, rubbing it between her finger and thumb. 'Twas of a fine texture—too fine to have come from a servant's garment.

The evening breeze wafted again, summer-warm, rustling the straw at their feet and bringing with it the familiar scent of horses bedded down in the nearby stable. Shaking her head, Gwynne walked closer to the wall, stepping up onto the mounded straw where the intruder had obviously been standing. After examining the area at her vantage point for a moment, she announced, "There's a large hole here in the boards. Whoever it was intended to spy on us."

"But why?" Dafydd scoffed. "We've sworn peace with the bastards for these three months."

"Your guess is as good as mine."

She squinted and peered into the hole again. The dim light made it difficult, but just in view jutted the end of the pallet where she'd been lying. Chances were, then, that she'd been seen. And there was only one person she knew of who would feel he had the right to check up on her like that without her knowing of it.

"De Brice," she murmured, brushing her fingers along the rough edge of the peephole. Anger pierced through her, hot and sharp. But as annoyed as she was at the thought of Aidan spying on her, she couldn't deny the forbidden pleasure that flared beneath it. Of all people, he would have known that her men hadn't returned yet—he would have known that she'd gone into their chamber on her own. But he'd come anyway.

*Because he wanted to watch you . . . alone.*

The little voice inside her whispered its seductive message, and Gwynne swallowed, wishing she could obliterate it from her mind. Instead, she cleared her throat and stepped down from the mounded hay.

Glad that the dusk of approaching night hid the heat in her face, she motioned for Owin and Dafydd to follow her back inside their chamber. She shoved the tingling thoughts of Aidan as deep as they would go, chiding herself for allowing them at all. She and her men had much to discuss, not the least of which was how to prevent anyone from spying into their private domain again.

By the time Gwynne took leave of Owin and Dafyyd, securing inside her tunic the sealed missive from Marrok that they'd brought back from the messenger, she'd agreed to demand that Aidan provide them with tapestries to hang inside the chamber on every wall.

It was a good plan, Gwynne decided, as she walked down the narrow pathway back toward the castle courtyard. And in the process of making her demand of Aidan, she'd have the chance to watch his reaction, to see if his expression betrayed him as the culprit this night.

Catching herself smiling at the thought of his discomfort, Gwynne grasped her layers of skirts more tightly around her legs and picked up her pace. Aye, 'twould be interesting to see just how Aidan would react when he realized that she knew what he'd been up to tonight.

Very interesting, indeed.


Diana pressed back into the shadows, fisting her hands as her breathing slowed. That had been close. Only a few seconds more and she would have been spotted.

She closed her eyes and leaned her head against the smooth stone of the brewhouse wall. She'd gotten one good look inside the Welshmen's chamber before they'd surprised her with their return. She'd been so startled that she'd almost fallen from her hay perch; as it was, her skirt had caught on something and torn when she'd jumped away to hide.

She looked down now at the ragged edge of her gown, her heart beating faster as she remembered the way the younger of the two men—the one they called Owin—had looked right to the place where she'd been crouched in the gloom, his mysterious dark gaze leaving her breathless and tingling.

But then he'd gone inside with his older friend, and she'd made her getaway.

Diana wrapped her arms around her waist now, excitement and fear giving way to dark anticipation. Because in the one moment she'd had to look inside the men's chamber, she'd seen something that was worth all the aggravation she'd endured thus far. Something that, shocking as it was, might prove exceedingly useful in her plan to rid Dunston Castle of the troublesome woman whom Aidan had taken in, claiming her as one of their own.

Diana tapped her fingertip against the soft, full curve of her bottom lip, thinking about exactly how she might make the most of this unexpected boon. She would have to be careful, to be sure, but the possibilities were too delicious to resist. Because tonight she'd seen Gwynne ap Morrison reclining on a pallet in her countrymen's empty chamber, calm as could be . . .

And she'd been dressed as a *man*.

# Chapter 9

❦

"**W**hat do you mean, I've been spying on you?" Aidan asked, trying to sound indignant, even as he turned his face aside to prevent Gwynne from seeing the guilt he knew must be there. They'd met here in the clearing for her first dancing lesson, and the last thing he needed was for her attention to be diverted from the pleasure of the activity by a dose of righteous anger at him.

"I've no need to spy in my own castle," he added for good measure. Pretending to dismiss the idea, he unsheathed his sword, dropped to one knee, and ripped off a handful of dry grass to rub down the blade, wondering how in God's name the woman had learned that he'd been watching her train.

"There's no need to hide it, de Brice. I know it was you. Just admit it and be done."

Aidan stopped what he was doing and looked up at her, almost certain he'd caught a whisper of pleasure in her voice as she'd berated him. Her complaints rang more with feigned outrage than anything else, he'd bet his boots on it.

Deciding to play out his hunch to its end, he leaned back and asked, "Even if someone *were* spying on you, Gwynne, what makes you think it was me?"

"No one else would have reason to watch me," she answered, tipping up her chin to look down at him, though the disdainful gesture lacked conviction.

He kept his gaze intent upon her, and his attention was quickly rewarded with a delicate flush of pink on her cheeks. Ah, yes, his intuition had been right; there was more going on here than met the eye.

A smile pulled at his lips. A skillful warrior she might be, but it appeared that when it came to the subtle tensions that could play between men and women, she was as much of an innocent as ever. Slowly he stood to face her, so near that he felt her startle and heard her breathing go shallow at his movement. He leaned in closer . . . then a bit closer . . .

"And what do you think was *my* reason for watching you, Gwynne?" he countered softly.

"I . . . I think it was because . . ." She closed her eyes as if feeling a momentary pain, then turned her face away, her voice trailing off to a whisper.

He stood very still and close, breathing in the fragrance of her hair. It was incongruously gentle, like fresh air and rain, and it made something catch deep inside him. He wanted to brush back the errant curl at her temple and press his lips to the soft, warm skin beneath, just as the boy he'd once been had done so many times before; the urge returned now as naturally as if twelve long, painful years of separation hadn't passed between them.

Steeling himself against the yearning, Aidan pressed his fists to his sides and reminded himself to keep a clear head. He was not the same youth of years past—and she was most certainly not the same woman. They were here together now only because of his need to repay the life-debt he owed her, that was all. True desire had no place in the mix. He was going to marry Helene—he *had* to marry Helene—and he was only doing what was necessary with Gwynne to make her remember him and the love they'd shared, so that he could resolve his obligation to her and go on with his life.

Aye, this was necessity, nothing more . . .

She shifted suddenly, trying to back away, but he gripped her upper arms with a firm intensity that made her gasp and look up to his face. He started to say something but found that he couldn't for the emotions sweeping through him. She stood still in his embrace, seeming to understand as he did that there were forces at work between them more powerful than either could explain.

He held her gaze as long as he could before the temptation of her mouth beckoned. Even knowing that he would regret it, he glanced down to the full curve of her lips. Her tongue darted out nervously, its pink tip moistening the tender flesh in its wake, and his belly twisted with a jolt of hot, hard need. He dragged his gaze upward again, hoping for salvation, but the look in her eyes only devastated him more—silver softened to misty gray, inviting warmth that battled with a shadow of wariness. And above all, pure, unadulterated wanting . . .

*God in heaven, help him . . .*

"Gwynne," he murmured, tilting his head down, a whisper away from brushing her lips with his own. He felt her exhale on a sigh, and her exquisite eyes fluttered shut as she leaned toward him . . .

"Aidan, I—"

"We're here! We're ready to play for you!" called out Clara as she danced into the clearing, followed by a more sedate Ella, who clutched a handful of reed pipes. The two girls jerked to a halt when they saw Aidan and Gwynne standing so close together, and Clara frowned, stamping her tiny foot. "You didn't wait for us," she pouted. "You're dancing already, with no music. But you promised to wait!"

Gwynne jerked away from him, and Aidan closed his eyes, blowing out his breath. He swiveled to face the girls, trying to smile. "We've waited, Clara, never fear. I was just helping Lady Gwynne to . . . relax a bit before we began." He heard her cough behind him. "Ready yourselves to play, and we'll be right with you."

Clara seemed to accept his explanation, for after a moment she busied herself with sorting through their pipes, while Ella found a comfortable mossy spot for them to sit. Aidan turned back to Gwynne. Trying to recapture at least a bit of the intimacy they'd shared, he murmured, "You were saying . . . ?"

"Hmmmm?" Gwynne had succeeded in backing away from him this time, and now she fiddled with the draped edges of her sleeves.

"You whispered my name, as if you were about to say something more . . . but you never finished." Unwilling to give up, he bridged the distance between them, just brushing her chin with the caress of his fingers before she jerked her head up to meet his gaze. She might as well have slammed her forearm into his chest. The warmth that had been in her eyes had fled, leaving naught but a brilliant gleam that cut him like glass.

"I was merely readying to voice my demand that you provide my men's chamber with tapestries."

"*What*?" Now it was his turn to step back. "What in blazes do tapestries have to do with what was happening between us just a moment ago?"

"Nothing was happening, de Brice, except in your own

vivid imagination," she answered coolly, though she looked away as if she knew that what she spoke was a falsehood. "I want tapestries to hang on the walls in my men's chamber to prevent whoever was spying on us," she glanced back to give him a pointed look, "from doing it again. Will that pose a difficulty?"

He didn't answer at first. An aching pain lanced through him, though he would have denied it to anyone who claimed it true. After a long pause, he forced a smile that felt more like a grimace and inclined his head to her in courtly fashion. "Nay, milady, 'tis no problem—your desire is my command. Tapestries it is, then."

He had the satisfaction of seeing her give a tiny flinch at his response, but other than that, she remained without expression. They readied themselves for the dance lesson, the girls' enthusiasm for their undertaking masking, for the most part, the uncomfortable silence between him and Gwynne. She moved through the positions he instructed her to take with as much life as a wooden doll, her face as hard as if it were carved from stone. It reminded him of the look she'd worn while driving herself through her series of training exercises, and he couldn't help but wonder if she didn't consider their dancing together as much of an arduous duty as those daily exhausting drills.

That sent another swell of pain through him, and so he forced himself to stop thinking about it. He pushed himself through the remainder of the lesson much as she did, managing to thank Clara and Ella when they were done, and arranging for them to return to the clearing again the next day. After they'd left, it was silent again. Agonizingly so.

Aidan stood there in the empty quiet for as long as he could bear it. Then he bowed to Gwynne without a word and stalked into the comforting embrace of the woodland beyond the clearing. But he was unable to prevent himself

from stopping a few feet into the concealment of the trees
to turn and take one last look at her.

She stood as motionless as a statue, her arms crossed
over her chest just as she'd been when he'd taken his
leave. He thought for a moment that she might show some
response, now that she believed herself to be alone. A
muscle in her jaw twitched, and if the distance between
them hadn't been so great, he'd have sworn that he saw a
suspicious sheen in her eyes. But he was too far away to
tell, and in the next instant she'd turned away, her movements rigid and controlled as she, too, left the clearing . . .

In a direction exactly opposite the one he'd taken.

Gwynne broke into a run once she entered the cover of
the trees, crashing through the woods until everything in
her vision blurred. But she wouldn't cry. Damn it to everlasting hell, she couldn't. She didn't cry. Ever. Through
the burning in her eyes she saw a huge, moss-covered log
lying on the ground ahead of her. Stumbling the rest of the
way to it, she collapsed against its damp surface, feeling
her breath rasp in her throat.

*It hurt. Oh, God, it hurt more than she'd ever thought it
could . . .*

How could he have taunted her like that? Tempted
her—made her feel emotions and desires she'd thought
long dead, buried beneath the steel she'd long ago forged
round her heart? Anger fought to find release, and she
struggled against it, sucking back the agony that filled her.

Aidan had almost kissed her, damn him—and to her
shame, she'd almost let him. She'd wanted him to. Pulling
away and acting like nothing had happened had been pure
torture. It had been nigh impossible, like refusing a cup of
ambrosia after years of agonizing thirst. She remembered
the strangely erotic sensation of his breath brushing over
her cheek, the warm, masculine scent of his skin as he'd

stood so near to her . . . she could almost taste his lips, tantalizing hers in the moment before they were to kiss. A rush of excitement and longing had swept through her then, pounding in time with the fevered beating of her heart.

*They'd come so close, so close . . .*

Jamming her fists into her eyes, Gwynne doubled over and held herself so stiffly that her muscles ached, not wanting to recognize the faint keening sound that came from deep inside her. *Damn, damn, damn . . .*

She couldn't let him get to her like this. Marrok was counting on her, as were Dafydd, Owin, and the rest of her clan. She had to remain strong in the face of de Brice's tender assaults on her. She was the Dark Legend, a creature of myth, bloodshed, and war. An instrument of duty for the Welsh patriots who followed her. She couldn't risk it all by indulging herself in carnal temptations she had no right to experience or enjoy.

Sucking in her breath, she squeezed her eyes shut at the images that hammered through her brain to remind her of that fact. Clear memories of those first dark days in the Welsh encampment when she was simply a frightened girl, her mind an empty canvas, her past somehow horribly erased. Memories of the man who'd called himself her father railing against her, enraged by her feminine weakness.

She'd felt as if the black intensity of Prince Owain's eyes would swallow her whole every time he looked at her. His face would twist into a mask of anger and disappointment, and he'd push her to the ground. When she wouldn't get up, he'd stand over her, shouting his curses and taunts . . . until one day, she'd shot to her feet again and flailed wildly at him, crying and screaming with all the hate that was inside her.

He'd smiled when she did that—the only time she

could remember seeing that expression on his handsome face—and then he'd handed her over to his trainer of warriors, his own brother, Marrok. Her transformation into the Dark Legend had begun that day, and she'd never looked back. Not when the other young women her age began to attract suitors—not when they married and had babies and settled into the homes they'd made for their families. Not even after Prince Owain died, killed during a battle against the English in her twenty-first year.

Nay, looking back was pointless and painful. Yet now she was being confronted with a threat to her identity that was far greater than any other she'd faced thus far. A danger that attacked from within, triggered by feelings and sensations barely recalled, and hot, full-blown desires only just now being realized . . .

Desires that came in the virile form of her arch enemy, Aidan de Brice.

Swallowing hard, Gwynne forced her eyes open and lurched to her feet. Slowly, she lowered her fisted hands to her sides and tried to relax each of her muscles in turn, willing her mind to calm and focus as Marrok had taught her to do years ago.

There, that was better. The sounds of the forest, the music of the leaves brushing against each other in the cooling breeze, the fertile scents and vivid colors filled her senses again, and she breathed more easily.

She would resist her desires, that was all. Aidan could ply her with tender looks, sweet caresses, even claims of an amorous past with her, and none of it would matter. She would stay strong in the face of his most tempting attacks. Aye, she would stay strong, she thought, as she headed back to Dunston Castle. It might take every ounce of inner strength she possessed, but she would do her best to resist Aidan de Brice.

*Pray God that it would be enough.*

\* \* \*

Much later that night, after avoiding both her men and the usual evening feast in the great hall, Gwynne crept to her chamber and climbed into bed. Sleep eluded her for the first hours that she waited for its sweet release. But when she finally drifted off, it wasn't into peaceful slumber. The old dream came again, winding seductive tendrils around her as always, keeping her immersed in its vivid and disturbing world of images and feelings . . .

*The misty woodland beckoned her, a damp blanket of fog veiling her sight as she strode forward. The woman's voice called to her again, wispy as the swirling breeze, her haunting melody an irresistible force.*

*Gwynne's heart beat thickly, her breathing harsh as she pressed forward, searching the wood. The wind picked up force, howling through the branches and tangling in the dark canopy of leaves before lifting them to the black sky.*

*Her eyes stung, and the awful choking feeling filled her throat. As always, she tried to answer the woman's call, but the words strangled before they reached her mouth. She thrust forward one gauntleted arm, moving aside a branch thick with rain-drenched leaves . . .*

*And saw her.*

*She floated in the cool shaft of moonlight, her form pale, her delicate hands reaching out to Gwynne. She was so beautiful. Long, golden hair cascaded past her hips from the jeweled circlet she wore on her brow; her white gown glowed in the moonlight, lustrous and pristine.*

*Pristine.*

*Gwynne frowned in confusion. There was no blood; the crimson stains that usually besprinkled the material of her gown had somehow vanished. The woman held one hand up to her throat, the gaping slash that typically disfigured her there covered now with clean strips of linen.*

*Her face looked calm as she reached out to Gwynne, still unable to speak, but nodding and expressing volumes nonetheless with her beautiful eyes . . .*

Gwynne jerked awake, her mind still spinning with the remnants of the dream. It had been different—so different from ever before—but why? In all the years that she'd been plagued by it, beginning with that very first time, the night after she'd begun her training as the Dark Legend, it had always been the same. The woman floated before her, bloodied and ravaged, her throat slit, her life flow spilling onto her gown as she reached out to Gwynne, begging for help.

But not this time . . .

Shaking her head, Gwynne leaned back on her pillow and tried to make sense of it. Why was the woman changed now—her wounds wrapped and the viciousness of her attack hidden from the eye? Why had she looked so calm and nodded her head that way?

The questions prickled through Gwynne's brain, a mystery with no easy solution; they left her fitful and restless, allowing her to fall into uneasy slumber again only after hours of mulling—not until dawn began painting hues of shimmering rose and gold across the delicate canvas of the sky.

Aidan grabbed the long-handled curry brush and stalked ahead of Kevyn into the stable, waving away the boys who jumped to their feet at his entrance.

"Do you wish your steed saddled, milord?" young Davey Gilbert asked, trying to sound manly, as befitted his position as head stable boy; he stood as straight as he could, as he hurriedly brushed straw from his breeches.

"Nay, lad. I've no need of your services this afternoon. All of you have my leave to go to the pond for an hour's fishing or other sport, if you like."

Several of the boys whooped their enthusiasm, while Davey gave a jerky bow and smiled wide enough to make the freckles on his cheeks nearly disappear. "Aye—thank you, milord! I'll have the lads back in plenty of time." With another quick salute, he turned and ran, still grinning, through the open stable door.

Aidan felt Kevyn's heavy gaze and heard the tread of his steps behind him as he walked the remaining distance to Revolution's stall. He resisted saying anything, knowing that it would be futile. Kevyn wasn't about to give up; if Aidan had learned anything about him in the years they'd fought together in their battles against the Welsh, it was that his friend's present silence was bound to be temporary.

As the son of a minor nobleman who lived a league east of Dunston, Kevyn was used to speaking up for himself and his ideas; he'd had to, having little other clout in terms of power and gold. His persistence—and his dogged loyalty to those who befriended him—were what had brought him to the more prosperous station in life that he enjoyed now.

Revolution began to make low noises in his throat and to toss his head as he sensed the approach of the two men. With a soothing murmur, Aidan held out his hand and the massive steed instantly quieted, calmed by his master's voice and scent. In the next instant, Aidan had stepped in next to him to brush him, keeping his gaze studiously on the task at hand rather than on Kevyn, who leaned on the wooden rail of the stall.

"I've never pretended to understand your motives, Aidan," Kevyn finally said, his thick blond brows knitting together as he frowned at him. "But what I'm saying has nothing to do with censuring you for them."

"Nay? Last I knew, you were telling me that I'm a fool to be taking an hour each noontime to teach Gwynne court dancing." Aidan picked up the pace of his brushing, determined not to get into this again with his friend, whose opinion he normally valued above anyone's but his own.

Kevyn shook his head, looking like he was losing the battle for patience. "I was simply trying to give you some advice on making Gwynne remember her past with you—if that's still what you want."

"It doesn't matter if it's what I want," Aidan said tightly, surprised that he hadn't been able to deny outright his own feeling in the matter. "It's the only honorable thing for me to do. I have no other option."

"Then you're going about it all wrong."

"What?" Aidan stopped what he was doing to glare at Kevyn. "Since when have you become an expert on handling women?"

Shrugging, Kevyn answered, "I'm not making claim to that, but I do know something of the ways to soften a woman's heart." He gave a small smile. "At least, that's what Ailyse says."

"*Ailyse?*" Aidan stood straight up, making Revolution snort and stamp at his sudden movement. Aidan quieted him with a few pats and an apple he pulled from the fold of his tunic. "Ailyse the laundress?" he asked, astonished at Kevyn's matter-of-fact revelation. He couldn't help but envision the woman, a good-natured widow from the next village, whose buxom curves and sunny, welcoming personality attracted a great deal of attention from men of all ranks. She was comely in an untamed sort of way, with a shock of russet hair that she favored wearing tied in a velvet ribbon she'd received from a noble lover years ago.

"Ailyse is a remarkable woman," Kevyn said, moving away from the rail to step into the stall's opening, "with a warm and generous heart."

"I wasn't aware that her heart was considered one of her more notable assets," Aidan said. He joined Kevyn outside the paddock after patting Revolution's shoulder one last time.

"Be that as it may," Kevyn said archly, "she's seen fit to share with me some of the secrets to winning women over."

"Is that so? And what, pray tell, might they be?" Aidan was thoroughly amused now; he leaned his elbow against the wall and awaited the fall of Kevyn's pearls of wisdom.

Appearing to ignore his friend's gibing tone, Kevyn said, " 'Tis wise to try to *talk* with a woman you wish to entice romantically—or in your case, a woman you hope will remember her romantic past with you."

"Talk? That's one of the big secrets?" Aidan shook his head and laughed again, moving toward the tack room to get Revolution's bridle. "I'm afraid you've been duped, my friend. I talk to Gwynne every day and it hasn't gotten me anywhere."

"Discussion of arms, warfare, and rebellion don't quite qualify."

Aidan sent him a sardonic look. " 'Tis *she* who initiates talk of that sort between us." When Kevyn said no more, Aidan crossed his arms over his chest and sighed. "All right, then. What topics should I be broaching with the recalcitrant Lady Gwynne?"

"Something deeper. Something she would consider meaningful," Kevyn answered, looking pleased to be asked for his opinion on the matter.

"Such as?"

"Her heart's desires. What she fears, what she enjoys doing . . . the things that make her happy. Try to get her to open up to you."

Aidan's jaw might have dropped if he was the kind of man prone to such displays. "You're jesting," he said at last, almost choking on the words. "You must be jesting. I'm fairly certain that the only opening up Gwynne is interested in doing right now involves her blade and my skull."

Kevyn scowled again, as he had when they'd first come into the stable. "It worked with me, I tell you. Ailyse found me very attractive after I asked such questions of her. She said it showed that I appreciated women and their finer feelings."

Aidan made a scoffing sound in his throat. "That I might believe. But Gwynne is an entirely different case from Ailyse—or any other woman, for that matter. What works with them won't work with her."

"What will, then?"

"I haven't figured that out yet," Aidan finally confessed, turning to inspect the remainder of Revolution's tack.

"Well, I can tell you one thing: you won't have much success with this dancing ploy you've come up with."

"Ah, so you're a soothsayer, now, in addition to being the world's greatest lover?"

Kevyn just shook his head and leaned against the wall with his arms folded. "Anyone with eyes can see what the outcome will be." He gave Aidan a pointed look. "Did you ever dance with Gwynne back then, when the two of you courted and betrothed yourselves to each other?"

Aidan frowned and glanced away, busying himself with polishing the iron bit-piece of Revolution's bridle. "Nay. We were forced to see each other in secret; my father never would have approved of our union, and we knew it."

"Then the dancing doesn't have much chance at achieving your goal of making her remember you. 'Tis possible, perhaps, to entice her physically with it, but once she realizes what you're doing and how you're making her feel—if you're lucky enough to inspire such a renewed attraction—" he raised his brows, making Aidan want to pummel him, "she's liable to withdraw from you."

Aidan knew that his expression revealed far more than he would have wished when Kevyn pushed away from the wall, shaking his head and making a clicking sound with his tongue. "I see. She's already done that, has she?"

"Nay," Aidan retorted, feeling more than a little defensive. "Not exactly, anyway."

"What happened, then?" Kevyn asked, bending over to pick up a girth strap Aidan had dropped, to hang it back on the wall.

"Nothing," Aidan admitted. "We spent a painful, silent hour dancing."

"Aye, that's what I predicted."

"Not entirely. It was in the moments *before* the lesson began, when we were alone . . . God help me, Kev, but it was like the last twelve years had never happened. She accused me of spying on her, but she was secretly flattered by the idea—enough to make her blush as she said it. And then we almost kissed . . ."

"Almost?"

Aidan grimaced, remembering. "Aye, almost. The girls came into the clearing then, and by the time I'd gotten them settled, Gwynne had retreated to what you were just talking about. Cold and distant—and angry, like she was the day I tracked her into the mountains and made her come back here with me."

Kevyn shook his head, making that annoying clicking sound again. "Take my advice, friend. Keep the dancing if you must, but try something more besides. Something that you used to do together, that might spark her memory of you."

Aidan frowned again, stilling as he considered Kevyn's suggestion. *Something she used to do with him* . . .

The memories came gradually at first, then harder and faster, causing the bittersweet pain he was learning to expect whenever he remembered what he'd shared with

Gwynne. 'Twas the same rush of hurt that always held him back from looking into the old wooden chest that sat in the corner of his solar; he'd thought Gwynne dead the last time, when more than a year ago, he'd opened the lid to peer at the precious objects inside. He'd been biding his time since then, and even more so in the past weeks, uncertain of how he would react to the trunk's contents, now that he knew she was alive.

But Kevyn's suggestion initiated a sense of excitement and hope, dispelling some of the pain. There was something more he could do, perhaps, to make Gwynne remember him. Aye, it just might work.

He turned to his friend, clapping him on the back hard enough to make him growl and return a good-natured shove.

"Kev," he said, grinning, "it'll take some preparation, but I'm going to try what you suggested—because even though it doesn't happen too often, this time I think you might actually be right."

# Chapter 10

~~~~∽∞∽~~~~

**G**wynne stamped through the underbrush on her way to the glen, kicking stones out of her way and grumbling to herself. How dared Aidan summon her like this, at this time of the day? Their cursed dancing lesson—their fourth so far—wasn't until this afternoon, yet he'd had old Alana send her out here instead of completing her normal morning training in feminine skills.

If she'd been allowed to escape the old woman's penetrating gaze and gentle instruction for any other reason, she'd have been glad for it, but as it stood, this reprieve was worse by far. It always took so much energy to appear impassive when she was with Aidan. *Lugh*, every minute in his presence was more difficult than she'd ever thought it could be. Especially after what had happened during that first lesson . . .

Unbidden, the memory of their almost-kiss came again, sweeping over Gwynne with surprising intensity. Tingles raced up her spine at the remembered feeling of his mouth so close to hers—of his warmth and his seductive gaze on her. Shaking her head, she gave a little growl of frustration and jerked to a halt. She had to pull herself together before she reached the glen. 'Twas bad enough that she'd need to face Aidan at all, without revealing how disturbed she was that he filled her every waking moment.

Closing her eyes, Gwynne clenched her fists and breathed slowly in. She could do this. Aidan de Brice, handsome and persuasive as he might be, was but a man. She'd faced countless others like him without so much as blinking an eye, even when she knew it would be necessary to kill them. At least she didn't need to muster that kind of steel will toward de Brice.

*Not yet, anyway.*

Ignoring the jolt of pain that shot through her at the mere thought of facing him again in a life and death battle someday, Gwynne stilled her thoughts as she strode the remaining twenty paces to the glen. What he had in mind for her this morning was anyone's guess. Perhaps a little sparring match out of the sight of prying eyes to remind them both of what they really were—and weren't—to each other. A sardonic smile twisted her mouth, but she found that she felt no real pleasure in the thought.

Finally, she approached the spot, but right at the edge of the clearing she paused, wanting to catch at least a glimpse of Aidan before he saw her, in hopes of getting better bearings on his intent. With a stealth born of years of practice, she lifted her arm and silently pushed a branch sideways to peer unseen into the lush glade. What greeted her gaze nearly made her stop breathing.

Aidan reclined on his back just to the right of where they'd done their dancing the day before, his hands cupped behind his head and his eyes closed to the sun beaming down on him. A bleached linen cloth was spread beneath him, and a basket rested at his side. Just behind him lay a finely polished lute with inlaid flowers traveling along the edge in a beautiful outline.

He looked, for all intents and purposes, like a noble gallant awaiting the arrival of his ladylove for an intimate rendezvous. Gwynne swallowed hard, a sudden lump unexpectedly filling her throat.

*Lugh's bones, what was she supposed to do now?*

She was so startled at the peaceful scene he'd created that she did the unthinkable, shifting her weight without paying attention to her surroundings; her movement caused a twig beneath her foot to snap with a resounding crack. Such a stupid error would have had fatal results in the midst of an ambush—and she wasn't so sure that the consequences were going to be any less damaging now. But there was no turning back. Wincing, she stepped into the clearing, just as Aidan sat up and looked in her direction, a smile edging his lips.

"Ah, you've arrived at last." He shaded his eyes in order to see her as she approached. When he lowered his hand, it was to gesture to the edge of the woodland from which she'd come. "Hiding there, were you?" he cajoled. "I should have expected as much. You always liked to keep me guessing when we were younger, especially if we'd arranged one of our secret meetings."

She frowned at the twinge his words sent through her; something in her head swirled, unbalancing her as a shadow voice rang out in her memory—Aidan's voice, only from another time and place: *"Gwynne, are you here? Gwynne, answer me!"* An image of bright sunlight and falling flower petals followed, catching her off guard and befuddling her senses, making that strange sensation sizzle through her brain again, as if she stood poised at the brink of something important. Something she couldn't quite grasp . . .

Biting down on the inside of her cheek to keep from displaying her confused emotions, Gwynne raised her brow and managed to ask dryly, "If we were so close all those years ago, why did we meet in secret? Why not let the whole world know of our feelings for each other?"

"Because you were a humble Welsh lass and I was heir to an English Earldom," Aidan answered, his smile a little less bright. "My father would have been furious."

"Aye, well, mine would have been as well, if it were true, instead of a fantasy you've created in your own mind." She pursed her lips. "Speaking of your imagination, how is the dissolution of our supposed union coming along?"

"You had no father then," Aidan answered, quite obviously avoiding her question. "None that you knew of, anyway," he added, when she glared at him. Then he shrugged and gave her a charmingly lopsided smile, spreading his hands in front of himself. "But enough of all that. What say you? Will you sit and join me?"

"Not until you answer my question."

"What question?"

Gwynne folded her arms across her chest. "I want to know how the dissolution of this betrothal you claim between us is coming along—and whether or not I'll have the good fortune to leave England sooner than I'd anticipated."

Aidan's expression didn't change. " 'Tis all going exactly as planned—so nay, you'll not be leaving before the agreed upon three months have elapsed." He slid over and patted the blanket next to him. "Now, will you come and sit here with me?"

"Why?" she demanded, cocking her hands on her hips in what she hoped was a decidedly unfeminine pose.

"I did go through a good deal of trouble to arrange this

repast for us," he said, seeming nonplussed as he gestured to the basket, overflowing with what appeared to be bread, some berries, a round of cheese, and a skin of wine.

She jutted out her chin, determined to stand firm. "For what possible purpose, de Brice? We're enemies—the leaders of two opposing armies. These—these kinds of *niceties*," she grated, her voice rising with her own sense of weakness as she gestured to the things surrounding him, "aren't part of what I agreed to when I came to England with you!"

"Heaven forbid me. I was simply trying to give you a respite from what I know must be tedious lessons of comportment with Alana," he said, shaking his head and leaning his forearm on his knee to gaze up at her. "I thought you might take pleasure in a summer day out in the fresh air doing nothing but sitting and perhaps eating—a chance to enjoy yourself for once. 'Twas nothing more than that, I assure you."

Whatever part of her she'd managed to keep firm until now turned completely to jelly at the warmth in his velvet gaze. She sighed, letting her hands fall to her sides.

"Fine," she growled in defeat, slumping to a cross-legged position next to him. It appeared that he'd won this round, at least, of their battle of wills.

After a length of silence spent trying to ignore the fact that Aidan continued to look intently at her, Gwynne finally muttered, "If we're going to be eating together, then you might as well get on with it and pass me the bread. I'm famished."

He laughed aloud, and she twisted to look at him before she remembered that meeting his gaze again would probably be a mistake. A fluttering sensation erupted in her belly at his expression; his eyes crinkled at the corners in that way that always made her want to smile; but it was the look in them—the deep appreciation, the welcoming and accepting of her—that nearly did her in.

"What do you find so entertaining?" she managed to ask.

"Ah, Gwynne, I never thought I'd say this, but I think I'm beginning to understand you. And I rather like that feeling."

Mortified to feel the heat rise in her cheeks, she scowled and looked down to her hands, which, to her horror, were folded in her lap like any proper lady's. *Lugh's head*. Deliberately changing her position, she reached for the basket and began to drag it toward her.

"Allow me," Aidan said, gripping its handle and stopping it in its tracks. Then, flipping the lid open the rest of the way, he gestured to the contents with chivalrous flair. "Would you care for some wine with your bread? Perhaps a wedge of cheese?"

Mumbling some sort of response, Gwynne scowled and looked down at her hands again; they seemed clumsy and useless, suddenly—a feeling she couldn't ever remember having about them when they were wrapped around the hilt of her sword. Giving up, she folded them again on her lap, casting a sidelong warning look at Aidan when he dared to continue smiling.

"You seem awfully pleased with yourself today," she ground out, taking the slice of bread with cheese that he offered her.

"I'm enjoying the day, with all its infinite possibilities," he answered, seeming to pierce her again with that meaningful gaze of his. "Is that so wrong?"

"Nay, I suppose not," she admitted finally, taking a bite of her food. " 'Tis wise to take pleasure in what comes our way, never knowing which day will be our last."

"Ah. Spoken as a true warrior."

She looked over at him quickly, to see if he mocked her. His expression showed no trace of derision—just the opposite, in fact. She finished chewing and swallowed, before setting the bread down. "A warrior's life is all I know, de Brice. Anything that happened, anything I was before that time is a blank for me. I remember none of it."

"But I do," he said quietly. "And I'd be happy to share it with you—to help you remember it if only you'll let me, Gwynne."

She remained silent, uncertain how to answer through the familiar pain that filled her at the thought of once again owning such knowledge about herself. "I don't want to remember," she said at last. " 'Tis too difficult."

"Why?"

"Because—" She broke off, trying to harness her feelings. Aidan was the last man on earth who should be privy to her innermost secrets. "Nay," she said, scowling. " 'Tis not something I wish to discuss."

"Why, Gwynne?" he demanded. "Why won't you let me help you remember?"

She bit her lip, holding herself stiff and still against the feelings coursing through her. But then he touched her hand, and the floodgate seemed to burst, the words spilling from her almost of their own accord.

"Damn it, Aidan! I don't want to know because it's not who I am anymore—can't you understand that? From as far back as I can remember, it was hammered into me that I was born to be the one and only salvation for all of Wales. I cannot be the Dark Legend and a woman too!"

She sucked in her breath when he grasped both her hands now, pulling her around and making her look at him. What she saw in his eyes pushed her emotions higher, making her heart race and her throat feel tight.

"But it *is* part of you, Gwynne. You are a woman as much as I am a man. To continue to fight that fact is futile and destructive."

She tried to look away again, overwhelmed by the torrent of emotions sweeping through her, but he wouldn't allow it. He released one of her hands to grip her chin, keeping her gaze locked with his. "You feel something for me, Gwynne. You remember something. Deep in your heart you know I'm not imagining all that happened between us—you know it!"

Taking her by surprise, he stroked his fingers softly down the side of her face, and she closed her eyes, feeling the pain caused by his gentle touch gradually subside and shift into a yearning that blossomed like wildfire, consuming every fiber of her being.

He leaned closer, his breath warm and moist against her lips as he murmured, "Somewhere inside your soul you do remember me—and by God, I know that you remember this."

His lips brushed hers, gently at first, then harder and more demanding. He slanted his mouth down, his tongue flicking inside, and a soft, guttural sound rose up from a place deep within her. Heat bloomed in her belly as they kissed, the hum of pleasure swelling until it converged into a tingling river of sensation that shot down the length of her spine to the tips of her fingers and toes.

Her hands seemed to lift to his arms with a will of their own, clenching into his shirt, feeling the hard contours of his muscles flex beneath her touch, all while he kept kissing her, over and over.

Oh God, she was falling away, losing herself in the glorious taste of him, the magnificent feel and warmth of him. He slipped his arms low around her back, his palms cradling her, stroking her rhythmically. And still he kept kissing her, his mouth hot and insistent, yet at the same time achingly tender against hers. All her senses felt aflame, swirling up to overwhelm her and making something inside coil tighter as he eased her down onto the linen cloth next to him.

"Gwynne," he whispered into her ear as he trailed kisses from that sensitive spot there to the place just beneath her jaw. " 'Tis so sweet, Gwynne. So good . . ."

She gasped with the pleasure of it and the feel of him pressed against her; her body arched, her eyes fluttering shut and her head tipping back as he dragged his mouth with sweet seduction down the length of her throat. As if spurred on by the languid remnants of some nearly forgotten dream, her hands drifted to his face, her fingertips threading through the hair at his brow before trailing down the strong lines of his cheek and jaw.

When she did that, he lifted his head, and she saw a flicker of surprise in the depths of his eyes, blended with fierce, stark need—an intensity of feeling that took her breath away. He took her mouth once more, and Gwynne cried out softly, kissing him back, giving herself over to sensation and the pure, unfettered passion that his touch, his nearness, sent coursing through her.

Instinctively, she nestled into his embrace, wanting to feel all of him, and as she did, her breasts rubbed with tingling heat against the solid expanse of his chest. In the next instant his hands were touching her there, warm and firm as they slid around one gentle curve, stroking . . . gliding to cup her in his palm and brush his thumb across the sensitive peak of flesh straining against the fabric of her clothing. His touch made her shudder with pleasure, consuming her with an aching need for something more.

She moaned as they kept kissing, reaching to pull him closer, wanting something she couldn't name, and not thinking, not allowing herself to consider anything but how good, how right this felt . . .

"Ah, Gwynne . . . love, you haven't forgotten. I knew you hadn't forgotten," Aidan breathed against her mouth, closing his eyes and pressing his brow to hers, even as he continued to caress her.

She stiffened suddenly, something jarring her from the marvelous fog of sensation that had enfolded her. It was the endearment he'd murmured; it yanked her back and slammed her down into cold, hard reality, making the dream of Aidan's touch splinter around her into a thousand shards of glass.

*She wasn't anyone's love.*

Nay, she was the Dark Legend, mighty warrior and leader of her people in their bloody conflict against England. Welsh rebel. Outlaw to the English Crown. And here she was, stretched out on a blanket and kissing Aidan de Brice, the Scourge of Wales. Their most bitter enemy.

*Her* enemy.

*What in heaven's name had she been thinking . . . ?*

"Nay," she gasped, sitting up and jerking to her feet, before stumbling back from him. "I can't do this. I won't."

She shook her head, the only sound coming from the strained breaths she took as she tried to hold herself rigid against the pain. Pressing her fingers to her mouth, she turned and ran toward the sheltering trees, not caring that he saw her weakness, not caring about anything but getting away. All she knew was that she had to go—had to get as far away as she could from Aidan de Brice and the desperate wanting that filled her whenever she was near him.

For she knew suddenly and without a doubt that if she didn't, she might very well lose herself in his arms forever.

Aidan watched her go, aching to run after her but knowing he couldn't. His heart thundered and his mind burned with the enormity of what had just happened—of how he'd felt when they'd kissed and he'd held her again at long last.

After twelve desolate years . . .

Ah, it couldn't be. He wouldn't let it. Not now. *Not ever.* He had his duty to think about—his honor and his responsibility to his family.

But he had felt it. It had been there as always before. The rightness, the connection between them, like the perfect melding of two separate souls.

He sucked in his breath and closed his eyes, feeling the pleasure and pain of it sweep through him in waves. There was no denying it. After all this time, it was still there, as potent and intoxicating as if they'd never been apart.

God in heaven, help him . . .

Because he didn't know what the hell he was going to do now.


Diana crouched in the brush beyond the clearing, her fists clenched and her eyes narrowed in rage as she watched Gwynne disappear into the forest that led to Dunston. Damn her, she'd been kissing her brother—practically *fornicating*, the harlot!

She began to calculate the damage, desperate to wrest a solution from this unbearable situation. It was disastrous, that's what it was. Swinging her gaze back to Aidan, Diana saw that he hadn't moved from the position he'd been in when Gwynne jumped up and ran. But then she looked at his face, and his expression sent her reeling anew . . .

*The fool. The poor, wretched fool.* He was in *love* with her. He'd actually allowed himself to fall in love with that hateful Welsh creature.

Nausea rolled in Diana's belly, and she sat back, feeling as if her limbs had turned to lead. What was he thinking? She jammed her fists into the tops of her thighs, biting her lips to keep from screaming out her rage and frustration.

This was it; he was going to ruin her—he was going to ruin them all. Father's shame had been bad enough, but at least they'd managed to salvage some self-respect, thanks to their own innocence and the hard work they'd done to rebuild their status in the years since. But if Aidan refused to go through with his marriage to Helene because of *this* insanity, it would mean another scandal to sully the family's reputation.

It would mean that she might as well give up any hope of becoming Hugh Valmont's socially prominent wife.

Gritting her teeth, Diana pushed herself to her feet and set into motion. She wasn't going to accept this without a fight. Not by half. She might be naught but Aidan's younger sister—a female with no say and no real rights in what would happen, even in her own life—but she still had resources. Aye, she'd need to be clever about it, as women always did, but she was going to take action.

Her legs carried her swiftly back to the castle, her movements jerky with the fury driving her. She needed to set several plans into motion in the next few days, the first of which she could initiate right now. The others would have to wait a bit, until she found the means to make them happen most effectively, but the first would be easy to bring to fruition.

Because she was going to march into her chamber right this minute and prepare a parchment filled to the brim with concern—a message full of anguish and sorrow and love for her poor brother Aidan, who was obviously suffering from the effects of too much war and not enough tender care, begging the recipient to come quickly to help bring him to himself again . . .

And she was going to send it to Helene.

# Chapter 11

**❝I** need to talk to you."

Dafydd turned away from the line he'd been setting in the water, obviously surprised at Gwynne seeking him out so early in the morning. "Aye, *Chwedl*," he said in that even, quiet way of his. "What is it?"

Covering the remaining distance to her bodyguard, Gwynne crossed her arms and looked out toward the pond, watching the rising sun reflected on its rippling surface though its brightness made her tired eyes ache anew.

"I have a request to make of you, Dafydd. 'Twill seem odd at first, I warrant, knowing me as you do, but 'tis vital for the continued safety of our mission here."

"It sounds important." He draped his line over a forked stick that he'd dug into the bank. "Tell me what you wish, and it will be done."

Gwynne would have smiled in gratitude if she didn't

feel like her face might crack from the strain. Instead, she leaned over to pick up a pebble that had been rubbed smooth by the constant lapping of the waters. Rolling it between her fingers, she paused, knowing that once she crossed this threshold, there would be no going back. She glanced up to meet Dafydd's gaze.

"I want you to accompany me whenever I am with de Brice. Any time I must meet with him, I want you there as well."

The older man paused before answering, "Of course, *Chwedl*. I am yours to command, as always." He gestured to a boulder jutting from the bank, inviting her to sit as he added, "But why the change? Has the Englishman been threatening you again?"

"Not exactly," Gwynne said, stiffening with the memory of yesterday morn. " 'Tis only that I—I don't wish to be alone with him if I can help it."

Dafydd didn't respond, and after a moment, she glanced sideways at him, trying to gauge his reaction. His face remained impassive but for a tiny frown that had etched itself between his brows.

"You are concerned, I can see," she said, sitting on the rock and leaning her forearms on her knees. "Aye, well I don't blame you. 'Twill be a most tedious duty, I am sure. Perhaps I should ask Owin to alternate with you."

"Nay, 'tis not that," he admitted as he sat next to her, though he still looked uneasy. " 'Tis just that—well, I cannot help but wonder . . ." He paused, then shook his head. "Nay, never mind."

"Cannot help but wonder what?"

He studied her for a moment. "You are my commander, *Chwedl*, and I will follow you anywhere, you know that. But I cannot help wondering if there isn't something more to your request. Something that comes not just from de

Brice's actions, but from your own feelings as well." He swallowed. "Feelings that perhaps you are finding . . . difficult to resolve."

Now it was her turn to remain silent, though her mouth twisted in a sardonic smile as she looked away. It was painful enough to admit her weakness to herself; she could never burden Dafydd with it.

But 'twas true, the confusing feelings had eaten away at her bit by bit at Dunston, her guilt rising to unbearable proportions in the hours since she'd been fool enough to kiss Aidan. She'd spent the entire night unable to sleep for the agonizing thoughts and worries that swirled through her brain—realizing, finally, that the pull between what she was, and what she couldn't seem to stop herself from wanting, wouldn't ever be made whole. Understanding that had hurt, as much as if someone were digging the point of a blade right into her heart.

And that was why she was doing something about it, she told herself. Right now.

"You've nothing to fear, Dafydd," Gwynne answered at last, her voice husky around the lump in her throat. "De Brice is our enemy—he is *my* enemy—and I know my mission here. I will not fail it. I just need your help in order to do that."

Dafydd kept looking at her for a moment before nodding once and turning his face again to the pond before them. She did the same, calling on whatever peace she could find to seep into her body and soul. They sat together in the early morning calm, listening to the water ripple over stones at the entrance of the spring and watching the swishing dance of leaves overhead.

Dafydd broke the silence first, his voice quiet as he glanced to her. "*Chwedl*, I want you to know that you are not alone in this. Owin and I—we both want to help you in any way we can."

She frowned, uncomfortable as always with overt gestures of kindness or understanding.

"I was there all those years ago when you first began your warrior's training at Prince Owain's command," Dafydd continued, apparently undaunted by either her expression or her silence, "and I have watched you and served proudly with you in the years since." He glanced down at his hands, clasped loosely between his knees. "It cannot be easy for you, this path you walk in life. But know that I will back you in anything that comes your way, *Chwedl*. This I swear as a warrior—and as a friend."

She looked at him for a while without speaking, the burning ache blooming again behind her eyes, before she managed to nod and glance away.

Gazing back at the water, she swallowed hard against the thickness that would not subside in her throat, wishing that what Dafydd said were true—that she could have a friend to share the burden of loneliness that was her life. He meant well, she knew that, but what he'd offered couldn't be. There was no one like her on this earth. She was an anomaly, a freak of nature.

A Legend reborn.

Yesterday, she'd allowed herself to fantasize for one brief moment that she was naught but a woman like any other, free to enjoy Aidan's kisses—free to feel heated passions and simple pleasures. But it had been only a fantasy. What had happened between them had brought her nothing but more pain and conflict, and she'd had enough of that to last her a lifetime.

A lifetime that was more than half a blank to her . . .

"Did you mean it when you said you would aid me in any way you could?" she asked Dafydd, careful to keep both her emotions and her voice in check.

"Aye, without hesitation."

"Then answer me this: do you know aught about my

early life? Anything about the person I was before Marrok brought me home?"

Dafydd frowned, shaking his head. "Nay. Nothing more than that you were stolen away at birth, and your mother, the princess, died shortly after." His frown deepened. "It took Prince Owain fourteen years to find you. You had been badly injured and had no memory when you came to us. Only the signs made it clear to everyone that you were his child—the Dark Legend. Once you finally embraced that truth, 'twas easier for us all."

"Aye, easier," Gwynne murmured. She brushed her hand over the spot just beneath her collarbone—the spot bearing the uniquely shaped birthmark that, along with her silver eyes and ebony hair, had proclaimed her to be the Legend reborn. She clenched her jaw, her mouth as dry as dust. Acceptance of her sacred duty had come at a bitter price. Bitter, indeed.

"Answer me one last question, Dafydd," she said, fisting her hand as she brought it down from where it had rested on her chest.

"Anything, *Chwedl.*"

"Do you think that de Brice is telling the truth? When he claims that he knew me during those lost years . . . when he claims that he loved—" she stopped and gritted her teeth, "—that we were betrothed . . . is he speaking true?"

Dafydd's face twisted in sympathy, his eyes reflecting a pain that she refused to acknowledge in herself. "That I do not know, *Chwedl.*"

"Neither do I," she said, trying to block out the tender agony. "And I'm going to do my damnedest to make sure that I never find out."


"What in bloody blazes is your henchman doing, standing over there in the trees and looking as if he'd like to skewer me through?" Aidan scowled as he pressed his palm against Gwynne's to guide her through the next dance step.

"I asked him to come."

"Why?"

Her chin lifted, but she refused to meet his gaze, instead focusing on a spot just beyond his shoulder; it maddened him, though he said nothing, waiting for her answer. When she still hadn't responded after three more steps and a gracefully completed circle around him, his annoyance pitched higher, and he drawled, "What, does he crave a bit of dancing himself? It can be arranged, you know."

That got her to look at him.

"Don't you dare," she muttered. " 'Tis bad enough that I suffer this humiliation. There's no need to make Dafydd endure it as well."

"I'll wager you'll be glad that you learned these dances in a few days' time."

"Why?"

Aidan continued through another step, breathing in the delicate scent of her hair and reveling in the warmth of her skin beneath his palm. But he kept silent, looking past her and humming along with Clara's piped tune.

"I said *why,* de Brice?" Gwynne demanded, stopping in mid-step and planting her hands on her hips.

"Ah, so bad manners are allowed only if you exhibit them, I gather?"

She glared at him for a moment before making a grumbling noise and turning on her heel to stalk to the edge of the glen, mumbling something about shade and a drink of water.

He followed her to the spot, calling out to the girls that they were going to take a break. Groaning, Clara and Ella put down their pipes and fell backward in mock exasperation. But soon they began to frolic in the high grasses around them, ripping up great handfuls to sprinkle over each other and giggling at the results before they raced down the path to their favorite playing spot near the pond.

When she was finished drinking and had handed him the water-skin, Aidan took a swallow and then glanced again toward Dafydd, who still watched them intently.

"So, are you going to tell me why he's here?"

"That depends on whether or not you're going to tell me why I'll be glad that I can muddle through a few dance steps."

"Fair enough." He grinned. "You first."

She slid her gaze from his. "He's here because I've ordered him to accompany me wherever I go from now on."

The jolt of displeasure Aidan felt quickly melted into a shock of realization—and then triumph. "My, my, my . . ." He grinned as he folded his arms and rocked back on his heels. "I always knew my kiss could make women swoon, but this exceeds even my own expectations."

She fixed him with a glare. "It has nothing to do with that."

"Of course it does." He went still, leaning closer to her to whisper, "You don't trust yourself to be alone with me."

Her cheeks bloomed with color. "That's ridiculous!"

"Oh, no, it's not." He chuckled, thoroughly enjoying her outraged expression. "Though I never thought I'd see the day when the mighty warrior would run away from a challenge." He shook his head, making a clicking sound with his tongue. " 'Tis a shame to see you hiding behind one of your men."

"You're insane."

"Nay—only truthful."

"Is everything all right here, *Chwedl*?"

Aidan had been so caught up in teasing her, that he

hadn't noticed Dafydd's approach. Now her bodyguard stood only a few paces away, his beefy arms akimbo as he stared evenly at them.

"Everything is fine," Gwynne answered through gritted teeth, unsuccessfully trying to hide her flushed face. "De Brice here was just going to tell me why I would find myself glad to have learned these ridiculous dance steps." She directed a warning look at him. "*Weren't* you, de Brice?"

"Oh, aye—something like that," he agreed, nodding.

She cleared her throat and turned away, the rosy hue of her cheeks intensifying. Obviously trying to avoid looking at him, she bent to fiddle with the basket he'd brought to keep the water-skins cool. Dafydd scowled, moving to her side to help her find what she sought, only to back away, frowning, when he realized that the basket was empty.

Deciding that she might appreciate it if he covered for her, Aidan pulled open a sack that was lying nearby, reached in, and grabbed an apple. "Is this what you were looking for?" he asked, tossing it to her when she straightened at his question.

She caught it with a look of surprise, glancing from the apple to him, before she was able to gather her wits enough to paste on a placid expression and say serenely, "Aye, thank you. I was feeling a bit hungry."

She met his gaze as she lifted the fruit to her mouth, clearly annoyed at his amusement, but unable to call him on it without giving herself away. Taking a large bite, she chewed with deliberation before swallowing and lifting her brow. "So . . . ? Are you going to enlighten us?"

"*Hmmmm*?" he murmured, entranced by the tiny drop of juice that clung to her lower lip.

She must have felt the focus of his stare, because she swiped the back of her hand across her mouth and flushed again, frowning. "Why, exactly, am I going to be glad to have learned these dances?"

"Oh, aye—of course." Inclining his head, he smiled again and announced gallantly, "You, my lady, will be attending a gathering of nobles, to be held six days hence. For your entertainment there will tumbling fools, music, an array of delicacies, story-telling . . . and, of course, dancing."

"Why?"

He was taken aback for a moment. "Well, for the pleasure of it, of course. The neighboring gentry plan such festivities regularly—only this time they're calling for it to be at Dunston, since they have all heard rumor of your arrival and wish to meet you."

"*What*?" She looked to Dafydd, her expression a mixture of dismay and shock. "What is he talking about?"

Her bodyguard shrugged. " 'Tis beyond me—though I've never understood the English."

Aidan made a sound of disbelief, laughing, "I'd almost believe that neither of you has ever attended a celebration of this kind before."

"We've had plenty of experience with feasting, de Brice, but 'twas always for a good reason—like to mark a victory in battle over our enemies," Gwynne said, directing a pointed stare at him. "We don't waste our energy by indulging in dances and silly games whenever the mood strikes."

"Then I'm afraid you don't know what you've missed," he answered, ignoring her gibe. "It promises to be an enjoyable evening, and you will have the chance to display your dancing talents before all who attend."

She made a scoffing sound. "You've lost your senses if you think I'll waste my time dancing with your English friends."

"They're not my *friends*," Aidan ground out, subduing the familiar dull pain he felt in admitting that fact. Since his father's execution for treason, most of England's powerful families had treated him and Diana with begrudging tolerance at best. His own efforts for the king against Wales and his betrothal to Helene were all that had prevented them from excluding him altogether from their important social functions. "They're simply other nobles from the area," he added evenly.

"They're *Englishmen*," Gwynne argued. " 'Tis likely that I've sacked their lands and killed some of their men." She shook her head. "Nay, de Brice. Celebrate with them to your heart's content, but I'll be staying in my chamber on that night."

She'd taken a position next to Dafydd as she spoke, seeming to gain some sort of comfort from his presence, even though she was almost equal to him in height and possessed, Aidan knew, far superior combat skills. A sharp jolt of resentment swept through him at her easy reliance on the man. He scowled, facing them as they stood, shoulder-to-shoulder, arms crossed over their chests in virtually identical positions of obstinacy.

"I'm sorry," he said at last, his voice tight with the effort to keep the unfamiliar emotion contained. "But that sounded like a refusal."

"I stand corrected, then," she said, arching her brow again. "Your sense of hearing is apparently intact."

The last of Aidan's calm dissolved, and he took a step toward her, noticing that Dafydd stepped forward as well. Ignoring her bodyguard's none too subtle attempt to intimidate him, he grated, "Refusal is not an option, Gwynne. We covered this weeks ago. You agreed to go along with the pretense of my arranging a marriage match for you, and you must attend this function—or any other like it that I deem necessary—in order to do that and allay suspicion about who you really are."

"You never said I'd need to be shown about like some sort of prized livestock."

"It won't be that way at all, I promise you." He took another step toward her, intending to explain and allay her fears, but he was forced to stop short thanks to Dafydd's solid form between them.

Scowling again, he snapped, " 'Tis devilish hard to have a conversation with you like this." He swiveled to glare at her bodyguard, adding, "Do you think you could allow us a few moments of talk in private? I promise not to attack or brutalize her in any way during that time—you can stand over there and keep an eye on us, if it will make you feel better."

Now 'twas Dafydd's turn to go red; the color spread from his neck all the way to the roots of his hair. He glanced to Gwynne, who had the good grace to look abashed as well. She nodded quickly, and Dafydd offered her a bow before he backed off twenty paces or so, returning to his former spot near the wood.

She settled her gaze on Aidan again. "You didn't need to be so harsh with him. He was only doing his duty."

"Aye, well, 'tis a foolish duty, if you ask me, to have to watch over you like a mother hen with a chick," Aidan growled, still bristling with annoyance at their solidarity against him. " 'Tis not as if you're a delicate female in need of protection; Christ's blood, you're the only woman I know who could possibly succeed at slicing me in two if you had a mind to do it."

As soon as the words came out, he could have strangled himself for uttering them. A look of hurt lanced across Gwynne's face, and he felt as if he'd been punched in the gut, knowing 'twas he who'd put it there.

But in the next instant, her expression tightened, her mouth twisting sardonically, though she couldn't mask the huskiness in her voice when she spoke. "Don't look so stricken, de Brice; you've spoken the truth for once. I'm *not* like other women, and I never will be. You'd do best to remember that."

"I didn't mean—"

"No need to take it back," she broke in, cocking her head in that defiant way he remembered all too well from the battlefield. " 'Tis good to be reminded of the truth now and again. Perhaps you need it even more than I do."

Her eyes glittered like chips of silvery ice, the last traces of pain shuttered behind them. "You should strive to recall that *this* is but an illusion," she said, fisting her hand in her skirt and pulling it away from her like something distasteful. "A farce. I am a warrior, through and through, sworn to fight, maim, and kill to set my people free.

"I will attend your celebration next week only because I promised to uphold this charade of yours—but I tell you, I will not be offered up in display for your noble guests. If I must dance to maintain appearances, 'twill be with you alone, for I vow I'll not be able to restrain myself from bloodshed if another cursed Englishman tries to put his hands on me."

"I understand," he said, still wishing he could do something to take back the hurt he'd inflicted. "I will do all in my power to ensure that you are treated with respect."

She gave a jerky nod. "We see eye to eye on it, then. But just remember, de Brice—a little more than two months. That is all I have left to endure. After that, all bets are off between us."

Her gaze chilled him for a moment longer before she turned on her heel and stalked away, gesturing to Dafydd to join her as she departed the glen.

Aidan watched her go, left behind to deal with the aching emptiness he felt inside of him in the best way he knew how . . .

Which turned out to be not at all.

# Chapter 12

Gwynne watched Diana flitter around the great hall, already worked into a tizzy over the celebration that was still two days off; the sight of her excitement only increased Gwynne's angry thoughts. Would that she was done with this cursed castle and all its inhabitants—most especially Aidan and his voluptuous twit of a sister.

She banged her empty cup down on the table, directing a black look at any of the castle dwellers who dared glance in her direction because of it. Owin, sitting across from her, lifted his head from his food for a moment, looking first at her and then over at Diana's lush, silk-clad form. Gwynne scowled, her annoyance spiking higher at Owin's constant and appreciative notice of the wretched woman. Dafydd, sitting a little farther down the bench, didn't react at all to either Gwynne or Diana. Unusually subdued, even for him, since the unpleasant incident with Aidan in the glen a few days ago, he kept his gaze on the table in front of him.

135

She'd tried to get him to ease up—to join with her and Owin last night as they'd sat together, joking and talking about conquests and victories past—but he'd remained quiet—brooding, no doubt, about de Brice and his biting tongue.

"I can't say that I blame you," Gwynne muttered, sliding her gaze from her bodyguard to the man who was behind both her and Dafydd's ill humor. Aidan sat near the enormous hearth that graced nearly the entire length of the wall, discussing something with Kevyn, and laughing, every now and then, as he raised his cup to drink.

"Cursed Englishman," she said under her breath, feeling the same sharp pain from three days ago course through her. *You're the only woman I know who could possibly succeed at slicing me in two if you had a mind to do it.* Aidan's brutal assessment of her rang out in her mind again, mocking her. And that, in turn, made her angry, since she knew that his thinking of her as a warrior first—a dangerous and powerful warrior—was exactly as it should be.

*Then why the devil did it bother her so much?*

"He can go to hell, for all I care," she said, pushing herself up from the table, followed close behind by both Owin and Dafydd, who rose to their feet as well. Aidan looked over when they all stood, his penetrating gaze locking with hers and seeming to see more of her inner turmoil than was comfortable. Swallowing hard, she turned to Owin and mumbled, "I need to go train. Ready my equipment for me, will you?"

He nodded. "Aye, *Chwedl*. 'Twill be waiting for you."

Dafydd glanced up as Owin strode by him with a murmured wish for safe travel; then the older bodyguard shifted his gaze to Gwynne, his concerned expression cutting her to the quick.

"Have you a message for Marrok, *Chwedl*?" he asked quietly. "I'll be leaving soon, to meet with our envoy in the wood."

"Aye, Dafydd." She reached into her tunic for the sealed parchment she'd completed last night, feeling a twinge as she handed it over to him. It contained none of the troubling thoughts she'd struggled with these past weeks; as with each missive before, she'd tried to sound encouraging about their progress, not wanting Marrok to worry about her unduly during their stay with the enemy.

*The enemy.*

The jabbing ache inside her increased, but she did her best to ignore it, instead clapping Dafydd on the shoulder and wishing him Godspeed on the daylong journey. He paused for a moment, meeting her gaze in silence, as if he were about to say something. But then he simply bowed his head and strode from the hall to undertake his duty.

*Damn.*

She watched him go, more disconcerted than before. Dafydd's obvious unease was not a good sign. Not good at all . . .

Frowning, she stepped back from the table, readying herself to leave the hall and prepare for her training session, when a sharp-fingered hand clamped down on her arm. She wrenched herself free and whirled to face whomever had been so foolish as to touch her, just barely restraining herself from gripping the idiot by the throat and slamming him up against the wall.

'Twas Diana.

*Damn again . . .*

"Going to practice your dancing?" Aidan's sister all but purred, wearing an expression of smug superiority as she confronted Gwynne.

" 'Tis none of your business what I'm going to do,"

Gwynne answered sharply. "Now, if you'll excuse me—"

"Nay, not quite yet," Diana said, stepping to block her path. A wicked smile curved her lips, making her look more feline than female. "I have something to say to you first," she glanced over at Aidan, whose back remained to them, "while we have a moment of privacy out of my brother's hearing."

"How exciting." Gwynne shifted her weight back, crossing her arms over her chest and raising her brow. "Please begin, so that I can hang onto your every word."

Anger sparked in Diana's green eyes. "Go ahead. Enjoy yourself while you can. It won't last long." She raised her chin, flicking a silky auburn lock over her shoulder with practiced skill. "I'm here to warn you to stay away from Aidan. He is already spoken for and needs no distraction from that truth by the likes of you."

"You must be joking," Gwynne grated. "Your brother means nothing to me. I have no intention of distracting him from anything—or anyone."

"That's not what it looked like the other morning in the glen," Diana snapped.

Heat rose to Gwynne's cheeks, and she cursed herself for the reaction. "I don't know what you're talking about, and I'm in no mood to try to figure it out. Suffice it to say that you've nothing to worry about." She gave Diana a cold stare, trying without much success to rein in her anger. "Now, if you'll get out of my way . . ."

She started to push past her, only to be waylaid again by the woman's surprisingly solid form. Diana leaned in toward Gwynne and hissed, "This is my last warning—leave Aidan alone, or I promise you will regret it!"

Gwynne froze still, her foul mood, the nagging guilt, and a too long suppressed battle rage all coming together in a riotous torrent. With a growl, she grabbed a fistful of Diana's gown just below the neckline and jerked up, taking Diana off the floor with it to deposit her none too gently at the side of the walkway. Still clenching the silky fabric, she yanked the woman toward her, halting when they were eye to eye.

" 'Tis *you* who will be sorry, lackwit, if you ever dare to threaten me again," she said through gritted teeth. "Now, I told you to get out of my way, and I meant it!"

Releasing Diana abruptly enough to make her fall back onto the bench, Gwynne turned to go. But a commotion at the front of the hall gave her pause; even Diana's loud gasps of indignation faded to silence when little Ella broke through the gathering of people across the hall, near the door, shrieking, "Oh, help—someone, please help!"

Aidan twisted around from his position at the hearth, his face concerned. "Ella—child, what's the matter?"

" 'Tis Clara, milord," Ella sobbed, nearly falling into his arms. "We were playing near the pond when she fell in and—"

The little girl began to weep uncontrollably, her slim form shaking as she cried out, "I tried to save her, milord—I swear did! But I couldn't reach her, and . . . Oh God, milord, but I think Clara is drowned!"

Aidan crashed through the brush that led to the pond, his heart racing and his throat tight. *Please let me be in time.* The simple plea repeated itself over and over in his head, his mind shutting down to the possibility of anything else. She was just a child. A sweet and sunny, loving child . . .

He heard the others close behind him, people from both the castle and the village racing down to the water's edge to help if they could, or to offer support and comfort, if need be. Pray God it would be the first.

He was almost there now. Just a few paces more . . .

Breaking through the last of the brush, Aidan jerked to a halt, searching both the water and banks for any sign of the little girl. A gentle breeze blew, and at first he saw nothing but the piercing glint of the sun on the pond's surface; he shaded his face, trying to make out anything unusual in the water, his eyes straining and his heart heavy.

And then he saw her.

She was floating at the far end of the pond, face down, her coarse-spun bliaud fanning out from her waist like tiny, misplaced angel's wings.

Roaring with anguish, Aidan threw himself into the water, moving as fast as he could to reach her. After what seemed an eternity his fingertips brushed the sodden edges of her gown; he grabbed ahold of it, pulling her up to cradle her against his chest. She felt so small, so slight in his arms. Several of the villagers splashed into the water after him, to help him drag her onto the sandy bank; there he rolled her onto her side, trying to get the water from her lungs.

She didn't respond. Her hair clung in wet strands to her cheeks, her cherub's mouth turned to a pale, sickening shade of blue. And she wasn't breathing . . .

"Give us some room," Aidan rasped, gesturing for the people surrounding them to back away. "She needs some air."

The onlookers shuffled back, silently forming a half-circle around him as he rubbed his fist up Clara's back again and again, trying to make her cough. Trying to make her expel the fluid that filled her lungs. But she remained limp and cold.

God help him, she wasn't breathing.

"Clara," he whispered harshly, pressing his fingers to her neck to check for a pulse that wasn't there, even as he half-lifted her from the sand. "Clara, lass, you've got to breathe. Come on, child, breathe!"

"Let me through. Now, damn it."

Aidan heard the commanding voice moments before its owner sank down onto the ground next to him.

*Gwynne*.

Ah, yes, Gwynne. Thank God . . .

His gaze locked with hers, and he felt the familiar jolt of connection pass between them.

"Can you do it—can you save her?" he murmured, watching surprise shadow her face when she realized that he knew full well the healing power of which she was capable.

"I don't know." She frowned as she bent over Clara's tiny body. "I never know until it happens."

A shriek suddenly ripped through the crowd, and the people began to shift, jostling each other in an attempt to make way for the woman running toward the pond's bank. Clara's mother burst through the throng, her headrail askew, and with bits of wool still clinging to her skirts from her weaving. Her face was red, her eyes brimming with tears as she reached out, desperately crying her child's name.

"My baby! Oh, Clara, my sweet baby, oh, God . . ."

Aidan lurched to his feet to grab the woman before she could throw herself on her daughter's body. "Hush, Anna, 'twill be all right," he said, cupping his hand to the frantic woman's cheek and trying to make her look at him, to calm her. "You must stay back though now for Clara's sake—please."

Glancing past Anna, he saw Kevyn, who'd been standing close by since their arrival at the pond. Kevyn nodded as he met Aidan's gaze and then walked up to slip his arm around Anna's waist. Supporting her against him and murmuring words of comfort, he led her a few feet away.

Anna buried her face in Kevyn's chest, continuing to sob as Aidan turned to the crowd again and said gruffly, "I

need you all to keep back—just for a few moments, so that
we can do everything that is possible for Clara."

Water dripped from his clothing and his breath felt
harsh in his chest as he murmured a prayer and sank down
in the sand near Gwynne and Clara. Using his body as a
shield, he kept them both from the onlookers' view. Several of the villagers coughed or shuffled their feet nervously in the sand, but save for that and the muffled sound
of Anna's sobbing, all was deathly quiet.

Vaguely, Gwynne sensed Aidan's movement as he
kneeled near her, but she blocked out any awareness of
him, knowing that she needed to focus on Clara alone. Her
stomach tightened and her head felt compressed in a vise,
as it did every time she attempted a healing.

Bending over the little girl's body, she cursed softly,
squeezing her eyes shut. Her hands rested, fingers spread,
on Clara's chest, and now she tilted her chin down, grinding her teeth into her lower lip. She bade the power to
form, the heat to rush into her center—struggled to make
it surge through her body and along her arms, to flow into
the child.

*I can't fail again. Oh, please, God, don't let me fail like
I did with Damon . . .*

A smoldering sensation erupted behind her eyes, burning heat that spun and spread down, swirling into her
shoulders and chest, gathering in intensity before finally
stabbing down her arms and into her hands. As if from a
great distance she heard her own sharp intake of breath,
felt her body stiffen with the power coursing through her
and into the little girl. The blessed healing power . . .

Clara arched violently upward, a gasp wrenching from
her throat. Gwynne's hands fell away and she leaned back
on her heels, her vision blurring for an instant while Aidan
reached for the girl to tip her on her side again. Water

came from Clara's mouth in retching gushes—volumes of it as she coughed and choked until it was all gone.

And then she began to cry.

The sobbing sounded thin and watery at first, but it gained in strength as Aidan sat her upright, lifting her into his arms. In the next instant Anna was on her knees in the sand, grasping little Clara to her breast and weeping as she rocked the precious gift of her child rhythmically back and forth, murmuring words of praise and thanksgiving that she could hold her again.

Gwynne somehow managing to gain her feet and stumble a few steps back, slipping out of the way as the crowd closed in around them. Through the potent energy swirling inside her, she saw Aidan, Clara, and Anna swallowed up by the cheering, joyful throng; she turned from them, knowing that she needed to get as far from everyone as she could.

Her vision jumped and wavered as she made her way to one of the boulders jutting from the pond's bank, intending to get to the other side of it; but the rush of power sweeping through her made her sink down on the stone; it wasn't a bad feeling, but it made her body react and shake—much the same, she'd noticed, as what happened to some of the women in her clan after they'd birthed their babes. Her legs trembled and her hands shook as she cradled her head in them.

"Gwynne . . ."

She raised her gaze; Aidan had somehow broken free of the group and now stood before her, concern shadowing his features.

"Christ, is it always like this for you?"

"Aye," she said, the warm flow of intensity still filling her. " 'Tis not painful, just overwhelming."

"How long does it last?"

She closed her eyes again, willing the healing forces to dissipate. "Sometimes only a few minutes, other times a day or more."

She opened her eyes and pushed herself to her feet, not wanting him to think her weak for what had just happened. " 'Tis of little consequence."

"Perhaps," he conceded, seeming as if he would reach out to steady her when she swayed, but dropping his hand back to his side at the scowl she sent in his direction. "But 'tis no less a gift to give so freely of yourself to others."

She remained quiet, unaccustomed to hearing praise from him, and uncomfortable with the sudden rush of pleasure it sent through her. She concentrated instead on steadying her breathing and bringing her vision back into line, finding that her equilibrium was returning far more quickly than she'd have expected.

"How is Clara?" she asked finally, leaning to look beyond him at the dissipating crowd. "Is she alert—was she able to sit up and talk?"

"Aye, she'll recover, thanks to you," he assured her, glancing back over his shoulder. "Her mother has good care of her now, and will watch to see that she stays quiet for a few days, until she is fully healed."

She nodded, her jaw tight, allowing herself a latent flash of joy. It had worked. Thank God it had worked this time.

"Come," Aidan said, gesturing toward the path back to the castle. "Let me walk you to your chamber. You need rest."

"Nay, I'm fine."

She shrugged off his gentle touch, moving a step away and fixing him with her gaze. His clothing was still soaked from the pond, his shirt clinging to him, molding to the rock-hard planes of his shoulders, chest, and abdomen. She watched the steady rise and fall of his breathing—that mysterious key to the rhythm and essence of life—and remembered how he'd looked cradling little Clara against that powerful chest. The man of war brought to his knees for the sake of a child.

Frowning, she glanced away. *Lugh*, why did he have this effect on her? She shook her head, trying to get her thoughts back in focus.

"Back there," she said slowly, working through the remnants of healing intensity that still held her in sway, "You seemed to know—" she broke off, frowning again, before steeling herself to meet his gaze directly. "You asked if I could save Clara. How did you know 'twould even be a possibility?"

"Because you did it for me."

A shock went through her, racing down her spine to the very ends of her fingers and toes. She'd saved *him*? Impossible. Her fists clenched with denial. "That cannot be. I remember every healing I've ever attempted."

"Yet you don't remember anything from the first fourteen years of your life, do you?"

His answer gave her pause, making her waver for an instant before she shook her head. "Nay, I'd remember something like that. Each time, every life won or lost—'tis ingrained upon my soul like fire. If I'd healed you, I'd know it."

"Perhaps you do know," Aidan murmured, "but you just haven't accepted it yet."

Without warning, he reached down to grip one of her hands, bringing it up to press it against the damp, warm expanse of his chest, just above his heart. " 'Twas right here that the arrow pierced me . . ." he said quietly, looking deep into her eyes as he spoke, "and right here that you laid your hands on me and took the pain and death away."

She felt his heart thudding beneath her palm, its cadence as intense and compelling as the force of his gaze.

"You saved me, Gwynne," he murmured, placing his hand on top of hers, "And if you do not want to remember it now, you will someday. This I vow on the life you gave back to me twelve years ago."

"Aidan!"

Gwynne jerked back to look at the man who'd called out Aidan's name, even as Aidan himself swung around to see him as well. It was Kevyn. He came toward them with purposeful strides, his face settled into grim lines.

"What is it?" Aidan asked, taking a step toward him.

"Riders approach." Kevyn stopped in front of them, looking from Aidan to Gwynne and then back again before adding, "They bear royal banners."

Gwynne sensed more than saw Aidan's entire body stiffen. Then he cursed under his breath and set into motion toward the path muttering, "What the devil can the king want now?"

Kevyn cleared his throat. " 'Tis not the king, Aidan."

Aidan paused in mid-step, his form even more rigid than before as he looked back over his shoulder, seeming both to want and dread the information he was about to hear.

Kevyn frowned, clearly trying not to look at Gwynne, and she felt a warning tingle go up her neck just moments before he said, " 'Tis the king's cousin, Lady Helene, and her father, the Duke of Rutherford. They've come to Dunston—and by the look of their baggage, they intend to stay for a while."

# Chapter 13

Gwynne fought the urge to straighten her circlet as she stood waiting with the rest of the household for the entrance of Lady Helene and her father. Though she longed to take her dagger and hack off the hair that had grown enough to curl annoyingly about her face and neck during her time at Dunston, it still wasn't of a length to secure the ridiculous golden band properly. It kept slipping. If not for her hurried promise to Aidan that she'd try to maintain a genteel appearance while Helene and her father were here, she'd have snatched the circlet off her head and tossed it into the fire.

It would have served him right if she did, she thought darkly, recalling his barked command that everyone change into finer garments before assembling to greet his noble guests in the great hall. He'd been preoccupied since Kevyn's startling announcement at the pond, dashing up to the castle with hardly a backward glance at her, and muttering orders all the way.

Leaning now against the comforting span of the wall near the hearth, Gwynne watched everyone bustling around her; she tried to brush aside the burning sense of hurt that had filled her at Aidan's sudden abandonment and disregard, knowing that she had no right to feel anything of the kind where he was concerned. Knowing that it was dangerous to do so. But it continued to plague her anyway, refusing to let go and leaving her brimming with dark, pent-up emotions.

She'd spent the past quarter hour containing the feeling as best as she could, but she'd found herself unable to be rid of it entirely, even when she caught Owin, who'd come up from the stables upon hearing the commotion, studying her with a concern similar to what she'd seen in Dafydd's eyes. To make matters worse, Diana appeared entirely unbowed by their earlier confrontation, taking the opportunity now to direct several smug glares at her.

*Lugh's* head, it seemed she was losing her power to command anyone.

A trumpet of arrival sounded. Clenching her teeth, Gwynne braced herself, watching the entrance to the great hall. Her position allowed for her to be partially hidden behind Diana, Alana, Kevyn, and a half dozen others so that she could observe Aidan's reunion with his sweetheart without being seen so readily herself. 'Twas a good thing, she decided a moment later, when the lady and her father entered the great chamber, for once she saw Helene, it was all she could do not to turn and flee the castle altogether.

Lady Helene de Jardens was a study in feminine perfection. She might as well have stepped from a stained glass window gracing any one of England's great cathedrals, she was so beautiful. Where Diana was all lush curves and vivid colors, Helene was petite and fair-haired, with a gentle, innocent expression that would compel any man who looked on her to want to spend his life protecting and loving her.

Gwynne's eyes burned as she stared at this graceful creature who had captured Aidan's heart. She watched Helene's sweet face alight with pleasure—with love—as she spotted Aidan and ran to him, winding her arms around his neck, though Gwynne remained too distant, thankfully, to hear the endearments they no doubt murmured to each other. She dragged her gaze away, forcing herself to look at anyone or anything else, certain that if she didn't, she might find herself losing the contents of her stomach.

In shifting her glance away, she noticed a man standing just behind Helene. It had to be the duke. But as soon as she looked at him, her battle instincts rose to the fore; she pushed herself away from the wall almost without thought, the strange thrum of warning she usually got just before combat unfurling, suddenly, in her belly.

The nobleman's feelings were concealed beneath manners he'd obviously long practiced and perfected, but she'd been trained years ago to read an enemy's face and the intentions hidden there, and there was animosity—nay, outright *hostility*—seething deep within this English lord when he looked at Aidan.

Before she could come to grips with her reaction, Aidan called her name, catching her off guard. She snapped her gaze to him as he approached, seeing the unmistakable shadow of conflict in his eyes. For some reason, he wasn't happy about the arrival of his betrothed, and that knowledge made the already taut spring that seemed to be winding up inside her crank tighter.

"Gwynne," he said more softly, this time stepping a bit to the side to allow Lady Helene to approach as well. The woman walked gracefully up next to him, sliding herself against his side as if she'd been made to fit there. Aidan's mouth tensed slightly at her movement, but after a brief pause he rested his arm around her slender waist.

"Lady Helene," he murmured, before turning to nod and direct the duke forward as well, "your grace—I'd like you to meet Gwynne ap Morrison, my distant cousin from the north. I believe that you've been apprised of her travails and the reason for her stay here."

Through the humming that had started in her ears, Gwynne heard the duke make a grunting noise in his throat; but Helene swept out of Aidan's embrace toward her, reaching down and grasping both of Gwynne's hands in her own. Shock kept Gwynne from pulling back, though her fingers tingled with the desire to yank away from Helene's velvety touch. The compassion in the woman's gaze seemed so genuine that Gwynne refrained from what certainly would have been construed a rude gesture.

"You poor dear," Helene said, her voice as soft and smooth as the tresses that shimmered to her waist like honeyed silk. "What you must have endured during the attack on your home." With a murmured sound of distress, she leaned forward and tipped her face up to brush a gentle kiss across Gwynne's cheek.

Gwynne froze, Helene's delicate rose scent filling her senses and making her breath seize in her throat. Helene seemed not to notice, having already released her to gaze up at her again, tears welling in her blue eyes. "But we shall do our best to endeavor that only happy memories be in store for you from now on, dear Gwynne. Isn't that right, darling?" She glanced to Aidan as she spoke, her lovely face so earnest that a lesser man might have crumbled at her feet with assurances for whatever she desired.

Aidan, however, simply nodded his assent, his jaw

tight as he shifted his gaze briefly to Gwynne before looking away.

Oh, heaven help her, Gwynne thought, for she'd never faced anything like this before. She'd never met the like of Helene de Jardens. The woman was sheer, sweet perfection—not only beautiful, but truly good to the soul as well. Kind, loving, caring—

*And Aidan's betrothed.*

Gwynne stood there, stunned from Helene's touch and the raging of her own turbulent emotions. She watched as the lady bestowed greetings and embraces on the others. When she and her father finally followed Aidan to the opposite end of the hall, Gwynne hastened to leave. She couldn't wait much longer or she'd lose whatever composure she had left. Her skin prickled and her senses were on edge.

*Her sword.*

God, she needed to hold her sword again—needed to go train, as she'd planned to do before Clara's mishap, and lose herself in something she could handle, something she could control. Because whatever was going on inside her right now was frightening and wild and unthinkable. She looked round the area, searching for Owin, to direct him to meet her again in the old stables.

Looking behind her, she felt a little jolt of surprise; old Alana sat at the opposite end of the immense hearth, quietly watching her. Her gaze was kind, but also perceptive, as if she'd been studying her for quite some time.

Trying to recover her wits enough to display at least a pretense of calm, Gwynne nodded to the old woman. For all of Alana's fussiness, as well as the demands she made during her lessons in feminine behavior, Gwynne couldn't help but like her. She could see why Aidan favored her as his most trusted servant. Old Alana possessed an insight uncommon to most, likely as much from enduring the constant pain that her twisted joints inflicted on her as from her many years of living.

Alana nodded back in greeting, a half smile on her lips. It was an evocative smile—and though Gwynne knew that Aidan had confided her true identity as the Dark Legend to the old woman, she didn't want to guess what else the servant's discerning gaze had led her to think.

Spotting Owin near the other end of the hall, Gwynne scowled and took a step away from the wall. But as she moved, she tripped on her skirts, and her circlet slipped again. With a growl, she straightened herself and yanked the jeweled band from her head, just managing to keep herself from flinging it against the stones.

"When we meet in your chamber for your lesson tomorrow morn, I'll show you how to fasten that on properly."

Gwynne whirled around. Old Alana had approached from behind, her speed remarkable, considering her ever-present pain.

"Why aren't we meeting in our usual place?" Gwynne muttered, trying to seem as if nothing was amiss.

"Our regular room is Dunston's only other extra bed-chamber, and Lady Helene will be using it during her stay here."

"Oh." Gwynne said, searching for something else to say that would show how composed, how unaffected she was. "What about her father?"

"He will stay in Lord Sutcliffe's chambers. The duke ranks above him and is therefore entitled to the best bed in the castle."

Gwynne frowned. "Then where will Aidan sleep?"

Alana's mouth edged up in that half smile again as she replied, "Why, in the small chamber connected to yours, of course."

"What?" Gwynne choked, only managing to add after a few moments, "But that is impossible!"

" 'Tis the only room left above stairs," the old woman replied, "unless he were to mingle with the servants, which would be unseemly."

"But that tiny chamber isn't fit for sleeping! I've looked in before—'tis but a room for storing linens."

"Be that as it may, Lord Sutcliffe has decided that he will sleep there until Lady Helene and her father leave," Alana answered calmly.

Gwynne fell silent, the enormity of what the old woman was saying finally sinking in. She gripped her circlet tight in her grasp, until she felt the edge of the metal bite into her palm, barely noticing when Alana patted her arm and shuffled off for the rush of panic overwhelming her.

*Aidan would be sleeping right next to her.*

There would be nothing separating them but a little distance and the thin scrap of linen that served as a door. Dafydd wouldn't be able to help her; he'd be asleep in the stables at night, far from the main keep. Nay, she'd be on her own, to resist the confusing feelings and desires that Aidan provoked in her, knowing that he rested but a few paces away . . .

God save her, she thought, as she forced her legs to move, woodenly making her way toward Owin—for she knew that sleep wouldn't come easily again until Aidan de Brice was back in his own rooms, with the impenetrable barrier of a hundred yards of castle and stonework firmly between them.

Aidan sat in his customary spot in the hall, feeling more miserable that he could remember. Kevyn leaned back next to him, his feet stretched out and his head resting against the wall. They nursed their cups of ale, their gazes trained on the cluster of women who sat embroidering at the end of the long table near the fire.

Gwynne was hunched over her bit of fabric, every magnificent inch of her looking uncomfortable and cramped as she attempted the task for which Aidan knew her to be completely ill suited. And though she'd tried to hide it from him, he was well aware that she continued to don her masculine attire beneath her smock and gowns; the resulting layers of clothing made her look strange, her figure seeming almost square with all the extra padding.

Perched next to her, Helene posed an undeniable contrast. She was a vision of delicacy, her face lit with one of her guileless smiles as she leaned close to Diana, who whispered something while surreptitiously flashing yet another self-satisfied look in Gwynne's direction.

"Feeling the heat of the flames, yet, my friend?" Kevyn murmured dryly as he glanced over at him.

Aidan favored him with one of his blackest scowls. "I don't find this situation humorous in the least."

"Nor do I," Kevyn answered. " 'Tis a shame all the way around, if you ask me." He gestured toward the women with his cup. "Just look at that. There Lady Helene sits next to Wales's most fearsome warrior, completely unaware of the intrigue and danger swirling around her, while Gwynne is forced to play a part she obviously despises and probably doesn't deserve. And your sister— suffice it to say 'tis clear Diana enjoys nothing more than to be sharpening her claws in Gwynne's back."

"Aye, my sister," Aidan said, allowing the dark swell of emotions to sweep through him anew. "If not for her meddling, I'd have been able to avoid this entirely."

"Did she admit to being the one who sent early for Helene, then?"

"Only after I threatened to keep her locked in her

chamber during the festivities tomorrow night if she didn't confess it. Valmont cannot attend the gathering, but his uncle, Lord Langdon, will make an appearance." He took another swig of ale, his mouth twisting. "Heaven knows my lovely sibling finds it difficult to resist any opportunity to display her charms—especially in this case, since she thinks word of her beauty may travel back to the ears of her marital prey."

Kevyn shook his head and sighed. " 'Tis a fine mess, it is. And you cannot have missed how the duke watches Gwynne. He studies her with hawk's eyes, trying to perceive any unseemliness in her living here with you. You should consider yourself lucky that she dresses as she does and pays you little heed in front of others."

Aidan didn't answer. Gritting his teeth, he gazed into the swirling golden liquid in his cup. But as always, Kevyn wasn't going to give up easily.

"I'd be careful not to let any more scenes occur like the one I walked into near the pond when Lady Helene arrived. You were standing close enough to Gwynne that at first I thought you were going to kiss her, by God." He took a drink of his ale before adding, "Lord Rutherford won't have to learn that she's the Dark Legend; he'll just need to see you with her like that again, and you'll lose Lady Helene for good."

Aidan remained silent, though it took all his self-control not to answer back. Kevyn glanced sideways at him, obviously not pleased at his lack of response. "You had better take this seriously, Aidan. Not only will the alliances that are so important to you crumble, but feelings will be wounded as well—most notably, Lady Helene's. And she deserves it least of all—"

"Damn it, man, enough," Aidan finally growled. "You're right—'twas a foolish risk, bringing Gwynne to

Dunston. I shouldn't have done it. Are you satisfied now?" He contented himself with glaring at Kevyn, though he'd have preferred to knock his head off his neck.

Kevyn just stared back, the look of quiet reproach in his eyes almost making Aidan ashamed of his outburst. Almost, but not quite. After a moment his friend shook his head again and leaned forward to rest his forearms on his knees, his big hands balancing the cup between them. " 'Tis your life, Aidan, not mine. I just don't want to see you or Lady Helene get hurt because of all this."

Aidan felt his ire cool a little, and after a pause, he leaned forward as well. "I won't let that happen, Kev, never fear. I can't afford to." Yet as he spoke, he knew such a result would be a forgone conclusion unless he took the step he'd been mulling over and resisting for the past five hours.

Gripping his goblet tightly in his fist, he muttered, "For the remainder of the time Helene and her father are here, I plan to cease my efforts to make Gwynne remember her past with me. I'll avoid being alone in her company as much as I can. 'Tis the best I can do." He glanced back over to the women, his mouth tightening as he did. "I just hope that Lord Rutherford doesn't get it into his mind to stay too long."

"Perhaps you'll get lucky and he'll leave right after the celebration."

"Not likely. Helene has it in her head that she needs to spend some restful time with me—something about keeping my mind off war and bloodshed for a while—a belief she maintains, no doubt, thanks to my dear sister."

Kevyn sighed. "Ah, to be so fortunate as to have a woman like Helene wanting to soothe my spirit."

Aidan glanced over to him in surprise, allowing himself a smile. "What—the world's greatest lover, and you cannot find such a boon with any one of your many women?"

Now 'twas Kevyn's turn to scowl. "Lady Helene is as unlike other ladies as a jewel is to a stone. You know that, Aidan. Any man in the kingdom would spill his blood for the honor of championing her, even without her fortunes or her connection to the king."

"Aye, I know, old friend," Aidan answered, looking back over at his betrothed as his smile faded. "And in truth, I know that I am not worthy of her affections. Would that you could take my place in worshipping her as she deserves."

Before Kevyn could answer, the castle hounds distracted him; the dogs began to whine and get up as the main keep's door swung open. 'Twas Dafydd, looking as solemn and focused as he always did. He brushed by the dogs and made a path straight to Gwynne, obviously startling Helene and Diana as he approached.

"What the devil is the man doing, stalking through the hall like he's come to announce a war?" Aidan muttered.

Gwynne looked up from her sewing and set it aside as Dafydd leaned in and murmured something in her ear. Her face stiffened with the news. In the next moment she turned to Helene and Diana, apparently making some kind of excuse before getting up and walking with her guardsman from the hall.

Aidan watched her until the door closed behind her; then he set down his cup and stood. "I'm going after her."

"What happened to leaving her alone?" Kevyn chided.

"Dafydd's been gone all day to meet the Welsh messenger in the wood. I want to know what's happened."

Kevyn sat still, arms crossed and brow raised as he stared up at him; his condemning expression made Aidan set his jaw. " 'Tis a matter of security, Kev, for Dunston and for England. Now, be a good friend and see to my sister and Helene for me, will you?"

After a pause, Kevyn nodded, and so, without waiting for Kevyn to try to argue him out of it again, Aidan set off in the direction of the door, intent on finding Gwynne and her bodyguard—propriety be damned.

Gwynne held the parchment up to the rush light in the corridor, examining the seal she'd broken just moments ago. 'Twas Marrok's insignia, of that she had no doubt.

"Did my cousin say more about why he is acting as messenger in Eldred's place?"

"Nay," Dafydd answered, "Only that his father wanted to ensure safe delivery of this important message, and that he'd be serving as go-between from now on. He said he'd offered himself for the position, as he craves some activity during these months of enforced peace."

Gwynne's mouth tightened. "Aye, that sounds like Lucan." She frowned, her heart pounding as she glanced briefly through the message again. "I just cannot believe that Marrok would command this of me."

Dafydd glanced at the parchment, having also just read its contents. "You can choose not to follow the order, *Chwedl*. Marrok is not like his brother Prince Owain was—he will understand if you feel the need to disobey."

"Perhaps," she said, "yet he is the clan's leader now. If I ignore his order, 'twill encourage others to do the same once they hear of it."

Dafydd remained silent for a moment before saying, " 'Tis your decision to make, *Chwedl*. But I know something of the struggle within you, and I feel it is my duty to caution you. If you feel that you must undertake Marrok's command, be very careful." He went quiet again, nodding in that thoughtful way of his before adding, "The heart is a powerful thing, *Chwedl*. Make no mistake."

"Aye, Dafydd, I know." Gwynne's mouth felt dry as dust. "Yet my duty must be to my people. I will complete my mission here in whatever way Marrok thinks I should, no matter how difficult the task."

"What task is that?"

Whirling around, Gwynne met Aidan's gaze, her pulse leaping at the spark of warmth in his eyes. He'd approached them almost silently from the shadows of the corridor, and her surprise made her clench down so hard on the parchment that it crackled. Sucking in her breath, she tucked it in the front fold of her bliaud.

"What is it?" he repeated, his expression unreadable. " 'Tis obviously of concern to you. Perhaps I can help."

Gwynne's mind raced with what answer she could give that would sound plausible to him, but her thoughts refused to cooperate, fixed as they were on the last lines of Marrok's message:

*You are a great warrior, Chwedl, but you are also a woman. Do not overlook that special gift or the power it can give you over a man. Use all the skills at your disposal—all of them—to lull de Brice into complacency.*

Dafydd cleared his throat, breaking the awkward silence. "In his latest message, Marrok has asked *Chwedl* to consider perfecting a difficult new series of sword exercises that they'd begun to practice before the advent of our treaty with you. He wants her to teach it to some of the younger warriors when we return to the village."

Gwynne threw her bodyguard a grateful look.

"Ah, I see," Aidan said, rocking back a little on his heels. His expression suggested otherwise, however, revealing just how much he doubted Dafydd's glib response, but unless he wanted to grab the parchment out of her bliaud and read it, there was no way he could refute the statement.

" 'Tis a challenging sequence of moves, and we were just discussing whether or not we would be able to perfect them in the time we have left here," Gwynne added, trying not to wince at the higher pitch her voice took with the lie.

Aidan cocked his brow. "Would you like some help, then? I'd be glad to come down to the old stables and work with you through the exercises."

"Nay—" Dafydd began firmly.

"Aye." Gwynne cut Dafydd off, giving him a brief but pointed stare, before swinging her gaze back to Aidan again. "I think 'twould be a welcome change. But only on one condition."

He smiled. "Back to your old penchant for making bargains, are you?"

She tipped her chin up defensively, flushing. *Damn him.* She crossed her arms over her chest to show her disdain for his teasing, then widened her stance a little to increase the effect. "The bargain would be this: I'll teach you my series of sword exercises," she said at last, "if you show me one of the training sequences that you use with your men."

Aidan crossed his arms as well, then, his brows knitting together as he nodded in an exaggerated display of considering her proposal. "I can see the logic behind that."

Her temper pitched higher at his mockery. Scowling, she snapped, " 'Tis the only fair way to do it. Now what say you—does the idea interest you or not?"

"Aye, it interests me."

All pretense of playfulness had vanished, suddenly, from his voice; she found herself the object of his full attention. His velvety gaze focused on her—completely on her—making a swirl of butterflies erupt into flight in her chest at the same time that a slow ribbon of heat uncurled in her belly. Vaguely, she was aware of Dafydd shifting from one foot to the other and looking down at the floor.

She swallowed, forcing herself to breathe before she could speak. "So it's settled, then."

"Aye," he answered, and she somehow felt as if he were caressing her with his voice. "It only remains for you to tell me when."

"Just after dark. 'Tis my accustomed time."

"I know," he admitted, his mouth quirking into another soft smile as he continued to gaze at her. "I've made it a point to learn your habits."

Gwynne flushed again, glad for the relatively dim light in the corridor. "Within the hour, then."

"Within the hour," he repeated. "I anticipate the moment."

With that he tipped his head in a bow, never breaking his gaze with her, before finally pulling away to turn and walk back toward the great hall.

She watched until he disappeared into the shadows, only then releasing the breath she hadn't realized she'd been holding. Dafydd stood silently next to her, shaking his head with an expression that told her he thought she was making a mistake. A very big mistake.

"Don't say it," she muttered, rubbing her neck with one hand, while wrapping her other arm around her waist and twisting to face him. "It will be a good opportunity to begin what Marrok has commanded of me."

Dafydd just looked at her; she'd never seen him appear more unconvinced. "What exactly are you planning to do with him during this training exercise?" he asked gruffly.

"I don't know yet. But at least it provides me a chance to be alone with him."

"But you will not be alone. I will be there, as always, by your order."

She met Dafydd's stare with her own. "My orders are

going to have to change. Marrok's command makes that clear. I must be alone with de Brice. 'Twill be difficult enough to find my way in doing what I must without having an audience as well. Don't worry—I will be fine, I promise you."

Dafydd didn't answer; he just continued to look at her with that same worried expression in his eyes.

"All will be well, Dafydd—never fear," she added, trying to sound reassuring, though the desperation tingeing her voice rather ruined the effect.

Dafydd seemed as if he would continue to argue, but then just shook his head again, sighed, and turned to go and do her bidding.

"Be careful, *Chwedl*," he called softly over his shoulder as he went. " 'Tis a dangerous path you're about to take."

"I'll do my best, old friend," she murmured to herself as he disappeared down the hall. "God help me, but I will."

# Chapter 14

**A**idan glanced into the great hall on his way out of the main keep a half hour later. He wanted to go and prepare for his meeting with Gwynne, but first he had to check to make sure that all was under control with Helene and her father. Through the sliver-shaped opening of the door, he could clearly see Helene, Diana, and Kevyn sitting where he'd left them; all three were engaged in conversation. Just then, Kevyn leaned in and murmured something to Helene, and she smiled, gentle laughter spilling from her as she shook her head at him.

"Thank you, old friend," Aidan murmured. He knew Kevyn could keep Helene amused with his tales for a while—long enough for Aidan to spend what time he could with Gwynne before he'd need to make another appearance in the hall to wish his betrothed a peaceful night's rest.

Carefully, he creaked the door open a bit further, to get a wider angle of vision into the chamber. The duke sat against the far wall near the one lit hearth; he leaned back in his chair with his eyes closed. A castle musician strummed a lute nearby, and though Aidan wasn't near enough to hear anything, he knew by the duke's gaping mouth that he was asleep.

*Good.*

Quietly, Aidan pulled the door shut and headed for the portal that would lead him outside the main keep, taking a rush-light torch with him as he went. The coming night lent a fresh, cool feel to the air compared to the heat of the day, and he breathed deeply of it as he made his way to his weapons chamber. He'd need to bring a few different swords with him, he decided.

Entering the darkened building attached to the main keep, he chose what he wanted, then went back out and headed for the abandoned stable room. He kept to the shadows as he went, for though activity in the yard slowed dramatically at nightfall and few castle-dwellers and villagers made their way through the area, he didn't want to risk being seen.

Soon enough, he reached the old stable door. Glancing around, he checked to make sure that no one loitered nearby and then ducked silently inside, planning to gain his bearings before he let Gwynne know he'd arrived.

He looked around, not having been in the chamber since handing it over to Gwynne and her men to do with as they wished. They'd dismantled all of the old stalls and stacked them against the walls, so that the place was like a large and empty arena, lit all around with wall torches perched in sconces.

In the middle of the dirt-packed floor Gwynne herself stood with her back to him; she was alone, and his breath caught to see her once again in her masculine garments, her long legs encased in the form-fitting laced braies of a warrior. She wore a leather sword-belt slung at an angle from her waist to one hip, bunching her linen tunic in a provocative display of slender form and shadow.

He swallowed, reminding himself to stay focused on the work at hand. He'd agreed to this for the chance to learn a Welsh exercise, he told himself—not for the pleasure of being in her company. 'Twas his duty to keep current on any tactical strategies England's enemies might employ against her in battle. Aye, that was it.

But God help him, Gwynne was like a siren's song to him. He couldn't stay away, no matter what he'd told Kevyn. She tempted him, teased his senses—tugged at him from memories that were lodged deep down inside, near his heart. Even something as simple as imagining what, exactly, lay beneath those warrior's clothes lent all sorts of vivid fantasies to his thoughts—fantasies he hadn't needed to contend with when he'd faced her on the battlefield and believed her to be a man.

"Are you coming in, then?" she said, still with her back to him.

He stiffened in surprise. "How did you know I was here?"

She shrugged. "I can usually feel it when someone approaches me. 'Tis a sense I think I've always had—though of course it helps knowing of the imminent arrival beforehand."

Turning to face him she gave him a brilliant smile, and the heat inside him turned to a molten rush. Jesu, but she was beautiful when she smiled at him like that. He'd almost forgotten, it had been so long. He willed his legs to move, trying to shake off the stunned feeling as he walked up to her. This was *his* castle, *his* territory, he reminded himself. She was his hostage, and he needed to stop reacting like a tender lad in the throes of first love every time he was near her.

Forcing himself to pull his gaze from her, he glanced

around the room before clearing his throat to ask, "Are either of your bodyguards joining us tonight?"

"Nay. They needed some rest, so I told them to do what they wished. In truth, we'll be quite alone." She arched her brow at him, the inviting look in her eyes making his mouth go dry.

*What in the blazes . . . ?*

"Besides, as you've said," she continued, "I'm more than capable of taking care of myself." Smoothly, and so quickly that in his stunned state he didn't realize what she was doing, she slid her sword from the belt at her waist and dragged the tip lightly from his belly to his chest, murmuring, "The only woman you know who could possibly slice you in half if I'd a mind to do it, remember?"

His mind finally caught up with his senses, and he smiled, a surge of pleasure rising along with the competitive spark she always managed to incite in him. Ah, yes—if she wanted to play, he'd oblige.

"I'd be careful with that if I were you," he murmured, slipping his fingers beneath the edge of the sword to push it away from him. "One never knows what kind of retaliation one's opponent might take."

"My opponents are usually unable to retaliate, once I've done with them," she answered, letting the blade swing back toward him, dipping just above his manhood.

He quelled his instinct to flinch, instead murmuring, "But I am not like any other opponent you've ever faced."

"And I am not like any other warrior, either," she clipped, winking as she pulled the sword up and stepped back to move through a few practice sweeps. "But come, let us begin, or we'll be here all night bantering instead of working on the exercise."

Aidan chuckled, bowing gallantly to her before turning to go toward the door and take up his favorite of the two swords he'd brought with him. Aye, she was in a rare mood tonight. He sensed that he was going to find this training session far more pleasurable than any he'd ever undertaken with his men.

Half turning, Gwynne watched him retrieve his weapon, then deliberately put her back to him, so that she could concentrate on easing her breathlessness and quieting her pounding heart. It raced more with this flirtatious repartee than it ever had before the start of a battle. 'Twas far more challenging—and enjoyable—to spar so with him than she'd thought it would be.

"Where do we begin?"

Aidan's voice tickled her ear, and she jerked her head to see that he stood right next to her again. He looked rather pleased with himself for sneaking up on her this time; she allowed the point, giving him a crooked smile as she directed that he take a position in front of her. Then, widening her stance, she lifted her weapon with both hands and paused until he did the same.

"Does the series include one of those unusual jumps I saw you do on the field that first day, by any chance?"

"Nay," she answered, slowly working through the first sword stroke, a classic move that Aidan met easily with his blade.

"Why not?" he asked, locking his gaze with hers and following her lead into the next move. "Afraid that I might decide to use it against you someday?"

"Hardly." She swung her blade up, meeting his stroke above their heads, sweeping down with another near the floor as they both lunged in toward each other. They stilled for a moment, their faces inches apart. His warm breath caressed her cheek, and she felt herself flush as if its feather-light touch had tinted her skin the delicate hue. "No one knows that move but me," she continued, trying

to seem unaffected by his nearness. " 'Tis far too difficult
for anyone else to master."

"Then who taught it to *you*, Legend?"

She paused, taken aback for an instant before she
grinned. "What makes you think I didn't conceive of it
myself, to have at least a bit of an advantage over brutish
louts like you?" Pulling away, she whirled around, sword
upraised in both hands, before slicing down, stopping her
blade but a hair's breadth from his throat.

She held the position, noticing that he didn't look as
dismayed as she'd thought he would by her besting of him
with the move; a moment later she realized why. His
sword dangled, useless, from his right hand, but she
couldn't see his left; then she felt something bump against
her side, up high, next to her breast. It was the hilt of his
dagger—drawn, apparently, in the instant that she'd made
her spinning move: now he held it poised in perfect position at that vulnerable spot beneath her upraised arm.

"Well done," she whispered, her eyes widening in surprise. In the last seven years of training and battle, no one
had managed to sneak beneath her defenses so.

"And you," he murmured, shifting his neck a bit away
from the edge of her blade, even as he continued to gaze at
her. She felt herself unable to look away, mesmerized by
the powerful emotions at play in his eyes. "But it appears
that we have reached a draw," he added, sounding
strangely neutral compared to the heat—the *desire*, she
realized with a jolt—that she saw in their depths.

In the next instant she gasped as she felt his hand
brushing forward along the curve of her breast. He took
advantage of her shock to disengage from their locked
stance; backing up a few steps to their starting position, he
sheathed his dagger and rested his sword, point down,
against the dirt-packed ground.

"So, is that it, then?"

The exaggerated nonchalance of his expression would have made a saint choke with disbelief—and Gwynne had never been known for her piety. In a smooth movement she sheathed her own sword, sucked in her breath, and vaulted into the air, tucking and twirling, to land directly in front of him. Their upright position brought them physically nearer than they'd been before; they stood chest to chest now, her lips a whisper away from his.

"That depends," she murmured.

"On what?" he asked softly, his gaze flicking down to her mouth; she licked her lips and heard his breath catch before she watched him drag his gaze up to her eyes again.

"On whether or not 'twas too hard for you."

A slow, sensual smile curved his mouth and smoldered in his eyes. " 'Tis never too hard, Gwynne. In fact, I always say, the harder the better."

Gwynne felt her cheeks heat again, but she couldn't back down now. "I'll have to take your word on it," she finally managed, struggling to keep her breathing even.

"Perhaps . . ." He paused. "Though as my instructor tonight, 'tis within your rights to assess for yourself . . ."

Her heart bumped a frantic rhythm in her chest as he tilted his head down fully now, his lips brushing lightly over hers. Her eyes fluttered shut as she breathed in and kissed him back, tingles of pleasure spreading like wildfire through her. He tasted so good. She tipped her face to the side to kiss him more fully, the smooth, warm sensation of his mouth sending a ribbon of longing spooling through her.

Their kiss went on and on, full of slow, sweet yearning, and for the first time, she allowed herself to relax and truly revel in the moment. She didn't need to berate herself for what she was feeling. She was only doing her duty by kissing him, after all—and 'twas pure heaven. His kiss was a little taste of paradise, made all the more erotic by the teasing heat of their bodies so close together, yet not quite touching.

All too soon Aidan pulled back, and she forced herself to open her eyes, struggling to regain both her balance and her senses. Her limbs felt loose and heavy with the desire coursing through her, and her mouth was still moist, aching for more. But when she met his gaze, a jolt of dismay filtered through those feelings. He looked torn; conflicting emotions showed full in his face—his own longing and need battling with something else. Something painful . . .

"Gwynne," he said, his voice rough with feeling, "Gwynne, I—"

"Damn it, Aidan, I've been looking all over the castle for you!" Kevyn stopped short in the doorway, spotting them both and realizing, suddenly, just what had been happening.

"Ah, hell," he muttered. "Christ, man, did you hear nothing I said earlier?" After another oath he just shook his head, growling over his shoulder as he spun on his heel to leave again, "If you can spare the time, it might interest you to know that your betrothed and her very powerful father even now await you in the hall. They've been lingering for nigh on a quarter hour, hoping that you might grace them with your presence."

Cursing under his breath, Aidan sprang into motion after Kevyn. He took a few stiff steps, then jerked to a halt, glancing back at Gwynne, as if he would speak—as if he might say something to ease the horrible strangeness that had suddenly blossomed between them. But he didn't. After a strained pause, he simply frowned and muttered an apology before stalking ahead toward the door.

And then he walked through it and was gone, leaving her alone again.

Alone with her racing pulse and panicked thoughts, trying to figure out how she was ever going to fulfill Marrok's command where Aidan de Brice was concerned. What had just happened here had proved to her without a doubt that she was in great danger—not the kind that threatened her life; nay, that was as secure as always, with her fighting skills as ever at their peak. But this . . . this danger was far greater, for she knew now that if she continued down the path of sanctioned seduction Marrok had commanded of her, she might well lose her heart to the one man she could never have.

The man it was her duty to destroy.

Stars covered the sky as if someone had flung them up in great, sparkling handfuls when Gwynne finally trudged up the stairs to her bedchamber. After Aidan's departure, she'd spent another hour in hard training, hoping to burn off some of the frustrations he'd left brewing in her.

It hadn't worked.

A long swim in the pond had done a little better. The place was barren of any human life so late at night, and she'd shed her clothing gratefully, sliding into the cool embrace of the moonlit water. The frogs and crickets chirping on the banks had soon forgotten that she'd disturbed them, taking up their resounding night chorus once more. Floating there, she'd been neither Gwynne the woman nor Gwynne the warrior any longer. She just was.

But now, as she approached her room, the jittery feeling inside her began to return. The hour was late and all who lived at the castle were abed—but one very important difference marked this night.

Tonight Aidan would be sleeping in the tiny chamber connected to her own.

With any luck he was asleep already. She could just slip in unnoticed, exchange her wet smock for a dry one, and climb into her pallet with none the wiser. She usually rose before dawn; if she planned it well, she and Aidan would never cross paths during the nights that Lady Helene's visit necessitated his stay in the tiny chamber.

Approaching her door, she slowed, hoping to hear a snore or other evidence of his slumber. All was silent. She took a few more steps, the tallow candle she gripped lighting the way. It cast eerie shadows on the wall, stretching as full and long as the peaceful silence that had descended over the castle.

The door creaked slightly as she entered, and wincing, she pulled it shut behind her and padded over to her bed. Before proceeding with preparations for bed, she glanced over at the curtain that served as a partition between her chamber and Aidan's room. The fabric was as always before, hanging still and undisturbed.

He must be asleep, then.

Relief mingled with a hint of regret. 'Twas better this way, of course. It was what she'd planned, even—and yet a part of her couldn't help wanting to see him again. She'd done everything in her power to put his kisses from her mind tonight, but the thought of them kept coming back to tempt her.

Even now, she relived the moments, felt again the soft, teasing caress of his lips against hers, the warm, languorous swell of desire swirling through her . . .

Squeezing her eyes shut at the memory, she turned to set the candle in its holder by her bed. Then, tossing her cloak on the chair, she reached into the trunk full of clothing that Aidan had provided and took out a clean shift. Unlacing her bliaud, she removed it and its smock, as well as her own soaked masculine tunic and breeches worn beneath. All that remained was her shirt. Released from her breeches, the creamy fabric hung halfway down her thighs, and, like her other garments, it was damp from her swim. But something made her pause before removing it.

Hesitantly, she lifted her hands to her body, high up,

near her breasts, and let her palms slide slowly down her sides past her hips. She was a tool of combat, her muscles firm and strong. But she wasn't all warrior, she decided; her breasts, small as they were, rounded out, as did the gentle flare of her hips. Was she so different from other women, then? When Aidan kissed her, had he felt the same kind of desire that she had, fierce and true?

His kiss had been like nothing she'd ever known before, leaving her hot and cold at the same time, tingling with a strange need for something more—what, she didn't know for certain. She only knew that it had felt good. So good and—

"Gwynne?"

Her breath caught as she tensed and spun to face the curtain. Aidan had pushed the crimson fabric aside, and now he stood in the doorway, shirtless, his face shadowed in the flickering light of the candle behind her. He lifted one arm, leaning it against the door jamb.

"I was worried about you," he murmured. She couldn't read his expression clearly in the gloom. But his eyes . . . his eyes showed everything, glowing deep and intense with emotion.

"I—I'm fine," she said, her voice sounding throaty. "I went for a swim."

"I can see that." His mouth edged up on one side as his gaze traveled a leisurely path from her toes, up her bare legs to the clinging fabric of her shirt. A rush of heat filled her as she realized, suddenly, that the wet garment outlined every contour of her body as if she were naked before him.

She looked at him uncertainly, anxious about what to say or do. She should try to entice him to kiss her again, she knew; Marrok's command had been to use every weapon at her disposal, including feminine wiles, to lull him into complacency. But she couldn't seem to move when he looked at her like that, though her pulse leapt in her throat and her breathing came shallow. Desperate to do something—anything—to parlay this moment into the kind of temptation she'd been ordered to initiate, she shifted her shoulder, allowing the damp fabric to slip down and bare her skin.

At first Aidan didn't react, but then, as he gazed at her, his expression shifted again, his mouth tightening and his eyes turning dark. He swallowed, and she watched his hand clench into a fist where it rested high up on the doorway.

"Gwynne, I—" He glanced away, and a muscle in his jaw twitched. When he looked at her again, she recognized the hard and fast purpose in his gaze.

"I just wanted to wish you goodnight," he finished, not waiting for her to respond before he nodded once more and murmured, "Sleep well." Then he stepped back into the dark of his chamber and let the curtain swish down into place between them.

She stood without moving for several long moments before numbly blowing out the candle and changing into her dry smock. Then she climbed into bed, trying to ignore the strange pain spreading through her. Pulling the covers up to her chin, she rolled onto her side, her heart thudding with slow, achy beats.

*What in heaven's name was she doing?*

She was completely out of her element, that much was clear. The humiliating truth beat relentlessly at her, hammering its message over and over into her brain: she couldn't tempt Aidan if her very life depended on it. She'd stood half-naked in front of him, her clothing wet and clinging to every meager curve she possessed—and he hadn't even been enticed enough to cross the room and try to kiss her again.

*You're a freak of nature,* the harsh voice inside of her grated, *a tool of war. What makes you think you could tempt any man? Aidan has Lady Helene with all of her beauty and softness to fill his senses—he has no use for a woman like you.*

Gwynne's eyelids burned with the knowledge, so she squeezed them shut, clenching her teeth until the voice began to fade. But it was no use. She couldn't hide from it altogether. The truth remained, biting and scratching at her from the inside out . . .

Leaving her with no escape.

Aidan sat on his pallet and then forced himself to lie down, his muscles screaming in protest against the action, his groin burning with a hot, heavy erection the likes of which he'd never endured before. He wanted to go to her. God, he wanted to go to her.

It was all he could do not to jump up and rip aside the curtain—to take her in his arms and fill her with all the passion blazing inside him. She'd been so beautiful standing there in the candlelight, her hard nipples jutting from under the wet fabric, her smooth legs, so long and powerful, rising up to disappear in the shadows beneath her shirt . . .

Groaning, Aidan clenched his teeth and closed his eyes, rolling so that his back was to the curtain. It had taken every bit of will he possessed to let that curtain fall back into place between them. To shield her from his gaze. But he'd had no choice. He couldn't allow himself to indulge his own desires—not with his betrothed sleeping a mere twenty paces down the corridor.

His and Diana's future success was contingent on his marriage to Helene. He couldn't be the same kind of selfish brute his father had been, caring only for his own needs at the expense of his family's well-being. He wouldn't. He had to stay away from Gwynne . . .

But God in heaven help him, he thought, staring into the endless dark. For he feared that it was going to be the most difficult thing he'd ever had to do.

# Chapter 15

Gwynne paced the confines of her chamber, glad that Aidan had woken and left his room hours earlier; she was impatient for her morning session with Old Alana to begin, and she needed no spectators—particularly Aidan himself—for what she hoped would happen here today.

'Twas a fine turn of events, she thought, actually to *want* to commence her meeting with Alana. If anyone had told her a month ago that she'd feel this way about her feminine comportment lessons, he'd have received naught but a hard cuff on the head for it. Yet now here she stood, itching for the old woman to arrive.

It had been a long night. She'd finally managed to fall asleep a few hours after seeing Aidan, but only by deliberately forcing herself to stop thinking about her shortcomings. She hadn't been able to entice Aidan to kiss her last night, 'twas true; no amount of wishing could change that fact. But she'd decided in those cold, dark hours just before dawn that there was something she could do about it today—and she was about to take that step as soon as Alana decided to arrive.

As if on cue, the chamber door creaked open and the old maidservant shuffled into the room. Alana came to a halt just inside the portal, pulling the door shut before her perceptive gaze swept first over Gwynne and then the rest of the chamber.

"I trust you slept well last night?" she asked in her gravelly voice, her mouth flirting with a smile.

Gwynne scowled. "Well enough." Her hand was clamped down on the back of the chair near where she was standing, and noticing the nervous grip, she let go and came around to plunk herself into the seat. "I've been waiting nigh on half an hour for you," she complained. "What kept you?"

"I was seeing to the preparations for tonight's celebration." Alana looked askance at Gwynne and moved slowly toward the bed, which was straightened, already, in the meticulous way of a soldier. Sitting down on it with a sigh, she added, "It promises to be a fine event. Perfect for showing off your newly acquired skills, I'd say—though Lord Sutcliffe told me that the premise of seeking a husband for you among the English nobles attending is naught but a ruse."

Gwynne looked at the floor, the dark feeling inside her chest coiling tighter. "Aye. I still don't like it. But I've agreed to go along with the plan, so I've no choice but to attend." She glanced over at the old woman. "Which brings me to what I wish to discuss with you today."

"What is it?"

Gwynne shifted uncomfortably in her seat and looked down to the wooden slats of the floor again. "I—I need you to teach me how to look—" She swallowed, trying not to grimace. "How to look like a real lady. Not just the wearing of a gown, but I want to look . . . pretty."

Alana foided her gnarled hands, one over the other, not responding for what seemed like an eternity, other than to nod and make some indefinite humming sound in her throat.

"What—do you think the result will be so difficult to achieve, then?" Gwynne finally burst out, sounding harsher than she'd intended, thanks to the strain of those very thoughts running endlessly through her mind these past twelve hours.

Alana stilled, fixing Gwynne with her calm gaze. "Not necessarily. 'Twill depend on what you're willing to do to make it happen."

"Just about anything, at this point," she mumbled, glad that Alana hadn't felt the need to ask her why she wished to be helped so.

"Very well, then," Alana nodded, pushing herself to her feet and shuffling closer—close enough to reach out and rub a wavy lock of Gwynne's hair between her thumb and finger. "You will need to release many of your old ways for this to work, child, at least for the amount of time you wish to maintain the appearance you desire. 'Tis a transformation we undertake. Are you willing to do that—to be schooled by me?"

Gwynne twisted her head to look up at the old woman, a strange sense of peace enveloping her at the thought of giving herself over to Alana's guidance. 'Twas but a fulfillment of her duty, she thought, that was all. Her desire to look more feminine, to be more alluring to Aidan, had no other basis to it but that.

"Aye, Alana. I will do as you say," Gwynne murmured, as if to herself, blinking back that heat that stung the back of her eyes. "Just teach me how to be beautiful."

Aidan made his way to the end of the great hall, stopping here and there to talk with guests as he went, before finally taking a position near the jutting stonework of the hearth. He sipped at his spiced wine, looking around the chamber. As instructed, the minstrels continued to play an array of pleasant tunes, just as they had while the two score of noble guests had made their entrances into the main keep this past hour. Nearly everyone had arrived already—the first time all of the nobles had deigned to gather at Dunston since Father's execution. Now the hall echoed with the muted sounds of their conversations as they awaited the start of the feasting.

Everyone, that was, but Gwynne.

Aidan glanced again to the stairway that led to the upper bedchambers, only just stopping himself from going up there to bring her down. What the devil was taking her so long? After last night he almost dreaded seeing her again, knowing as he did how difficult it would be to keep his thoughts from straying to the way she'd looked then, standing before him in the candlelight, her damp shirt clinging to sweet curves and giving him tempting glimpses of shadow. Even now, the memory of it sent a lance of desire through him, making him shift with restlessness.

But no matter his reaction to her, she needed to come down, and soon. She was virtually the guest of honor. Distasteful as it was, he should be showing her off to the nobles if he wanted to maintain the illusion of her as a potential bride for one of them. Many of the bachelor lords were interested, he knew; overheard snippets of conversation as he'd mingled with his guests had made that clear. It seemed that even though they believed tainted de Brice blood ran through her veins, Gwynne was deemed an acceptable match, thanks to his upcoming nuptials to Lady Helene de Jardens.

'Twas amazing how the power of that name and his imminent connection to it had shifted perceptions about him among King Henry's elite; the change was so compelling that a part of him couldn't even fault Diana for her schemes to get Helene here early and save him from any distractions. He understood why his sister would do everything she could to ensure that his marriage came to pass. 'Twould be Diana's only chance at respectability again, after having had to face the decline of her own worth as a bride, along with their family's good name, when Father had committed his treason. Aye, his marriage to Helene was a forgone conclusion—he had to go through with it in a few weeks, whether he liked it or not.

But that didn't mean he couldn't try to fulfill his life-debt to Gwynne in the meantime.

After glancing around the hall to ensure that everyone seemed content, Aidan swung his gaze to Helene, who stood, graceful as always, chatting with Lady Anne Herrick, the daughter of the Marquess of Wellesley. Helene outshone the Marquess's daughter like a torch to a firefly. His betrothed was one of the loveliest women in England; of that there was no doubt. And her sweetness surpassed her beauty, though he'd had a difficult time believing that possible when he'd first met her, years ago.

His father, still a political force before the discovery of his treason, had consulted with the duke and arranged the match between them; it had been only a few months after the Welsh attack that had left him wounded, and Gwynne, so far as he knew, dead. Even so, his father had been furious to learn of his only son's illicit meetings with a common Welsh girl. The betrothal had been the earl's attempt to seal Aidan's fate in a way that he saw fit—and Aidan had been too distraught over the death of the woman he'd loved to protest overmuch.

Once Father's treason had come to light, his betrothal to Helene had been all that had kept the de Brice family from complete ruination. Oh, the duke had done his best to break the marriage contract between them—but Helene, believing herself already in love with him, had wept and begged King Henry for intervention. The king had complied, unable to refuse his gentle cousin a boon in her favor. He'd declared the betrothal valid and allowed Aidan to continue his fostering with Rexford de Vere. Then, once he'd proved himself in battle, the king had taken him on as his champion in the wars against the Welsh.

Over the years, Aidan had let Helene maintain her fantasy about loving him, though he knew that it couldn't be true. She didn't really know him. Not the real him. That had belonged to Gwynne alone, and when she'd been taken from him, it had been as if he'd died as well. But he had known that Helene deserved a life of happiness, and so he hadn't told her that he would never—could never—love her back. 'Twould have been a cruel repayment for her generosity.

*Yet 'tis nothing compared to what she would think if she knew you were harboring England's most dangerous enemy within your walls.* Aidan's hand clamped down on the stem of his goblet. Tilting his head back, he took a healthy swallow. Kevyn had been right, damn it. He was playing with fire here, and if he wasn't very careful, many others less deserving of it than he stood a good chance of being burned.

" 'Tis quite a triumph, bringing all the nobles to Dunston again. It's been, what, nigh on ten years since they've gathered here, hasn't it?"

Aidan glanced over at the man who'd spoken; 'twas his mentor, Rexford de Vere, the fourth Earl of Warrick, who had raised him, for all intents and purposes, from the age of fifteen. A rush of happy warmth filled Aidan as he faced the man who had been more of a father to him than his own sire.

" 'Tis a change, I'll grant you that," he answered, taking another drink and gesturing back to the gathering. "Though I cannot claim sole responsibility for their acceptance of my invitation. 'Tis due to my imminent marriage to Lady Helene, more like."

"Perhaps—though there is also great curiosity about the mysterious Welsh cousin you plan to present here tonight." Lord Warrick glanced around the chamber before looking back at Aidan. "Who exactly is she, Aidan, and why wasn't I told of her before?"

"She's a distant relative of my mother's," Aidan said glibly, pretending an interest in what the mummers were doing at the far end of the hall and hoping that his expression didn't reveal his guilt over the lie. "And 'tis as I've said—Welsh rebels ransacked her home once they learned of her English blood ties—especially her connection, remote as it is, to me. Her family was killed, so I decided that it would be best to bring her here for a while, to try to get her settled on safer ground."

He took another drink and went silent, feeling the weight of his mentor's stare. He hated lying to Rex, but 'twas better that he didn't know the truth. King Henry was notorious for handing down swift punishments upon discovery of treachery—and if Gwynne's true identity was discovered, Aidan didn't want his old friend swallowed up in the shame and death that would undoubtedly result.

After a long silence, Lord Warrick turned to view the crowd as well, taking a sip from his wine as he did before asking, "So, then—why hasn't this . . . kinswoman of yours made her appearance yet?"

"Her name is Gwynne," Aidan answered, wincing at Rex's cool tone, "and I cannot say what is keeping her." He gestured his friend forward, steering him back into the crowd, toward where Diana had joined Helene, after Lady Anne had moved off to speak with another guest. He hoped that a new conversation with the women would distract his mentor from his inquiries about Gwynne.

"My lady," he said to Helene, as they approached, "I trust that you remember my foster father, Rexford de Vere, the Earl of Warrick? He will be staying on at Dunston tonight after the celebration."

Helene gave him a welcoming smile, the expression reaching up to sparkle in her blue eyes. "Of course I remember you, Lord Warrick. 'Tis a great pleasure to see you again. Aidan never tires of telling me tales of his years with you—and of the many adventures you undertook together, once his training time ended."

"Call me Rexford, please, my lady," Lord Warrick murmured, bending over her hand. "And I would be honored if you would consider me your humble servant, eager to serve and defend you."

Helene's gentle laughter spilled forth like a bubbling stream. "Oh, sir, you are too kind. Pray God I shall never need to call upon your services of defense, Rexford," she said, still smiling. Then she turned her vibrant gaze on Aidan. "I know that I will not, once my dear Aidan and I are married. Then, I trust, he shall champion me against all who try to bring me harm."

Aidan cleared his throat, wanting to wither under her obvious adoration. Forcing a smile, he readied to make some kind of response, when someone knocked into him from behind. It caused him to lurch forward, and he muttered a curse. After righting himself, he whirled to face the miscreant, scowling when he saw that it was young Stephen de Segrave, the Marquess of Haslowe.

The marquess lifted his cup in greeting to Aidan, showing a face already ruddy from too much ale. "Ah, Sutcliffe—I didn't see you there, man."

Lord Haslowe was the same age as Aidan, yet he enjoyed nearly unsurpassed favor in the kingdom, thanks to his family's overflowing coffers and their decades of loyal service to the Crown. Stephen, however, preferred his cups to any honorable activity, a fact borne out in his current condition. After nodding to Rex, the marquess took in the ladies as well, and Aidan's back stiffened at the leering expression on his face as his stare traveled too slowly over Diana's lush form.

"Lady Diana, it has been far too long," the marquess murmured, taking her hand in his free one to plant a wet kiss on her palm.

She yanked away, frowning with distaste, and Aidan stepped up to block the man's further view of her.

"Enjoying yourself, are you, Haslowe?" he asked coolly.

The marquess recoiled almost imperceptibly. But he recouped quickly enough to grasp the arm of a serving boy, grabbing the ale pitcher out of his hands to refill his cup before shoving the container back at the boy, sloshing ale all over him.

The lad went on his way, wide-eyed, as Lord Haslowe drank deep. Then, swiping the back of his hand across his mouth, he grinned. "I am having a fine time, Sutcliffe. A fine time. The only thing that would make it more enjoyable would be a beautiful woman on my arm, to sit by me and feed me tidbits at the feasting. But that shall come later, I hope."

"Perhaps. There are many in attendance here tonight," Aidan said, for no other reason than to try to ease the man into moving on so that he would leave Diana and Helene alone.

Lord Haslowe leered once more. "Aye, there are. Many lovely morsels. Mayhap even your Welsh cousin—what is her name? I hear that she's a fine, sturdy piece of—well, you know . . ." He lowered his voice conspiratorially. "A welcoming sheath for my sword, eh, Sutcliffe?" he smirked, winking. "Your timing is impeccable, I must say," he added, nodding to another of the nobles across the chamber and starting toward him with an unsteady gait. "I am in the market for a wife," he called back over his shoulder, "and if your cousin is attractive enough, I suppose it might as well be her."

"You'll rot in hell first," Aidan muttered, doing everything in his power not to reach out, jerk the bastard backward, and throttle him senseless. If not for Helene's presence he'd have done just that.

"I am sorry you had to witness that, my lady," he said, meeting her wide-eyed gaze.

She cleared her throat nervously, her delicate hand pressed there as if to soothe a jittery pulse. "He's rather more rude than I recalled," she murmured, glancing to Diana, who was following Lord Haslowe's movement across the hall.

"Aye, he seems quite full of himself," Diana added. But the expression on his sister's face made warning bells go off in Aidan's mind. His eyes narrowed. Diana was up to something, he'd wager his boots on it. Something devious, which usually meant—

"Good God, Aidan, you never alluded to this. If I weren't so old, I'd try for a chance with this one myself," Rexford suddenly murmured next to him, pulling him from his thoughts. He twisted around to see what his mentor was alluding to, hearing Diana gasp as she, Helene, and nearly everyone else in the great hall turned to face the door as well.

What he saw in the stairway door made his throat close and his lungs seize up. The room fell silent as his gaze locked with the woman standing in the doorway, his mind awhirl with memories of the girl she'd once been, his soul colliding with thoughts and feelings that he'd done his best to keep at bay for twelve years.

'Twas Gwynne. *His* Gwynne, almost as if she'd stepped back through time to return to him, whole and achingly beautiful. He stared at her in awe, and she returned his gaze, her stunning silver eyes soft with uncertainty. But in the next moment she blinked, her mouth edging up in a tremulous smile, and his heart melted, its liquid heat seeming to seep out and slide down his limbs, settling in the very tips of his fingers and toes.

*Oh Gwynne, Gwynne . . . my sweet Gwynne . . .*

His mind raged, and though he schooled his features so that none could see his reaction, he swallowed hard, knowing that he was lost for good this time. Aware that the fires Kevyn had spoken of were even now rising up like an inferno to engulf him . . .

And realizing that no matter how hard he tried, he was never going to be able to extinguish them.

# Chapter 16

Gwynne stood in the doorway, her heart racing. Her palms felt damp and so she pressed them into the folds of her skirts. Her movement made the fabric swish around her legs, gathered as it was under the jeweled silver belt slung low round her hips; its sapphire gemstones matched the intricate design-work edging her long, draped sleeves, as well as the fitted smock cuffs that peeked out at the top . . . and for the first time that she could remember, she wore nothing beneath her female clothing.

She took a step forward, the close fit of her bodice unfamiliar against her skin, the sensation of her skirts brushing her thighs making her shiver. Everyone was staring at her, she suddenly realized. Her belly gave a twist, and she jerked to a halt. Oh, they were all staring at her—especially Aidan—and he looked . . . well, sort of stricken. Another twinge of worry gripped her; was her circlet askew again? Was the color of her gown unbecoming?

She remembered Old Alana's thoughtful consideration of all the gowns and bliauds spread out on the bed this morning. She'd finally picked this one, a midnight blue creation, shot through with silver, its yards of flowing silk like the ocean sky before a storm, she'd said—a fitting blend of hues to highlight her unusual eyes and ebony hair.

She'd gathered together Gwynne's unruly coal-black curls at her nape, weaving in a blue ribbon. 'Twas barely shoulder-length and difficult to plait, but Alana had tucked the short ends under, leaving a few tendrils loose around her face. She'd topped it all off with a delicate silver circlet, claiming, when she was finished, that Gwynne looked like a princess true born.

And she *had* felt completely different from her usual self, as she'd made her way down the stairs and to the hall. She'd felt almost . . . beautiful. Until now, anyway.

Hesitant and a bit foolish was all she could think of to describe herself at the moment, thanks to more than two score people studying her.

She looked at Aidan, waiting for him to do something, say something—anything—to end the stunned silence that had reigned since her entrance into the hall. But he remained still, his expression unreadable, having shifted at last from unabashed shock.

The first fingers of disappointment twisted inside her, along with hurt. She was a fool. All of this—the effort, the embarrassment of asking Alana to help her—had been for naught. She wasn't any more enticing to Aidan in this finery than she'd been covered in blood and grime atop her steed on the battlefield. *Lugh* save her, but she—

"My lords, my ladies!" Kevyn called out to the assembly, striding up to her and tucking his hand firmly beneath her elbow. "Allow me to present the Earl of Sutcliffe's lovely Welsh cousin—Lady Gwynne ap Morrison!" Then he propelled her forward with his grip, even as she tried to pull back so that she might flee to her chambers and end this travesty.

"Stop fighting me and come along," Kevyn tilted his head to murmur at her. " 'Twill be all right, I promise you."

"Let me go," Gwynne muttered back, pasting a false smile on her face. "I need no further humiliation to know that I've failed completely at—"

"My lady Gwynne! I would be honored if you would allow me to share your trencher this eve!" called one of the noblemen from the crowd.

"Nay, consider me, my lady!" another cried, jostling the man next to him to get a better view.

"Say that you'll promise me the first chance to dance with you during the entertainments!" shouted a third, though he was soon drowned out in a cacophony of masculine voices, all staking claim to her this evening.

She looked around, as stunned now, herself, as the collected gathering had been when they'd first viewed her.

"What does this mean?" she whispered, swiveling her head to Kevyn in panic.

"It means that you've outdone yourself—and every other woman in the room." Kevyn paused, looking at her for a moment with a flicker of admiration in his eyes before he inclined his head to her and murmured, ". . . my lady."

"I'll take over from here," a low voice rumbled near them, and Gwynne snapped her gaze to its enigmatic owner as he edged Kevyn out of the way and took her arm himself. 'Twas Aidan. He looked none too happy, however, and she could only assume that either her choice of clothing or the shouted offers on her behalf had put him in such a sour mood.

'Twas the first, she decided, knowing as she did how he

wished to make all of England believe that she was anyone but the Dark Legend.

Her hurt faded under a dose of righteous anger as he steered her away from the crowd to get her a goblet of wine from the table. "I thought that this was what you wanted—for me to try to dress and behave like a real lady," Gwynne muttered as he handed her a cup. "Yet you act as if I've arrived at your celebration wearing my mail and gauntlets. You are impossible to please!"

Aidan stiffened as she spoke, looking away from her at first as he nodded to an older man, who was staring as he approached on the pretext of seeking some refreshment. Once the man had gone on his way, Aidan slowly turned, and as his eyes connected with hers, she felt like the air was being sucked from her lungs.

"You are beautiful, Gwynne," he murmured. "Even more so than I remembered. In truth, you take my breath away."

But in the next instant, her stomach dropped when he added, "But I would have been far happier to see you in your least becoming gown, with your circlet askew, as it usually is."

She bit down on her tongue, reminding herself of all that Old Alana had said regarding her behavior if she wished to seem enticing. "Perhaps you'd better explain," she ground out as sweetly as she could manage, succeeding in something that sounded more like a choked growl.

Aidan held her gaze, unable to keep a half smile from his lips. He still felt overwhelmed at seeing her like this, but as befuddled as his emotions were, he realized the effort she was making to be polite; the Gwynne he'd come to know these past weeks most likely would have thrown a forearm into his chest and challenged him to swords in the yard for the apparent insult he'd just dealt her.

And yet her appearance didn't truly displease him.

Nay, just the opposite—but that didn't mean they weren't going to face enormous problems because of it.

He sighed. "Do you remember a few days ago, when I told you about today's festivities? You made it clear to me then that if you attended, 'twould be on the condition that no other Englishman would touch you—that you would dance, if you had to, with me alone."

"Aye, what of it?"

"I'm afraid that you've made that condition nearly impossible to achieve, looking as you do."

She flushed. "What is wrong with how I look?"

"There's nothing wrong with it. That's the problem."

She frowned at him, but even so, he found he couldn't go on right away. Grabbing another cup of wine from the table, he downed it in one swallow. God help him, but he was having a hard time concentrating with her standing so near to him and looking so damn beautiful. He forced himself to finish what he needed to say, knowing that he didn't have much time left. His guests were beginning to prowl around them like packs of wolves lured by the scent of fresh blood.

"You need to understand something," he said, struggling to hide his incredible need to kiss her, to taste the warm, delicate skin just below her ear. "In addition to the married guests in attendance here," he managed, "there are another dozen *unwed* English lords. You heard them; they're all chomping at the bit for a chance to win you over."

" 'Twill never happen," she said, punctuating her words with a little snort, then flushing again as if she realized that such a noise probably wasn't very ladylike.

"You may know that, but they don't," he continued. "You've made a spectacular entrance, and they'll be like stallions after a mare in season, vying for your attentions all night."

Though he hadn't thought it possible, her cheeks bloomed brighter—but from anger this time rather than shame. "I am no mare to stud," she said lowly, setting her goblet on the table hard enough to make it clang.

Young Richard de Gambol, heir to the Earl of Fennwick, had been standing nearby, obviously trying to work up his courage to approach them, but he startled at Gwynne's display of temper, moving off with a few of his friends to mumble amongst themselves and cast wary glances at her.

Clearing his throat, Aidan raised his brow. Perhaps this was the solution, he thought. Rile up Gwynne enough so that she frightened away every potential suitor. 'Twould solve their dilemma most effectively.

But even as the thought crossed his mind, he knew that it couldn't be. The whole point of her attendance at this gathering was to ensure that her true identity remained hidden, as well as to explain her continued presence at Dunston. Should any rumors leak out, he wanted all the noble houses from here to London to feel confident in dismissing her as just what he'd claimed her to be: his unfortunate Welsh cousin, taken in for the sake of family ties.

"There is only one way around this, as I see it," he said, pulling his gaze from young Richard back to her.

"And what is that?" She was making a valiant attempt to sound conversational, but he saw that she stood ramrod stiff, her arms having crept up into their usual position folded across her chest.

"You'll have to mingle with the nobles more than we'd planned."

She looked ready to burst out with a resounding denial to his suggestion, so he added, "Conversations and the like, of course. You'll need to sit at the feasting amongst them, perhaps, and talk and stroll about to view the entertainments with some of the others afterward."

He waited for her response, trying not to breathe in the sweet fragrance of her hair—doing all he could not to lean in and press his lips to the silken tendrils at her temple.

"Will any of those activities require them to touch me?"

He paused, surprised to realize he found the idea as unsavory as she seemed to. "Only in courtesy," he admitted. " 'Tis common for a man to place his hand on a lady's elbow as he walks with her. Beyond that, you should be safe—unless you choose to dance," he added, glancing at the guests milling around them with an increasing sense of interest and impatience.

He looked at her again, reminding himself to sound nonchalant, in control. "I would suggest that you come up with some excuse that exempts you from the activity altogether."

Gwynne pursed her lips. "Aye, well, I must have forgotten to mention that I twisted my leg during our training. My ankle suddenly feels a bit swollen, I'm afraid."

Smothering another smile, Aidan turned to see William Gerard, Lord Fenton, approaching them with a gleam in his eye. The man was a good enough sort, Aidan knew, possessed of both humor and integrity; in addition, he boasted a long and honorable association with the Crown, having fought for nearly a decade as one of the king's personal champions.

"What's this, Sutcliffe?" William called out, his voice light with jesting. " 'Tis not fair of you to keep such beauty to yourself, especially when you have a lovely lady of your own to consider."

Looking past him, Aidan saw Helene standing in the group William had left; she didn't come closer, but remained in place, staring at him with a solemn, sad expression in her eyes as she shifted her gaze between his face and Gwynne's. His gut dropped to realize that he'd forgotten all about her. From the moment Gwynne had entered the great hall, Helene had ceased to exist for him. 'Twas clear that his betrothed had felt the slight—not to mention her father, who stood nearby, glowering at Aidan.

Stiffening, he turned his attention back to William and Gwynne, offering introductions, and trying not to notice the desperate look Gwynne cast him when William announced that she must share his trencher during the feasting.

He couldn't respond, he told himself—couldn't step in and champion her. *Damn it, he couldn't*. Not here, of all places, before the probing gazes of two score guests, Helene, and Lord Rutherford. And so he simply nodded his compliance, his neck feeling rigid enough to crack, as William led Gwynne away toward the end of the hall where the tables were arranged and awaiting the feasting that was about to begin.

" 'Tis quite a change in our *cousin's* appearance," Diana's sharp voice echoed in his ear. He remained silent, unwilling to chance revealing any of the turbulent emotions roiling inside him.

"I'd almost thought you planned to ignore the rest of our guests—and Helene—this night, in favor of cloistering that Welshwoman over here like some sort of sacred relic," Diana continued with a sniff. " 'Twas becoming an embarrassment, the way you fawned over her, Aidan. Helene was hurt by it."

Steeling himself, Aidan faced his sister. He reminded himself of his obligations to her and to his family's name, knowing it was all that had allowed him to carry his loveless betrothal to this point. "Gwynne was nervous about her first appearance in English society," he answered, "and I tried to ease her way, that is all. I will make sure that Helene understands as much."

Then, forcing himself not to glance, even, in the direction that William had led Gwynne, to see how she fared, he gave a cursory bow to his sister and murmured, "Now, why don't you try to enjoy the rest of the evening without your usual dose of criticism, sarcasm, and back-biting? 'Twill net you far greater prospects for a husband, I assure you."

Diana sucked in her cheeks and narrowed her eyes as her brother turned on his heel and made his way toward Helene and the duke. Anger coiled through her like a snake. How dared he mock her desire to make a prosperous marriage match? Rather, he should be helping her to achieve it. 'Twas the least she deserved after all that had happened to them, first with Father's dishonor and then with Mother's horrible death. But instead, her brother was choosing to hinder her with his foolish and dangerous infatuations.

Oh, aye, he'd tried to hide it beneath a facade of cool disdain, but Aidan's tender feelings for that wretch of a Welshwoman were painfully obvious as far as she was concerned. And it couldn't be allowed to continue. She'd thought that bringing Helene and her father to Dunston would nip the entire, foul problem in the bud, reminding Aidan of where his loyalties and their good fortune lay.

But it had barely slowed him down.

'Twas clear that she needed to take further measures, and the idea that had come to her earlier, just before Gwynne had made her flamboyant entrance, would suit perfectly. If Aidan couldn't be made to reconsider what he was doing, throwing away their future for the sake of lust, then perhaps Gwynne would.

Aye, if her plan worked, Diana thought, she'd wager her best gown and jeweled girdle that Gwynne would soon realize the error of her ways and cease this dangerous flirtation with Aidan. She'd be too humiliated to do else.

Keeping that positive thought in mind, Diana set off

across the great chamber in search of the one man who would undoubtedly enjoy participating in what she had planned—the man most fitted to helping her achieve a satisfactory result: Stephen de Segrave, the Marquess of Haslowe.

# Chapter 17

---

Gwynne needed to leave; she didn't know how much longer she could bear it. If she had to listen to even one more slobbering, fawning Englishman praise her complexion, her eyes, her hair, or her attire, she thought that she might lose the little bit of dinner that she'd managed to swallow during the feasting.

The only thing that had kept her from tossing a bowl of steaming soup at her admirers, or simply getting up and heaving the table over on them, was the enjoyable thought of how shocked all these lily-faced wretches would be to learn that they were trying to court England's foremost enemy—the same Dark Legend who had robbed their castles and held their men at sword-point time and again.

Of course, she hadn't been able to tell them. Nay, she'd had to endure their maddening attentions in silence. But even imagining the possibility had been enough to sustain her for a while. Thank God that the feasting portion of the evening, at least, was over; even now, servants worked to clear the tables and move them back against the walls, taking away the benches as well so that there would be more room for the dancing and entertainments. Perhaps now would be a good time to make a quiet departure.

She'd done her best tonight to make Aidan proud of her—to behave in a refined, feminine manner, though her cheeks ached from enforced smiling and her fists yearned to pound some sense into the simpering women and drunken nobles surrounding her. Yet she'd borne it all in the hopes of pleasing Aidan, of attracting his favorable attention. And all it had gotten her was a throbbing skull and nerves pulled tight as a bowstring.

Since taking his leave of her back when William had escorted her to the feasting tables, Aidan hadn't looked in her direction even once. He'd been studiously attentive to Helene, who'd been seated right next to him at dinner. Further, he'd been conversational with the duke, as well as with most of the other nobles seated near him. But he'd managed to avoid any kind of contact with her altogether.

'Twas about all she could take. The twisting, grinding pain it caused inside her was wearing her down in a way that the grueling rigors of her training had never done. She yearned only to leave and spend some time in peaceful empathy with her men, who rested and awaited her return from this celebration in their rooms back near the old stable.

Sighing, Gwynne watched the people moving and talking all around her, glad to be alone for the moment. Though she couldn't deny that William had been pleasant enough during the feasting, he, like the others, had complimented her far more often than she knew could be sincere. He'd left her side, finally, a few moments ago, but several other lords kept looking her way, noticing that she stood alone; if she didn't go, no doubt she'd be stuck exchanging more mindless pleasantries with one of them.

Now was her chance to leave.

A last glance toward Aidan confirmed her decision. He smiled at Helene; his betrothed had taken hold of his arm and seemed to be trying to lead him to where the dances had already begun. Gwynne watched Aidan shake his head as if to decline, but then the duke frowned and said something to him. Even from this distance, she could see the muscle in Aidan's jaw twitch as his face tightened. With a stiff little bow, he put out his arm and led Helene to the dancers, where, palm-to-palm, they began the graceful series of movements.

*The same movements he practiced with you, time and again in the glen where he kissed you for the first time . . .*

Shutting off the mocking voice inside of her, Gwynne squeezed her eyes shut, blocking out the sight of Aidan and Helene at the same moment that she turned, intending to slip, unnoticed, through the door that led to the kitchens and then to the yard and outbuildings. But instead she slammed into a seeming wall of stone. Snapping open her eyes, she met the gaze of the most arrogant-looking Englishman she'd ever had the displeasure of bumping into.

"Stephen de Segrave, Lord Haslowe, at your service, milady," he said in a silky drawl, standing far too close to her. Cocking one eyebrow, he bent forward in a bow, his gaze fixed on her breasts with a leer that even Gwynne, in all of her inexperience, couldn't mistake.

Using every ounce of reserve left to her, she quelled her initial reaction to double him over with a well-placed fist to the belly, instead taking a step back to glare at him and mutter, "I was just leaving. Now, if you'll excuse me . . ."

"I am afraid that is one request I cannot satisfy, fair lady," Lord Haslowe murmured, even as he moved so swiftly that she didn't realize he'd taken her arm until she felt her elbow clamped in his immovable grip. "Come.

You must allow me a dance before you leave me bereft and alone."

Shock made Gwynne go still for an instant, but then her instincts leaped to the fore. Yanking her arm free, she tried to remember Alana's instructions for behaving in a feminine manner. Quietly, she said, "I do not wish to dance. I wish to leave. Now, please step aside so that I may go."

"Nay, lady. I will have a dance with you—if not at the end of the hall where the others are enjoying the activity, then right here." He wrapped his arms around her waist. "Right *now*," he added, punctuating the comment by pulling her toward him, so that her breasts pressed hard against the slab of his chest.

"Let go of me," she said through gritted teeth, jerking back in an effort to free herself, yet still trying not to make a scene. She couldn't. As much as this bastard deserved it, she couldn't strike him down—not if she wished to maintain the outward illusion of femininity required of her.

*Just behave like a lady and all will be well. Behave like a lady, behave like a lady . . .*

"Ah, you're a live one," Stephen growled softly, his voice thick with excitement as she struggled in his grip. "Perhaps you'd rather a kiss, then," he said, his breath hot in her ear. "Or a bit more—"

Reaching down, he cupped one hand roughly over her buttocks, squeezing as he dragged her flush against him, so that she couldn't help but feel the hard, rutting length of him pressed into her belly.

And then something snapped inside of her.

A red haze washed before her eyes; she felt it seep into her veins, unleashing feral, dark rage. She swiveled her head to Haslowe, hearing his sharp intake of breath even as she twisted out of his grasp and slipped one of her arms beneath his, jerking up and throwing him off balance.

Then, with a growl of fury, she shoved him bodily away from her. He went flying, crashing to the floor and skidding another ten paces before he eased to a stop near the feet of a half dozen of Aidan's startled guests.

For the second time that night the hall fell deathly silent.

Gwynne stood there, her breath rasping in her ears, her heartbeats coming painful and fast as she looked all around her. The music had ground to a screeching halt and everyone had stopped what they were doing to turn and stare at her, faces aghast; Lord Haslowe, even, lay frozen in place on the floor, half-reclined on one elbow, and gaping at her as if she were the devil incarnate.

Numbly, Gwynne shifted her head to look at Aidan, and their gazes connected with a sharp jolt. She read the shock, the dismay in his eyes, and her heart felt like it was cracking in her chest. And everyone just kept staring . . .

Oh, God, what had she done . . . ?

Biting the inside of her cheek to keep the hot prickles behind her eyes at bay, Gwynne took in a ragged breath and spun around, heading for the door. After what seemed an eternity, she lurched through to the cool, blessed oblivion of the dark corridor beyond it; leaning back against the wall for a moment, she wrapped her arms tightly around her middle.

Her mind reeled with the pain and embarrassment of what had just happened. *Lugh's bones*, she'd just tossed one of Aidan's guests clear across the floor. Whether he'd deserved it or not didn't seem to matter. Not if the expressions of horror on everyone's faces were the judge of it. She closed her eyes against the memory. She was unnatural, their expressions said. Unrefined. Violent. Most certainly not a lady . . .

Suddenly, she felt a hand on her arm. Gasping, she whirled, prepared to finish off Lord Haslowe once and for all—if nothing else, for being stupid enough to follow her here after what had happened inside the great hall.

But she stopped short.

'Twas Aidan. He stood in the shadows of the corridor outside his ruined gathering—the celebration of nobles he'd worked so diligently to arrange—and he reached out to brush his finger under her chin, forcing her to look at him.

"What happened in there?" he asked gently.

"Do you need to ask?" she managed, choking out a harsh laugh, even as she pulled away from him, unable to bear the pain of his touch. "You saw it for yourself—I just attacked Lord Haslowe in front of the entire assembly."

"Aye, I know—the question is why?"

She paused, her mouth twisting into a grimace as she considered telling him the truth. But 'twould do no good, she knew; the damage was already done, and besides, she needed no commiseration from him after an entire evening of his neglect.

She grated out, "Perhaps it is just my nature to react violently, Aidan." The damnable burning behind her eyes increased, but she blinked it back. " 'Tis bred into my blood and bones, it seems. The man offended me, I tried to restrain myself, and I ended up throwing him across the room."

She turned, closing her eyes and pinching the bridge of her nose between her fingers, even though she knew she needn't fear the possibility of crying in front of him; she hadn't indulged in that release for nearly twelve years, and after so long, she didn't think she could, whether she wished it or nay.

"I have to go."

She pushed away from the wall, desperate to get away from Aidan and this other life—this other person—she'd tried so hard to mold herself into being. Even if 'twas only for the rest of the night, she had to get away, out of these clothes and back into her own safe and familiar warrior's garments. To somehow rebuild her sense of self, so that she could face donning this false persona again tomorrow and every tomorrow after that, until the rest of this cursed bargain between them was fulfilled.

"You can't leave," Aidan murmured, gripping her upper arms and keeping her near him. "Damn it, Gwynne, I won't let you."

She stiffened in his grasp, but she wouldn't look at him. Not yet. She hadn't the strength for it. "There is naught more to be done here, Aidan," she managed to say. "Unless I am to further damage this illusion you've created for me by causing another scene like the one with Lord Haslowe, I must leave."

She paused, calling on all of her inner focus, on the icy sense of calm that had carried her through battle after bloody battle. When she finally lifted her gaze to his, she filled it with as much cool indifference as she could muster. "But there is something more that you can do— that you *must* do, right now. Return to the celebration. Your betrothed will surely be looking for you, distressed that you've strayed from her side for too long."

"I've done my duty by Helene all evening," he answered, his voice gone husky. "She can wait a few moments more. I need to know that you're all right."

Gwynne's heart lurched at his words, but she subdued its traitorous motions. "I'm fine," she said, surprising herself with how calm, how unaffected she sounded. "Now, let me go."

"Nay, I cannot." Releasing one of her arms, Aidan brushed his fingers gently along her temple, where the delicate silver circlet rested, down the side of her cheek to just below her jaw. "Ah, Gwynne, I don't want you to go," he murmured, following the path of his fingers with soft kisses, feathered across her skin like little bursts of heat.

He continued to kiss her neck, the tender spot just below her ear, and suddenly, she couldn't suppress the tremble that went through her, or the shuddery, hitched breath that escaped on a sigh. Warmth unfurled through her, languorous desire and sharp need swirling together in a heady mix; she tipped her head back, arching into him, barely stopping herself from sliding her hands up his shoulders to tangle in the dark waves of hair at the nape of his neck.

*'Tis your duty to let him kiss you—to kiss him back and make him desire you!* the voice inside her shrieked, but she knew she couldn't obey its command. Heaven help her, she wanted to, wanted to kiss him with all the emotion and need inside her. But something held her back. Some understanding that told her being here with him was far more dangerous than she'd ever thought possible.

*You're falling in love with him.*

The shadow voice sang out its seductive claim, jolting her to sudden and complete awareness. She wanted to deny it, wanted it to be a lie of the most vicious kind. But she knew it wasn't.

During these past weeks together her feelings for Aidan had somehow mysteriously changed. She'd witnessed so much that flew in the face of her previous notions of him that she no longer recognized them.

He wasn't the brutal, cold-hearted Englishman she'd convinced herself he'd be. She'd watched him lavish kindness on Clara and Ella, observed his humor and good-natured friendship with his man, Kevyn—seen the fair way he treated everyone around him, including her. Even when she deliberately provoked him, he'd remained patient, attentive, and generous with her. And all at once she understood that it was more than simple duty that drove her to want to be with Aidan, to try to please him and entice him. It was much, much more. It was desire, and passion, and the sense of intimacy they shared . . .

And it was love.

Oh, God, she was falling in love with her enemy.

*She was falling in love with Aidan.*

Blindly, she pulled back, doing everything in her power to resume the controlled facade she'd feigned throughout much of their conversation. But she couldn't. There was no way to hide what she was feeling right now. She looked at him, the torn, confused emotions inside of her burgeoning with every additional moment she spent near him, in his arms, feeling him breathe and move against her . . .

"Let me go, Aidan, I beg of you," she whispered. "Please, you have to let me go."

"I cannot," he growled softly, holding her closer. "God help me, Gwynne, but I want you with me. When I first saw you tonight, standing there in the doorway, it was as if the past twelve years hadn't happened, like you'd never been taken from me. But it was also something more . . . something I cannot explain—" he broke off, cupping her face in his hands, so sweetly, so tenderly, that she thought her heart would break.

She struggled, trying to maintain any trace of self-control, to stem the shaking in her hands as she eased out of his embrace. "If you will not allow me to leave this gathering freely, then I must call in your debt. Weeks ago, when you tricked me into learning to dance with you, I told you that I would let you know later how and when you could repay me for your deception. It is now."

She swallowed, praying that she had enough fortitude to finish the rest. "Honor demands that you release me from the remainder of tonight's celebration, since that is what I wish for repayment. You owe me that, at least."

He looked more stricken, if that were possible, than he had when she'd first made her entrance into the hall. "Ah Gwynne," he murmured huskily. "If only you remembered. In truth, I owe you far more . . ."

He shook his head and swallowed, his face shadowed with resignation and pain before he nodded once and stepped back, allowing her to pass. "But I cannot deny you. Go then if you must," he added, clasping his hands behind his back as if he too doubted his ability to stop them from reaching out, from reclaiming her. "I will not try to prevent you further."

She stood still before him for a moment, all her need for him rising up to twisting, throbbing life. But then the specter of Duty reared its head above the rest, strangling her heart once more into submission.

"Good night, Aidan," she finally whispered, her voice like a disembodied soul's as it crossed the gulf of time and circumstance separating them.

He didn't respond, but only stood there as before, gazing at her with the same intensity, his entire body rigid with repressed emotion, his eyes glittering with anguish, longing . . . and something more.

Before she could falter in what she knew she needed to do, Gwynne turned away from him, her heart pounding and her throat aching, as she forced herself to walk toward the stairs that led to the upper floor. She mounted the steps, choking with the need to go back to him. But somehow she kept going; when she finally reached the landing, absolute silence surrounded her, dark and empty. As barren as the solitary life it was her destiny to lead until the day death took her. 'Twas the only way it could be, damn it.

*The only way.*

Her legs felt weak by the time she entered her bedchamber and pulled the door shut behind her. Unable to support her own weight on them any longer, she slid slowly to the floor, her borrowed finery pooling around her in waves of blue and silver. After a long moment, she reached up and removed the delicate circlet from her brow, placing it carefully next to her on the floor of the chamber . . .

And then she bent over and buried her face in her hands, rocking silently in the yawning shadows of her room, and aching for the release of tears that she knew would never come.

# Chapter 18

Diana crouched behind the massive wooden table in the darkened corridor outside the great hall, all alone, and for the first time in her life, not caring that the fabric of her best gown would surely be ruined by the dust and dirt in this unwashed corner. Just moments ago, Gwynne had fled upstairs. Shortly after, Aidan had turned and walked stiffly back into the great hall. But Diana couldn't seem to move for the thoughts whirling through her head.

When she'd sneaked out here and hidden after Gwynne had run from the celebration, it had been with no further thought in mind than to view the fruits of her labors; the humiliating scene she'd arranged in the hall had gone perfectly, with Gwynne, hot-tempered as always, reacting to Haslowe's advances just as Diana had hoped. But her desire to gloat over Gwynne's certain anguish—to watch the arrogant creature at last reduced to tears—had been crushed within moments of Aidan rushing from the hall to comfort her.

But it wasn't the fact that her brother had come out to comfort Gwynne that had made Diana feel woozy. It was what they had said to each other . . . the information she'd just learned . . . that made this entire situation seem suddenly so much more dangerous than she'd ever dreamed.

*God help me, Gwynne, but when I first saw you tonight, standing there in the doorway, it was as if the past twelve years hadn't happened, as if you'd never been taken from me.*

Aidan's impassioned statement rang through Diana's mind again, just as shocking as it had been when she'd heard him say it a few moments ago. Her brother knew Gwynne—had known her for years, from the sound of it. Closing her eyes, Diana did the calculations in her mind. Twelve years . . . that would have been when she was six and Aidan fifteen.

*When Aidan was fifteen. Sweet Mother Mary . . .*

Diana's eyes snapped open, and she gasped aloud in the quiet of the corridor. That was the summer he'd almost died at the hands of the Welsh rebels! Though she'd been only a child, she remembered how frightened everyone was, and how angry Father had been—angry because Aidan had been out in the dangerous border woods without protection, sneaking off to meet a girl. A commoner. Alana had found Aidan that afternoon on Dunston lands, where he'd managed to drag himself after the attack, wounded and babbling incoherently about devils with blue faces who'd killed the girl he loved and stolen her body away.

*A Welsh girl . . .*

Diana lurched to her feet. Images from those long ago days merged with memories of the past few weeks—of her brother's eyes, filled with suffering and pain. With love and longing and anguish . . .

Oh, nay! Was he planning to break off his betrothal with Helene because of Gwynne? He couldn't! But if he was planning such a foolhardy action, then why did he and Gwynne continue to lie about her identity and her past with him?

The questions raced through Diana's mind, stunning her with their ferocity. She had to find out what was going on here. Her head swiveled to the door of the great hall, and through the sliver of opening, she saw the bustling of activity and merriment that had resumed within minutes of Gwynne's embarrassing scene. Her brother would be engaged, most likely, in soothing any remaining discord among the guests; she couldn't approach him and demand answers in front of everyone—and she wasn't willing to wait until they all departed for their own estates to talk to him.

That left Gwynne. She'd disappeared above stairs to lick her wounds after her humiliation, no doubt. 'Twas a good time to confront her in the privacy of her chamber and make her tell what she and Aidan were up to.

But before she could make the move toward the stairs, someone emerged from the darkened opening there and headed down the corridor that led outside. Diana's eyes narrowed. It looked like a young man, though 'twas difficult to tell, since he wore his hood up. It wasn't one of the servants, of that she was fairly certain—and it couldn't be one of the guests; this person's garments, though well made, weren't of the quality anyone would wear to a gathering of nobles.

Suddenly, she remembered the glimpse she'd caught of Gwynne that one time, when she'd been spying into the Welshmen's chamber; Gwynne had been wearing boy's clothes that night—why, Diana had never discovered—but it appeared she was doing it again. Squaring her shoulders, Diana followed the retreating figure, determined to persist, whatever her destination. It mattered little to her whether Gwynne wore a dress, breeches, or nothing at all; she planned to get some answers to the secrecy surrounding her connection to Aidan, and she wanted to get them tonight.

As expected, Gwynne led her toward the outbuildings; but instead of entering her countrymen's chamber, Gwynne kept walking, past the men's darkened lodgings to the abandoned stable building. There she slipped through the door and shut it behind her.

*What in blazes was she doing?*

Frowning, Diana took a few steps closer. She considered the idea of simply charging in to see what Gwynne was up to, but something stopped her. Instead, she approached the door quietly, carefully, nudging it open a crack.

The place looked deserted, the light of one torch at the far end of the building flickering over the whole gloomy expanse. 'Twas set up like a training ground, Diana realized, empty to the walls, with a hard-packed floor of dirt. And in the circle of light thrown off by that solitary torch, Gwynne stood still as a statue, her back to the door where Diana was hiding.

Of a sudden, Gwynne moved, shrugging out of the cloak and tossing it to the side. Diana stifled a gasp; it wasn't only boy's clothes Gwynne wore, but the garments of a warrior, complete with sword belt and leather hauberk. But when she reached down and gripped the hilt of her sword, drawing it out and raising it so that the blade glinted in the torchlight, Diana felt so shocked that she couldn't have moved from her position even if Gwynne had turned around and charged at her with it. She watched mesmerized as Gwynne began to work through a series of motions with the weapon, swinging it with a precision and strength to rival the best of the warriors Diana had ever known, including Aidan.

Sensation returned to Diana's legs and arms with sharp jolts, and she finally managed to stumble back, away from the door; she stood in the cool night air, motionless, trying to grasp the meaning of what she'd just seen. It had been upsetting enough to realize that Gwynne was almost certainly Aidan's long lost love, but that she favored dressing as a man and could wield a sword like this as well was just too much.

What in God's name did it all mean? Diana squeezed her fingers together, trying to gather her thoughts as she leaned in and took another peek inside the old building. Gwynne continued to work through her movements, only now she'd added lunges and thrusts to the mix. Diana shuddered, imagining herself at the point of that wicked tip. She knew that Gwynne would relish such a thing, too, if their previous interactions were any indication.

Backing up again, she let the door creak shut and prepared to return to the castle as quickly as she could. One thing was certain: knowing Gwynne's temper, she wasn't going to confront her right now—not with that deadly three-foot blade locked in her grip.

"You there—what are you doing?"

The deep masculine voice echoed in Diana's ear an instant before she felt its owner's iron-muscled hand clamp down on her arm. Gasping, she tried to jerk away and run, but she might as well have been a butterfly pinned to a board, for all the good it did her.

Gritting her teeth to keep them from chattering, Diana swung to face the man who restrained her, half-hidden in night shadows as he was—up his bulging arm and shoulder to a chiseled chin, full, sensuous lips, tightened into a scowl, and onto piercing black eyes. Eyes that were focused directly on her.

Her heart quivered at the look in those eyes, and instinctively, she did what always came to mind whenever she was caught doing something she shouldn't by someone of the masculine gender: she lowered her chin and tilted one shoulder forward a little, presenting him with an enticing view of her cleavage even as she gazed up at him through her lashes.

"My goodness, Owin," she breathed, shifting the tiniest bit into his grip, so that her breasts brushed lightly against his arm. "You startled me."

She felt a flare of disappointment when the stony set of his face didn't change—though the unmistakable flicker of interest that burst to life in his eyes mollified her a bit. Another delicious shiver traveled up her spine; challenges were always more exciting than men who simply fell at her feet.

"I asked you what you were doing here," he said, his tone as firm and as wonderfully gruff as before. "Why were you spying?"

"Spying?" Diana echoed, her free hand fluttering up to rest at the base of her throat. Her mind raced ahead, trying to decide how she should play this out. The leashed power emanating from this virile Welshman made it clear that she had better be convincing, whatever she did. She called up her most innocent expression. "I wasn't *spying*, Owin. I was just checking on Gwynne to make sure that she was all right."

"Why—is something amiss?" He frowned, and Diana's heart leaped again.

"There was a bit of . . . unpleasantness at the gathering of nobles a little while ago," Diana said, shrugging and looking away as if wounded by his accusing tone. "She was obviously embarrassed, and I wanted to see if she needed some comfort." She glanced at the Welshman sideways, deciding that she might as well just leap in the rest of the way with her pretended knowledge and see what happened. "I'd forgotten that she likes to work through her troubles this way, easing her mind with these exercises."

"Aye," Owin nodded, still frowning as he released Diana's arm and moved to glance in at Gwynne himself. Apparently satisfied that nothing was out of place, he turned back to take her arm again and as if to lead her toward the castle. "Come, I'll see you returned safely to the main keep."

The swell of triumph Diana had felt at her success thus far withered under his declaration. She couldn't leave yet; she hadn't learned enough about all this to abandon the unexpected opportunity to speak to Gwynne's kinsman.

Taking a few steps along with Owin, she suddenly uttered a cry, acting as if she'd turned her ankle on the rough ground of the yard. For a moment she thought he might allow her to slump all the way to the dirt, but at the last instant he pulled up on her arm. Gasping, she used the momentum to propel herself into his chest, clutching little handfuls of his tunic as she did to keep herself pressed as close as possible to his entire muscular form.

With a breathy moan that wasn't entirely feigned this time, she looked up at him through her lashes again, gratified to see that his frown had shifted to wide-eyed shock and then blatant hunger before he managed to shutter his expression again.

"Oh, thank goodness you were here, Owin," she murmured, shifting as if to regain her balance, though her movement ensured that her breasts rubbed with tingling friction against him. She heard him choke back a groan. Biting her bottom lip to smother a smile, Diana realized that for the first time in ages she was enjoying this little flirtation—far more than the cruel and fruitless teasing that she usually inflicted on others of Owin's gender.

"Are you hurt?" he muttered, keeping himself rigid, as

though he was afraid to move and cause more of the delicious sensations to burgeon between them.

"I—I think I'm all right. If you could just help me over to the side of the pathway, to sit for a moment, perhaps . . ." Diana answered breathlessly, easing herself away from him in apparent shyness.

Soon she was settled on an old crate that had been left near the wall; Owin stood in front of her, looking down. His expression seemed more gentle now, she thought, though she couldn't be sure in the dark, with the shadows playing over his face.

An awkward silence settled over them, their breathing and the chirping of a few crickets the only sounds to disturb the quiet. Astonished to feel herself blushing at the unexpected intimacy of the moment, Diana leaned over and made a show of rubbing one of her ankles.

Owin cleared his throat, and she glanced up at him from beneath her lashes, almost certain that she wasn't imagining the reddish hue creeping across his cheeks. "Shall I go to the castle and get your brother or some of his men to assist you?"

"Nay. I think I am able to walk," she answered, tilting her face up to meet his gaze fully now, and giving him a soft look. "If you will agree to escort me to the keep, I am sure that I will be fine. Just give me a moment more."

He looked as if he might return her smile, but then cleared his throat again and looked away. Diana took a deep breath and pushed herself to stand; it seemed that if she was going to find out more about Gwynne's reason for being at Dunston, she needed to do it before her maddening reaction to this handsome Welshman got the best of her.

"So," she began, taking his proffered arm as they started slowly back toward the castle. "Do you find living in England to be terribly different from your life in Wales?"

"Aye."

At first she thought he would say nothing more, but then his brow furrowed, and he added, "Though in truth some of the people in England are more . . . friendly to us than I had believed they would be."

Diana couldn't stop the bubble of laughter that escaped her then. "What—did you think the land populated by ogres, to be so wary of your welcome?"

Owin stiffened and ceased walking. "Considering the years of war between our countries, lady, I did not quite know what to expect."

Feeling somehow chastised by the dignity of his response, Diana blushed again. What could she say now to draw him into a more revealing conversation? The main keep loomed ever closer; 'twas best, she decided, to try to get back to the topic that had made this conversation necessary in the first place.

"With all that Aidan has told me about Gwynne and her reasons for being here," she lied, "he didn't mention your connection to her. Are you related, perhaps?"

Owin looked askance at her. "Nay. She is my leader."

"Ah, yes—your leader," Diana repeated, trying to sound as if she knew what he was talking about. "Silly me, but it seems that I've forgotten—what exactly is it that she leads you in?"

Frowning, Owin glanced at her again. "Battle, of course. I am one of *Chwedl's* warriors."

Diana stopped in her tracks at that, barely noticing that they'd reached the main door of the keep. "*Battle* . . ." She forced herself to nod knowingly, though her voice sounded as if it came from far away, thanks to the blood that had started pounding in her ears.

"We fight as often as possible for the freedom of our people," Owin added, not seeming to notice her stunned stare as he guided her, weak-kneed, to a place where she might sit on the steps; 'twas a position for which she was profoundly grateful in the next moment, when she heard the rest of what he had to say.

"And a better warrior you'll never find," Owin added, looking out over the walls of Dunston to the mountains beyond, shaking his head in remembered awe. " 'Tis why we call her *Chwedl*—a Welsh word meaning myth, or as you say in English, 'legend'." He swiveled his head to look at Diana again, his ebony eyes glowing with a passion and fervor she'd only ever seen sparking Aidan's gaze.

" 'Tis one of the reasons, lady," Owin finished in a reverent voice, "that I joined her here as a protector. In truth I would die a thousand deaths in defense of her. For regardless of what your English king or your countrymen claim against it, the once and future king *has* returned to this life. Gwynne was born to lead all of Wales to freedom— the finest warrior ever to take breath—for she is the one, true Dark Legend."

# Chapter 19

"**D**amn it, Aidan, just deny it and be done with it. 'Tis too early in the morning for such foolery."

Aidan stood before the hearth in his solar, leaning his arm on the mantel and staring into the cold gray ashes inside. Though the sun shone weakly through the shutters on the far wall, he hadn't been to bed yet, and fatigue pressed in on his temples, adding to his black mood.

The churning in his gut was worse than before, too; it had begun the moment he'd been forced to release Gwynne from the celebration last night, and it hadn't lifted since—a sick, hollow feeling that he'd had to grit his teeth and pretend didn't exist as he'd returned to the great hall to face his betrothed, her father, and the rest of his guests. Clenching his jaw against it now, he swung his gaze to Diana, who sat on the elaborate carved bench near the table, her expression both nervous and accusing.

After raising a mocking brow to her, he looked back at Rex. "And where, exactly, did my dear sister supposedly happen upon this . . . information that she decided to share with you?"

"Owin told me," Diana snapped, every self-righteous inch of her demanding recognition. "Though he bears no blame, since he thought that I knew the truth already."

"A belief I'm sure you encouraged in your own unique way," Aidan said, flicking his gaze to indicate the clinging, provocatively cut gown she still wore from last night.

She gave him a black look, but before she could utter a fitting rejoinder, Rex broke in again.

"I told her 'twas ridiculous, but she was so insistent that I agreed to bring her to you, to let her hear you deny it herself." Rex frowned. "However your silence is becoming as frustrating as her prating about outlaws and traitors. Just refute the allegations and let us all get back to bed where we belong."

Aidan didn't answer, his sardonic smile fixed, it seemed, as if it were frozen onto his face. Part of him wished that he could carry on the pretense and act as if he didn't know what Diana or Rex were talking about; but another part of him knew that he could never do it. Indirect falsehood was one thing—an outright lie was another.

"I cannot refute it," he said at last, his voice quiet as he held Rex's gaze. "Gwynne is the Dark Legend, and I have been keeping her here under an assumed identity."

"What?" his foster father choked.

"I knew it!" Diana burst out, shooting to her feet. Her hands clenched into fists. "You're going to ruin us all with this—we'll be executed for treason, just as Father was!" she cried, her words raking Aidan's heart as surely as their shrill sound pierced his brain.

Rex hadn't moved a muscle since Aidan's confirmation of the charge, but now he lurched into motion, stepping forward to take Diana's arm. "I think you'd better return to your chamber now, lass," he said, leading her to the door. "I need to talk to your brother in private for a few moments."

"Nay." Her eyes welled as she twisted in Rex's grip to look at Aidan. "I want to hear him explain why he has done this to us. Why he has let lust override reason and honor. We will all end up paying the price for it! God help us, we will—" She broke down then, collapsing against Rex's shoulder and sobbing so that her tears wet his shirt.

"Hush, child," Rex soothed. "I will sort this out with your brother, you have my word on it. No more talk of tragedy, now. Go to your chamber and try to get some rest. I'll speak with you later about this."

Diana pulled back from him and sniffled a few more times, casting another wounded look at Aidan before she allowed Rex to lead her the rest of the way to the portal.

"Go on now," Rex murmured, patting her on the back. "And say nothing to anyone of what the Welshman told you or what was discussed in this room, do you understand?"

Wordlessly, Diana nodded, wiping the tips of her fingers beneath her eyes to remove the last traces of tears gathered there. Fixing her watery gaze on Rex, she pleaded, "You are the only one who might be able to make him see some sense. Promise that you'll make him remove Gwynne from Dunston before 'tis too late."

"I will straighten all of this out with your brother, Diana, never fear," Rex cajoled, nudging her the rest of the way out of the room.

When the door had shut behind her, he turned to Aidan again, staring at him for a long moment before he finally said, "I think you have some explaining to do, son. Not the least of which is why you seem to think 'tis possible that this Welshwoman could be the Dark Legend. I saw Gwynne quite clearly last night. She is a beautiful woman; I cannot believe that she is also England's fiercest enemy."

"Were you there when she threw Haslowe across the room?" Aidan asked dryly.

" 'Tis beside the point. He was drunk. He could have slipped."

"He didn't slip. Gwynne tossed him." The weariness pressed harder into Aidan's temples, and he sighed, jabbing his fingers through his hair. "I know it sounds daft, Rex. Hell, if anyone had told me this same tale six months ago I'd have written him off as a fool," Aidan answered. "But I've seen Gwynne in action, the first time on the battlefield where we'd set up that surprise attack on the rebels two months ago."

Aidan looked back to the ashes in the hearth. "Even at the moment when I realized it was her, I tried to convince myself that it was some kind of dream, sprung from my twisted imaginings. And it almost worked—until she sliced me with her blade." He closed his eyes, remembering. "My arm felt the sting of her weapon as readily as my eyes saw the truth. Gwynne is the Dark Legend."

His foster father scowled. "If that is the truth, then why haven't you handed her over to the king to face the justice she so clearly deserves?"

Aidan looked at him, a bittersweet smile curving his lips. "Ah, yes. 'Tis the question of the hour, isn't it?"

"Aye, it is," Rex grated. "How about answering it?"

Aidan continued looking at him. "I cannot hand Gwynne over to the king for her crimes as the Dark Legend, because that is not all she is to me."

Rex scowled more deeply. "You have qualms, then, about handing her over because she is a woman?"

"Nay—because she is a woman I loved. The same woman who was stolen and killed, or so I thought, by the Welsh rebels who attacked us in the wood beyond Dunston when I was a lad." Aidan swallowed hard, struggling to keep at bay the memories of that morning and all of the painful, bitter feelings they evoked. Rex's sympathetic gaze bore into him, and Aidan knew his foster father was remembering the little he'd been told of the events that had occurred just a few weeks before Aidan had come to live with him.

"Gwynne feels a similar connection to you as well, then?" Rex asked. "That is why she agreed to come to Dunston—to aid in hammering out a peace between her people and England?"

Aidan paused. "Not exactly. She doesn't remember me, or anything about the first fourteen years of her life. She's here because I convinced her that I need her in England for three months in order to dissolve the childhood betrothal I alleged between us. We've struck a peace for that span of time."

"By the Rood, Aidan, what were you thinking to claim such a thing between you?"

"I have reason enough."

Rex cursed under his breath, but Aidan continued his explanation, frowning, as he looked away. "My father told you about the raid in the wood that morning—that I took a Welsh arrow in the chest and was found later by Alana, incoherent, wandering the edges of de Brice land." The backs of Aidan's eyes felt like hot coals as he relived the moment in his mind.

"What he didn't tell you, however, was that it was Gwynne who saved my life that day. We *had* pledged ourselves to each other in secret, that morning, full in the flush of young love. Right after, the Welsh warriors attacked. Gwynne could have run away and hidden when I was wounded, but she chose to stay and help me. The rebels were able to grab her because of it. She hit her head in the struggle, and they disappeared with her, carrying her, lifeless, between them into the woods. 'Twas the last sight I had of her."

Gritting his teeth, he finished, "Suffice it to say that, though I believed her to be dead, she apparently survived—only without her memory intact. She lost all knowledge of herself and of me. What the rebels did to her after that is anyone's guess, but the result is that she believes herself to be the Dark Legend—and she has the battle skills to prove it."

Aidan's foster father shook his head. "By all the Saints, this just gets worse and worse," he muttered.

"Aye, it does. 'Tis a pain that I've lived with for twelve years—now turned into a dilemma I've spent the past two months trying to resolve. You can see why I had no choice except to bring Gwynne to Dunston once I found her again. I owe her a life-debt, Rex, and I couldn't very well repay it by handing her over to be executed."

Rex let out his breath in a whistle. "Christ, I shouldn't even be hearing any of this, Aidan. I am one of King Henry's justiciars. 'Tis my duty to uphold the law—and there is a price on her head." His eyes were shadowed with conflict. "Kinsman or nay, by rights I should be taking the both of you in for what I've learned here today."

"I know, Rex, and I am sorry for it. I never wanted to involve you. 'Tis why I'd kept the truth from Diana as well, to protect her as much as I could." Aidan gave a mocking smile. "I should have known that she'd suspect something eventually—and that she'd use her considerable wiles to get to the truth."

"Aye, well, Diana can be handled for now; she's too frightened about what may happen to gossip of it. But how many others at Dunston know the truth of Gwynne's identity?"

"Most of my men, though they are sworn to silence."

"And what makes you think one of them won't decide

that the king's favor outweighs the honor of his own word?" Rex argued.

"My men are loyal to *me*," Aidan ground out, frowning as he met Rex's challenging stare. "Besides," he added more quietly, knowing the unfavorable reaction he was about to provoke, "several of their comrades' lives weigh in the balance. They will not endanger them by talking."

"Several of their comrades' lives . . . ?" Rex sputtered. "What in blazes did you do, Aidan?"

"The men volunteered," Aidan answered, striding over to the table near the window to pour a goblet of spiced wine. He needed something stronger to drink right now than ale, regardless of the early hour. "We traded with the Welsh. Four of my men for Gwynne, though she ended up bringing two of her bodyguards as well, at the insistence of an older warrior who was with her when I tracked her into the mountains."

Aidan took a long drink, relishing the liquid's bite as it slid down his throat. "I cannot hand her over to the king, because the bargain between us stipulates her safe return to her people for the safe return of my men. I must see her well back to Wales, or my men will die."

"Damn it, man, then send her back to Wales now and be done with it!"

" 'Tis impossible. I would only end up facing her in battle again, and I cannot—I *will* not—raise a weapon against her," Aidan countered, swallowing the bitter taste that rose at the thought of that possibility. He directed his burning gaze on Rex again. " 'Twould be poor repayment for the sacrifice she made for me all of those years ago."

"What alternative do you have? Unless you plan to re-sign your position as the king's leader against the rebels, 'tis your only option."

"Nay, there is another possibility—one I've already commenced. I mean to make Gwynne remember her past with me so that she will refute the Welsh on her own and cease to lead them in their rebellion against England."

Rex stared at him, incredulous. "You cannot be serious . . . ?"

"Aye—'tis the perfect solution. The king will get what he wants, and I will be able to fulfill my life-debt to Gwynne at the same time." Aidan jabbed his hand through his hair again, blowing out his breath in frustration. "God's blood—first Kevyn, and now you . . . why does everyone seem to have such difficulty in seeing the benefit of this plan?"

"Because 'tis idiotic, that's why."

Aidan glared at him.

"What do you really think your chances are of succeeding in this?" Rex asked, returning his glare. "Each day that passes 'tis more dangerous to keep her here; you're inviting trouble, just waiting for someone to discover who she really is. Diana is merely the first, for 'tis the nature of things that sooner or later the truth will out." Rex cursed again. "How long has she been with you already—nearly two months? She hasn't remembered anything yet. What makes you think she ever will?"

"I've seen glimpses of recognition—flashes of memory. I just need a little more time to bring it back the rest of the way, that's all."

"How much more time?" Rex demanded. "I want to know exactly how long you plan to let this go on, Aidan. 'Tis my neck stretched toward the chopping block now as well, you know."

A rush of shame flooded Aidan, followed close by surging resolve. "You won't be complicit in this, Rex, I swear it. You, Diana, or anyone else. 'Tis my choice. I will take full responsibility and face the consequences if it comes to that. It is just something that I need to do. I cannot explain it otherwise."

After a long pause, Rex let out his breath and shook his head. "Much happens in this world that we do not expect, Aidan—outcomes which cannot be controlled by force of pure will. I fear 'tis another of your father's legacies that you try to do so nonetheless, and have since you were a boy." He shook his head again, muttering something about the sins of Gavin de Brice being visited on them all. But then he looked back at Aidan, grim acceptance etched in the lines of his face as he repeated, "So—how much more time do you need?"

"A month," Aidan answered, conflicting feelings of gratitude and regret causing him to speak quietly. "I am close, Rex. I know I am. I will make her remember."

Rex gave him a tired smile. "And what if it comes to naught, Aidan? What if she remembers and still chooses to continue leading the Welsh rebellion?"

Aidan looked away, not wanting to reveal just how often that same question had tormented him in the past weeks. "I will deal with that possibility when I am faced with it," he answered. "But I cannot rest until I have done everything in my power to prevent her from returning to the dangers of the battlefield—or losing her life under the executioner's blade."

"Even if it means losing your own?" Rex countered gently. When Aidan didn't respond, Rex lifted both hands as if in surrender. "Never mind answering. Your mind is made up; I can see that." He walked to the door, his steps heavy, stopping and turning to face Aidan again once he reached the portal. "Just know 'tis a dangerous road you've chosen, lad. I will do my best to help you in any way that I can, but I have my own duty and honor to contend with as well. I will not be able to conceal this forever."

"I know. I wouldn't ask you to."

"One month . . ." his foster-father repeated, and for the first time Aidan noticed how deeply the lines around

Rex's mouth were etched, how dark the circles under his eyes had become . . . signs of age and weariness that had escaped him until now.

"Aye, Rex. I promise," he answered. "One month."

Giving him one long, last look, filled with all the cautions and warnings that Aidan knew he wanted to give but wouldn't, Rex nodded and left the solar.

Aidan stared at the closed door for a moment, the ache in his gut blooming anew. Then, turning to the shutter opening, he gazed out at the pink flush of dawn spreading across the summer sky beyond the castle walls. Before the heat of day set in, everything looked green and fresh, covered as it was in a layer of dew. Another promising morning to mock him, reminding him of the swift passage of time.

*One month.*

'Twas all he had left. After that, it would all come to an end—one way or another, Gwynne would leave him again—with any luck for a future life with a home, a husband, and children. He couldn't keep her here. God help him, as much as he wanted to, as much as the secret, guilty pleasure of being near her haunted him, he knew that he would have to let her go. His duty to his family and to the de Brice name demanded it. And yet the very thought of Gwynne as another man's wife, as the mother to another man's children, set his teeth on edge and shot a pang of agony deep inside him.

But unless he wanted to see her dead in battle or awaiting an ax-blow on the block, it was his only choice.

Breathing deep, he sank into his chair. He'd have to speed things up, intensify his efforts to make her remember. Time was running out, and 'twas getting more complicated by the day. He trusted that neither Diana nor Rex would speak of what they'd learned, but even so, 'twas only a matter of time before someone else figured out the truth in all this. And then there would be bloody hell to pay.

Leaning his head back to rest against the cool, hard wood of his chair, Aidan closed his eyes. There was no help for it; it had to be this way. He'd balance himself on tenterhooks for the next month, doing what his conscience demanded he must for Gwynne, regardless of the pain her eventual leaving would cause him.

And then he'd do his duty to his family and marry Helene.

He gritted his teeth, his hands fisted atop the arms of his chair. 'Twas the only way that he could resolve these two divergent paths in his life, even if it resulted in a bitter ending for him. In his mind he knew the soundness of this truth, even if his heart tried to deny it. Releasing himself to the crippling power of that realization, he thought about all that had gone by in the past, and all that could never be . . .

Knowing that when the moment came for Gwynne to leave him—when he lost her once more, for the last time—his life would become naught but an empty shell again, and he a hollow man.

And it would remain that way forever.

# Chapter 20

Gwynne paused before the solid span of the door to Aidan's solar, overcome with a strange feeling of reticence. She'd experienced that mood more often in these past months than she could ever remember before in her life, and it unsettled her. Clenching her jaw, she resisted the urge to lift her arms into their protective pose across her chest, instead clasping her hands behind her back.

She'd show no weakness, damn it. She'd be strong, even in the face of this new and unexpected assault from within. No matter what, Aidan couldn't know of the tender emotions he'd unleashed inside her. They'd tormented her, growing into sweeping waves of longing that had only intensified last night, and no amount of physical training had been able to ease their power. But she could never let Aidan know that. She'd face him this morn for the sake of her men, and then she'd spend the rest of her enforced time at Dunston keeping as much distance from him as she could.

Ignoring the prick of pain that came at the thought of leaving Dunston and Aidan for good, she blew out her breath. The weight of Dafydd's stare fell on her from his position by her side, and she knew that he sensed her disquiet. But she kept looking straight ahead at the door, fearing that if she met her trusted guard's gaze, he might be able to read the confusion in her eyes.

Last night had made one thing very clear: she couldn't go through with Marrok's request of her; she couldn't keep trying to tempt Aidan. 'Twas far too dangerous. Her emotions for him were becoming so strong and real that she couldn't deny them, but at the same time they filled her with shame. She'd forgotten her duty—her commitment to her people—by allowing herself to soften toward Aidan; he was the Scourge of Wales, embodying all that she'd sworn to fight until death. She was undermining everything she stood for if she allowed herself to fall in love with him.

And yet a part of her couldn't deny the renegade thrill that tingled through her whenever she allowed herself to think of being alone with him at Dunston during these next few days. All alone with him, her men off on the quest she'd directed them to undertake.

*Are you sending them away for that reason, then, and not to forewarn Marrok that you intend to disobey his orders, as you so vehemently claimed?*

"Shall I scratch to gain admittance, *Chwedl*?" Owin murmured from her other side.

"Nay." She tried to put the disturbing thoughts from her mind for the moment, taking another step toward the door. "I'll do it."

Swallowing, she reached up to make the sound to gain entry. A few tense seconds passed, and then the heavy wooden panel creaked open.

Aidan stood just within the portal. Gwynne tried not to

meet his gaze, but even so, the faint whisper of his clean scent—the almost tangible heat of his nearness—sent a twinge through her. She sensed rather than saw him go rigid as he realized who his visitors were. After a pause, he spoke.

"To what do I owe this boon? I'd have thought you all still abed."

"We have some business we need to discuss with you," she answered, lifting her gaze to him at last, and struggling not to react to the ache that filled her as she did. " 'Twill only take a moment, if you'll allow us entrance."

He kept staring at her, and she cursed silently, feeling her face heat under his scrutiny, but then he inclined his head and stepped back, freeing the way for them to come in. Moving a few paces further away, he took up a flagon and lifted a cup toward her.

"Can I interest you in a drink?"

" 'Tis early for spirits," Dafydd said gruffly, as he took his stance next to Gwynne, his arms folded over his chest and his frown centered on Aidan. Owin moved into position as well, his pose identical, so that they flanked her with a seemingly solid wall of protection.

"Perhaps 'tis early for those who've been to bed this night," Aidan answered, nonplussed. "But for the rest of us," he glanced to Gwynne, taking in her training attire and giving her the hint of a smile, " 'tis more like very late." He poured himself a glass and then filled one for her, bypassing Dafydd and Owin when they shook their heads.

Gwynne downed her drink in one swallow, glad for the burning heat of it sliding down her throat; then, leaning forward, she set the empty cup on the table in front of them before resuming her position between her men.

"Owin and Dafydd need to leave Dunston for a few days, to deliver a message directly to Marrok. We came to tell you of our plans," Gwynne said, pausing before adding begrudgingly, "and to make sure that you harbored no concern about it."

Aidan looked startled for a moment, but he recovered quickly enough to ask, "*Both* your men are going? You will remain here alone?"

Heat swelled in Gwynne's cheeks again, and Dafydd stiffened beside her. Neither he nor Owin had been keen on the idea of leaving her here without them, but she'd insisted, claiming that she was well capable of caring for herself for a few days, while the journey into the mountains would be safer with the two of them traveling together.

Now she tipped her chin up as she faced Aidan, her arms drifting up to fold across her chest. "Aye. I will stay on alone for the time being to continue fulfillment of our bargain. Dafydd and Owin will rejoin me here once they've completed their journey."

Aidan studied her, trying to determine her motivation in sending her men off without her. She'd been upset last night; there was no denying it. Hell, what had happened had nearly torn him to pieces as well. It had been all he could do to let her walk away from him after she'd demanded that he let her leave the hall. Later, after most of the guests had departed and he'd gone to check on her, Alana had told him she'd left the main keep dressed in her masculine garments and short cloak. She hadn't returned to her chamber until a few minutes before Rex and Diana had come looking for him.

Aye, the feelings that had raged between them last night had shaken her as much as they had him, he knew; he'd seen it in her eyes, the softness and longing, mixed with confusion. 'Twas what had made her flee to the old security of her training. And yet now she was standing here and telling him she was sending her men away, knowing full well that it would ensure she'd be alone with him for what could be near a week's time.

"Didn't the Welsh messenger just make his appearance the other day for the usual exchange of missives?" he asked, flicking his gaze from Gwynne to her men, in hopes of reading something there that would give him a clue as to what this was really all about. "What is so important that it cannot wait for his next visit?"

" 'Tis something I forgot to include in the message I sent then. It must needs be delivered without delay."

Owin and Dafydd continued to look directly at him, their expressions unreadable, though he picked up an almost imperceptible twitch of the muscle near Dafydd's eye.

"What does it concern?" he asked evenly, maintaining his gaze on her men for another moment before shifting it back to her. He felt a rush of heat fill him at the look in her eyes. 'Twas the same look as last night. But before he could be sure that it wasn't just his own misplaced longings making him see what wasn't there, she glanced away, her mouth tight.

"Sharing the content of my written messages was never part of our agreement."

"Aye. And yet I would have your word that 'tis nothing plotting harm to me or anyone on English soil."

Her cheeks deepened to a bewitching pink. "You have my word. 'Tis nothing of that ilk."

Aidan's heart skipped a beat. Perhaps 'twas just that she wished to be alone with him, then, and she was sending her bodyguards away on a pretext to clear her way to that end. He studied her, trying to cool his unexpected reaction to the thought, before finally nodding. "I have nothing against your decision, then."

"Good. It's settled," she answered, turning with Owin

and Dafydd as if to go. As if she couldn't wait to put distance between herself and him.

"Wait," he called out.

She swiveled to face him. "What is it? My men need to begin their journey soon if they are to make good time."

He paused, surprised at how much he wanted to keep her near him. "I thought you should know that your true identity was discovered by two others last night."

"Who?" she demanded, scowling. "And how?"

"My sister, and through her, my foster father, Rexford de Vere." Aidan glanced to Owin, who, like Dafydd, had twisted around to stare at him from the portal. "Diana bluffed her way into confirming her suspicions with someone close to you."

Owin cursed and took a step forward. "Nay, it cannot be. She acted as if she knew everything when I caught her watching *Chwedl* train last night."

"She was spying on me while I trained?" Gwynne growled, shifting to glare at her younger bodyguard. "Why does no one tell me these things?" She looked back to Aidan, her eyes glittering. "Your sister sorely needs a lesson in respect for others' privacy."

"Aye, I imagine you're right, but for now the damage is done." Aidan sank into a chair, leaning back and rubbing his top lip with his finger. "However, Diana already knows of the dangers involved in telling anyone what she's learned. She will remain quiet about your identity."

"Why should she? She's made no bones about her feelings for me; 'twould be no difficulty for her to see me carted off by King Henry's soldiers," Gwynne scoffed.

"Perhaps, but there is more at risk for her than that," Aidan answered. "If you are arrested, I will be taken also, for harboring you here. And as difficult as it may be for you to believe, my sister does have feelings for others beside herself."

"I can believe it," Owin mumbled, frowning and gazing into the coals in the grate.

Aidan shook his head. "Diana can be quite charming— a caring person when she wants to be. She'll do whatever is necessary to protect me from harm, as angry as she may be with me for bringing you to Dunston. And she's no fool, either, to endanger her own potential marriage match for the sake of indulging pettiness. She will not gossip of your true identity, I assure you."

"And your foster father?" Dafydd asked, again stepping up next to Gwynne, who continued to stand still, her expression black over what he'd told her about Diana.

"He has promised to keep what he has learned to himself as well, for the remainder of your time with me."

" 'Tis too dangerous, *Chwedl*," Dafydd said, frowning as he swung his gaze to her. "We cannot leave you alone here now. De Vere is one of the king's men—he cannot be trusted to remain quiet."

"He can," Aidan grated, standing to face them again. "He has given his word. His oath is equal to mine at the least."

"I do not like it," Dafydd grumbled.

"That cannot be helped." Aidan's temper bit sharper than usual from too little sleep as he faced down the man.

Gwynne sighed, sounding exasperated as she stepped between them. "Enough. All will be well. We go ahead as planned, Dafydd." She gestured toward the door, motioning Owin to go with him. "You'd better get started or 'twill be nightfall before you reach camp."

Dafydd looked as if he might offer more in the way of argument, but Gwynne shook her head, walking with him toward the door. " 'Tis as de Brice said—if I am discovered, he pays the price as well. We've nothing to fear from

Lord de Vere. He would not want his foster son implicated in treason."

Dafydd stopped at the portal. "I still do not like it, *Chwedl*. But as always, I will obey." With a nod to her, he ducked out of the chamber, followed by Owin, who kept his head down as he left.

"Gwynne," Aidan called softly, as she made a move to follow her men.

"Aye," she answered, stilling in the portal.

"I'd have a word with you in private, if you would."

He sensed her tensing—could almost see the long, graceful muscles along her neck tighten, exposed by the hair pulled back at her nape. But after a moment, she leaned out the doorway and murmured something to her men. Then, slowly, as if 'twas difficult for her, she turned to face him again.

"What is it?"

She held herself rigid and in control—but those eyes gave her away. They always had, even when she was a girl, and Aidan fought against the aching well of sadness and longing that opened up at the bittersweet memory of it.

"We have to decide when to complete the second half of our latest agreement," he managed to say.

"I don't know what you mean."

"The arrangement we made when I offered to help you perfect the training exercise Marrok commanded of you—you agreed to teach it to me, as long as I promised to show you one of those my men use. I'd like to do that today sometime, if 'tis meet with you."

"Nay—it isn't necessary."

"Why not? 'Tis what we agreed to," he said, stepping closer, so that they were near enough to touch if either of them possessed the courage to do it.

She looked ready to turn and flee; her hands trembled, though she tucked them behind her back before he could take them in his own as he longed to do. But in the next instant, she'd drawn herself up to her full height, as if shoring up her inner defenses.

" 'Tis not necessary, because it wouldn't be fair," she said. "You learned only a small portion of the Welsh exercise before you were called away so suddenly." Her gaze sharpened, cutting into him. "To attend to your *betrothed*, remember?"

"Aye, I remember," he answered, determined not to let her rattle him. "But I learned enough that 'twould only be right to repay the favor."

"Then I forgive you the repayment."

"Ah, but my honor demands otherwise."

Gwynne made a sound of exasperation, cursing under her breath as she looked away. "I don't wish to spar with you again, Aidan—can't you just accept that?"

"You don't wish to spar with me, or you fear being that close to me again?" he asked softly, touching one finger beneath her chin to ease her gaze back to his.

She went dead still at his touch, though she didn't try to pull away. "We cannot have one without the other."

To anyone else observing, she appeared to be in complete control of herself, but Aidan knew better. She blinked twice, a faint pink staining her cheeks, and her lower lip quavered. But when her tongue darted out to moisten that rosy flesh, a jolt of raw desire shot through him, devastating in its power.

Oh, God, he wanted to kiss her right now. And she wanted it, too, try as she would to deny it. Every inch of her seemed to strain toward him, her mouth full, and moist, and inviting . . .

But he wasn't supposed to be seducing her, damn it. He was only supposed to be trying to help her remember.

Forcing himself to lower his hand from the silky curve of her jaw, Aidan inclined his head in a little bow before taking a step back. "You are right, of course. There is really no need for us to engage in training to satisfy the agreement."

"I am glad you see the wisdom of that," Gwynne murmured, turning away stiffly, looking drained, somehow, by their encounter. She cleared her throat. "And now I'm afraid I've tarried too long. I should see to my men. If you'll excuse me . . ."

"Wait—I didn't say that our agreement needn't be satisfied at *all*." He feigned surprise at her attempt to leave. "I'm sure that there are several other interesting ways that we might conclude this bargain between us."

After a stunned silence, Gwynne muttered, "By the Rood, I don't think I can endure it." She cast a baleful look at him. "What's it to be, then—more berry picking? A new kind of dancing perhaps?" Jamming her arms into place across her chest, she added, "Do me a courtesy, will you, Aidan? The next time I'm foolish enough to think about entering into one of your so-called wagers with you, remind me to run in the other direction."

He smothered a smile. "You make it sound so unpleasant. And here I thought I was providing you with some peaceful diversion from the life of a warrior."

"I'll take battle and mayhem any day."

"Mayhem, hmmmm . . . ?" he echoed, rubbing a finger across his upper lip as if considering the possibility. "Unfortunately, I was thinking of something less violent— like an offering of music, perhaps." He raised his brows and wiggled them at her. "I've been known to play the lute on occasion. If you agreed to let me play some tunes for you . . ." He nodded, acting pleased with himself. "Aye, it might just be enough to satisfy my end of our bargain. What say you to the idea?"

"I'd say you're as unbalanced as ever," Gwynne mumbled, shaking her head at him, though he noticed that she couldn't completely suppress the glint of humor in her eyes at his outlandish suggestion.

"Come—'twill be painless, I assure you." Flashing her a grin, he cocked his head, giving an exaggerated glance to the ceiling. "At least, I think it will. I admit, it has been years since I played, but I'm sure I couldn't have completely lost my skill in that space of time . . ."

She shook her head, a smile flirting over her lips. Then she sighed, giving him a look that, though he knew she didn't intend it, still set his blood afire. "God help me for saying this, but I suppose it sounds harmless enough. All right. If it makes you happy and will satisfy that damned *honor* of yours, then I have no objection to going along with your plan."

"I'm afraid 'twould take far more from you than that to make me truly happy," he answered, giving her a teasing look. "But it will do for a start."

She flushed again, this time walking away from him, toward the door. "Just tell me where and when I should expect to receive this boon, Aidan—because I believe I'll need to fortify myself for it."

"Tonight, I think," he called after her retreating form.

She flashed him a sideways look the instant before she disappeared out the door, a glance filled with an array of emotions—caution, yearning, and humor all mixed together—that made his heart flop in his chest. And then she was gone.

He ached to hold her again, to caress away her fears. 'Twas a feeling he'd experienced countless times with her, both in their early years together and since he'd found her again—an urge to comfort her and share the burdens of life in a way that he'd never known with any other woman. Whether or not she was a legendary warrior now, she still inspired that same instinct in him.

Shaking his head at his own foolish musings, he slowly

walked over to the large chest tucked into the corner of the chamber. He'd been contemplating whether or not he should use its contents all morning; kneeling down now, he rested his hand on the clasp, hesitant. It had been a long time since he'd last steeled himself against the surge of emotions that came from daring to peer inside it. But perhaps 'twould be different this time, he thought. Before, he'd believed that Gwynne was dead. Now that he'd found her again, it might finally be different.

Leaning back on his heels, he unfastened the lid; it creaked open, the hinges groaning from disuse, revealing a tumble of creamy fabric that he'd long ago placed over the objects inside to protect them from dust and damp. He lifted the cloth aside, and the movement sent up a whisper of fragrance. 'Twas the perfumed scent of springtime leaves, a hint of mountain breeze . . .

*Her* scent . . .

Closing his eyes, Aidan paused, swept back to that other place, that other time. His heart thundered; he felt every beat course through his body, each throb bringing back another moment, another sweet memory of Gwynne. He opened his eyes again, clenching his fist to still the trembling before pushing aside the fabric to reach the items beneath. His touch first brushed over his old tunic, still bearing the bloodied, ragged-edged hole ripped by the Welsh arrow. He'd kept the ruined garment as evidence of Gwynne's sacrifice—a tangible reminder of why 'twas his duty to be relentless in battle against the rebels. Of why he must continue to be the Scourge of Wales.

A half dozen other objects rested at the bottom of the chest as well, all gleaned from the scene of the attack; he'd dragged himself back there the day after, sneaking from his chambers, hunched over and wracked with pain in order to do it. Old Alana had tried to begin nursing him back to health, but he'd resisted, needing to go back, to see the destruction left in the wake of the ambush—to touch the gouts of dirt that had been dug from the ground during their struggle, and hear the wind whistle through the empty shell of the cottage Gwynne had shared with her mother.

Aye, he'd combed the area, desperate to find any scrap, anything to tell him that she had been there—that his Gwynne had been alive and real, and that their time together hadn't been just a dream, crushed under the onslaught of those blue-faced devils.

That day he'd gathered all he could find and then stumbled back to Dunston, swathing them lovingly in cloth and placing them into this chest, to be opened and thought about as often as his brutalized heart could bear. It had been more than a year before he'd been able to look into the trunk for the first time. Each time after, the emotions and memories had ripped through him anew, making him feel raw inside. But he'd kept scraping the wound, reliving every moment. He'd felt he owed Gwynne that, at least.

This time was different; he could sense it. He could look at these things with fresh eyes—feel new emotions that might banish the others for good.

Next to his bloodstained tunic lay a wreath of wildflowers that Gwynne had worn in her hair that day—a circlet of woodland blooms he'd fashioned for her—crumpled in the attack and dried now from age. He set it carefully aside, seeking the other items . . . a shawl of Gwynne's, taken from the cottage . . . a feather from one of the crows she'd healed . . . the old, scratched up lute, broken now, that he used to play for her during their secret trysts . . . a few of the acorns she'd playfully thrown at him that last morning . . .

And then finally he saw it: their rumpled, silken betrothal cloth, cradling the braided lock of her hair.

These two things he touched last, as always. Gingerly,

he took them out of the shadowy protection of the chest, holding them up to the light. Remembering.

His heart swelled as he held them, but not with an unbearable ache, as before. This time there was a fullness of feeling he was at a loss to explain. Lifting them up, he pressed them to his face, breathing in their scent, so delicate after all these years; he felt the smooth quality of the cloth, and the even more silken texture of her braided tresses, soft against his cheek. Aidan closed his eyes again, his throat tightening. He sat that way for a long time, his pulse beating shallow and uneven, a burning sensation gathering behind his eyelids.

Finally, he exhaled and swallowed, opening his eyes to lay everything except the lute back into the trunk; then he arranged the cloth atop them once more, and closed the chest.

Rising to his feet, he picked up the old instrument and carried it to the window, still caught up in his thoughts. His fingers absently stroked its roughened wooden surface as he peered out the open shutter to the courtyard below.

The bustle of the day was already well under way, with villagers and castle folk going about their business. In the far distance, near the castle gate, he caught a glimpse of Gwynne; she'd changed once again into her feminine garb, and it seemed that she was readying to see her men off on their journey. When Owin and Dafydd rode their mounts through the open portcullis, she turned to disappear back into the maze of buildings near the old stables.

Aidan held the lute tightly in his grip, rocking back on his heels as his gaze trained on the spot where she'd last been.

"Ah, Gwynne," he murmured, "it seems that you and I have our work cut out for us in the weeks ahead."

In a few short hours, Helene and her father would leave for home; then he would be free to begin his part of the work in earnest. He'd never planned to use the precious items in the trunk in his efforts to jar Gwynne's memory; they were too personal, too dear to him. If she didn't remember their meaning, or, worse yet, did and scoffed at them anyway, he wasn't sure that he could bear the pain of it.

But the alternative was worse, he knew, and he had only one short month left to make this work. He needed to use every method at his disposal to bring back her memory in that time, even if it meant wrenching his own heart from his chest and laying it bloodied at her feet to do it.

Clenching his jaw in resolution of his plan, he stepped back from the open shutter and tucked the lute under one arm, jabbing his other hand through his hair as he braced himself to begin the painful process ahead of him.

"Aye, Gwynne, you will remember me," he repeated softly. "You will remember *us*, and the love we once shared . . ." Pausing, he reached out to brush his palm over the cool, grainy lid of the closed chest once more, thinking, planning how to use the objects nestled within, no matter the pain it caused him. Then, raising his hand, he touched his fingers to his lips in a kiss to seal his vow.

"I do so swear it."

# Chapter 21

Gwynne slumped in her chair in the corner of the great hall, uncertain whether she wanted to scream, laugh, cry, or shout. 'Twas a feeling she'd been struggling with for more than two days already, ever since Owin and Dafydd had departed for Wales—the same day Helene and her father had left for their own estate; if she couldn't get rid of the unsettling urge soon, she knew she would snap. Perhaps she'd rip the tapestries from the walls or throw a few chairs from atop Dunston's crenellated towers; whatever she did, she knew that she needed to take some kind of action to dispel her edginess, or there would be disastrous results. 'Twas but a matter of time.

People bustled around her, everyone busy doing something to prepare for the morning meal. Only Diana was conspicuously absent, having kept mostly to her chambers since the day after the celebration. It was just as well they hadn't faced each other, Gwynne thought. 'Twould be uncomfortable at best, now that the woman knew the truth about her. Besides, she'd have gone into conniptions over her brother's actions lately, if she'd witnessed them.

Curling her fingers so that her nails dug into her palms, Gwynne breathed in deeply; she tried closing her eyes to ease the burning there, but 'twas no use. What happened whenever she did that was exactly why she hadn't slept for the past two nights; images of Aidan blended with those awful, nagging sensations she'd experienced when she'd first come to Dunston, leaving her no rest.

And then there was the nightmare. It had returned with a vengeance, though, as with the last time, the dream woman looked healed and pristine compared to her earlier condition in the visions.

"Did you enjoy Lord Sutcliffe's performance last night?"

Gwynne swung her gaze to Alana, who was sitting nearby, sorting through a bowl of fruits that sat perched on her lap. The old woman flicked a sideways gaze at her and smiled as she spoke; Gwynne scowled in response, the question having sent another burning image of Aidan through her, unbalancing her emotions the way it had every time he'd insisted on playing that old, scarred lute for her—the way it had last night, when, just before his performance in the hall, he'd gifted her with a circlet of fresh wildflowers from the fields beyond Dunston.

"Nay. I don't recall much of it," she lied, hoping to end the conversation before it began. "I was too tired to pay attention."

"Ah," Alana murmured, nodding. "How unfortunate. Those old songs—it seemed his heart was bleeding into the words he sang . . ." She shook her head, still smiling as she clucked her tongue. "Why, it made me long for my younger years, it did. He used to play so when he was a lad, in love for the first time. 'Twas a good deal of time ago, but I remember it well."

Gwynne shifted uncomfortably, the nagging sensation swelling anew at the back of her brain. Damn the old woman and her chatter. She'd thought it safe to spend her time this morn in the great hall, away from any possibility of finding herself alone with Aidan.

She'd been unable to stop the yearning that overwhelmed her every time he was near, most especially when no one else was around. Even though he hadn't made an effort to kiss or hold her again since the night of the celebration, his very presence continued to send waves of longing spooling through her, a yearning for the kind of closeness she would never—*could* never—have with him. 'Twas becoming too painful to bear. She'd thought that by coming here, where activity reigned and the people of Dunston could serve as a buffer between them, she might find some peace.

But she hadn't taken Old Alana into account when she'd made her decision.

Humming a few bars of one of the tunes Aidan had played last night, Alana continued sorting through the berries, only glancing up to murmur, "So . . . having trouble sleeping again, are you?"

Gwynne squirmed even more under her knowing stare; she answered in a mumble, "A bit. I—I must be coming down with something, is all."

Inwardly cringing at how foolish she sounded, Gwynne suddenly curled to sit forward, balancing her forearms on her knees. She picked at her skirts before lacing her fingers loosely, tapping them together and fidgeting in her seat. Curse it, but she felt unsettled. And it was all thanks to Alana's pestering, she told herself. 'Twas the only thing it could be.

It had nothing to do with Aidan's imminent arrival to the hall, for example. Nothing at all.

"Do you feel ill otherwise?"

"What?" Gwynne asked, pulled from her brooding.

"You said you were coming down with something," the old woman persisted, her expression inscrutable. "Aside from your sleeplessness, do you have any other complaints—aching muscles, sore eyes—anything?"

"Nay—" Gwynne frowned, before remembering that she needed to sound convincing in her complaints. "—I mean, aye. I've some aching in my back and neck."

"That's as like from all the training you've been doing as anything else," Alana cackled, fixing her with that sidelong gaze again. "Are you planning to burn off your troubles with more of the same again today?"

"I suppose I am," Gwynne growled, her black mood rising as she glared at the old woman. Alana's amused expression did nothing to ease her chagrin. " 'Tis my duty to maintain my skills while I'm held captive here," she added, even knowing that it sounded defensive.

"I see," Alana murmured, looking suspiciously like she was about to smile. "Of course, Lord Sutcliffe allowing you unlimited time for your pursuits must help a great deal; 'tis very kind of him, considering your . . . *captive* status."

" 'Twas part of our bargain, is all," Gwynne retorted. "I hardly think he deserves congratulations for it."

Alana nodded wordlessly, making a noncommittal sound while that same smile toyed with her lips. "So, are you beginning your exercises for the day soon?"

Gwynne gaped at her. If she didn't know better, she'd think Alana was trying to get rid of her. With a snort, she pushed herself to her feet, reaching down to swipe up her discarded veil in one hand. "To be honest, I wasn't planning to go until after the noon meal, but somehow the idea suddenly seems more appealing right now." She headed toward the door that led to the upper chambers, where her training gear was stored while her men were away, but before she'd reached halfway to the portal, it swung open, and Aidan walked in.

Pausing for but an instant, Gwynne braced herself for the torrent of feeling that she knew would follow next. His gaze locked with hers and yearning, swirled together with regret for what could never be, swept through her in waves. Gritting her teeth against it, she dragged her stare from his, ignoring his cheerful "Good morn!" as she veered around him to go out the door.

Curse it, but she couldn't go on like this much longer. She covered the length of the corridor outside the great hall in a few strides. Bunching her skirts around her knees, she took the steps to the upper chambers two at a time, lurching into her room to yank her training garments and cloak from her clothing trunk. Then she stalked to the corner of the chamber and pushed aside the tapestry, revealing the little niche where she'd been concealing her sword, its sheath, and her practice shield while her men were away and unable to hold them for her. But what she saw struck her like a blow to the chest.

*Her sword was gone.*

In the next instant, prickles of stunned disbelief shot to the ends of her fingers and up her spine to encase her skull in a tingling web.

*Someone had stolen her sword.*

The culprit must have sneaked into her chamber without notice sometime this morn, between the time she'd gone to break her fast and now, because she'd checked on her weapons before she'd descended to the great hall.

It had to be someone who knew about who she really was and what she was doing here—and other than her own men and Aidan's friend Kevyn, who never came above stairs, that left only three possibilities. And she'd bet her boots she knew just exactly who it was.

*Damn the shrew to everlasting hell . . .*

"Diana!" Gwynne roared, tossing her masculine clothing and cape onto her bed as she slammed out of her room and into the hall. "Get out here and show your face if you dare! For once and all, you and I are going to—"

"She's not in the castle at the moment, I'm afraid. She's been out all morn."

Gwynne slid to a halt; whirling around, she saw Old Alana standing near the top of the stairway, hunched over as always, her sparkling gaze both kind and penetrating.

"Tell me where she went," Gwynne managed to say, still breathing heavily through her rage. "Because I'm going to hunt her down. She's taken my sword, and—" Her voice drifted off at the sight of Alana shaking her head. Soft clicking sounds came from the old woman's lips, and she was smiling.

" 'Tis unwise, child, to leap to conclusions as you do."

Gwynne scowled. "What—are you saying that she didn't take it?"

Alana just kept shaking her head and smiling, until Gwynne thought that she'd go mad with the repetition of motion. With another growl of rage, she spun away from the old woman and stalked down the hall. Flinging open the door to Aidan's chamber, Gwynne swung around, seeking a likely hiding place. Why he'd take her weapon and hide it on her now, she had no idea, but he'd been doing so many strange things lately that nothing would surprise her.

Her gaze lit on the massive bed that dominated the room, her rage ebbing just a bit as the realization that she was intruding on his personal domain took hold. The place where he was most vulnerable each night as he slept. But in the next instant she pushed aside her guilt, and all her softer thoughts of Aidan with it; she needed to concentrate. 'Twas his fault she'd been forced to barge in here. His alone. He had no right to take anything of hers, especially her weapon, and if she invaded his privacy by being here to search for it, then so be it.

Swallowing hard, she yanked her gaze from the bed to peruse the rest of the chamber. Other than a standing closet, there was nothing in the room large enough to conceal her sword. Walking over to the closet, she pulled the door open, ignoring the heat that filled her cheeks anew at rifling through Aidan's most personal belongings. She found some garments and a cape or two, but aside from that the closet was bare. She spun to face the center of the room again.

There was nothing. Not even a tapestry on the wall with which to hide her blade.

*Of course.* Aidan wouldn't keep her sword or any weapon in his bedchamber. He'd store the bulk of his equipment in his armor room—though she doubted he'd bring her sword there, even in an effort to tease her, as all the weaponry he possessed would be carefully inventoried and kept in good order by his chief armorer. He'd not want the man to question the sudden appearance of a strange blade among the supply; 'twould raise the possibility of further discovery, which would only endanger them all.

Nay, he'd have taken her sword somewhere else. Somewhere where he alone would have it, without interference of maidservants, squires, or other castle-dwellers.

*His solar . . .*

Aye . . .

Crossing Aidan's bedchamber in three strides, Gwynne threw open the door and stomped into the hallway, her gaze focused on the stairs that led to the lower floor and Aidan's solar. As she passed by, she could just see Old Alana from the side of her vision, still standing where she'd left her moments ago; the old woman absently rubbed her gnarled, wrinkled hands together atop her walking cane.

"The trunk in the corner," Alana called out softly, as Gwynne began to descend the stairwell. "Check the old trunk in the corner . . ."

Her words hardly sank in until Gwynne gained entrance to Aidan's solar chamber. Her fury had swelled with each action taken to regain her weapon, until now her vision seemed blinded by the hot, surging emotion engulfing her. 'Twas as much a build-up of the other confusing feelings that had been tormenting her of late, her conscious mind knew, but her body reacted only to the moment. By the time she closed the door of Aidan's quiet haven, her muscles felt strung tight enough to snap.

Heat burned the backs of her eyelids, and she clenched her fists, chest heaving as she took in the burnished wooden surfaces of this tasteful room, the chiseled stone hearth and polished metalwork, paralyzed from moving, for a moment, thanks to the force of her rage.

How dare he mock her so with this latest prank? 'Twas bad enough when he'd teased her with the dancing lessons, the picnic, the sweetly sung tunes, the circlet of flowers—treating her as if she were some Court lovely and he an enamored swain. But *this*, she thought, dumping out the basket of metal rods and pokers that perched near the hearth, in quest of her sword—this crossed over into *her* realm, *her* life, scoffed at what had always meant most to her and had served as her salvation when all else seemed lost.

She lurched forward, rifling through the stack of parchments on the massive table in order to look beneath them, and then stomped to the center of the chamber for a better vantage point.

*Curse his eyes, but this time he'd . . .*

Suddenly, she stopped, her gaze fixed to one corner of the room. There it was. The old, battered trunk that Alana had spoken of in those last moments above stairs. Perhaps the old woman knew something more than she'd wanted to admit, after all. Stalking over to the chest with jerky steps, Gwynne dropped to one knee and examined the latch. It didn't seem to be locked. She rattled the metal clasp and then lifted the piece that jutted below the rest; it made a popping sound and the clasp released.

Without hesitation, she raised the lid and pushed away the soft covering inside, looking for her weapon. The gentle whisper of a familiar scent floated up to her, sending a tingle through her brain, and she stiffened as her gaze fell on what had been resting just below the protection of the fabric.

A dried-up circlet of flowers, aged almost to dust.

*Wildflowers,* her mind somehow supplied. *From the meadow beyond Dunston. . . .*

Of a sudden, her throat tightened, and a heaviness gathered behind her eyes. She frowned, feeling disjointed and staring down as if from a distance at her own body going through its motions; reaching out, she brushed her hands over what lay beneath the circlet. Her fingers stroked a shiny black crow's feather, lying amongst a small pile of cool, shiny acorns . . . then, below that, a woolen shawl, obviously homespun, yet softened from much wear, resting atop a young man's bloodied tunic, the ragged-edged hole in the chest showing where the wound had been delivered.

*What the devil is all of this?* her mind screamed through the stretching, aching feeling that began to burgeon inside of her. *And what in God's name is happening to me . . . ?*

All thoughts of her missing sword vanished under the assault of painful sensation. She felt as if she were teetering on the edge of a whirlpool—a huge, grasping tide of something that would swallow her whole.

At that moment her hand touched a swath of rolled fabric—a length of silk, deep emerald in hue, embroidered with a faded white cross. As she lifted it up, phantom pain lanced up from her palm, cutting a path along her arm and shoulder to bury itself in her chest, high and to the left. A burning spot that felt as if she'd just been pierced by an arrow.

With a gasp she dropped the cloth, and it rolled onto the floor of the solar, the folds of material falling open to reveal a braid of ebony hair, thick and glossy.

*Hair the same exact shade as her own . . .*

As if struck by a blow, Gwynne doubled over, burying her face in her hands as she fought against the images. They spun slowly at first, then faster and faster as they rose from the depths of their black prison in her mind, crackling bits of light and color that started to come together . . .

Oh, God . . . Oh, God . . . Oh, God . . .

*Aidan gazed at her, smiling so that it reached up to the velvety depths of his eyes; then he took a deep breath and began his vows.*

*"I, Aidan de Brice, son of Gavin de Brice, second Earl of Sutcliffe, do take thee, Gwynne ap Moran, to be my wife. I love thee with all my heart and soul, and will bind myself to thee forever, with this my eternal vow. I do so swear it."*

*Gwynne glanced down at the embroidered betrothal cloth draped round their joined hands, feeling the late summer sun beat down on their heads. A pair of sparrows danced and chirruped through the sky above them, and she smiled up at Aidan tremulously. "And I, Gwynne ap Moran, take thee, Aidan de Brice, to be my husband. I love thee with all that I am, and will keep myself only to thee until the end of time. This I so swear and will abide, heart and soul, until I die."*

*Ducking her head, she dared a glance at him from be-neath her lashes. Her heart throbbed with the love she felt for him. He was so wonderful, so caring. Her one true knight and lord of her heart, even if she was but a peasant lass and he the heir to an Earldom. They were as one now; they'd sworn their love in this ancient circle, and none could ever part them now. They would be one, always.*

*Always . . .*

A blinding flash erupted again in Gwynne's mind, yanking her out of that memory and into another. She cried out and pitched forward, her palms slamming against the open edges of the old trunk as she groped for the bloodied tunic at the bottom; when she found it, she pulled it to her chest, clinging to it, as the second memory hit with staggering force . . . images of the attack and Aidan's wounding. Of the warrior snatching her away after she'd healed Aidan, and the pain and blackness when she'd hit her head . . .

A sound in the doorway wrenched Gwynne from her agony, dragging her back to the present. She blinked a few times, dazed as she sat in front of the open trunk, trying without success to absorb the shock of what she'd just experienced. Her head throbbed, and her body felt numb—yet somehow she managed to turn to see who had opened the door and found her here.

It took a moment for the sight of Aidan to seep into her awareness; the Aidan of here and now. Her mind still sizzled and ached with the disjointed images of her past—of the entire first fourteen years of her life, jabbing, now, into her awareness with razor-sharp intensity. She took in a shuddering breath, keeping her gaze fixed upon Aidan, her hands gripping his old tunic as if it were her rope to salvation.

"Gwynne—?"

The sound of her name uttered in his husky voice, so

uncertain, so filled with concern, shook her from her numbness, unleashing a rush of love for him that rocked her to the core. She choked back a sob; wet heat slid down her cheeks—tears that, released now by her memories, seemed to flow without end.

She searched Aidan's face with her gaze; his eyes were shadowed, the expression in them as stunned and anguished as she felt. A thousand memories of him—the perfect completion of their life together up to the moment of her kidnapping—clicked into place, blending seamlessly with new memories of the past few months, and making the ache inside her bloom anew. She sobbed again, his blood-stained tunic falling from her hand as she lurched to her feet.

Blinded by her tears, she shook her head and charged forward, pushing past Aidan and out the door, needing to get away—to run from him, the memories, and the truth. The painful, awesome truth.

*Aidan had loved her, and she had loved him in return.*

It was true; they'd promised themselves to each other in the ancient stone circle, vowing to be one for eternity. And then her people—the same people she'd served all these years, the people for whom she'd sacrificed herself on the altar of the Dark Legend—had crashed into her peaceful existence and stolen her away, destroying whoever she'd once been, forever.

She ran, choking back sobs, from Aidan's solar, the damning knowledge crashing into her, relentless and brutal . . .

Hammering into her the realization that, from this moment on, the world as she knew it would never be the same again.

# Chapter 22

Gwynne's breath rasped in her throat, burning her lungs as she made her way through the keep, heedless of the stares; she fled out the main door of the hall and through the castle gate with its raised portcullis—just running, trying to escape the agony rocking inside of her. She had no plan or intent for where she was going, but by the time she stopped, she grasped in some cloudy corner of her mind that she'd escaped to a familiar place.

Her chest heaved as she gasped for air, and her eyelids felt swollen; sitting back on her heels in the grass, she looked around, trying to regain some sense of balance. God help her, but she'd come to the spot where Aidan had taught her to dance. Right next to where he'd staged their false berry-picking contest . . . the same spot where he'd kissed her for the first time.

But something else nagged at the very back of her mind. Narrowing her gaze the best as she could, Gwynne looked around once more, with the fresh and aching wisdom of her regained memories—and in that instant her insides wound tighter, her heart feeling as if it had just been yanked from her chest.

Oh, God, this wasn't just the spot where Aidan had spent so much of his time with her these past weeks—'twas the clearing that had been nestled inside the ancient circle of stones all those years ago.

*The very place where they had pledged themselves to each other forever on the day the rebels had stolen her away.*

*Oh, God . . .*

Stumbling to her feet, Gwynne staggered forward again, toward the edge of the glade, where the grasses shifted to forest bracken; she searched the area, desperate to find the stones that should mark the circle. Naught met her vision but waving ferns and wildflowers, backed by the darkening fringe of forest beyond.

*Where were the stones?* 'Twas the spot, her ravaged mind insisted. But the jutting sentinels that had encircled this clearing were gone—gone, as if they'd never been.

Gone like the life she and Aidan had been meant to share.

Sinking to her knees again, she gave in at last to the pain; it took hold of her, and she buckled under its weight. Crying out, she curled forward, unable to stop it from filling her, unleashing its crippling power.

"Gwynne!"

Aidan knelt down in the grass next to her, and the touch of his hands somehow pushed her over the tenuous edge of control; she twisted into his arms, pressing her face to his chest and gripping fistfuls of his shirt as if she'd never let go.

"I feared I wouldn't find you," he murmured, stroking her hair as he cradled her against him, rocking her in his arms. "Why did you run? I want to help you—I can help you get through all of this . . ."

"Where are the stones?" she croaked, the question suddenly seeming more important than anything to her. As if the answer might somehow unlock the mystery of this entire tragedy for her—make sense out of that which defied reason.

Aidan didn't answer at first.

"The stones of our circle," she repeated hoarsely. "What happened to them? I remember them . . . I remember them being right here . . ."

"I knocked them down."

He still held her close, and she reveled in the warmth and safety she felt in his arms; his breath riffled her hair as he continued quietly, "After the attack, I couldn't bear the sight of them. A few months later I came out here and took the rage I felt at losing you out on them." He loosened his hold on her, enough to let her look in the direction he indicated.

"Look over there. You can still see a piece of one on the ground."

She followed his gaze and saw it, finally—a gray lump of stone lying flat, almost obscured under a thick blanket of moss. She stared at it for a moment before looking around the little clearing again, all the memories of her time here with Aidan washing over her anew. So much time spent living her sweet, simple existence—time spent loving Aidan—and she had lost it all to a life of violence and war . . .

"My God . . ." she whispered, her voice cracking with the strain. "I still cannot believe 'tis real . . ."

Looking back to him, she studied his face; her eyes felt hot and achy, and her hand trembled as she stroked it across his brow, her fingers smoothing down his temple and cheek, to the firm line of his jaw.

"It has all come back to you, then?" he asked. He took

a sharp breath as he caught her hand and brought it down from his face to cradle it in his own warm grip.

"Aye." She swallowed against the thick feeling in her throat. "It hurts, but I remember it all."

She touched her hand to his chest, on the same spot where the arrow had pierced him during that long-ago ambush.

"I remember you leaping into the clearing to save me, to give me time to get away," she said softly. "And I remember the arrow striking you—" She broke off, overcome with the pain the memory brought, fresh as it was, now in her mind.

"Then you must remember healing me as well. Like you did with Clara."

"Aye." She looked at him, wanting him to see in her eyes all she felt for him. "It seems we saved each other that day."

Aidan shook his head. "I should have done more. I should have found a way to stop them."

The memory of their last moments together surged up again, tiny, aching bursts of light in her brain. She sucked in her breath, reaching up to brush her fingers against Aidan's temple, the place where the warrior had kicked him. *Futile*. It had been futile to try to stop them from taking her, but Aidan had given all he had . . .

"You couldn't have done more," she whispered, the ache swelling and her heart beating heavy in her chest, "Not then. They were grown men to your fifteen years; 'twas a miracle you survived at all."

Aidan looked stricken. "I wished I hadn't afterward." He held her, gazing deep into her eyes. "I kept asking myself over and over why it couldn't have been me—why they wanted you, even after it seemed that you were dead to us all . . ."

"Aye—I remember hitting my head," she murmured,

frowning as the rest of the shadowy image sliced through
her, a memory of throwing herself backward in her cap-
tor's arms, only to feel pain bursting over her skull, followed by blackness.

" 'Twas one of the cottage joists," Aidan supplied quietly, brushing her hair back from her brow and holding her
against him again as he spoke. "You hit your head struggling to escape. You went limp and so still, I thought your
neck had been broken," he said, his voice gone hoarse
with emotion. "I tried to follow you—I swear I did. I
wanted to hunt them down and reclaim your body, but I
was too weak from the arrow wound, and Father refused
to send any of his men to search."

She closed her eyes, pressing her cheek to him and listening to the steady beating of his heart; after a moment he
continued, "I thought that you were dead, Gwynne, you
must believe me. 'Tis why I was so shocked to see you on
the field near Craeloch Castle—I couldn't believe you
were alive—that it was really you standing in front of me,
swinging your blade like a virago."

"I am sorry about that," she murmured against his shirt,
her mouth curving into the nearest thing to a smile she'd
been able to muster in days. "I had no idea 'twas you."

"Aye, well, the fault was mine for standing there like a
fool while you took a swing at me."

"I believe the word I used when describing you to Marrok was *idiot*," she said, hearing Aidan's chuckle even as
her grief sharpened at the latent thought of her mentor. He
had betrayed her, kept her in the dark about the person
she'd been and all that she'd lost after her injury in the abduction, telling her instead that she'd been stolen as a babe
by the English and rescued by her own people years later.
Her entire life from the moment she'd lost her memory
until now had been a lie.

She closed her eyes again, too exhausted by the rush of

emotion to think on it further. Tired to the bone of the upheaval and shadows that had been stirred up inside her by it all . . .

"*Lugh*, but my head hurts," she murmured.

"I'm not surprised," Aidan answered. "You've endured a great deal in the past half hour."

"But I'm not used to feeling so shaky; if I tried to get up, I'd likely crumple right back to the ground."

"There's no shame in that, after what you've experienced," he answered, still stroking her hair back from her face, soothing her as he held her against him. "By God, you've been stronger through all this than anyone I've known could have been."

Aidan looked down at her, saw the way she held herself so carefully against him, trusting him implicitly. *Just as before*, a voice inside him whispered, *just as it was all those years ago, when she loved you*.

Jesu, but he wanted to kiss her right now, wanted it more than he'd ever wanted anything. He could lean down and take her lips with his own this very moment; he knew it. She'd not resist. As vulnerable as she was feeling right now, she'd surely kiss him back, press herself against him, and wrap her arms round his neck. 'Twould be so easy to shift his weight and tilt his head just a little . . .

Aidan cleared his throat and rose to his knees, stifling his baser instincts as he gently tugged her into the same position. "You need some rest after all that's happened. Come—I'll take you back to your chamber, and when you awaken, I'll order a warm bath and some food sent up."

"Nay." She clenched her fingers in the fabric of his shirt, locking her arms. "Let's not go back yet—please." The fervor in her voice surprised him. She sounded sure of herself, as if she knew exactly what she wanted . . .

He met her gaze, startled at the passion he saw there, the softness and longing. The silvery depths of her eyes

were turbulent now with emotions that held her in sway—
and awareness crashed into him with staggering force.
Aye, she knew what she wanted; she wanted *him*.

Oh, God . . .

She shifted on her knees, and he was acutely aware of
the way her breasts and belly brushed against him. 'Twas
just barely, but it was enough to send a thrill of heat
through him—a spiraling, burning sensation that scorched
him to his soul. Instinctively, his body tightened, all his
muscles contracting beneath her touch.

"Gwynne—"

He broke off to a little growl. He glanced away before
exhaling and swinging his gaze back to her, feeling like a
drowning man about to lose his battle with the waves
crashing over his head.

"I don't think 'twould be a good idea to stay here
longer." He swallowed hard. "You need your rest, and—"

Uttering a husky moan, Gwynne jerked him closer by
fistfuls of his shirt, taking his mouth with hers and stilling
any remaining arguments he might have offered. She
melted into him, clinging tighter as they kissed. It felt so
right, so natural, that he simply kept kissing her back, his
mind shutting down to all of the reasons why he shouldn't
be doing this with her, why he had no right, now that she'd
regained her memory, to allow this kind of affection between them.

"We have to stop," he managed to mutter hoarsely
against her mouth, barely keeping himself from kissing
her more, so great was his craving, his need for her. "We
have to stop now, Gwynne, or I don't think I'll be able
to—"

"Then don't," she murmured. "Don't stop, Aidan,
please."

She pulled back a little, and he saw that her cheeks
were flushed; with a gentle smile, she lifted her hands to

cup his face, stroking her fingers lightly down until her thumbs brushed a sensual pattern over his lips.

"I remember it all, Aidan," she said softly, one of her hands drifting down along the line of his jaw, across his shoulder to his chest, and he closed his eyes and sucked in his breath at the exquisite sensation of her touch.

"I remember what we were to each other all those years ago," she continued. "What we'd planned for our future . . . what we were about to do when the attack began . . ."

She pressed her lips to his neck, a tender caress that wound the heat inside of him higher. "Heaven help me, Aidan, but I've spent my life since that day fighting and killing—training to be a warrior. To be a Legend." She gazed into his eyes, staring deep, touching his soul as she had that long ago day. "Teach me to be a woman again. Teach me to be *your* woman, as I was meant to be from the start . . ."

"Oh, God, Gwynne, I want to," he answered, his voice ragged with the desire pulsing through him. "I want it more than you could ever know."

"Then stay here with me now."

A war waged in Aidan's heart, a fierce, violent battle, whose outcome, he knew, would be more crucial than any he'd ever fought on the field. He struggled with it, the force of his desire matched against his sense of duty, uncertain which would prove the victor. But when Gwynne touched him again, leaning into him, he knew that it had gone beyond his control—a realization that was sealed with the words she uttered next.

"Make love to me now, Aidan," she murmured, her eyelashes fluttering against his cheek as she tipped her head to press another kiss to his jaw. "Love me here, in our magic circle . . ."

He shuddered once—a subtle rippling that dissipated into a sound that was half growl, half groaning need. Muttering a curse, he suddenly gripped the back of her head and pulled her to him; then he took her mouth with his, hungrily, greedily, like a man who's been denied his soul's sustenance for too long.

They fell to the deep grasses together, cradled and hidden in the soft green cushion of it. Gwynne felt heat rising in her, felt the tingling contact between them—the hard warmth of Aidan's chest pressed to her own. She shifted, moaning as his knee slipped between her thighs; he balanced himself on his forearms above her, leaning over her, still kissing, tasting her, touching her face with the soft caress of his fingers.

Gwynne closed her eyes and breathed in, releasing Aidan's name on a whisper; it almost felt as if it was that long-ago summer day all over again, the way it had been meant to be before the attack had destroyed everything. Only 'twas better now . . . so much better, like some cherished gift that had been lost and unexpectedly regained.

The sun beat down through the trees, soaking them with light and heat, and making Aidan's shirt glow brilliant white. The sharp, tender scent of the grasses bit into her senses, and she arched back into their softness as Aidan kissed a burning path down the column of her throat to the hollow above her collarbone.

"I love you, Gwynne ap Moran," he whispered a moment later, his voice husky as he paused to lean his forehead against her. "God help me, but I've always loved you."

Her heart leapt at his words, her eyes stinging with the sweetness of his admission. So long . . . she'd waited so long to hear him say that to her, only she'd never known it.

But it was *him*—it was Aidan her heart had been waiting for, searching for, all along. He was the missing piece of her soul, and being with him here and now, with all of her memories regained, she finally felt complete.

"I love you too, Aidan de Brice," she said, her throat aching with bittersweet joy as she repeated some of her original vows to him. "With all that I am, I love you and only you, until I die."

He cradled her face in his palms as he gazed down at her. The sun cast his face in shadow, his dark hair brushing the fine, aristocratic tilt of his cheeks and the strong line of his jaw. But it was the look in his eyes that sent another thrill of longing through her—the softness of love mingling with a passionate heat that set her pulse to racing. And yet his expression was serious; her Aidan, so careful, and deep of heart as always.

"Are you sure that this is what you want, Gwynne?" he asked softly, as if it was difficult for him to speak. "Heaven help me, but if you need me to stop, this is probably the last time that the power to do so will be left to me."

"Aye, I am sure," she answered, reveling in the feeling of him pressed close to her, of his arms on either side of her, enfolding her with his strength. "Are you?" she asked in return, reaching up to brush her finger over the full, sensuous slant of his lips, stifling another moan when he took the tip of it into his mouth and suckled gently.

He released her from that tender assault to murmur, "Aye, love, I am sure." Breathing in deep, he closed his eyes, kissing her forehead, softly, as if she were sacred to him. "I want to be one with you, Gwynne, as we were always meant to be."

She smiled and tilted her head up to kiss him again, even as her hands pulled up at his shirt, freeing it from his breeches and tugging it up and over his head. The sun spilled down, tawny on his skin, and she couldn't resist running her hands over the warm, muscular expanse of him—across his chest and the strong contours of his ribs, then around to his back, making him groan.

But in the next instant it was her turn to gasp as he retaliated in kind, shifting to loosen her belt and bliaud, undoing the laces and then lifting the dress off her in one smooth movement. Her smock followed soon after, and, breathless, she lay there in the sun, naked before him, feeling strangely shy at being exposed so to him, though she couldn't remember ever experiencing that emotion when her body had been only a weapon of war.

"You are beautiful, Gwynne," Aidan murmured, after gazing at her for what seemed an eternity. He reached out, the muscles of his arm and chest rippling with the movement, to drag his fingertip lightly down her throat, continuing on a gentle path between her breasts, so slowly that she ached with the anticipation of his caress.

Her breath caught when he finally slipped his hand sideways to stroke over the creamy swell of her flesh, his touch warm and smooth and sure; he stroked gently, feather-light, leaving delicious shivers of pleasure in his wake. And when he finally cupped her breast in his palm, she choked out a little moan, arching into him and closing her eyes.

"God, you're beautiful," he whispered again, leaning down to press soft kisses to her shoulder, her collarbone, the curved birthmark just below. "So beautiful." His lips continued their path to where his palm rested, finally taking the delicate peak of her breast inside the moist, warm haven of his mouth.

She cried out, then, the throaty sound rising from somewhere deep within her. Threading her fingers through his hair, she held him close, letting him suckle and trail kisses from one breast to the other, loving each in turn. She was gasping by the time he lifted his head; once she managed to open her eyes and quiet her thundering pulse enough to see what had made him pause, a chill of anxiety wound through her. A tiny frown creased his brow, framing the suddenly dark expression filling his gaze.

"What is wrong?" she whispered, half afraid to hear the answer. Worried that somehow she'd done something amiss in her innocence of this act between men and women.

"What is this?" he asked quietly, nudging her up on her side to reveal a jagged white line that began near her right breast and then dipped down, curving to her hip.

" 'Tis a battle scar." She paused for a moment, puzzled at his reaction. Then, frowning, she twisted her head to meet his gaze. "Surely you've seen the like before, Aidan— dozens of them, I'd think, in your years of fighting."

"Aye, but never on you."

His voice sounded as tight as his jaw looked, and she tried to roll back to face him, wanting to smooth away the twitch of muscles in his cheek. But he held her still, his scowl deepening as his finger traced a different scar, one that was higher up, she knew, and threaded across her back.

"And this?" he asked, his voice echoing with an even darker emotion than before, as he touched it and several others of similar appearance. "These are lash marks, Gwynne, and I know of no warriors who carry whips as their weapons."

She paused, the shadows of her past curling up like dark serpents to sting her. "The man who called himself my father did," she murmured at last, "though only in his battle to make me into a Legend."

She heard Aidan curse under his breath, and rolling in one swift movement atop him, Gwynne took his face in her hands. " 'Tis of no matter now," she said, shifting until he was forced to meet her gaze. "That time is over and done. Prince Owain died years ago, well after I was strong enough that he could no longer use such measures against me."

"He was a barbarian ever to lay a hand on you like that."

"Aye, and yet he believed he was only using every means available to him to mold the future savior of Wales."

She shivered, pleasure replacing the remembered pain of those days as Aidan stroked his hands along her sides and down to her hips, holding her tight against him. Reaching down to touch the puckered arrow-scar that marred the smooth expanse of his chest, she said quietly, "It seems that we were both fortunate to have survived his plans for us." Then, tilting her head, she kissed the whitened flesh and continued across his chest, letting the tip of her tongue dart out to tease the flat of his nipple, hoping to distract him from his darker thoughts.

It seemed to work; before long, Aidan groaned, pressing up into her, and she moved her hips instinctively against him, feeling the coarse-woven cloth of his breeches rasp against her inner thighs, the friction teasing the hot fullness at their juncture. Uttering a low growl, Aidan gripped her by the waist and rolled her beneath him again, cradling her head to kiss her.

Gwynne closed her eyes, wrapping her arms around his neck and letting her hands tangle in the waves of his hair, lost in sensation. She felt his heart beating steady and fast, and she arched up as he kissed a path down her neck again, her nipples tightening into aching points of pure pleasure as they rubbed against his chest.

"Make love to me, Aidan. Let the past go, and live with

me here and now, please . . . don't make me wait longer," she whispered, running her hands from his shoulders, down his sides to his hips, helping him to loosen his breeches and ease them off so that he would be as naked as she. He kicked them aside, and she exulted in the warm, smooth feel of his skin, the rippling of his muscles beneath her touch—the hot length of him pressed against her belly as he shifted and positioned himself over her, preparing to complete this expression of love that had been denied them for so long. But then he paused, locking his gaze with hers.

"I need you to know something, Gwynne," he said hoarsely, the muscles in his arms flexing and his entire body seeming to strain as he spoke. "I am yours. Yours alone." He looked into her face, gazing deeply, making her eyes sting with the force of love that she saw there.

"No matter what else happens, in my heart I will always be yours, forever."

His enigmatic words sent an aching stab through her, but it was soon washed away by another rush of passion as he shifted, bringing their bodies into more delicious, tingling contact.

"I am yours as well, Aidan," she answered softly, taking in a tremulous breath; she smiled and then kissed him with all the love and passion she felt for him now—with all the yearning that had been locked up inside her for twelve long years, released again by this man who was her second self, the half that completed her. "I will love you always," she added in a whisper, her voice gone husky.

With a kiss of sweet surrender, he groaned and rocked his hips, sliding against her, his rigid heat rubbing along her slick folds until she moaned aloud at the exquisite sensation. Stroking her hands up around his back, she pulled him closer, arching up into him as he tipped away and then finally glided deep, burying himself in her; she felt a slight sting at his entry, but it was followed by a flood of pleasure so intense that she feared 'twould overwhelm her senses and leave her unable to breathe.

Tears of joy sprang to her eyes, clouding her vision. "Oh, God, Aidan," she gasped against his shoulder as they began to move together, their bodies joined in a flowing, sacred rhythm that consecrated everything she felt for him—freeing all that was inside of her in a storm of swirling, starry light. " 'Tis so beautiful . . . I never knew it could be so beautiful . . ."

"Aye, Gwynne . . . 'tis perfection." He groaned in blissful agony as he kissed her again and cupped her face gently in his palms. Through her own haze of passion, she was astonished to see the glistening in his eyes as well; he bent down to touch his lips to the dampness of her clumped lashes, the tiny hollow of her temple, the wetness of her cheeks, all as he continued to stroke deeply and smoothly inside of her. "I love you, Gwynne," he murmured. "God help me, but I've loved you for so long . . ."

Their tempo increased, and she cried out, her body tightening with the overwhelming feelings, the pleasure that was building, spiraling higher in her. She felt Aidan tensing, too, and she clenched her fingers into his back, arching into him again and again as the sensations began to peak, until suddenly she was tipping over the edge of a wondrous cliff.

She sobbed his name into the salty heat of his shoulder at the same time that he stiffened and growled out his own oath of ecstasy, plunging deeper than before, to release a flood of warmth inside her that blended with the dancing sparks of light, a tingling bliss that washed over her body, filling her soul . . .

Shattering once and for all the protective shell she'd long ago erected around her heart—and healing in that one sweet moment wounds that had been nearly a lifetime in the making.

# Chapter 23

**A**idan rested beside Gwynne, his body spent and his spirit strangely content in a way he couldn't ever remember feeling before. The caress of the sun, the sounds of the woodland around them—the very scent of the breeze seemed more intense than it had just a few hours ago.

'Twas because of her, he knew. He and Gwynne had come full circle at last, pledging themselves with their bodies as they'd done so long ago with their hearts. The feeling it left him with was difficult to describe, almost as if the missing part of him—the part that had been gone for so long that he'd begun not to notice its absence—had finally been returned. 'Twas a gift. A sacred, precious gift, that he was loath to give up.

And he needn't just yet, he reasoned. Not just yet.

The familiar ache lanced through him anyway, despite his attempts to fool himself. He was here with Gwynne on borrowed time. He knew that better than anyone. But God, how could he give her up again?

She stirred where she lay next to him, sighing and stretching like a cat in the sunshine. Rolling up onto his side to face her, he pulled her toward him, and she stretched again, pressing herself flush against his body and causing delicious twinges of desire to jab through him anew. Her eyes were closed, though the smile curving the lush, kiss-softened curve of her lips told him that she was as satisfied as he was.

"So that is what all the excitement is about, is it?" she murmured, opening her eyes to gaze at him with a playful intimacy that took his breath away.

He smiled back at her, running his hand lazily along the powerful, silky length of her side. "What do you mean?"

She arched one brow, teasing him with the look, and he felt an answering warmth bloom in his belly, twitching down to his groin, though he'd have sworn just a moment ago that the explosiveness of their climax had rendered him incapable of stirring again for a very long time.

Her eyes sparkled. "I mean that I've often heard my men discussing their attraction to various women— details of their dalliances and the like, when they thought I couldn't hear them. But I always wondered what they found so compelling about the act, that it would occupy their thoughts so continuously." Her smile curved deeper, her gaze more mischievous. "Now I know."

Aidan laughed in response, stroking his fingers down her arm and taking her hand in his. "Well, I'm glad it met with your approval."

"Not it, Aidan. *You*."

"Ah, then I stand corrected," he murmured, experiencing an unaccountable surge of joy at her compliment. He lifted her hand to his lips and kissed her fingers. "I feel the same, you know."

She flushed, dropping her gaze to the crumpled grass.

"I wasn't sure if you would, considering my inexperience and your . . . well, your obvious—"

"Skill? Knowledge? Unsurpassed mastery, perhaps?" He grinned as she ripped up a handful of grass and threw it at him.

"Lechery, more like," she muttered, laughing as she rolled to reach for her smock and pull it on over her head. Then she stretched out again next to him.

He found himself laughing too as he brushed the bits of grass from his hair; swiftly donning his breeches, he resumed his position beside her, intertwining his hand in hers as they stared up at the blue canopy of the sky. They'd lain just like this on their betrothal day, he thought, his heart throbbing almost painfully as he turned to her, taking in her breathtaking beauty, that powerful elegance of her that blended into the natural setting around them, seemingly as effortlessly as the sparrows that swooped and chirped high above them.

And he found himself praying with every ounce of strength in him that this moment would never end.

Gwynne breathed deep where she rested next to Aidan, smiling up at the antics of the birds before closing her eyes and just soaking in the warmth of the sun, the gentle weight of his hand clasped in her own. It felt so right, so good, being with him here like this. Like it was meant to be. Her only regret was that it had taken so long to come to this place again in their lives. So many years of wasted time . . .

But that was all in the past now. She was Aidan's and he was hers. They'd shown each other their deepest feelings, shared the most intimate part of themselves. A few shadows lurked, still, she knew—she needed to confront Marrok. And she didn't know how she was going to reconcile her role as battle leader of her people with all of the truths she'd just learned about herself and her past. But that would come later. Later, once she and Aidan had worked out the details of rebuilding their life together, as they'd planned from the start.

"Aidan?" she murmured, her cheeks flushing as she stroked her thumb along the strong, sensual length of his palm, remembering how his hands had felt on her—those hands that were powerful enough to match her, swing for swing, in battle, yet still tender enough to caress her into a fever-pitch of mindless ecstasy.

"Aye?"

"What will we do, now, about the dissolution of our betrothal?" she asked, feeling a little shy at her boldness, but needing to know how they would go about making things right between them. "The process of ending our union must be almost complete, if 'tis not finished already. Will we need to betroth ourselves again, or can the entire action still be stopped?"

She felt Aidan stiffen next to her. He went so completely still that even his breathing seemed to cease for one awful moment, and she swiveled her head to look at him, filled with concern.

"Aidan?" She sat up, a heavy dread settling in her middle. "What is it?" she asked, keeping her gaze fixed on him as he slowly sat up as well, the muscles at the flat of his belly rippling with the movement. He wouldn't look at her at first; his jaw seemed painfully rigid, and he just stared down at the ground, at the wide area of grass that was crushed from their lovemaking.

"I need to tell you something, Gwynne," he said finally. "I had to remain silent until your memory returned—and God knows I wish I never needed to say it at all—but 'tis clear that there can be no more delay now, whether I wish it or nay."

Another wave of dread hammered into her. He sounded

so resigned. Resolute. Like a doomed man uttering his last words. Her back ached, she was holding herself so tightly. "What is it?" she repeated, though her mouth felt as dry as dust.

He closed his eyes, his cheek twitching again. Then he breathed in deep, holding in the air for a moment before letting it out in a sigh as he swung his gaze at last to her.

"I haven't been entirely honest with you, Gwynne. There is no need to try to stop the dissolution of our betrothal, because there never was an agreement between us to break. Not legally, anyway."

"What?" The word slipped past her throat on a horrified whisper, and the world suddenly narrowed to a pinprick, shutting out the sun, the trees, the humming of the insects around them, the breeze, soft against her skin—closing out everything but the sight of Aidan's face, so grim and anguished before her.

"I never wanted to mislead you, Gwynne, I swear, but I could think of no other way to get you back to England with me." He reached out and took her hand, but she barely felt his touch for the numbness that was spreading through her. "You must believe me. I had no other choice but to use this falsehood if I wanted to keep you safe."

"But 'twas real, Aidan." She scowled with confusion, looking all around them. "We pledged ourselves right here, in our circle of stones, just before the attack. 'Twas no falsehood; I remember it all. It happened—you know it did!"

"Aye, it happened." He glanced away, his gaze tormented, as if he couldn't bear what he was saying. "But to the rest of the world it might as well not have. 'Tis not legal, Gwynne; not to anyone else. Hand fasting is not enough to make a union binding among members of the nobility. And there were no documents signed, no witnesses to the pledge."

Her shock receded, suddenly, under a wave of nausea. "None but us," she murmured, and Aidan closed his eyes again, wincing as if he'd been struck.

With a slow, even motion, she removed her hand from his clasp, tucking it into her lap. A hot aching had begun behind her eyes, and she frowned, swallowing hard, trying to find the words she needed to say to him. "Then all this—" she murmured, swallowing again and trying to maintain her composure, "—all these weeks that I've lived at Dunston with you—they've been naught but an amusement for you? If there was never a true betrothal to dissolve, then there was no reason for me to—"

"Nay, there was a reason," he said, looking back to her. "I owe you my life, Gwynne, and you deserved to have yours back as well. I needed a way to have you near me, to help you remember, so that you could know for yourself what the Welsh rebels had done to you. So that you could decide what to do with your own future, with the full knowledge that they had denied you after the attack."

"My *own* future . . ." she echoed dumbly, the pain seeping in more, spreading to cripple her very bones, it seemed, with the excruciating burden of it. *Her* future, he'd said. Not theirs together. Hers. Alone. *Oh, God . . .*

"Then your betrothal to Helene . . . ?" She barely managed to breathe out the woman's name, for the choking, aching sensation that filled her throat. She searched Aidan's gaze, desperate to see some sign to tell her that their lovemaking had meant something to him. That it had been more than just a physical consummation after a twelve-year intrusion . . . that he yearned to share his life with her as much as she wanted to be with him.

But his expression remained flat, his eyes sad. So sad and resigned. *Oh, sweet God in heaven, no . . .*

"My wedding to Helene will take place as planned, three weeks from now," he answered quietly, sounding as if the declaration was being wrenched from him, word by bloody word. "I have no choice, Gwynne. There are things that happened in the years you were away that are forcing me now to go through with this marriage; 'tis not what I wish, but it is my duty and the way it must be."

"Nay . . ." she mumbled, shaking her head and scooting back away from him when he tried to reach out to her. Lurching to her feet, she swung her head in frantic search of her gown and belt. She spotted them and took them up, even as Aidan sprang to his feet as well.

"Gwynne, please . . . if you'll only let me explain, I can—"

"What in *Lugh's* name is this?"

Gwynne froze at the familiar voice. Still clutching her bliaud in a death-grip, she turned toward the sound. Her head throbbed, and her body felt stiff, still filled with pleasurable aching from her recent lovemaking with Aidan as she faced her cousin, Lucan. Owin and Dafydd flanked him on either side, but while Lucan looked like an enraged bull, ready to charge, her bodyguards seemed embarrassed to have come upon her and Aidan like this. Owin coughed and looked away, and Dafydd's ears glowed scarlet, his large form unmoving as Lucan strode further into the clearing.

Her cousin's gaze swept from her, clad only in her shift, to Aidan, who stood behind her, bare-chested and with his breeches barely laced. Dragging his glare back to her again, Lucan growled, "Traitorous whore."

Aidan took a step forward at that, danger emanating from every powerful inch of his body. "Words like those could get a man killed."

"Stay out of this, Aidan," Gwynne murmured, keeping her gaze focused on Lucan. "I'll handle my cousin myself."

"Aye, *cousin*," Lucan repeated. "Though I never believed I'd live long enough to see any kin of mine whoring herself to a damned Englishman."

"You go too far, Lucan," Gwynne snapped, her anger rising enough to eclipse, at least a bit, the agonizing hurt that had been pounding relentless at her heart.

"I could go much farther, and you know it," he growled. " 'Twas only chance that my father was out on scouting patrol and didn't receive the parchment you sent to him; 'tis more than obvious now that the maidenly reticence contained in your message is naught but a lie."

A muted pulse of heat beat into Gwynne's face, making her cheeks flame, not only with the shame of his accusation, but with the knowledge that her actions here today had done nothing to prove him wrong.

"*Lugh's* bones," he continued, "your orders were only to tempt the Englishman, not to—"

"That's enough," she broke in, stepping in front of Aidan as if it might somehow keep the diatribe from his hearing.

Lucan's expression shifted, his face taking on a sharper cast as his glance slipped to Aidan again. "Ah—what's the matter, cousin? Doesn't the Englishman know?"

"Know what?" Aidan ground out, moving as well to stand next to her.

"That your willing captive was under orders to seduce you," Lucan said, obviously relishing the disclosure. "That she was told to use her feminine wiles to lull you into a false sense of security." He jerked his head to indicate their partially clothed forms. "Apparently she decided to take it a bit farther than that."

Aidan froze beside her, and Lucan raised his brow, shifting his gaze back to her, his expression more malevolent than any Gwynne had ever seen him wear openly toward her. "Go ahead, cousin," he challenged, mocking her. "Tell your lover all about it."

"It wasn't like that, Aidan," she murmured, the sick feeling inside her swelling with every new moment.

"Is it true or not?" Aidan asked quietly. "Were you commanded to do what you did . . . what *we* did, today and before?"

She clenched her jaw at the hurt she heard in his voice. "Nay," she said, "I mean aye, I was ordered to try to tempt you, but that is not why I—"

"I think what my cousin is trying to say is that she was never commanded to rut with you, Englishman. That part she did all on her own."

"Go to hell, Lucan," Gwynne growled, finally swinging away from Aidan to round on her cousin, itching for the old comfort of her sword at her waist.

Lucan backed off, but only slightly, giving her a sneering look as he did. "In good time, dear cousin—in good time. But before then, I intend to ensure that our people learn just what kind of traitor their *Legend* has turned out to be."

Disdain shown in every chiseled line and shadow of his face, and though he tried to hide it, Gwynne couldn't help seeing the gleam of satisfaction in his eyes. With one last glare and a disapproving grunt, he turned on his heel and slipped back into the woods, on his way, she knew, to do exactly what he'd promised.

Everyone remained still for a moment after his departure. Finally Gwynne turned away, unclenching her hand from her bliaud and pulling it, wrinkled as it was, over her head. Her heart throbbed with dull, heavy beats, as from the side of her vision she saw Aidan bend slowly to retrieve his shirt and put it on again. Owin glanced at Dafydd, who nodded, and both men approached from the position they'd maintained while Lucan had been there, at the edge of the clearing.

Her cheeks still felt hot, and the silence in the glen was

thick and awkward, but she forced herself to meet first Dafydd's gaze, then Owin's. "If you wish to follow him back to camp, I wouldn't blame you. In fact, 'twould probably be better if you did, so no one could call into question your loyalty in this."

"Are you all right, *Chwedl*?" Dafydd asked gruffly, not seeming to care about her caution to them as he frowned his concern for her; she noticed that his gaze kept shifting from her to Aidan, who still stood, unmoving, where he'd been during her confrontation with her cousin.

She paused, not daring to look directly at Aidan herself for fear of the weakness and emotion that she knew would rise up to paralyze her if she did. But she felt his gaze on her nonetheless—a warm, penetrating stare, as he waited, too, for her answer to Dafydd's question.

She glanced down at her hands; then, for want of anything better to do with them, she clasped them loosely in front of her. Lifting her gaze, she said quietly, "Aye, I am fine, Dafydd. But I have learned, recently, that much of what Aidan—" She broke off, her persistent, shameful longing for him surging through her, even after all that had happened between them. Stiffening, she continued, "I have learned that much of what the English claimed about my early life, before I became part of our clan, is indeed true."

"How did you discover that?" Owin asked, scowling.

"I have regained my memories from that time." She willed herself to maintain outward control.

Owin shifted uncomfortably, but Dafydd kept his gaze steady. "What will you do now, *Chwedl*?" he asked.

She looked at her bodyguard, trying to concentrate on breathing evenly, on acting as if her heart hadn't been shattered and her entire world hadn't collapsed around her in the past few hours. The answer she would give Dafydd would seal her lonesome, desolate fate, she knew. For no matter how she felt about Aidan—no matter that her returned memories made her love and commitment to him feel as fresh, as poignant as on the day she'd pledged herself to him twelve years ago—she knew she couldn't force him into denying his responsibilities on her behalf.

She wouldn't.

"I am going to gather my things and then return to the mountains to confront Marrok," she said at last, taking a few steps to reach for her discarded belt as she spoke. "He was part of the raiding party that stole me from my home twelve years ago; he knew the truth, and yet he lied to me all these years. I want to know why. Beyond that, I do not know what I will do."

"I think you should reconsider, Gwynne," Aidan said quietly, breaking his silence at last. "Lucan will reach your people first, and 'twill be dangerous at best to be amongst them again once he has had his say about you."

She braced herself for the impact of emotion as she swung her head stiffly to look at him; even so, she was shaken by the waves of aching loss and yearning that swept through her when their gazes locked. It took her a moment to recover enough to respond, though when she did, she was forced to call on all her old strength, all the battle steel she'd forged in her years of training, in order to speak.

"You seem to forget that your men will die if I do not return to my people to show them that I am safe following my captivity here."

" 'Tis too risky right now. If you will but wait for—"

"I don't think my safety is your concern any longer," she broke in, her voice husky with the effort. "You did your good deed. You restored the rest of my life to me. We are even now, and you owe me nothing more. Let us leave it at that."

Intending to walk back to the castle, she turned away,

knowing she needed to separate herself from him physically and emotionally right now, before what little was left of her resolve deserted her. When he took a step forward and laid a hand on her arm, she sucked in her breath and jerked to a halt, his light touch stilling her as effectively as if he'd clapped shackles on her wrists.

"Don't go, Gwynne," he said—adding a plea for her hearing alone. "Please."

His whispered entreaty made the ache inside of her blossom into pure agony; her body began to tremble, a faint shivering that she did her best to conceal as she pulled her gaze slowly from where his hand rested on her arm, up to his face, feeling the pain rock through her.

"I must," she said finally, mustering all the dignity she could into that hoarse reply. "You see, I know a thing or two about duty as well, Aidan; I've lived most of my life under its power. You have your duty to fulfill in the path you have chosen to take from here . . ." She gazed into the warm depths of his eyes one last time, unable to stop herself from doing it, even though it made her feel like she probed the wounds in her heart with a red-hot knife. ". . . and I have mine."

With that, she very carefully raised her shoulder, lifting her arm up and away from his touch. And then, though it was the most difficult thing she knew she would ever have to do, she turned her back on Aidan de Brice—on the gentle youth who'd grown into a tender warrior—the one man who would ever hold her heart and soul in his hands . . .

And she walked away.

# Chapter 24

Aidan stood atop Dunston's battlements less than an hour later, his gaze fixed on the door that led into the main keep. He ignored the bustle of activity that, as usual, occupied the yard; his sister looked up at him from where she stood near the ribbon-seller's cart, having emerged from her self-imposed confinement upon hearing word of the Welshmen's return, but Aidan pretended not to see her. The summer breeze riffled his hair like a mocking caress, and still he stood unmoving and alone, his hands resting atop the jagged stone of the crenellation as he waited for Gwynne and her men to reemerge from the keep.

Kevyn had taken one look at his face when he'd come back from the glen and started asking questions. His friend had tried to get him to talk, but when he'd gotten no more than a brief explanation of what had happened with Gwynne, he'd given up and stalked away, muttering, as he left, about the infernos rising up, finally, to consume them.

His leaving had suited Aidan just fine. 'Twas not that

he didn't appreciate Kevyn's concern; 'twas just that he couldn't stomach any kind of comfort right now. He wanted the godawful pain of what he'd done to sink deep into his bones, to eat at his soul and fester in his gullet, where it would sit, he knew, churning and tormenting him for the rest of his life. He deserved no less.

'Twas hell, pure and simple. A hell he'd earned when he'd held Gwynne's hand and looked into her eyes after making love to her, and then broken her heart by telling her that he'd still be marrying Helene in little more than a fortnight.

The door of the main keep creaked open, and Aidan's gaze riveted to it, his heart lurching. Owin came through first, fully geared for battle, as he'd been the day he'd arrived at Dunston; Dafydd followed him, similarly attired. Both men walked toward the three steeds that the stable boy held, saddled and ready to ride.

And then Gwynne strode through the portal.

He felt a shock go through him—heard the audible gasps rise from the people in the courtyard as everyone ceased what they were doing and turned to stare.

She was magnificent, looking every inch the legendary warrior once again—it was a startling transformation that made his gut clench with regret. In the time since the skirmish that had brought them together, her men had apparently cleaned and polished her long-sleeved mail hauberk; the metal links gleamed now in the sun, sending off sparks of light as she moved. Her scarlet surcoat had likewise been washed and stitched; the golden dragon, rampant, on her chest was an echo, he knew, of the device emblazoned on her true shield, which had been sent back to her people weeks ago.

She wore no helm but had pulled her shoulder-length hair back, revealing those startling silver eyes and the ele-

gant lines of her face in stark relief. He couldn't help but
see that the old grim and resolute set of her jaw had returned, and the sight of it made his heart twist anew.

She was really leaving. Oh God, she was going to walk
out of his life forever, and he had to let her go. He couldn't
be like his father, selfishly acting without thought to the
consequences. He wouldn't. He'd do what was best for
Diana, and for the honor of his family name. No matter
that he felt like his heart was being sliced to bits inside of
him, or that his soul would never recover from the agony
of losing Gwynne again. He couldn't stop her . . .

Without looking right or left, she stalked to her ebony-
coated steed, swinging astride and adjusting her sheathed
sword, which she'd recovered from Old Alana, before
tightening the long-bow affixed to her saddle. But in the
next instant she paused—a delicate stiffening of her back
that made Aidan's breath catch, made his eyes burn as he
stared at her, unblinking.

With a barely perceptible shift, she tilted her head a
fraction up and to the right, her gaze locking with his for
what was just a moment, yet seemed an eternity. Surges of
longing, need, and grief pummeled through Aidan then,
slamming into his middle and seizing his lungs; he struggled with everything in him against the need to shout
down to her, to call out his love for her until his throat was
raw and his voice hoarse.

To make her understand that her leaving would kill him
as surely as if she drove her blade clear through his heart.

But he forced himself to remain silent, his chest
aching—until finally she looked away. The muscle in her
cheek twitched as she gripped her steed's reins, uttering a
muffled command before wheeling about to lead her men
at a canter from the courtyard.

And as she thundered through the gates, the Welsh banner raised and billowing behind her in Dafydd's grip, Aidan's heart felt as if it cracked open and began to bleed inside of him, splintering, it seemed, into so many pieces that he knew he'd never be whole again. He swallowed hard against the tightness in his throat, leaning back against the wall of the battlements, his spine tense and his legs locked stiffly, as the gates swung shut behind her for good.

He could hear his blood roaring in his ears in the terrible silence after her leaving. Swallowing hard, he blinked, trying to rid himself of the dry, scratchy sensation that lodged behind his eyes. Then, wordlessly, he slid down the wall until he sat on the floor, not caring if he would ever rise again.

Kevyn found him there a few minutes later. His friend stalked toward him with purposeful steps. "We have a problem, Aidan. Riders are approaching Dunston from the south."

" 'Tis of little matter," Aidan muttered, not moving from his position. "If they be traveling in peace, order some food and drink sent down to them."

"They bear Rutherford's banner."

That statement cut like a knife through the fog surrounding Aidan. He lifted his gaze to Kevyn's, finally, the ache from Gwynne's loss dulling a bit under the swell of unease that filled him. "*Rutherford*?" he frowned. "Why in hell is the man back here to plague me? Christ, he only left two days ago."

"I'm not so sure 'tis a friendly visit, Aidan." Kevyn reached out and gripped Aidan's forearm, helping him to his feet. "Look," he said, indicating their approach far off, on the road that trailed away from Dunston's main gate, "he comes with a troop of men behind him."

Aidan cursed under his breath, springing into motion along with Kevyn, calling out orders for readiness, getting

the castle and its inhabitants prepared for whatever the
duke's visit might bring. The yard was cleared of people,
vendors either leaving through the back gate or accepting
lodging near the stables, while everyone else retreated to
positions of relative safety within the walls of the keep.

By the time Lord Rutherford's company reached the
main gate, Aidan had positioned himself near the hearth
inside the great hall, with Kevyn next to him and his men
lining the walls, at readiness; Diana and Old Alana sat,
quietly, a little behind Aidan, where they would be most
protected should there be any sign of trouble.

He was trying his best to appear unconcerned—to pretend that the readiness he'd ordered stemmed from his desire to be available at a word to help his betrothed's father
and lend the power of his own forces, should the request
be made. But Aidan knew that the duke would never stoop
to ask him for help. Nay, not even if he was on his last bat-
talion of men. There had to be another reason for his coming here today . . .

"Will you try to stall his entrance at the gates to learn,
first, why he has come?" Kevyn asked him quietly, so that
the women wouldn't hear.

"I cannot, whether I'd like to or not—the man is to be
my father by marriage in a few weeks time."

Kevyn nodded, at the same time giving a grunt of assent. "Aye, well, at least you can rest easy, now that
Gwynne and her men have gone. As difficult as I know it
was for you to let her go, 'tis best that you need no longer
fear her discovery," he murmured gruffly, offering what
Aidan knew was his best attempt at comfort.

Aidan didn't answer at first, keeping his jaw clamped
tight for the sharp pain that still jabbed him whenever he
thought of Gwynne and of the danger she faced, riding up
into the mountains after Lucan with only two men beside
her.

"We shall see," he murmured, finally, in response. He rose to his feet and walked calmly toward the door at the signal of the sentry, preparing to greet Lord Rutherford's imminent entrance to the hall.

He never had the chance to utter a welcome. The duke stalked through the door with grim purpose, leading nearly two score of his fully armed men, the lot of them shoving aside furnishings and people alike as they spread to fill the chamber. Aidan's men leapt from their positions along the wall, prepared to battle the intruders, but Aidan held up his hand, stilling their action.

"To what do I owe the pleasure of this . . . *unusual* visit?" Aidan asked quietly, once the commotion had settled. He directed his question to Lord Rutherford, his anger at the violence of the intrusion overriding his concern for the moment.

But in the next instant a new rush of emotion nudged the anger aside; the men around the duke shifted at a woman's low-uttered command, and his betrothed pushed through to stand near her father.

"Helene . . . ?" he murmured, taken aback, startled that she would be accompanying her father on what was clearly a warlike expedition.

"I had to come, Aidan," she said, the worry in her voice as evident as her troubled expression. "I told father that it wasn't true, that it couldn't be true, but he—"

"Silence, Helene," Lord Rutherford commanded, giving her a stern look. "You've no call speaking with him anymore." He swiveled his gaze to Aidan, his face dark with animosity. "The man is unworthy of you, as I've said all along. The traitorous son of a traitorous father."

A pit opened in Aidan's stomach. "You had better explain yourself, Rutherford, or, betrothal or not, our houses will be at war."

"There is no more betrothal, de Brice," the duke

growled. He took a step forward, his face sharp with contempt. "You gave up any right you might have claimed to my daughter when you plotted against the king and all of England by harboring a known enemy of the Crown within your walls!"

Kevyn cursed softly next to Aidan; he heard Diana's gasping cry, saw from the side of his vision how she jumped to her feet, then looked as if she might collapse while Old Alana rushed to support her. He turned to Helene, but though her eyes looked huge in her face, she maintained her composure, keeping her gaze fixed on him as her father nodded to one of his soldiers.

"Do you deny the charges?" Lord Rutherford demanded of him, as the soldier brought forth a large, linen-wrapped bundle.

"Deny it, Aidan; there is no proof," Kevyn urged quietly where he stood next to him. Aidan remained silent. The only sound in the huge chamber came from the clinking of metal from the uneasy shifting of Rutherford's men and his, facing each other down, and Diana's soft sobbing behind him.

Kevyn muttered another oath and took a step toward the duke, calling out, "Where is your proof, that you make such a charge against the king's noble servant?"

"This parcel arrived at my estate some time ago, though it went unnoticed until recently, thanks to my frequent absences to attend King Henry, and my visit here last week," the duke said evenly, taking the linen-covered object from his guard. He pulled the wrapping from it with a snap, revealing a magnificent golden shield, emblazoned with a red dragon—Gwynne's shield—to the stunned assembly. "As you can see, it is the shield of the Dark Legend—the only one of its kind. It came with a parchment, detailing the arrangement that had been made with this Welsh criminal, allowing him to remain at Dunston, safe from capture, for a price unknown." Lord Rutherford locked his big steely gaze with Aidan's. "Unknown to anyone but *you*, that is, de Brice. And so I repeat, what say you to these charges?"

Aidan met the man's stare and his query in silence. *Him*, he repeated to himself. The duke had said *him*. That meant that he didn't know about Gwynne. Not really. Whichever one of his men had betrayed him, Aidan decided, he'd kept the language of his condemning message vague—realizing, no doubt, that Lord Rutherford, like everyone else, would never give credence to a claim that the Dark Legend was female. How his betrayer had achieved possession of Gwynne's shield was a mystery, however, to which Aidan's troubled mind could find no easy answer. Gwynne's men had delivered her shield to their envoy themselves, he'd thought. Whoever had done this, whether by switching the shield or stealing it, had gone through a great deal of trouble to achieve this end.

Still forbearing to respond to the duke, Aidan looked around the chamber, lighting on each of his men in turn, wondering which of them was guilty of the treachery. Rex had been right. Currying favor with the Crown had won over honor and loyalty, it seemed, for at least one of his men. The pit in his gut opened wider, and a hammering ache began in his brain. Damn the man who had done this. If the power was left to him after all this was over, he'd ferret out the culprit and ensure that he paid with his life for his disloyalty.

"Come, man!" the duke snapped—tired, it seemed, of Aidan's prolonged silence. "Will you not have the honor, at least, to admit the deed—or will I need to order other, less pleasant means of forcing the confession from you, once I have you secured in a cell, awaiting your trial?"

Swallowing against the bitter taste in his mouth, Aidan swung his gaze to Lord Rutherford again. He fought the reckless urge to bark out a humorless laugh, as he faced the man who was trying to loop the same noose round his neck that had ensnared his father. And in truth, the trap was getting tighter; he could sense the doom getting closer with every passing moment, yet all he could seem to feel was the same persistent ache that had been throbbing inside him since the moment of Gwynne's departure.

He leveled his stare at the duke, dull to the peril facing him, and tired—so tired—of the pain gnawing inside him. "You can do anything you like to me, Rutherford," he said in a gravelly voice, lifting his brow at him in a mocking salute, "for I am long past caring."

Rutherford's face paled, and he took a step forward, fury making the vein at his temple stand out. "That is well and good, de Brice, and I will take great pleasure ensuring that your wishes are fulfilled. But keep in mind that you are not the only one whose comfort is at stake here. I have the king's authority to interrogate *anyone* at Dunston, as I see fit—to do whatever it takes to get to the truth."

The duke looked to Diana, who was still in the consoling arms of Old Alana, then around at the occupants of the hall. " 'Twill not be a tasteful task, putting your sister or your servants to the test, de Brice. But I will do it, let me assure you, if your continued silence in this matter forces me to the action."

Silence descended over the hall; even Diana's sobs broke off in shock at Lord Rutherford's threat. Aidan felt disbelief spill over him, a cold wash of sensation that shook him to the bone. He closed his eyes, feeling as if all of the air was being sucked from his lungs. God, he'd never considered that possibility, that Rutherford would use his loved ones against him: his vibrant sister or Old Alana, imprisoned, even for one night, in some dank hell-hole of a cell—any number of his other faithful servants tortured by who knew what horrible means into uttering confessions . . . his jaw tightened until he thought his teeth would break from the pressure.

"Damn you, Rutherford," Aidan said at last, very softly, opening his eyes to stare at him. "My sister and the servants have no part in this. Leave them alone."

"Admit your guilt, de Brice, and I will."

Aidan breathed in deep, looking from Diana and Alana, to Kevyn, his men, and all around the great hall. Everyone was staring at him, some in fear, some in dismay, while others, like Kevyn, showed in their expression their support of him, regardless of Rutherford's intimidation against them.

But no matter. He could never subject any of them to harm because of him. And as he looked around the chamber, the thought occurred to him that perhaps he'd misjudged his father all those years ago, when the soldiers had come to this very hall to arrest him and take him away to face charges of treason—to face the sentence of execution.

That perhaps, when all was said and done, he was much more like his sire than he'd ever known . . .

He turned back to the duke, a dark smile flirting over his lips. "Aye, well, it seems you've got me. If 'tis what you need to ensure the safety of my sister and the rest of my people, then aye, I admit to the deed. I harbored the Dark Legend here, at Dunston, for a period of nearly three months—a space of time which ended this morning when he departed again for the mountains, shortly before your arrival."

The chamber erupted into chaos at Aidan's admission; the duke's men scrambled to maintain control, clashing with Aidan's soldiers. Diana cried out, Kevyn and many of the other men, once they were subdued, cursing their denial of the charges against him. Helene raised her hand to her mouth to stifle her cries, her eyes welling with tears as she rushed forward; she threw herself at Aidan, grabbing fistfuls of his shirt and shaking him, then beating her fists against his chest.

"Nay!" she cried, "Tell him it isn't true, Aidan! Deny the charges! Tell him, tell him, tell him . . ."

She broke into sobs as the duke's men came forward, pushing her aside in order to clamp irons on Aidan's wrists; Kevyn reached out to her, and she collapsed in his arms, sobbing against his chest as Lord Rutherford shouted the command to depart. His men began to lead Aidan from the hall, but he yanked back on his chains, stalling their progress long enough to call hoarsely to Kevyn, "Watch over Diana for me . . . please. Do everything you can to find someone to take care of her, and—"

His friend shouted his pledge, still holding Helene in his comforting embrace, and straining to see over the heads of the soldiers surrounding Aidan as they pulled him roughly away. Suddenly Diana shoved through the crowd of men, flinging herself at him and wrapping her arms around his neck. Her face was wet with tears, and some of the guards holding him stopped for a moment, in pure shock, stunned as men usually were at the sight of her voluptuous beauty.

"Don't go—oh, Aidan don't go and leave me all alone," Diana sobbed, clinging to him and pressing her face against his neck.

Aidan swallowed convulsively, his throat feeling like it was closing again as he did everything in his power to keep from showing his weakness. "I'm sorry, Diana," he said huskily, holding her gaze for one precious moment. "I never wanted you to have to endure this again."

"Nay, Aidan, don't talk like that—please, it's going to be all right! It won't be like Father again—it won't, I won't let it! I won't let them hurt you—" she murmured over and over, crying and clinging to him, kissing his cheek, as the guards finally overcame their initial shock and pulled her off him.

He shouted at them to be careful in their handling of her, wrenching his neck as they pulled him through the door to call back to her one last time. "No matter what happens, know that I love you—look to Kevyn—he will help you in my stead—"

Diana stifled another cry, covering her mouth with her hand as she watched her brother being hauled away; the rest of what he said was cut off by the surging of the guards, pulling him out into the yard to lead him off through the gate toward some unknown fate.

*Just like Father*, a panicked voice inside her screamed. *They're taking him away to be executed, just like Father!*

"Nay!" she cried out, swinging away from the door to gaze frantically all around. Confusion reigned in the hall, with servants and soldiers scuffling and moving about; some of the women and children huddled in groups, crying, but in the turmoil of it all, she spotted Kevyn. He'd brought Helene to sit near the hearth, and he leaned over her, wiping the tears from her cheek as he talked to her.

Diana couldn't hear what he was saying, but it didn't matter. He wasn't going to be of any help at the moment, and someone needed to take action to save Aidan, right now, before it was too late. Diana looked for anyone who might be able to help her—but there was no one she could entrust with such an important task. She gritted her teeth and stiffened her back. So that was it, then; she'd have to do what needed to be done herself.

Turning on her heel, she headed for the door, going in the direction of the stables. Old Alana stepped from the midst of the thronging people, trying to grasp her arm as she went by, but Diana shrugged off her touch, intent on pursuing the plan she'd settled upon.

"Where are you going, child?" the old woman called after her, her wrinkled face gray with the worry and strain of the afternoon's events.

"I'm going to save Aidan," Diana called over her shoulder, defiant, not caring that Alana would probably run off to tell Kevyn, or some other man who believed himself in charge of her, about the dangerous thing she planned to do.

She kept going, stalking into the sunshine and stifling heat of afternoon, straight through the now-deserted yard to the stables. She smiled grimly with her good fortune when she found one of the mares already saddled, left so, unattended, when Aidan had issued his sudden command for everyone to take refuge inside the keep.

Swinging astride the horse, Diana offered up a silent prayer of thanks that her brother had taught her to ride years ago, indulging her whim to practice as often as she liked. It would serve her well with what she intended to do now to save him.

Wheeling the mare around, she kicked her heels into its sides and galloped at breakneck speed from the castle gates, rehearsing her plan in her mind— practicing what exactly she would say to make those whom she was riding off to find, agree to help her save Aidan. Because there was only one person she knew who might have any chance at all of rescuing her brother.

And Diana planned to ride, hell-bent, into the Welsh mountains to find her.

# Chapter 25

**G**wynne slowed her pace, deciding that her stallion needed to rest for a bit, even if she was loath to stop until they'd reached the clan's holding. 'Twould be another several hours' ride, at least, before they'd be forced to make camp for the night, and an hour or two beyond that once they started off again in the morning; 'twould serve no purpose to get their mounts too winded, and her stallion's sides already heaved from the steady uphill climb they'd been taking for the past hour.

Calling to her men, she reined in near a trickling stream, swinging down and leading her stallion to the water. Owin and Dafydd did the same, and an awkward silence settled over the two men and Gwynne again, as it had ever since they had been reunited in the clearing earlier that morn.

"If you wish to eat something, now would be the time," she said gruffly, nodding to the packs of provisions that were lashed to their saddles. "We'll ride farther once the horses are rested, then bed down for the night near Wickston crossing."

Neither man answered; both looked miserable. Dafydd moved first, trying hard, Gwynne thought, to act as if nothing was wrong. He reached for his pack, unlacing the leather flap and lifting out a chunk of bread and cheese. Offering her some with a nod, he met her gaze directly for the first time since the incident in the clearing, and a rush of shame filled her at the concerned expression—at the loyalty he still felt toward her—brimming in his eyes.

"Nay—I'm not hungry," she managed to murmur through the tightness in her throat, as she turned away. She walked over to her steed again, pretending to examine for slackness the perfectly cinched girth strap. 'Twas so difficult to face Dafydd—to face Owin as well, after what had happened—and she couldn't stop herself from wondering how in hell she was going to handle the accusing eyes and stares of scores of villagers and her other warriors, who were bound to be less forgiving than these two men, who had become her most trustworthy allies.

They moved off a little from her position now and sat congenially with each other on some rocks, chewing their bread and cheese and speaking in low tones. And for the first time in all the weeks since she'd come to Dunston Castle, Gwynne was reminded again of how alone she truly was. Of the anomaly of her nature that would make the kind of easy communion that Owin and Dafydd shared a thing of impossibility for her.

Hunkering down next to the stream, she laced her hands loosely together between her knees and blinked away the gentle sting in her eyes. Worsening the feeling was the knowledge that she'd actually felt like she belonged for a short time while she was at Dunston. As much as she'd like to deny it right now, she couldn't; 'twas the truth. Those moments in Aidan's arms, loving him and feeling as if he loved her in return, had been the sweetest she'd ever known.

'Twas what made the need for her leaving all the more painful. It had wrenched something deep inside her—something that she feared could never be repaired again. When he'd told her that, regardless of what they'd shared, he would still marry Helene, she'd known she had to go. She'd had no other choice.

It was devastating and cruel—a feeling similar, she imagined, to what a man, crawling through a scorching desert and dying of thirst, would experience, were he offered a few sips of water, only to have the remaining elixir spilled before his eyes into the greedy maw of the sand.

Pushing off her knees to stand up again, Gwynne tried to stem the waves of grief that seemed never to cease threatening to overtake her. She'd been doing her best to put Aidan and all that he'd meant to her out of her mind, but thoughts of him kept creeping up on her unawares, catching her with a poignant memory, a remembered laugh or caress, when she least expected it.

She took a deep breath, deciding that perhaps it was time to remount and continue on—that perhaps action would accomplish more than sheer will, at this point, to drive thoughts of Aidan from her mind—when a cracking in the bushes made her stiffen. Dafydd and Owin heard it, too, she knew, by the way they went still, pausing in both their eating and conversation.

"Owin! Oh, Gwynne or Dafydd—any of you!" a woman's voice suddenly rang out from the woodland, plaintive, and near tears. "Please, you must be near—you must answer me!"

The pleas ended on a hitched intake of breath, followed by a faint sobbing sound that became louder in proportion to the nearer crashing in the brush.

"What the devil—?" Owin murmured, pushing himself

slowly to his feet, his bread dropping from his hand as he fixed his scowling gaze on the area of forest from which the noise was coming. In the next moment, he muttered a curse that was echoed by Dafydd and Gwynne, as they all charged toward the figure that stumbled from the woods into the small clearing near them.

"Diana?" Owin growled, holding her stiffly as she fell into his arms with a grateful cry; she seemed on the edge of hysterics as she sobbed into his chest, her gown ripped in several places, and her usually glossy tresses tangled and knotted with burdocks.

"By the blood of saints, woman—what the devil are you doing out here?" Gwynne asked her harshly, helping Owin to lead her to sit on the flat rock where he and Dafydd had been supping.

"Ai-Ai-Aidan," she sobbed, giving Gwynne an almost accusing stare as she swiped the back of her hand across her nose; dirt smeared her cheek in the process, but for once, she didn't seem to care about ruining her impeccably feminine appearance. "They've taken Aidan. You've got to help him!" she cried, swinging her teary gaze to the men. "Please—I know I made things difficult for you all when you were at Dunston, but I'm begging you now— you *must* help him. You've got to stop them from killing him—you're his only hope!"

"Hush, now, lass," Owin murmured, patting Diana's back, which earned him a biting gaze from Gwynne.

"We'll get more from her if she's calmer," he explained, shifting to look from her back to Diana again, continuing to stroke with a gentle caress. "There now lass," he said soothingly again, until her sobs had quieted to uneven breaths and a few stray hiccoughs.

"How did you get up here, lady?" Dafydd asked, when she seemed calmer, though the usual gruffness of his tone startled her into trembling again. She ducked her head into Owin's chest, peering up from beneath her lashes to murmur, "I rode a mare from the stables. A ways back, something spooked her and she threw me."

She frowned, the expression looking more endearing, if that were possible, because of her reddened nose and tear-spiked lashes. If she hadn't been so concerned about her frantic news, Gwynne might have rolled her eyes.

"The mare headed back down the mountain, for home, I think," Diana continued, swinging her pleading gaze up to Owin again as she grasped handfuls of his shirt, clinging pitifully. "But I had to keep going to try to find you. You must understand—Aidan's life is at stake! They're going to kill him if no one stops them!"

"Who is going to kill Aidan?" Gwynne asked, finally, her voice quiet. 'Twas against her better judgment even to ask the question. She shouldn't care, she told herself. She had no business caring about what happened to him anymore; he'd made that very clear. But she knew that she couldn't control how she felt about him any more than she could order the stars to stop glowing in the midnight sky.

"Lord Rutherford wants him dead," Diana answered, spitting out the duke's name like something vile. "He's wanted to destroy Aidan for a long time, but now he's had him arrested and carted off by his brutish soldiers, to face trial and torture and—"

"*Helene's* father?" Gwynne broke in. "Why would he do that?"

"Because he found out about you," Diana said, fixing Gwynne with that half-accusing stare again. "Someone sent a message to him, divulging that you were under Aidan's protection at Dunston—and sent your shield along with the message as proof. My brother was forced to confess the truth in order to save us all from the interrogation Lord Rutherford threatened if he didn't."

"Poor lass," Owin said, patting her back again.

"You've got to help my brother, Gwynne. Please," Diana murmured, beseeching. "He's protected you all of these weeks, putting himself and the rest of us at risk in order to fulfill his damned honor—to repay his life-debt to you."

Diana swallowed, releasing her grip on Owin's shirt to turn and face Gwynne fully. "I am begging you—I will get on my knees before you, if I have to—but you must help. My brother is in terrible danger. They are leading him off right now to be tried for treason, just as they did to our father." She met Gwynne's gaze, her emerald one echoing, for the first time that Gwynne had ever seen it, with a level of sincerity and grief that couldn't be feigned.

"God help him, but they will kill him, if they can. And 'twill be for the crime of harboring you at Dunston. Don't let Aidan die for your sake. Please."

Pushing up from the position she'd taken on one knee near Diana, Gwynne turned away and took a few steps, cursing under her breath. A myriad of emotions filled her, an undeniable urge to help Aidan mingling with the anger she still felt toward him at the way he'd deceived her. At the way he'd hurt her.

"What will you do?" Dafydd asked in a low voice, moving away from where Owin still sat, comforting Helene, to take a position at Gwynne's side.

"*Lugh's* blood, I don't know," Gwynne cursed again under her breath, lifting her hand to rub her temples.

"Much has happened since this morning, *Chwedl*. 'Twould be difficult for anyone to make sense of it all so quickly."

"Aye," she said, her voice tight, "but it appears that I don't have the luxury of time. I will either help Aidan or not. 'Tis as simple as that."

"And yet there is nothing simple about the way the two of you seem to feel for each other."

Gwynne snapped her gaze to him, familiar shame curling inside of her; she wondered if her bodyguard was finally going to chide her for the weakness she'd shown with the man who was considered one of the foremost enemies to her people. "Dafydd, I—"

"There is no need to explain, *Chwedl*," he broke in gently. "I am a warrior, but I am a man too. For many years, I have watched as you trained like someone driven by demons—watched as you were made to deny much of who you are." He met her gaze, his brown eyes kind with understanding. "You've said that you have regained your memories from the time before you came to the clan, and that what the Englishman claimed about your past, happened just as he said." He nodded once. "If that is true, then there is much more going on here than I or anyone else has the right to judge. 'Tis your decision alone, whether or not you wish to ride back and attempt a rescue of de Brice. You should do what you feel is right, knowing that I will back you, no matter what."

"And Owin?" Gwynne asked hoarsely, nearly overcome by this gentle giant's show of support for her.

Dafydd gave a wry smile—one of the few times that Gwynne could ever remember seeing that expression on his face—and jerked his head in the younger guard's general direction.

"Look at the lad," Dafydd growled, still smiling at the way Owin held Diana cradled against him. "He's besotted, and has been from the first time he laid eyes on the woman. Never fear—he'd charge into battle to help her brother, if he could, without blinking an eye, even if his loyalty to you didn't direct him to the same action." Dafydd nodded once again. "Worry no longer, *Chwedl*; both Owin and I will ride with you back to English soil. We'll fight by your side to try to free de Brice, if that is what you wish."

Gwynne reached out, clasping Dafydd's forearm against her own, her jaw clenching. "Thank you, Dafydd," she said, adding in a husky murmur and gripping his arm more tightly, "you are a faithful friend."

"I will defend you to the end, *Chwedl*, and follow you anywhere," he asserted, his voice rough with emotion as well, as he loosed her grip and stepped back a pace. "Only issue your command in this, and it is done."

"We ride back to England, then," she answered.

Dafydd returned to Owin and Diana, to tell them of the plans, and in a few moments, they were all mounted again; Diana sat astride Owin's horse in front of him, though they would be leaving her on the edge of Dunston property before they continued in search of Aidan and Lord Rutherford.

As they headed back down the path toward England, Gwynne couldn't stop the surge of bittersweet feeling that throbbed inside her, an awareness that increased with every hoofbeat of her steed on the rocky terrain.

She was going back to help Aidan.

For whether or not he'd hurt her with all that he had done—with the deception over their betrothal and his decision to follow his duty rather than his heart—he had loved her too; he'd shown her how to feel again, how to be a woman and not just a warrior. He'd given her back her past, brought to life her present, and assured, with the awesome gift of his heart, that her future would be of her own making, undertaken in the full knowledge of who she was. A future of her own choosing.

And she'd be damned if she was going to stand by and let him die for it.

# Chapter 26

Aidan stumbled for what seemed like the twentieth time in the past quarter hour; blood oozed, stinging, from the manacles biting into his wrists as the guard seated in the cart in front of him jerked him forward by his chains again. He might as well have been walking the road to hell. The sun beat down on his head, baking him, and his throat was parched, every muscle in his body screaming for relief from the grueling pace that Rutherford had chosen to take with him.

The duke had pushed their speed intentionally, Aidan knew. The man rode comfortably in the same padded cart that held Aidan's guard, while the remaining two score of his forces sat astride war steeds on this godforsaken path; Aidan alone had been forced to make the journey on foot, the ordeal serving as another way for Rutherford to extract payment from his protesting flesh. 'Twas clear that he relished the idea of inflicting as much agony on him as possible, even knowing that torture and a trial would surely follow their arrival at his place of judgment.

And that was all the more reason, Aidan swore to himself, that he'd fall down dead before he would willingly falter or beg quarter of any kind.

"Move along, Captain—you're slowing down!" Rutherford called ahead from the cart. As he awaited his captain's response, the duke looked back at Aidan, taking a moment to enjoy his prisoner's exhaustion—his level of thirst and discomfort—before giving him a dark smile.

The captain at arms cantered back from his position at the front of the line, reining in his mount to a trot beside Rutherford's cart; his face was red from the heat and his mouth looked pinched as he said, "I am afraid that we will need to stop for a short time, your grace. The horses require rest and water if we are to reach Lord Warrick's estate before nightfall."

Though sweat stung his eyes, Aidan blinked it back enough that he could see Rutherford scowl. "Can we not get another half hour from them?" the duke grumbled.

"Not unless you wish to stop in the villages along the way to replace those animals that collapse," the captain answered, clearly struggling to mute the disdain in his voice.

Rutherford gave him a sharp look then growled, "Very well. Call a halt for an hour—no more. Enough time for some water and rest. Then we push on."

With a nod, the captain rode to the front again, calling a break. The procession ground to a halt, the wheels of Rutherford's cart creaking as they slowed and finally stilled. Aidan stumbled to a stop as well, sucking air, the bliss of not moving almost overwhelming as he bent over, his manacled wrists pressing into his thighs.

"Water!" the soldiers called down the ranks a few moments later, as several of the men made their way down the line carrying bucketsful that they'd fetched from a nearby stream. Aidan eyed the drink, his thirst an almost tangible force, as he watched the soldier next to him set down a bucket for his mount. Noticing his stare, the man untied a skin from his waist, tipping it up to take a swallow before offering it to Aidan.

"Here," he said. " 'Tis still cold from the stream."

But as Aidan reached out to take the vessel, a voice rang out sharply, "Hold there!"

Aidan stilled, snapping his gaze to Rutherford, who had issued the command as he climbed from his perch in the cart. "Give it to me," the duke ordered the soldier as he approached, and the young man paled, handing it to the duke without a sound.

"Thirsty, are you, de Brice?" Rutherford gloated, measuring the weight of the skin, and jiggling it so that splashes of precious liquid spilled onto the dust of the roadway.

"You're a bastard, Rutherford," Aidan rasped.

"And you're a traitor," the duke replied smoothly. Then his pointed expression became subtler. "But I suppose I must keep you alive long enough to have the pleasure of seeing you drawn and quartered. Here—" he tossed the water skin, and Aidan was forced to jerk forward to catch it, wrenching his painful wrists, "—take it and drink. I'd hate to miss the amusement of watching you struggle to keep up."

Aidan didn't bother to reply, instead drinking deep, letting the water spill over his face. 'Twas a gift from God, and an enormous error on Rutherford's part; the water would give him the strength, he knew, to keep alert and ready for the moment when he might make an attempt to escape.

The bastard duke hadn't won yet, by God. Nay, not yet.

Aidan gave the water skin back to the soldier when he was through, noticing that Rutherford seemed to have contented himself for the moment with the spite he'd shown; he'd climbed back into his padded cart and leaned back, using a crude construct of several of his men's shields as a shelter from the sun. The arrogant wretch felt so secure that Aidan even heard snores coming from inside his makeshift haven.

The forty or so soldiers accompanying him seemed to feel similarly confident, by virtue of their numbers, Aidan supposed; as he gazed around from where he sat, still chained to the cart at the roadside, he saw that half of the duke's men rested in whatever shade could be found. The other half talked quietly, or laughed and played at dice, but all completely ignored him.

All except for the captain at arms, he noticed—who continued to walk the perimeter of the group, stiff-backed and watchful, checking on Aidan regularly. The rest of the time the man looked to the forest on one side of the road, then up to check as far as the eye could see both north and south of the thoroughfare, and finally over again to the wood on the other side of the road. His scrutiny of the area was more than thorough, Aidan thought, exhibiting an attentiveness worthy of one of his own men, even.

Which was why it was all the more surprising when an arrow suddenly whizzed a silent path from the woods, catching the captain unawares and piercing his thigh with a sickening thud.

*What the hell . . . ?*

It took a moment for Aidan's mind to grasp the import of what was happening, but in the next instant he'd scrambled for some semblance of cover near Rutherford's cart, watching the chaos swell around him as arrow after arrow flew a deadly course, each finding its target with uncanny accuracy. He wondered who was behind the attack; based on the sheer volume of arrows zinging at the caravan from the trees, he decided 'twas most likely Kevyn, leading a group of Dunston men to rescue him.

A feathered shaft whistled by his head, close enough that a waft of air brushed his cheek. Gritting his teeth, he dived farther under the cart, once there, slipping his chain beneath the wheel in an attempt to pull the links apart. As he yanked at the chain, the thought crossed his mind that he would have to have a talk with Kevyn, when this was all over, about his archery skills—not to mention the stupidity of taking a risk like this when he was the only one left in charge of protecting Diana and the rest of the people at Dunston.

But he could do that later; right now he was just damned glad that his friend had come at all.

Nearly half of Rutherford's men lay wounded or dead, it seemed, in the first five minutes of the attack. The duke himself had awoken at the shouting, but had remained hidden under the one shield not snatched off of him by his men as they clambered for their weapons. Aidan realized that fact when the man who'd owned the shield cried out and fell out of the cart, dead, at his feet; 'twas the same guard who'd been jerking him along the roadway—and from the position of the feathered shaft protruding from his chest, the arrow had pierced him straight through the heart.

"Mayhap your aim's not as bad as I thought, Kev," Aidan muttered, grinding his teeth again as he pushed the man's body aside with his foot in order to yank one last time on the chain. It broke free with a snap, and he fell backward, the momentum knocking the wind from him. But it wasn't the jolt of the fall that made him freeze still, or sent the tingling chill up his spine: 'twas the otherworldly battle cry that echoed from the woods at that very moment, followed by the hurtling mounted forms of three

Welsh warriors in full battle regalia, their helms on and visors down.

He felt pinned to the ground with shock when he finally managed to get a good look at the descending attackers as they rode past him, seeing the distinctive golden dragon, rampant, on the chest of the lead warrior. Then a growl ripped from his throat as he surged to his feet, the pure joy he felt at seeing Gwynne again drowning in a wash of utter fear at the danger she was putting herself into with this foolhardy attempt at a rescue. "*Gwynne?* Damn it, what are you doing here—?"

But his roared question was absorbed into the shouts echoing around him. Owin and Dafydd fought with her, he saw, and the three of them made quick work of disabling those men not already subdued by the earlier hail of arrows. Several of the soldiers took one look at the wildly fierce attack of the rebels—saw Gwynne's remarkable fighting skills in action against their comrades—and they threw themselves astride their mounts and rode, hellbent, down the road toward Warrick's estate.

Though the chains themselves still dangled from his wrists, Aidan's hands were free now; stumbling to one of the bodies, he picked up the man's sword and ran into the remaining melée, swinging and slashing alongside Gwynne and her men, unhorsed now and fighting on foot, until none were left standing but himself and them.

Gasping with the effort just expended, the four stood with their backs to each other once the fighting ended, gauging any further threat. All was silent for a moment. Then a soft cry rang out from behind Aidan, near the cart. Gwynne wheeled away from the protection of the group and stalked closer to the source of the sound, her blade at the ready. Aidan followed close behind, stilling, as she did, at what they found.

Three young soldiers—two of them looking to be no

more than sixteen or seventeen—huddled together behind
one of the cart's wheels; one of the young men appeared
to be wounded by an arrow-shot; the others were bleeding
from various cuts and bruises, but all three looked terrified
as they stared in awe at the famed Dark Legend standing
before them.

"Do you yield?" Gwynne growled, lowering her sword
tip toward them. Her voice sounded husky, low enough to
pass for a man's, Aidan thought, muffled as it was through
the opening of her helm.

"Aye," one of the young warriors called, his voice
cracking with fear.

"Aye, we yield!" another of the men choked. The third
had already fallen senseless and was unable to respond.

"Throw your weapons down and find mounts," she
commanded, still maintaining her pose of readiness.
"Then ride away from here and do not look back."

The young men remained in place for an instant longer,
still frozen with dread, until she growled a final, "Go!"

At that, the two on either side of the wounded man
jerked to their feet, supporting their friend between them
as they moved as quickly as they could to an uninjured
steed. Throwing the senseless man across its back, one of
the boys climbed astride behind him, while the third
found another horse and swung into the saddle. Casting a
last panicked glance in Gwynne's direction, the lone rider
dug his heels into his mount and took off down the road,
his two friends not far behind.

'Twas silent again after their leaving; only a few groans
echoed from the mass of death and destruction surrounding them. Aidan watched Gwynne survey the area again,
still not looking directly at him; Owin and Dafydd approached her as well, removing their helms to stand near
her, breathing heavily from their exertions.

"If there be any others capable of leaving who wish to

do so—go now," she called out. "No harm will come to you if you do."

As she waited for a response, Aidan glanced at the cart near her current position; he remembered Lord Rutherford's attempt to hide himself inside it, beneath the dead soldier's shield. The cart looked empty now, the shield discarded. Making a scoffing sound, Aidan took a few steps nearer, noticing the empty harness; its straps had been cut. 'Twas clear that the cowardly duke had taken the first opportunity to flee during the fighting, leaving his men to die in his stead, in the way of many great lords Aidan had the misfortune of knowing.

Gwynne had still received naught by way of response to her offer of reprieve by the time he turned to face her again, all those left being either dead or incapable of moving. Taking a step back, she sheathed her sword. Her shoulders seemed to sag with weariness, her arms dangling at her sides for a moment before she finally reached up and pulled off her helm.

She swiveled her head toward him, then, her gaze connecting with his and sending that familiar jolt through him. He couldn't seem to look away. She frowned, the expression etching tiny lines between her brows as she pulled off her gauntlets to wipe her face with the back of her hand.

"You're bleeding," she said gruffly, nodding toward his wrists and the blood that trickled, now, over his hands from handling a sword while still shackled.

" 'Tis nothing," he said, swiping the flow away with the edge of his tunic before raising his gaze to her again, adding in an attempt to coax a smile from her, "I much prefer it to the amount that would have been spilled on the block had you not come."

The statement got no reaction, except, perhaps, a deepening frown. "We should see to having those chains removed. The cuts could fester . . ."

Her words faded away for him as a sudden movement off to her side caught his attention—and though what happened next took place in a matter of seconds, it seemed to drag on through eternity, playing itself out with agonizing slowness before his eyes.

He threw himself toward her, his shout of warning echoing through the space between them, but he knew that, no matter how quickly he moved, he would never reach her in time to stop the man who'd sprung to charge at her from his hiding place behind the back wheels of the cart.

The man who was in the process of swinging a glinting, deadly blade right at her head.

Lord Rutherford bellowed with victory as he brought his sword down, but Gwynne, reacting to Aidan's shouted warning, managed to reach down and grip her hilt, drawing her weapon and spinning to face the duke in the same instant. 'Twas too late to avoid his blow altogether; Rutherford missed her head, but with her twisting, his blade sliced high into her side, stilling her for one heart-stopping moment before she followed through with her stroke, a growl bursting from her as she brought her blade down to cut deep into his shoulder.

They both fell away from each other, Gwynne scooting backward, gripping her side, while Rutherford, who seemed more seriously wounded, lay almost motionless in the dirt. Aidan reached Gwynne at almost the same time as Dafydd and Owin; the men surrounded her, trying to ascertain how badly she was hurt. Dafydd made her lean back against him while Aidan assessed the wound. Owin moved a little away to stand over Rutherford, guarding him, though from the shallow, gasping sound the man was making, 'twas most likely an unnecessary caution.

Gwynne winced, sucking in a hissed breath as Aidan examined the area, then helped her out of her surcoat and hauberk, before peeling back the cut edges of her shirt to reveal where the blade had sliced into her side. It bled heavily and would be painful when she moved, but Aidan saw that her hauberk had caught enough of the force from the blow that it didn't appear life threatening.

"Thank God," he murmured, blessed relief flooding him, before he added more loudly for her benefit, " 'Tis not too deep, but it should be stitched anyway."

"No stitches," Gwynne muttered, her teeth gritted tight from the pain. "Just get some strips of cloth and help me to bind it. 'Twill heal in time."

"Can you not use your gift to aid it?"

She grimaced, looking as if she might have laughed if she wasn't in so much pain. "Nay, it doesn't work that way. I cannot heal myself."

"I don't think 'tis a good idea to leave it with no stitching," he argued.

"*You* didn't want stitching when I sliced your arm near Craeloch. 'Tis the same with me. Binding it will be enough."

"My wound was different."

" 'Twas not," she retorted, wincing again when Dafydd, who had had enough of their bickering by now, shifted away from her to fetch the cloths she'd requested.

"Damn it, Gwynne," Aidan murmured, darkness filling him at the sight of her pain. At the hurt she was suffering because of him. The enigmatic look in her eyes unleashed a torrent of more tender emotions, obscuring the darkness for the moment. He shook his head. "You are the most strong-willed, stubborn woman I've ever known, Gwynne ap Moran," he added softly.

"No more stubborn than you are, Aidan de Brice," she answered, husky-voiced. But before he could say more in response, she lowered her gaze, taking in a hitched breath, her mouth tightening and her skin paling even more.

"Hurry it up, man," Aidan called to Dafydd, gripping Gwynne's hand and helping her to sit up a little, while the older bodyguard prepared the dressing for her wound.

" 'Twas difficult to find anything clean," Dafydd explained, handing strips of a brown-hued cloth to Aidan.

" 'Twill do, Dafydd. Thank you," Gwynne murmured, sitting stoically as Aidan pressed a pad of folded cloth hard against her wound, before wrapping the first strip of linen around it and then tightening, tying it snugly beneath her arm.

As much to get her mind off of what he was doing to her as anything else, Aidan murmured, "Why in hell did you come back here, anyway, woman? We were even, remember? You said it yourself."

"Perhaps I am lured by lost causes," she drawled, a hint of humor in her tone, though she gave another little groan when he pulled the next strip of linen tighter around her ribs. Gritting her teeth again, she looked at him with the familiar glint of challenge in her eyes. "Why—would you rather I'd left you unaided, to be dispatched by the executioner?"

"I didn't say I wasn't grateful. Just surprised."

"Then it seems we are truly even, since I've become acquainted with that feeling as well, during the course of this day."

He didn't answer at first, instead tugging the last of the strips into place. After brushing his fingers over the dressing to check that it would hold, he started to sit back on his heels, but something stopped him from pulling completely away from her. His job of tending her wounds was finished, yet still he tarried, trying to concentrate on anything he could other than the warmth of her skin beneath his touch and the pleasure of her nearness to him again—a nearness that he realized he was loath to give up.

Gwynne shifted a little under his ministrations, her

cheeks flushing with the most color he'd seen in her face since she'd pulled off her helm. She was as knowledgeable as he in the ways of war, he knew, to recognize that he was finished binding her, yet she too seemed unwilling to end this contact, brief as it was, between them. He cleared his throat, frowning. "Gwynne, perhaps we should discuss—"

"We've got a bit of a problem here," Owin interrupted, making a little clicking sound with his tongue against his teeth as he walked up next to them, away from his position guarding Rutherford. "The duke is dead."

Dafydd grunted before walking over to check the corpse; Gwynne remained silent, while Aidan cursed under his breath. 'Twas not from any misplaced grief over Rutherford's passing, but rather because 'twould lengthen the list of crimes against Gwynne even more than before.

*And Helene.* Helene would be devastated. He didn't have to be in love with the woman to feel saddened by what she would endure because of this. But there had been no help for it. Rutherford had been given the chance to leave unharmed, and he had chosen to attack instead.

Aidan shook his head, pausing before pushing himself to stand. He reached down to help Gwynne to her feet, noticing that she did her best, this time, to avoid any overlong contact between them.

"You've a price on your head, Aidan, and Rutherford's death is only going to make it worse," Gwynne said finally, breaking the silence between them. She stood with her hands crossed in their usual defensive pose across her chest; her jaw looked tight, but she kept her gaze even on him as she added, "I can tell you from experience that life as a wanted criminal is difficult at best. You should ride to the coast as quickly as you can; board a vessel for France, perhaps. 'Tis your best bet for staying alive."

"I don't intend to run, Gwynne," he answered, walking

to the cart to reclaim his sword and belt, which had been shoved beneath the seat after his arrest. "I will take care of my own affairs here, in due time." He fastened the belt round his waist before stalking over to Rutherford's body to retrieve the key to his manacles. Slipping the piece of metal into the lock-piece, he turned it, and the shackles fell off.

With a grimace, he kicked them aside, throwing the key after them as he faced her again, and rubbing his wrists gingerly. "However, right now, clearing my name will have to wait, because I'm going into the mountains with you."

"*What*?" Gwynne choked, rounding on him, her expression incredulous and her fists planted on her hips. "You must have lost your wits to think I will allow that."

"You will need all the help you can get up there, Gwynne, and you know it," Aidan said, adding, "There is nothing to hold me back, now—and 'tis the least I can do." He glanced to the horizon, noting the darkening hues of gold and russet that were spreading across the sky. "We'll have to hurry, though," he added, reaching down to pick up a dagger, dropped by someone in the fighting, before sliding it into his boot. "We'll only have light enough to travel for an hour more at best."

Dafydd and Owin had resumed their old positions on either side of her, and all three of them faced him now, scowling, the stiffness of their poses screaming rejection of his plan. "I didn't risk my neck saving you out here, Aidan, just to have you ride up into Welsh territory and get yourself killed," Gwynne said finally, shifting her gaze to Dafydd for a moment, and giving a slight nod. The large man stalked away, on a mission to gather their mounts, Aidan decided, after watching him approach one of their steeds and reach into the pack on its back.

He ceased following Dafydd's movements and looked

back at her. "But that is the point, Gwynne—you *did* risk your neck for me. 'Tis only fair that you allow me to return the favor."

"I am truly sorry, Aidan, but I cannot do that," she said quietly, and the apologetic look in her eyes—a look he thought he'd *never* see there, knowing Gwynne as he did—gave him a moment's pause. She gave another brief jerk of her head, and a tingle of warning shot down his spine in the instant before he heard the whistling descent of the club that Dafydd swung into the back of his head.

And as he crumpled into the dark oblivion dealt him in that mercy blow, the last thing he heard was Gwynne's husky voice, murmuring, "And you should know, Aidan, that I never promised to play fair."

# Chapter 27

⟨ornament⟩

**G**wynne awoke with a start. Wispy fragments of the dream still floated around her, pervading her mind, digging deep into her heart. 'Twas the same as always— the woman in white, her long, golden hair waving to her waist, holding her hand to her throat and opening her mouth in the soundless plea that Gwynne could never understand. Only this time it had been different at the very end. This time the vision woman had pulled her hand away, the bloody, gaping wound or bandages of the earlier times gone, to reveal a span of soft, fair skin, unmarred by any scar. And then she'd said something aloud, uttered in a melodious voice that had seemed to resound in Gwynne's very soul.

'Twas a phrase, Gwynne thought, squeezing her eyes shut, struggling to hold onto the image. A message of some kind . . .

*Gwynne . . . ah, my sweet child. Never fear to follow your heart . . .*

Gasping, Gwynne snapped her eyes open. Jesu, what did it mean? The woman had looked beautiful this time, healed and whole. And she had spoken out, after all these years of silence. 'Twas so strange . . .

"Are you ready to continue, *Chwedl*?"

Dafydd's quiet question scattered the remnants of the dream. She shook her head a little, trying to regain her focus. Then, taking a deep breath, she tucked thoughts of the vision into their usual place, far back into her mind, knowing that she had a great deal more to worry about today than just making sense of something that had troubled her for years.

"Aye. I'm ready," she answered. She swiped her hand across her eyes and pushed away from the moss-covered log against which she'd fallen asleep, wincing at the pain in her side as she stood—realizing that she'd forgotten, while she slept, about the wound. After checking her dressings to ensure that they were still tight, she looked to the horizon, just visible now through the interspersed shadows of the trees. 'Twas near dawn, the pink-tinged, thready clouds serving as harbingers of the new day.

Owin called a greeting to her, and she returned the pleasantry, glancing over to where he stood with their mounts already prepared for the remainder of their journey. They'd all taken a short rest, after having traveled the path up into the mountains for most of the night, but it appeared that she'd been the last to rise. Now 'twas time to go. Time to return to the home they hadn't seen in more than three months.

Time to face the accusatory glances and charges of treason that most surely awaited her there.

As she swung astride her mount and led her men on the final stretch to the Welsh settlement, she couldn't help but think of Aidan and of the way they'd left him last night, lying so motionless and quiet, still senseless from the blow she'd ordered dealt to him. They'd done their best to make him comfortable, and then they'd resumed their journey into the mountains.

Regret bit deep, followed by the bittersweet recollection of his earlier insistence to join her on this journey. It had been a noble gesture, to be sure, but she hadn't been able to escape the thought that it had been offered from a sense of obligation—a kind of repayment for her aid in freeing him from the duke.

And she'd had enough of duty and obligation to last her for two lifetimes.

Clenching her jaw, Gwynne picked up the pace that would lead her and her men toward home. Nay, the past was over and done with; as much as that truth hurt, she had to accept it. The only thing that she could control right now was her present, and the future that would result from it. Just what that future entailed was going to become crystal clear in the next few hours, when she rode back into the bosom of the people that had molded her into a Legend . . .

And took hold of her own destiny at long last.

Aidan paused as he neared the Welsh settlement nearly fours hours after dawn; his breathing was slow and steady, his hands tingling with anticipation of what he might be forced to do to keep himself—and perhaps Gwynne—alive long enough to get them out of here again. He'd paid hell to get up the mountain as quickly as he did, and still he feared he'd taken too long. 'Twas already mid-morning; if they'd traveled all night, as he knew she'd planned, Gwynne and her men would have reached this settlement hours ago. He'd lost valuable time thanks to Dafydd's club slamming into the back of his skull. Rubbing the aching knot on his head again now, he reminded himself of the need to repay the man for that little gift.

He'd awakened in one of the village huts just outside of Dunston to find Old Alana tending him—an arrangement Gwynne had apparently insisted upon, Alana had said; Gwynne had sought assurance that he was all right, waiting until Alana had examined him before she and her men had ridden off into the night.

He'd cursed aloud when he'd heard that, and, not caring whether or nay the price on his throbbing head made it dangerous for him to do it, he'd thrown himself from his pallet and gone in search of Kevyn, finding his friend still dutifully ensconced at Dunston. He'd asked Kev to go to Rex for him, to explain what had happened; then, after throwing together what he thought he'd need for the journey into the mountains, he'd saddled Revolution and set off as if hell's hounds pursued him, determined to reach the Welsh settlement by dawn.

Determined to reach Gwynne.

Her head start had made things difficult, a situation compounded by the lack of a clear trail for him to follow; her experience at organizing ambushes and leading expeditions had meant she'd expertly covered most of her tracks. But he'd managed, following what signs he could find, and they had led him here.

Now he dismounted almost silently, tethering his steed to a branch and creeping closer to the settlement's edge. He'd gone over the possibilities in his mind a hundred times on the way here, working and reworking his plans, based on what he might find. He knew that Gwynne might be imprisoned somewhere in the village for the crimes Lucan had levied against her, or perhaps even accepted back into the fold of the people, with all forgiven. Or anything in between. He had no way of knowing.

But he'd realized at some point after she'd ridden out of

Dunston yesterday that no matter what else happened, he loved her. Loved her with everything he was and ever would be. She was the one true constant of his life—the woman he would yearn for with his whole heart and soul, forever—and no amount of duty or family honor could ever change that. He didn't want to change it.

And so he knew that no matter what the risk to him, he couldn't bear the thought of her facing the specter of danger without him by her side, ever again.

Ducking down, he peered through the brush, seeing several huts along the perimeter of the settlement. The buildings blocked his full view, but if he'd had to, he'd have guessed that beyond the huts lay the village square. If Gwynne was in trouble, she'd be held somewhere near there, in the center of the settlement, where escape would be more difficult.

Making note of two large dogs he saw sleeping in front of the dwellings, Aidan felt in his pack for the scraps of meat and biscuit left over from the repast he'd all but inhaled on the way here. 'Twould come in handy when the time came to sneak past the animals in search of Gwynne.

Finally, after checking the location of his mount one last time, Aidan stepped from the wood and into the clearing, running to take cover behind one of the huts. A prickle went up his neck as he paused, focusing on keeping his breathing steady; he suddenly realized that he saw no people. Anywhere. The village was quiet. If not for the dogs and a few wisps of smoke that rose from the top of the huts, he'd have thought the place deserted.

Tossing a scrap of meat to one of the beasts that growled low in its throat as he passed, Aidan continued on, slipping ever closer to the center square. As he neared, he began to see some of the villagers; they clustered at the far end of the open area, involved in what seemed to be a confrontation of some kind, with two groups standing opposite each other, shouting and shaking their fists.

Scowling, Aidan squinted, edging closer from his position behind a pile of drying grasses, trying to see if Gwynne, Lucan, or either of her bodyguards were visible anywhere. With a start, he recognized Dafydd's broad back; the older man faced away from him, spine stiff, watching the shouting match rather than getting caught up in the fray. Aidan let his gaze sweep over the area again; Owin, Gwynne, and Lucan were nowhere to be seen.

Suddenly, everyone began to quiet, the shouts and insults fading to grumbled comments and whisperings. A tingle went up Aidan's back, and he crouched lower behind the grass pile, hoping that the unexpected hush didn't mean he'd been spotted. In the next instant, everyone seemed to shift, the opposing sides widening to form a circle—and then Aidan realized why.

The door to what appeared to be the main building of the rebel settlement swung open, and Lucan stalked out, followed by Gwynne, who was led forth between two warriors Aidan had never seen before. 'Twas clear that she was being held captive; her surcoat, mail and sword belt had been taken from her, and her hands were bound behind her back.

Aidan's heart thudded painfully, and he searched her with his gaze, praying that she'd not been harmed in any way since he'd seen her last. He held his breath, watching as the two men forced her toward the center of the makeshift circle; as she got closer he could see that her face showed signs of strain from whatever had been happening here this day, and she walked stiffly, no doubt from the pain of her wounded side—but otherwise she seemed unharmed.

*Thank God.*

Letting the air from his lungs out in a rush, he glanced quickly to the right and then the left before darting to the corner of the next building. As he crouched down, the fetid stench of rotting vegetables that had been tossed out the back door nearly choked him, but he tried to ignore it and focused instead on working his way ever closer to Gwynne.

Determined that, when the moment was right, he was going to make his move to aid her.

As she walked across the main square, Gwynne squinted, her eyes unaccustomed to the glare of the sun. Her head throbbed, and she tried not to think about the burning ache of the wound on her side, but that feat was near impossible; the pain had increased tenfold in the past two hours. Shortly after her entrance into the village, Lucan had ordered her locked in the council building, away from the watchful eyes of her supporters. He'd joined her there a brief while later and spent the time from then until now interrogating and trying to force a confession from her—which had included a few well-placed, brutal strikes to her injured side. It had taken all her strength to stand up straight again once he was done with her, and a burst of pure will to walk unaided into the center of the square just now.

"Speak, woman!" Lucan snarled at her yet again, repeating the command he'd made countless times while they'd been inside. "Confess your treason or suffer the consequences!"

She remained silent, not even condescending to look at him, in hopes that her disdain would incite him to strike her again here, in front of these people, many of whom still worshipped her as the Legend and would no doubt eschew altogether the trial he'd called, simply to take matters into their own hands. But as furious as he was, even

Lucan wasn't foolish enough to risk turning the people against himself.

He stood, almost shaking with anger, for a moment, before he stilled, a new idea seeming to cross his mind. Making a self-satisfied sound, he came close enough to bring his mouth next to her ear, growling, "Confess to the people, cousin—or I will ensure that our English hostages die."

"You wouldn't dare," she grated, speaking at last as she turned her head toward him and withered him with her gaze. " 'Tis against the agreement Marrok and I made with de Brice. I am back safely, and they must be returned home the same."

"I am in command, now, in my father's absence. The people will do as I say," he boasted. "If I wish them to die, they will die. Speak your confession now, and they will be spared."

"I do not believe you, Lucan," she muttered, "and I've told you before, I will not speak until I see Marrok."

Stiffening her back, she looked away from him again, letting him see her contempt as she ignored him; he stalked off with a curse toward the line of his men—discussing further strategies for bringing her to heel, no doubt—and so she was left alone, to gaze into the writhing, milling crowd. She frowned, looking over the square. It seemed that nearly the entire village had come to witness the open trial Lucan had called. But the confusion of emotion, condemning expressions on the faces of some, tear-filled sympathy or indignation for her on others, sent a pang through her, chilling her anger for a moment.

It wasn't supposed to be like this. Not like this, with division and conflict driving a wedge between these people. These were the same villagers she'd known almost all her life, most of them honest men and women, who believed in the fight for justice as much as she did. And now, thanks

to her—thanks to Lucan and his damned need for
retribution—they were in danger of falling into a war
amongst themselves.

Her gaze lit on Dafydd, standing, stalwart as always, at
the back of the crowd. He nodded, trying to bolster her
spirits, though the depth of concern in his eyes belied his
unease about what was happening.

Aye, he was worried, and rightfully so; Lucan and his
backers were out for her blood. Before she'd entered the
village this morn, she'd sent Owin ahead to find Marrok
and bring him back from the scouting expedition that had
prevented him from receiving her message four days ago,
but if her bodyguard came back empty-handed, she feared
that her cousin and his men just might get what they
seemed to desire so urgently.

"Make her confess before the people," she heard Isolde
hiss to her son from the edges of the crowd. "If they hear
her say it, they cannot support her any longer!"

"I have tried, Mother," Lucan muttered, though few but
those in closest proximity to him were able to hear the exchange. "She will not yield!"

Gwynne continued to stare straight ahead, unwilling to
give the woman the respect of looking at her; if there was
any way to accomplish it once this was over, she promised
herself to see Isolde stripped of her position as soothsayer
to the clan for the perfidy she'd shown here today.

Her cousin, meanwhile, had swung his attention back
to the throng, clearly desperate for a plan that would grant
him some success in influencing them. Gwynne felt her
mouth twist mockingly as she watched him struggle with
both the situation and his mother's pervasive interference.
No matter how hard he tried, she knew that Lucan would
never be the chieftain that Marrok was. He lacked both the
wisdom and the compassion that would enable him to

make the kind of solid decisions his father did—decisions to affect the multitude.

But that wouldn't stop him from trying anyway.

As the noise in the crowd burgeoned louder, Lucan raised his arms, calling out, "Hold—hold but for a moment if you wish to hear why I, as leader of this clan in my father's absence, was forced to call for this trial!"

The noise ebbed a bit, and Lucan flushed, filled with a taste of the power he craved. "A warrior's duty is to protect the people and uphold the laws"—he called out, flashing a hate-filled glare at Gwynne as he added—"and to obey the chieftain's orders. I saw with my own eyes how this, our most famed warrior, spit in the face of those beliefs, choosing instead to embrace whole-heartedly a life with the English bastards, indulging in the lustful pleasures of a traitorous bed—whoring herself freely with the English criminal she was sent to destroy!"

The crowd erupted into shouting again, some calling for her destruction, while others yelled denial of the charges. Gwynne stood, stony-faced and unmoving, forcing herself to remain quiet. Not trusting what she would say—or do—to Lucan if she were given the chance.

Out of the chaos, one voice bellowed more loudly, ringing through the square with righteous anger.

"What you speak is a lie!"

Gwynne shifted to see who had chosen to single himself out in defense of her, her stomach dropping when she realized that it was Dafydd. She tried to signal to him with her expression, not wanting him to expose himself to more danger for her sake, but he ignored her command, pushing through the throng to confront Lucan face to face.

"I was at the English castle with *Chwedl* the entire time of her stay, and never did she do what you say," Dafydd insisted. "She obeyed Marrok's commands and conducted herself always as a true and noble warrior!"

The crowd hummed their approval, until Lucan sneered, his face sharp with contempt. "Is that so?" He raised his brow. "Tell me something, Dafydd. Were you not with me just yester morn when we came upon my cousin and the Englishman in the clearing beyond the castle walls of Dunston?"

Dafydd hesitated, his face darkening. The crowd waited for his answer, the air thick with expectation. "Aye, I was there," he finally admitted in a low voice.

"Care you to explain what we saw, then, when we reached the clearing?"

Her bodyguard gave Lucan a glare that would have sent most men scurrying for cover. But her cousin was so engrossed in his plot of destruction that he seemed hardly to notice. Swinging to face her, he called out loudly, "And what of you, cousin? Will you not speak now to defend yourself in this?"

Gwynne gritted her teeth, aching to tell him exactly what she thought. But she wouldn't. Nay, he didn't deserve to be obeyed. Ever. "I will not speak until I speak with Marrok," she growled, still not looking at him as she maintained her stance, her spine rigid with anger.

"Then allow me to do the honors," he answered, undaunted, stepping toward the crowd with a flourish worthy of the finest traveling mummer. "What greeted me, good people, when I entered onto Dunston lands," he called out, rolling each word glibly from his tongue, "was the sight of my cousin, your famed Dark Legend, half-clothed and lolling in the field, fresh from a traitorous rutting with Aidan de Brice himself, the cursed Scourge of Wales!"

Through the uproar that followed, Gwynne tried to ready herself for the call to sentencing that would most likely come next, if Lucan had his way. She kept as calm as she could, looking to all points of the pushing, brawling crowd, seeking out those she might be able to count as allies, as well as those she should avoid if it came to a war between the factions that were aligning, even now, for or against her. She needed to plan how she could free her hands—how she could get hold of a sword so that she might defend herself and keep those who wished to harm her at bay. How she could—

And it was then that she saw him. He moved smoothly through the crowd, sidestepping the shouting, shoving groups of people as well as he could. At first she focused on him with disbelief, stunned, convinced that he was but a figment of her overtired imagination. But then he broke through the edge of the mob, stepping into full view of the circle's center, and she knew that it was really him.

*Aidan.*

His name whispered from her lips on a breath, the myriad emotions that flooded her with it keeping her from paying as close attention as she should have to Lucan and his men. Her cousin spotted Aidan but a moment after she did, and the crowd gradually fell into shocked silence to realize that a stranger was in their midst.

"If you wish to invoke the name of the Scourge of Wales and detail his crimes, man," Aidan called out, "then, pray, do so—but to his face. Here I am, in flesh and blood, awaiting your judgment. But do not blame this woman, my former captive, for my actions. She is innocent of all wrongdoing and should be freed immediately."

The people near the front of the mob went wild. "Seize him!" Lucan shouted in response, directing several of his men to take hold of Aidan. But he was losing control of the crowd, the very people he'd planned to use to his advantage against Gwynne, and he knew it. He sensed, just as she did, the way their anger was turning from her to Aidan—to the notorious English warrior that they blamed for the deaths of so many of their husbands, sons, and brothers.

The crowd surged forward, a horde, thirsting to taste his blood, and it was all that Lucan's men could do to keep them at bay and maintain order. The shouting and shoving increased, but after a few of the leading miscreants were beaten back by blows from the warrior's spears, the people shifted a little, forced to content themselves for the moment, at least, to let the trial commence with the promise of this new morsel to appease their vengeance.

"What the devil are you doing here?" Gwynne muttered as the soldiers finally managed to drag him to stand next to her. Her joy at seeing him alive and well again was tempered by the knowledge that he wouldn't long remain that way unless they found a way to turn this around.

"I could tell you the truth and admit that I came here because I've finally realized that I would rather die than live a moment of my life without you," he murmured, speaking to her but keeping his gaze fixed firmly on the people around them who were still calling for his blood, "but I think you'll be more likely to believe me if I say that perhaps, like you, I am irresistibly lured by lost causes." After he spoke, he looked away from the throng just long enough to glance at her, giving her a look that, even in the danger of the moment, set off a fluttering, twisting sensation inside of her.

*I would rather die than live without you.*

Those were his words, and the wondrous realization of them sank into her, deep into her bones, filling her with a warmth and light that made everything else happening around them seem a little less horrible. He'd come after her. Even after she'd done everything in her power to make sure it would be easier for him to follow his duty, he'd still risked his life to come here for her. And it hadn't been from a sense of obligation or duty, but because he'd wanted to do it, *for her* . . .

"Aye, well, I hate to ruin your pleasure," she said at last, suppressing her joy enough to give him a wry look, "but I am afraid that my cousin isn't going to release me simply because you told him to."

"Enjoying a little romantic chat, are you?" Lucan drawled, stepping closer to them. "How stupid of you to try to play the hero, de Brice," he gloated, though quietly enough that only they could hear him. "And how futile. You've accomplished nothing but to make my task today easier. When I am finished here, you'll *both* be swinging from the nearest tree."

"Only a fool believes in such certainties," Aidan countered calmly. "I may be an easy conquest, but many of these people still support Gwynne; you'll have a revolt on your hands if you attempt to harm her."

"We shall see." He turned his attention to Gwynne. "In the meantime, *cousin—*"

"What in *Lugh's* name is going on here?"

The shouted question rocked through the clearing, making virtually every man, woman, and child in the village cease what they were doing in order to turn and face the owner of that imposing voice. Marrok continued slowly toward the center of the square, guiding his steed's measured strides. Owin rode a little behind him, looking exhausted but pleased with himself; Marrok's other scouts—another half score of men he'd brought with him a week previous—followed behind, eyeing the tumult in the square with brooding interest.

"Father . . . !" Lucan yelped, jumping away from Gwynne as if he'd been burned. "I was just—well, what I mean is that I thought it necessary, as acting prince, to lead a trial before the people, according to custom, in a case involving these two," he gestured lamely toward Gwynne and Aidan, flushing as he added, "since a clear act of treason has been committed. I—I was simply readying to decide upon the method of—I mean the manner of resolution we should attempt to determine guilt or innocence," he finished, his face a dull brick color.

"Release her."

Marrok's simple command resounded through the clearing, echoing with a tone of authority that seemed to calm the crowd and ease, at least a bit, the tensions flaring between the two factions of villagers.

"But Father, I saw her treason with my own eyes!" Lucan argued. "She gave herself over to the Englishman. I caught them in the meadow, f—"

"I said, release her!" Marrok growled, making the men Lucan had appointed as her guards rush to obey him.

"And what of the Englishman?" Lucan called out after a moment of desperate silence. "Will you order *him* released without penalty as well—the Scourge of Wales, allowed to go free?"

"I will handle de Brice later," Marrok answered evenly, dismounting and handing the reins of his steed to one of the boys in the crowd; a path cleared for him as he made his way to the center of the square.

Gwynne stood unmoving as her bonds were loosened, meeting Aidan's gaze for another sweet moment before the soldiers pulled him to the edges of the crowd, under orders to hold him there until Marrok issued further command for what was to be done with him.

When her hands were free, she rubbed her wrists, looking back to her leader—to the man who was not only the just and noble prince of the people, but also her mentor as well. The man who had been more like a father to her than her own sire, who had cared for her, protecting and guiding her, as she made her way along the brutal path Owain had laid out when he'd shaped her into a legendary warrior.

The man who had lied to her about her past and, in doing so, had forever betrayed the trust they'd forged together in those years of pain.

Grief washed over her, gripping her throat in an aching vise; she looked away, trying to steel herself to confront him now, here in the square. To confront him as she'd known she must, ever since that moment when the awful reality of his betrayal had burst into her memory— a gushing tide that had muddied her world and driven her to seek, once and for all, the truth of who she really was.

"Owin told me some of what has happened, *Chwedl*," Marrok said, unaware of her feelings as he approached her; he nodded to one of the warriors, indicating that the man should return her swordbelt to her. Still moving stiffly from the pain caused by Lucan's earlier interrogation, she took it from him and fastened it round her hips.

"We need to talk," Marrok continued. "Come. Let us go inside to discuss what must be done from here."

"Nay, Marrok," she said huskily, facing him. Hurt lanced through her anew, but she forced herself to continue. "I will not go inside."

"Why—what is the matter, *Chwedl*?" he asked, frowning, his familiar concern for her ripping a larger hole in her heart.

"I need you to explain something to me, Marrok," she said, steeling herself to go on. "I want to know why you lied to me about who I was and what happened to me all of those years ago. Why you let me believe I was saved from a life of English captivity, when in truth it was you and the people of this clan who ravaged my home and stole me away by force from the man that I loved, and the only life I'd ever known."

She swallowed, leveling her gaze at him, trying to keep

her tone even and calm, though her heart pounded furiously with all the emotions churning inside her.

"I want the answers to those questions, Marrok—and I want them now."

# Chapter 28

The square had fallen silent with Gwynne's accusation; even Lucan seemed taken aback by the seriousness of her charges. Marrok, too, had stiffened as she spoke, and now he swung his head toward her, meeting her gaze.

"It wasn't like that, *Chwedl*," he said at last, quietly. "There were reasons for what we did—for what I—" He broke off, shaking his head. "Nay, there is much more to this than can be explained easily. So much more that you do not know . . ."

"But I remember everything, now," Gwynne asserted. "It has all come back—all of it—the happiness I felt in the peaceful, simple life I shared with my mother . . ." She shifted her gaze to Aidan, all that she'd cherished about him so long ago combining with all she felt for him now, filling her to overflowing.

"And I remember the love I felt for a young man," she added softly, drawing strength from the tenderness and

337

passion she saw reflected back at her in Aidan's eyes. The love he felt in return, deep, strong and true, for *her*.

"One morn," she continued, "while we stood inside an ancient stone circle, he asked me to share the rest of my life with him." Swallowing again against the thickness that had crept back into her throat, she pulled her gaze from Aidan, directing it at Marrok once more. "I gave myself in a sacred betrothal to Aidan de Brice that day, but moments later, I was forced to watch as your warriors cornered him near my mother's cottage and buried an arrow in his chest. Then they grabbed me and hauled me away so violently that I lost all memory of the life that I'd loved." Her face ached as she said huskily, "Damn it, Marrok, I want to know why."

As she'd spoken, her mentor's shoulders seemed to sag, his fists unclenching and his entire body drooping. He shook his head again, and when he finally met her gaze, he seemed to look at her through the eyes of an old man.

"Ah, Gwynne," he murmured at last, "you do deserve the full truth. God knows you do after everything that has happened." He took a deep breath. "Tell me what you want to know, and I will answer if I can."

"My mother—" Gwynne said quietly and without hesitation. "I remember her now, and I know she was still alive after your warriors ambushed us. What happened to her?"

Marrok took a moment, bracing himself it seemed, for the release of these secrets, kept hidden for so many years. "That woman you remember from your childhood," he said finally, "the gentle Druid who raised you for the first fourteen years of your life—she was not your true mother, Gwynne."

"But how can that be?" Gwynne scowled, anger and confusion jabbing her. "I remember her. I remember our little cottage, and the yellow cat that used to bask in the sunny window . . ."

Marrok shook his head. "She cared for you and raised you as her own, 'tis true, but she did so only at your real mother's request." His face tightened, his eyes showing the strain of calling up all of these memories again. "Your Mam was princess of this clan, as I told you on the day you were brought here. Her name was Gwendolyn, and she was as sweet and good as she was fair."

At the mention of her name, many of the people in the crowd began to murmur—a hushed swell of sound, as those who had been alive, then, whispered recollections of her, old memories of a time long past. Marrok rubbed his brow before continuing, "My brother Owain saw her but once and decided that he had to have her. The marriage was arranged, the ceremony took place." He paused, his face tightening. "And nearly nine months later, you were born."

"Why did she leave me, then?" Gwynne couldn't seem to stop herself from asking. "Why would my mother give me over to be raised by another?"

" 'Twas because of the prophecy. Gwendolyn refused to accept it. When you were two weeks old, she stole away with you, determined to keep you from being raised as the Legend Owain claimed you to be." He met her gaze, his eyes sad—so sad. "Your mother loved you more than her own life, Gwynne. She secreted you with the Druids, and then she ran, stumbling through the woods, trying to lead Owain away from you and them, so that he would never find you again."

A sick feeling had begun to settle in Gwynne's stomach, a vague sense of dread that churned with increasing ferocity. "And then?" she asked softly, terrified, in some hidden part of herself, of hearing the answer.

"Owain caught Gwendolyn not long after she'd hidden you with the Druids," he answered, his voice as quiet as Gwynne's had been. He closed his eyes for an instant, and when he opened them again, the grief she saw reflected there shook her to the core. "And when he found out what she had done with you, he killed her."

The aching, hollow sensation slammed hard into Gwynne; many of the villagers gasped aloud, the sound echoing through the square. Her ears were ringing, and she wasn't sure she was going to be able to breathe, but after a few agonizing moments, air rushed into her lungs, sweet and clear.

"How did he do it—how did he kill her?" she asked flatly when she could speak, wanting everyone in the village to hear, to know the monster her father had been—wanting to learn if the tingling, dark suspicion that had begun to swirl inside of her held any truth.

" 'Twas a cruel and brutal thing, *Chwedl*," Marrok said, his expression dark with the memory of it. "Better left unsaid."

"Nay—I need to know."

He gazed at her in silence, his pain nearly tangible. When he finally spoke, 'twas clear that he forced himself to it only because he knew that he owed it to her—that he owed her all of the truths she needed to hear right now, even if it would destroy him. Taking in a sharp breath, he looked away, the sheen in his eyes unmistakable. "Gwendolyn died when my brother slit her throat."

*He slit her throat . . . oh, God . . .*

The world began to spin, but Gwynne somehow kept her balance, locking her knees tight, so that she wouldn't sink to the ground. "Tell me what she looked like," she said, in a painful whisper that barely squeezed from her chest. "Please, Marrok—I need to know what my mother looked like . . ."

He seemed surprised for a moment, then his face twisted in a kind of agony, and he looked as if he might turn away to try to hide what he was feeling—to stop the pain of being forced to relive his memories. But, rubbing his hand across his eyes, he managed to compose himself enough to tell her what she'd asked. "Your mother was beautiful," he rasped at last. "She was tall and slender and strong, with skin of silk and a mouth that looked as if it was made to laugh." He let his gaze drift over her, giving her a sad smile. "In truth, you are much like her, Gwynne, except that her hair was light as the sun, like spun-gold, and she wore it long, hanging almost to her waist . . ."

Gwynne's legs gave out then, and she sank slowly to her knees. *She was tall and slender, with long golden hair* . . . Oh God, the vision—the dream-woman that had haunted her for all these years—it had been her mother . . . her true mother, trying to tell her what had happened. All this time . . .

"Aye, your mother was a beautiful woman, Gwynne," Marrok repeated, more vehemently, "and I loved her more than my own breath or life."

The shock of his admission caught her by surprise; she heard Isolde gasp and sensed the crowd stirring again. Bewildered, she looked to him. He met her stare with his own unflinching one, and then he stepped forward, no longer showing suffering, but rather in command again as he turned to include the people in what he would say next.

"For too many years," he called out to them, "I have kept the truth of those days secret, hidden in the darkness of my own soul—" He swung his gaze around, taking them all in, his eyes snapping with fire as he stood tall and strong before them. Gwynne was suddenly reminded of the man he had once been, the powerful warrior who had inspired terror in the hearts of his enemies and led his people in a revolt against England, a country led by a king whose army was one of the greatest ever to have seen daylight.

"I have committed two great crimes in my life," Marrok continued, resolute, "the first more than twenty-six years ago, when I stood by and let my brother take as his own the woman I loved, and the second, fourteen years later, when I found and kidnapped her child—the child she had died trying to protect."

Gwynne had risen slowly to her feet again as he spoke, and now he turned to her, his eyes moist and his voice huskier, as he continued, "For the first crime, I have no excuse, other than my own weakness; I gave in to Gwendolyn's pleas not to reveal our secret love, to protect myself and her by allowing Owain to marry her, as our two powerful clans had arranged." He swallowed hard, never taking his gaze from her. "But for the second—that of kidnapping you from the peaceful existence your mother had died to give you—I did have reason, Gwynne. Owain was determined to find you, no matter what the cost. He had searched already for nearly fourteen years. 'Twas only a matter of time, I knew."

Marrok took a step closer to her, seeming to reach out to her with his expression, asking her for understanding. For forgiveness.

"I led the search to bring you home, because if I did not, Owain would. And I wanted to be there, to protect you, knowing that I could not free you from the destiny that had marked you from the moment of your birth, but wanting to ensure, if I could, that you would possess the skill and power to survive it."

He looked down for a moment, as if he were gathering his strength, before lifting his gaze to her again. "And there was one more reason, Gwynne. A reason that damned the others to hell by comparison."

She felt her heart pound with slow, steady beats; her hands tightened into fists that she pressed into the outside of her thighs as she kept her gaze fixed on him, waiting for him to finish what he was going to say. Knowing, somehow, in her soul that what he was about to utter would change her world forever.

"I needed to lead the effort to find you, Gwynne—I needed to be the one pushing you, training you to become a legendary warrior as Owain wished," Marrok said slowly, painfully, "because I was afraid that he would discover the truth if I didn't. And God help me, but I feared that he would kill you as he had killed Gwendolyn if he found out—because, though everyone believed it so, you are not Owain's child."

The gasps and cries that greeted Marrok's confession faded for the rushing that had begun to fill Gwynne's head. But she kept looking at him, kept herself still, so still, controlling herself and her breathing, as he had always taught her to do.

"You were conceived more than a month before Gwendolyn and Owain wed—the child of a secret love—and that was why I had to do everything I could to protect you," Marrok continued gently, facing her as he spoke the final words, his eyes brimming. "Owain was not your father, lass. I am."

Gwynne couldn't move. Her breath had finally frozen in her chest, the ancient secret to that rhythmic flow of life forgotten under the force of her shock. She stared at Marrok, at this man who had been many things to her—her leader, her taskmaster, her mentor, her friend—and suddenly it all made sense. He was the one who had been there whenever she needed someone to turn to, who had given her the only affection she'd known among people who had viewed her as something untouchable, as a myth in their midst. The one who had held her, during those first few months, when she'd collapsed, retching and sobbing, from Owain's brutal attempts to make her strong.

The one who had stood up to his brother and demanded to be given control over her training so that she might live and grow in skill and power.

"*You're my father . . . ?*" she breathed, locking her gaze with him.

But before he could answer her, she heard Lucan roar a denial of it. He threw himself into the clearing, looking as if he would like to strike Marrok, but holding himself back enough to snarl at him, " 'Tis a lie! This traitor is no more my sister than she is the Dark Legend!"

"She is, Lucan," Marrok said darkly, approaching him as if to place a hand on his arm to calm him. "Now, come inside with us and we will all try to—"

"Nay!" Lucan shouted, pulling away from him, in the same motion sliding his sword, hissing, from its sheath and slamming his father in the temple with the hilt.

Caught unawares by the blow, Marrok crumpled to the dirt, and Lucan stepped over him, brandishing his blade as he came closer to Gwynne. She backed up a few steps, wary. Someone reached in to pull the chieftain's limp form out of harm's way, and the entire crowd moved, as if they would surge forward again, perhaps to try to stop Lucan—but then, with more muttered arguments and shoving, the circle reformed. The group hummed with tension, Gwynne noticed, but seemed content, for the moment, to watch as this struggle for power between the chieftain's two offspring played itself out.

Lucan directed his hate-filled glare at her, muttering at last, "No matter what my father says, I will never accept that you are either my sister or the true Dark Legend. And while there may be no way for me to disprove that you are his spawn, I can show everyone right here and now that 'twas his coddling and not any mythic ability that has kept you safe from death in battle thus far, *woman*."

He waved his weapon at her again, scoffing, "Come—draw your sword and prove yourself the warrior that our clan has been duped into believing you to be!"

Gwynne faced him, watching him carefully, her instincts prickling as they always did at the prospect of danger. Her hand tingled with readiness to grasp her hilt and defend herself, yet she knew she would avoid fighting him if she could. She had no wish to cross blades with him. Not here—not ever. That she knew he was her brother now would have been reason enough, but what she'd just learned about Marrok—what she'd learned about herself and the missing pieces of her life—had left her drained of everything but the wish to walk away. More than anything, she wanted to give over this life of war and violence, a life she'd never been meant to lead, to go back to Aidan and what they might still be able to build together, if only they were given the chance . . .

"Put away your weapon, Lucan," she said quietly, opening her hands in a gesture of peace. She almost felt sorry for him now, standing before her with so much hate and jealousy burning in his heart. "You need prove nothing to me or anyone else. It is over now. I will fight no more."

"Perhaps you will reconsider that decision once you learn that it was I who took your shield and sent it to the English bastard you killed yesterday," he retorted. "To the duke, whose daughter was to marry your lover!"

Stiffening, she frowned. "*You* stole my shield and gave it to Rutherford? But why?"

"I wanted you dead, or captured at the least and brought to trial as a traitor to the English king."

" 'Twas a selfish way of trying to rid yourself of me,

then," she said, unsuccessful in stifling her anger. "You had to know 'twould endanger Dafydd and Owin as well."

"Such extra losses are unavoidable in war—and this is war, woman, make no mistake," Lucan grated. Then his expression shifted again, becoming more mocking. "But you were so easy to defeat, 'twas almost pitiful. 'Twas also I, you know," he taunted, "who sent you the parchment in my father's name, urging you to tempt de Brice with your body. I knew you wouldn't be able to resist coupling with him. And you proved yourself to be as weak as any other female, when you bedded him at my command." He took another step toward her, sneering, "You have no claim to be called a Legend, woman—only a legendary *whore*."

"I warned you before about that, you bastard," she heard Aidan growl from behind her, and she turned, seeing him lunge forward, readying to attack Lucan, only to be wrenched back into place by several of the guards that were in charge of him. In the scuffle, he was struck, and he let go a string of curses, fighting back so fiercely that three other men needed to jump forward in order to help restrain him.

Gwynne called for them to stop and started to run toward him, but before she could take a few steps, her half-brother reached out and grabbed her by the arm, yanking her back and snarling, "Draw your weapon and fight. I'll wait no longer!"

She froze, stunned by his self-destructive obstinacy. *The fool was going to force her hand.*

Jerking free of his grip, Gwynne took two steps back, impaling him with her gaze. The shock and emptiness that had numbed her earlier faded under the prick of more biting emotions, but still she struggled to maintain control and walk away—knowing that if she came to blows with Lucan, 'twould be disastrous.

She shook her head finally. "The same hatred that has

destroyed your mother is ruining you, Lucan. I have told you that I will not fight you here—not today or ever. Now, let it be."

With a final glare, she stiffened her back and turned again to walk toward Aidan. But she felt a brush of air, a mere flicker of movement at the same time that Aidan shouted a warning to her.

Instincts that long ago had been honed razor-sharp slammed into place, then, and she whirled, ignoring the slashing stab of pain in her side as she cleared her sword from its sheath, raising the blade with a feral growl to meet Lucan's vicious stroke.

They clashed together, and she knew without a doubt that each blow her half-brother dealt her was meant to kill. But she held her own, and within moments, the heat of battle masked the searing agony of twisting and lunging as she wielded her sword against him. People scurried out of the way as they came together again, sparks flying from their blades as they tried to drive each other back, out of the circle. She saw his face as he came at her, contorted with the dark forces at work in him, felt his rage coming at her in waves, heard him sucking in air even over her own gasping breaths as they fought in this struggle of life and death.

Of a sudden Lucan lunged sideways and raised his blade to slash at her, but the sun glinted off it, blinding her for a moment. She stumbled, her balance lost. With a howl of triumph he took the advantage, swinging his blade high, and forcing her to lift her arms to meet his next deadly thrust—exposing her injured side to the force of his momentum as he deliberately rammed into her, pulling his elbow back at the same time to jab it into her wound.

Agony rocked through Gwynne, jolting her with shock for one paralyzing moment before a cry ripped from her throat and she dropped to the ground. Black spots converged on her vision and a buzzing sound filled her ears; more than anything, she wanted to give in to the welcoming blackness that would free her from the torment, the unbearable pain—but somehow she managed to roll to her feet again. Another of Lucan's strokes missed her by a hair's breadth as she stumbled back a few steps, hunched over now, with her left arm curled round her middle. She squinted at him through eyes that felt scraped with sand, grimacing, hissing her breath in through clenched teeth—little pants that kept the agony at bay enough for her to blink away the last of the dark spots and ready herself for his renewed assault.

"You're going to die today, woman," Lucan rasped, gloating even through his own exhaustion. Sweat beaded on his face as he flashed a malevolent smile at her. "And I am going to enjoy dealing your final blow."

"You are sick in your mind and your soul, Lucan," she managed to gasp, still reeling from the agony, but welcoming the flood of anger—and strength—that surged through her with his taunting. "I don't intend to die this day. Put up your weapon and end this—please. I do not want to hurt you."

He barked a sneering laugh. "Hurt *me*? Worry about yourself, woman," he scoffed, backing off a few steps to grip the hilt of his weapon in both hands, before leveling both the blade and his gaze at her, "And prepare to face the afterlife you've earned, because a *Legend* is about to end."

He roared a fierce battle cry as he came at her for the last time, and Gwynne's mind shut down to all but survival; at the last possible moment, she sucked in her breath and vaulted into the air, landing just beyond where Lucan had expected her to be, throwing off his aim and leaving him vulnerable to her return strike.

And then everything seemed to slow for her as it always did, her focus narrowing down to the motion of her weapon, everything fading but the pounding rush of blood in her ears, the weight of the hilt in her grip, thick and heavy, no longer something apart from her, but an extension of her arm, her body . . .

With a growl, she whirled, swinging her blade over Lucan's head in a lethal arc and then bringing it down with a precision borne of endless practice, to bury it in the tender flesh between his shoulder and neck.

Lucan stiffened in the instant following, his face going rigid with shock as she pulled back on the blade, yanking it up and away. Then he uttered a choked groan, blood gushing out over his shoulder, down his chest and arm, soaking his side with slick, red wetness. His sword thudded to the ground. A moment later, his eyes rolled back, and he crumpled to the dirt after it. Lifeless.

*Dead.*

Gwynne knew it as soon as her mind began to clear from the battle rage that had locked her down for the kill. Her breath rasped harsh in her chest, and the thousand hurts of her injuries came back to rip through her like the fires of hell, but she was able to ignore them all, feeling so far removed as she did from everything, from everyone. She just stood there, gazing at Lucan's body lying bloodied at her feet. With a gasping cry, she let her hands fall to her sides, let the tip of her sword gouge into the ground as grief and anguish swelled to a torrent inside of her, stinging her eyes and turning each breath into a raspy sob.

*He was dead—oh, God, Lucan was dead. She'd just killed her own brother . . .*

"Gwynne—Gwynne, look at me! Are you hurt? Have you been cut? Damn it—look at me, Gwynne!"

The insistence of the voice sliced through the haze in her brain, and, woodenly, she swung her head to see who was shouting at her. The fog began to lift, pieces of the present clicking back into place. She drew in a ragged breath, blinking to clear her vision; 'twas Aidan calling out to her. The crowd had fallen deadly silent around him, all of them staring. *Staring at her, standing over her brother's body.* Aidan was the only one moving; cursing, he struggled to be free of the warriors who still held him, his face showing his desperation to get to her, to make sure she was all right.

"Release him," she said, somehow managing to bark the hoarse command.

They stared at her, obviously uncertain whether or not they should obey. But then one of them mumbled something about her victory giving her the right, and without further pause, they did as she commanded.

Aidan reached her in three strides, enfolding her in his embrace with a groan of relief. And for the first time since this had all begun, she allowed herself to weaken, let herself sag against him, clinging to his warmth and his strength as if he was all that stood between her and the gaping jaws of hell.

"By all the saints, Gwynne, I thought I was going to lose you," he murmured, his voice breaking with emotion. "The bastards wouldn't let me go to help you."

"There was nothing you could have done," she said, her voice echoing hollow in her ears.

God, she was tired—so tired. Her breath hitched, and she closed her eyes, still leaning against him. " 'Twas my fight, and I had to see it through. I only wish it never had to happen."

" 'Twas unavoidable. I saw that—everyone did. You can't blame yourself for Lucan's hatred." Aidan held her close, cradling her against his chest and stroking her hair as he murmured to her what comforts he could. She relaxed into his arms, the relief of being able to give over to his strength like a blessed elixir to her soul.

After a moment, he pulled back a little, cupping her face in his hand and forcing her to look at him. "Are you sure that you're all right?"

"Aye," she answered huskily, her eyes welling with tears as she added, "But I didn't want to do it, Aidan. God help me, I didn't. He was my brother; I should have—"

"It wasn't your fault, lass," another, deeper voice said from behind her. "You had no choice but to do what you did."

Turning in Aidan's arms, she met her father's stare; he held a dampened rag to his temple, still trying to stem the bleeding from the blow Lucan had dealt him earlier, but it was the depth of sadness and resignation she saw in his eyes that made her heart contract anew. She stared at him in silence, unable to speak for a moment.

"I am sorry, Marrok—so sorry," she said when she could, though the words caught in her throat.

"Not Marrok, lass," he answered, giving her a soft look. "*Father*."

She struggled to hold back tears, overcome with the gift of his forgiveness. "Aye—Father," she repeated hoarsely. He stepped toward her, holding out his arms, and with a low cry, she fell into his embrace.

A few moments after, when everyone had had a chance to settle and begin the process of coming to terms with what had happened, Marrok called a meeting. He faced his people, not far from where his son's body lay, and Gwynne noticed that the villagers had already started preparing Lucan's body for burial. He'd been laid out on a small platform, a cloth spread beneath him, and much of the blood from his wound washed away. Finally, they'd placed his sword in his hands, resting it on his chest. Isolde was nowhere to be seen; shortly after her son's death, she'd been led away in hysterics from her grief, and so now Marrok stood alone as he addressed the crowd.

"Much has happened here this day—and much was learned that should have been revealed years ago." He looked down at Lucan's body, sadness seeming to overwhelm him for a moment before he could go on. He took in a breath and held it, his eyes glistening when he finally shook his head, exhaling. "My son died today, in part, because of these secrets, and my daughter almost lost her life as well. The legacy of bloodshed and hatred must end, and it must end now."

Turning to look at Gwynne and Aidan who stood, still embracing a little distance away, he nodded. "As chieftain of this clan, I have decided to propose a way to establish a peace between our people and England."

He held up his hand to quell the exclamations and sounds of surprise that rose from the crowd. "We will be following the example of many other of our countrymen— of other Welsh clans—if we undertake this," he assured them. "Prince Rhys ap Gruffyd, for one, signed a new treaty with England's king little more than three months ago. I will send a messenger to enlist his aid, should our council agree, in working out a truce of our own with our neighbors to the east."

Gwynne met Aidan's gaze as the discussion swelled around them again, feeling the first inklings of hope. A ray of light in the darkness of this day. But in the next moment, that hope was dashed; one of the clan's runners whose duty it was to patrol the area and serve as a watchman; hurtled into the square, his face ashen beneath a coating of sweat.

"Grab your weapons!" he gasped. "English forces— scores of them . . . they're nearly here . . . !" he shouted brokenly, before bending over, coughing, and trying to catch his breath.

Gwynne reached for her blade, the other warriors rush-

ing to gather arrows and spears, while the rest of the villagers scrambled for makeshift weapons—but they were
all too late. With a crashing sound, an English warrior
rode into the clearing at full tilt, wheeling his steed to a
halt not twenty paces from them. He was followed by an
army of more than five score soldiers, who strode into the
square with an impressive show of force, their armor
clanking as they stepped from behind the buildings that
circled the area. 'Twas clear that the rebels were outnumbered; the English completely surrounded them, facing
them down with three of their group for every Welsh warrior. They stood at attention, their finely honed blades
gleaming and at the ready, waiting only for their leader's
command to take the entire group as captives in the name
of England and her king.

"Rex!" Aidan said in surprise, recognizing the leader's
device. His foster-father paused before taking off his
helm to face them, as Aidan took a few steps toward him,
calling, "Kevyn reached you, then? He explained what
happened?"

"Aye, he found me." His face was grim, and a prickle of
apprehension went down Gwynne's spine; she kept her
gaze fixed on him, this man who loved Aidan as his own
son, but who also served as one of King Henry's chief
justiciars—realizing that whatever had brought him up
into the mountains today with this many fully armed warriors wasn't going to be good.

"Kevyn told me the details of what transpired in the
past two days," Rex continued, "—and that information
was supplemented yester eve by the surviving men of
Lord Rutherford's party, who threw themselves into my
castle yard as if demons pursued them, babbling about the
bloody destruction dealt them during a Welsh ambush to
free you." He shook his head. "I may sympathize in many

ways with what you've been through, Aidan, but I am under specific orders from the king, and I cannot—I will not—disobey him."

Aidan had gone silent, and now Rex dismounted, looking none too happy about the duty that had brought him here. Scowling, he strode toward Aidan, followed by five of his soldiers, who fell into formation behind him.

Gwynne clenched her jaw, watching them come, tension winding up tight again inside of her. This was not good. Nay, 'twas not good at all. Swinging her head to meet her father's gaze, she felt her stomach sink when she saw the same worry reflected in his eyes. 'Twas serious, then, as she'd thought. Gritting her teeth against the pain that jabbed her with every movement, she lurched forward. Marrok came close behind, as she walked toward Aidan, in her determination to face this latest ordeal, at least, at his side.

She reached him before Rex did, forcing herself to stand tall when the man finally came to a stop in front of them. His face was tight, his expression somber. In the next moment he shifted to acknowledge Gwynne as well, flinching at her appearance. *Of course.* He had never seen her in her masculine garments before; the sight of her now, bloodied and bruised from battle, was undoubtedly difficult for him to reconcile with the elegantly dressed woman he had met at the gathering of nobles.

He seemed to gather his wits again in little time, frowning and murmuring an apology to both of them, before he lifted his chin and called out in a loud, official voice, "It is my unfortunate duty to hereby place the Welsh criminal known as the Dark Legend under my arrest, by command of King Henry II, for the charge of treason, sedition, and murder." Ignoring the shouts of anger that rose within the square, along with the renewed scuffling of the stand off between his men and the rebels, he grimaced and added,

"I also arrest Aidan de Brice, third Earl of Sutcliffe, for the treasonous action of aiding and protecting the Dark Legend, in direct opposition to the task assigned him by the king."

Gwynne stood motionless next to the man she loved, watching the tumult swell around them and letting the shock of Rex's announcement seep into her bones. They were being arrested for treason, she thought; both of them. 'Twas almost like the trauma of twelve years ago all over again, only reversed: the Welsh had hurt her and Aidan last time; the English claimed that distinction today. Her breath stuck in her throat at the thought, and blindly, she reached out to clasp Aidan's hand, feeling him grip hers in warm response. It seemed that, once again, their time was going to be up before it had even begun, and her eyes stung with the cruelty and unfairness of it all. The realization pounded through her, hammering at her composure and her sanity, releasing a flood of anger, grief, regret . . .

*And an idea.* It sprang to life, suddenly, taking root even as Rex clamped his jaw tight and walked away from them, back toward his mount, to hand something from his saddle pouch to one of his men. She waited, watching the soldier return, manacles dangling from his grip, knowing that they would be clapped onto their wrists in a few moments. And it was then that the tiny seed of inspiration pushed up through the darkness, unfurling itself to bloom in the fullness of day . . .

"Lord Warrick!" she called out, his name ringing through the clearing and piercing the commotion surrounding them. The noise ebbed a little as she took a step forward, her heart pounding; then she just waited, standing straight and tall despite her injuries, her commanding presence gaining the attention of both the English soldiers and the crowd, just as she'd hoped, quieting them.

The Englishmen leveled their spears at her, but she met

their stares coolly, swinging her gaze to Aidan's foster-father, who had turned, now, to face her.

"I fear you are mistaken, Lord Warrick," she called out, "in ordering our arrests for the charges stated." Her statement drew a swell of renewed murmurings, but she continued on, undaunted, and somehow more certain in what she was about to do than she'd ever been during her years as the most feared and respected warrior of Wales.

Slowly, with measured, even steps, she walked over to where her half-brother lay, lifeless, on the platform. She stood over him, taking in a shuddering breath as she stared down at his body, sick to her soul at the waste—the terrible, pointless waste. It had been inevitable, perhaps. Envy and hate had eaten at Lucan, driving him to the evil deeds that had ultimately cost him his life.

But perhaps all was not lost, she thought. Perhaps some good could come out of it yet . . .

Looking up again, she let her gaze sweep over the crowd of people—the English soldiers and Welsh warriors, Lord Warrick, her father, and Aidan—and then she called out, "Aidan de Brice should not be arrested for the crimes leveled against him, Lord Warrick, because they are untrue. He is in fact a hero of England and should be celebrated for performing his duty to his king—for here lies the Dark Legend, defeated by the Scourge of Wales this day, in a hand to hand combat for justice!"

A rush of shouts and scandalized gasps filled the square, uttered by Welsh and English alike, before settling gradually to a stunned silence as the enormity of her claim sank home.

"Gwynne," Aidan said softly, walking over to her; he touched his hand to her chin to make her look at him. "Love, what are you saying . . . ?"

"I am saying that the Dark Legend is dead."

Her eyes stung a bit, and she gave him a gentle smile.

*Ah, Gwynne, my sweet child . . . never fear to follow your heart . . .* Her dream-mother's words rang through her soul again, giving her strength and courage. What she was doing was right. She had no more doubts; 'twas time to let go of the past and turn to a future with this man she loved—this man who also loved her in return. Time to reclaim the life they were meant to share together.

Slowly, she lifted her hands to her sword belt, unfastening it and tossing it onto the platform at Lucan's feet. "Aye, the Dark Legend is dead," she said again, her voice husky in the stillness that echoed through the square, "May he rest in peace, for his life of violence and bloodshed is done forever."

A muscle in Aidan's jaw twitched as he gazed at her, and she saw the pride and joy that filled his eyes; then he pulled her into his embrace, kissing her as if he would never let her go. She reveled in the comfort of it, soaking into his touch and knowing that this was where she was meant to be—where she had belonged all of her life.

Gwynne clung to Aidan, hugging him as tightly as her wounded side would allow. The square remained silent, even the grumbling of those still eager for warfare hushed for the moment. Except for those few lingering insurgents who would most likely break away from the clan now and join other rebel groups, the people would follow her decision, she knew. Their life of constant warfare was over, for without the Dark Legend to lead them, the rebellion would founder. From the side of her vision, Gwynne saw Rex gesture to his men, issuing an order for them to stand down. The tension in the square seemed to dissipate a bit; the people began to move about more freely, still wary but in less combative poses than before.

"You've a supple mind, lass, I'll grant you that," Rex murmured, as he approached them. "Yet, though what you've suggested seems a clever solution to our problem, 'tis still not entirely resolved. Your people, at least, know the truth about your identity as the Dark Legend, as do most of Aidan's men"—he gestured to the soldiers he'd brought with him—"and considering your battle-worn appearance right now, perhaps some of my men as well. How do you propose to maintain the illusion, with so many others who might someday reveal your secret?"

"I won't need to, Rex. No one will," she answered, filled with happiness when Aidan took her hand in his and squeezed gently. "We need not fear a revelation for the simple fact that I am a woman, a condition that for most men, the English king included, will preclude the possibility in their minds that I ever was also a warrior. Anyone who suggests otherwise will undoubtedly be opening himself up to naught but humiliation and ridicule."

"She's right," Aidan agreed. "Just think of your reaction, Rex—your disbelief—when Diana first told you that Gwynne was the Dark Legend; 'twill be so with everyone who doesn't see her in action with a blade—and that won't be a concern again. Not in the life we intend to lead as husband and wife," he added, smiling and giving her one of those looks that always set her pulse to racing.

"I will gladly give over my claim to the title of *Legend,* and all that went with it," she said softly, reaching around Aidan's waist as he tugged her carefully against him again. "And 'tis fitting that Lucan be given in death a share of the fame and glory he craved and could never seem to find in life." Pushing back the remembered pain of her final confrontation with her brother, she hugged Aidan and smiled. "What Aidan has in mind for our future sounds far more appealing than more training and battle, I think."

"Think? I was hoping for *know,*" Aidan teased, pressing a kiss to the top of her head.

"My daughter knows her own mind, make no mistake

about it," Marrok answered, nodding acknowledgment of their greetings as he walked up to them. He touched Gwynne's cheek in a fatherly caress, making her smile again when in the next moment he rounded on Aidan, adding in a mock growl, "And you'd be wise to remember, Englishman, that whether she's wearing bliauds or breeches, she still has the skill to bring you to your knees. I trained her well—do not forget it."

"I won't, Marrok, you can be certain of that," Aidan said, laughing with the rest of them as he clasped her father's proffered forearm to his own. "God save me from what might happen if I ever tried."

Gwynne let the joy inside of her seep a little deeper. This moment was all she could have hoped for and more; the banter between the man she'd respected and admired for most of her life, and the man that she'd loved for even longer was proving to be a shocking and happy change from the insults they had hurled at each other just three months ago. Still nodding and grinning with approval, Marrok sidled up to Aidan's foster-father and swung an arm around his shoulders. He leaned in, and as they ambled off, Gwynne heard her father murmur something to Rex about arranging a meeting between them at his estate, so that they could discuss the details of working out a treaty of peace.

Gwynne watched them go, her heart singing with more happiness than she could ever remember feeling, anytime in her life. Aidan pulled her close to him again, pressing a gentle kiss first to her cheek, before tipping her head back and trailing his mouth lightly down the length of her neck.

"Ah—alone at last," he murmured against her skin, and the warm little bursts of his breath sent delightful shivers down her spine.

"We're hardly alone, Aidan—there are at least five dozen people right here, not to mention the four score soldiers besides, all undoubtedly watching your display," she scolded playfully, unable to stop herself, however, from continuing to lean into the strong length of his body as he held her.

"I wouldn't say that *all* of them are watching, Gwynne." He pulled away a little, igniting the familiar fluttering in her belly when she saw his expression. "Would you like to make a wager on it?"

Laughing aloud, she shook her head. "I vow that was the only constant in all of my time at Dunston—you and those blessed bargains of yours."

"The bargains we made then were good, I admit, but this one will be even better. What say you—would you like to hear what I propose?" he asked, wiggling his brows and making her smile again.

"All right—go ahead."

"I wager," he murmured, leaning in so that his voice tickled her ear with warm little tingles, "that I could kiss you soundly enough, right here and now, to ensure that we gained the undivided attention of every single person in this square, for as long as we liked." While he spoke, he slid his hand behind her neck, his fingers stroking and rubbing gently, dragging a sigh of pleasure from her. "What say you, Gwynne—do we have a deal?"

"Aye, we do," she murmured, the huskiness in her voice giving away the irresistible effect of his caresses on her.

"What—so eager to accept . . . ?" he asked, looking at her in mock surprise. "I'm shocked. I never would have guessed you'd be so ready to bargain with me again, considering your dismal showings in the past."

Gwynne laughed again, then—a low, throaty sound. "Ah, but that is just it, my love," she murmured, turning the tables on him as she leaned back in his arms and gazed at him in a way that made his breath catch and his eyes widen. "I truly hope that my luck will maintain the same bleak course as it has in all our dealings before."

She brushed her finger across his lips, following it with a teasing caress of her mouth—her smile slow, sweet, and seductive . . .

"Because this is one wager that I think I will take great pleasure in losing."

.

# Epilogue

❧∽❧

*The castle yard at Dunston*
*One month later*

**T**heir wedding day shone clear and bright, the early autumn breeze lending a welcome balance to the heat of the sun; it beat down on the crimson silk tent that Aidan had ordered erected in the yard for the brides' convenience, lighting everything inside it with a rosy glow. Gwynne sighed, impatient; the ceremony was done, and the feasting about to begin, and she was stuck in here having her skirt hemmed, thanks to her usual clumsiness. She fiddled with her gown again, stifling a curse as Old Alana clucked and straightened the fall of smooth ivory and gold fabric one last time. Then she adjusted an ebony wave that had slipped free of Gwynne's jeweled circlet before declaring that she was done.

"Ah, you look like royalty, my lady," Alana said, beaming as she stepped back to survey her handiwork. "A queen, true-born."

"Then it appears I've stepped up in the world since the last time you helped to dress me," Gwynne teased, giving the old woman a warm hug and murmuring thanks at her tearful expression of congratulations. Then she turned with a swish of skirts to face Aidan, who stood a few paces apart, patiently waiting for her to be finished. Giving him a brilliant smile, she murmured, "Shall we go now, my lord husband?"

"Aye, Lady Sutcliffe," he answered, the heat that glowed in his eyes having nothing to do with the tent's fiery hue. He strode forward and took her hand, bending to brush her fingers with his lips—a feather light touch that she knew was but a hint of all that would come later, when they were alone in their bedchamber . . .

A pleasurable shiver raced through her at the thought, and Aidan paused, still bent over her hand, his mouth curving up as he met her gaze to whisper, "You look magnificent, my lady, but if I am to keep from ravishing you right here, we must needs find the others and make an appearance before our guests." Straightening in one smooth movement, he tucked her hand beneath his arm.

In a few moments they'd found Owin, Diana, Kevyn, and Helene; from the flush of pleasure on the other women's faces, Gwynne guessed that perhaps they'd been sharing some seductive banter with their new husbands as well—a prelude to what she hoped might be wedding nights as blissful as the one that she would enjoy with Aidan.

Kevyn and Helene were the first to leave the tent, but before they went, Aidan's friend turned and winked at them, his expression glowing with happiness, as it had every time that Gwynne had seen him since she'd returned to Dunston to learn that Helene had accepted his offer of marriage. Grinning now, he scooped Helene into his arms and carried her, blushing and laughing, through the tent flap. They were greeted with shouts of, "God bless the bride!" as they strode through the crowd of well-wishers, followed by a few more ribald comments from the back, addressing the hope of Helene's frequent fertility in the years to come.

"Your Welsh relations, no doubt," Aidan said dryly, laughing at the face Gwynne made at him in response.

"Careful, Brother," Diana warned, grinning as she twisted to face him from where she and Owin stood together, awaiting their turn to duck through the flap. "The Welsh guests are your relatives now, too."

"And yours, sweet," Owin reminded her gently, eliciting another stream of giggles from her before he kissed her cheek for what had to be the fiftieth time that Gwynne had witnessed this day alone. Giving them a laughing salute, Owin pulled his new bride out of the tent, and the crowd of former Welsh rebels and titled English lords and ladies shouted renewed, rollicking congratulations, before resuming their mingling amongst tables that groaned with food, or sampling from the casks of fine wine and ale that Aidan had purchased especially for this feast.

Finally it was their turn; they stepped up to the flap, and Aidan pushed it open a bit—just enough to tease the waiting crowd into beginning more of the shouts of congratulations that had come with the two couples before them. But then he paused, turning his head to gaze at her, that sweet, sensual smile hovering on his lips.

"Are you ready, Gwynne?" he murmured, the happy look reaching up to light his eyes, now, as he watched her, waiting for her answer.

"Aye, I'm ready." She smiled. "After all, I've already

been waiting more than half my life to do this with you."

"Then give me a kiss for luck, and we'll be on our way."

And as she leaned into him, tilting her head up to share the sweetness of their kiss—a caress full of passion and promise, love and redemption—she knew that this was where she was meant to be. Where she had always belonged.

"I love you, Aidan," she said softly, cupping his face in her palms as the happiness inside her danced about like sparkling bubbles of light.

"And I you, Gwynne—I will love you forever," he answered huskily. He held her close, leaning his brow against hers for just a moment before he pulled back and gave her a wink and a grin to match her own. "Come—'tis time to go."

Then, clasping hands, they threw open the tent flap with a joyful shout . . .

And stepped into the sunshine at last.

# Author's Note

The legend of King Arthur has roots in ancient Celtic lore: most likely he was a fifth century king of Briton who fought the invasion of the Saxons. As an historical figure, he is mentioned in numerous early texts, including the *Letter to Riothamus*, c.470; *De Excidio Britanniae*, c. 540; *The Battle of Llongborth*, c.480 (an English translation of a sixth century Welsh poem), and *The Anglo Saxon Chronicle*, 9th C. Regardless of true history, King Arthur's legend rose among the people, particularly in Wales, where the idea that their "Once and Future King" would return when the country needed him most, to lead them to freedom from England's oppressive rule.

The Welsh rebellion rose and ebbed numerous times through the course of several hundred years, culminating in a particularly seditious era during the reign of England's King Henry II. In the summer of 1189, just before Henry's death, a group of monks at Glastonbury Abbey "discovered" Arthur's grave between two stone pillars on the grounds; the bones—the shin of which was longer by nearly half than that of any man the monks or witnesses could find—were buried alongside those of a woman, presumably Guinevere's. A long, blonde braid lay with the remains, though according to testimony, it disintegrated to dust once touched.

The hollowed-out oak bole containing the bones had been buried sixteen feet below the surface of the earth— apparently to prevent Arthur's Saxon enemies from discovering and desecrating his grave—with a stone slab beneath it that bore a leaden cross with the inscription: HERE IN THE ISLE OF AVALON LIES BURIED THE RENOWNED KING ARTHUR, WITH GUINEVERE, HIS SECOND WIFE. The remains and stone slab were kept safe until the later reign of King Henry VIII; after his rift with the Church of Rome, he ordered the dissolution of England's monasteries. Shortly thereafter, the stone slab disappeared, never to be seen again; only a drawing of it remains.

Of course, many argue that the entire "discovery" of Arthur's grave was a calculated hoax, invented by King Henry and the Glastonbury monks in an attempt both to raise money for the abbey through the visitors who would flock to the site, and to hamper the Welsh rebellion against England by issuing a death blow to the patriotic fervor fueled by rumors of Arthur's imminent return. Whether the entire event was an elaborate ruse or not will undoubtedly be debated for centuries more. But researching the events at Glastonbury and the controversy surrounding them provided me with some wonderful inspiration for *The Maiden Warrior*.

In conceiving my story, I adjusted Arthurian legend and historical fact a bit to allow for the idea of the great king *reborn*, rather than simply returned from Avalon. In this way, Gwynne would be the infant bearing the "signs" that marked her as the future savior of her people in battle. But I reflected the original legend on at least one major point in my tale: just as Arthur was the son of an illicit union between the warlord Uther Pendragon and Gorlois's wife, Igrayne, Gwynne is also the fruit of a forbidden relationship between the warrior Marrok and Owain's noble wife, Gwendolyn.

Making the "Dark Legend" of my story female instead of male also has some basis in historical fact, as ancient Celtic culture actually revered women warriors: some of the most powerful Celtic war deities were female, and they came with requisite abilities in weapons and martial arts–style fighting. In fact, it is believed that women warriors were an accepted part of Welsh society and fought alongside men as late as the ninth century.

Gwynne was an irresistible heroine for me to write, not only because of the chance she gave me to express the kind of honor, strength, and courage that I think is too often downplayed in women, but also because of the agonizing conflict it allowed me to examine through her characterization. How much more emotionally fraught can a woman be than to be torn between an undeniable duty as her nation's most important leader—as their legendary warrior—and the fierce, unyielding desires of her still-tender heart? Then, of course, matching her up with a hero both worthy of her on the battlefield and gentle enough to win her love presented a challenge all its own—one I hope I did justice to in the person of her noble knight, Aidan de Brice.

All of it put together made for an engrossing writing experience—and I hope an engrossing reading experience as well. As always, I thank you for coming along on the journey . . .

MRM

### *Summer just got hotter
with romance from Avon Books . . .*

#### ONE NIGHT OF PASSION by Elizabeth Boyle
##### *An Avon Romantic Treasure*
Georgiana Escott attends London's notorious Cyprian's Ball, determined to find the perfect man to ruin her. She feels like a princess, looks like a siren . . . and tumbles into the arms of disgraced, yet dashing, Lord Danvers. Could this one night of passion turn into a blissful future?

#### MAN AT WORK by Elaine Fox
##### *An Avon Contemporary Romance*
Lady lawyer Marcy Paglinowski rescues a terrified puppy—and in the process is swept off her feet by Truman Fleming. He's a working man, who's got biceps and triceps galore, and is so wonderfully different from the stuffed shirts she's used to. But Marcy wants security, and Truman's not the man to give it to her . . . or is he?

#### LONE ARROW'S PRIDE by Karen Kay
##### *An Avon Romance*
Be swept back to the thrilling American West in Karen Kay's newest Avon Romance. Carolyn White was a child in danger when a young Crow Indian rescued her. Now, years later, she and Lone Arrow are together again, and though their cultures collide there is one thing that both share—passion for the other.

#### A GAME OF SCANDAL by Kathryn Smith
##### *An Avon Romance*
Lady Lilith Mallory is the most scandalous woman in London, but that doesn't stop the gentlemen of the *ton* from drinking her wine and gambling at her tables. Then, suddenly and shockingly Gabriel Warren, the Earl of Angelwood, comes back into her life. He had once broken his vow to make her his bride . . . and destroyed her reputation. Now, however, the tables are turned . . .

*Have you ever dreamed of writing a romance?*

*And have you ever wanted
to get a romance published?*

Perhaps you have always wondered how to
become an Avon romance writer?
We are now seeking the best and brightest undiscovered
voices. We invite you to send us your query letter to
*avonromance@harpercollins.com*

*What do you need to do?*

Please send no more than two pages telling us
about your book. We'd like to know its setting—is it
contemporary or historical—and a bit about the hero,
heroine, and what happens to them.

Then, if it is right for Avon we'll ask to see part of the
manuscript. Remember, it's important that you have
material to send, in case we want to see your story quickly.

Of course, there are no guarantees of publication,
but you never know unless you try!

*We know there is new talent just waiting
to be found! Don't hesitate . . . send us
your query letter today.*

*The Editors
Avon Romance*

MSR 0302